Also by Mia James from Indigo:

By Midnight
Darkness Falls

Sleeping Angel

A RAVENWOOD MYSTERY

MIA JAMES

Indigo

First published in Great Britain in 2013 by Indigo
An imprint of the Orion Publishing Group
Orion House, 5 Upper St Martin's Lane,
London WC2H 9EA
An Hachette UK Company

1 3 5 7 9 10 8 6 4 2

A CIP catalogue record for this book
is available from the British Library

ISBN 978 1 78062 079 4

Typeset by Deltatype Ltd, Birkenhead, Merseyside

Printed in Great Britain by Clays Ltd, St Ives plc

The Orion Publishing Group's policy is to use papers that are natural, renewable and recyclable products and made from wood grown in sustainable forests. The logging and manufacturing processes are expected to conform to the environmental regulations of the country of origin.

www.orionbooks.co.uk

Prologue

Highgate Cemetery, north London, six months ago

There was blood on his hands. Black and warm, it ran down his fingers and onto the path. He held them up, the stained skin catching the moonlight, mesmerised. But *whose* blood? Whose? And how had it got there?

Behind him, there was a snap and he dropped, his body tensed for fight or flight, ears alert. He could hear the rain beating on the leaves above him, hear as it condensed into drops and then fell, fat and ripe onto his soaked back. He could hear the scratch of an animal – fox? badger? – in the bush far to his left. And he could hear the wind from the east. The cars rushing up Highgate Hill. His own heart.

And something else.

He moved back into the shadows, allowing the darkness of the cemetery to envelop him like an embrace. This was his home, the one place he felt whole, freed from the frowns and the glances – and the hunger. For a while at least.

He looked down at his hands again. Too dark, but he could feel the scratches, deep welts, as if something had dragged its claws down them. And there was a swelling pain in his knee, his jeans were torn, caked in mud and leaves.

Have I been fighting?

'Think, dammit,' he said, pressing fingers against his temples. If he stayed very still, pictures came to him: there was a man, a man with dark eyes, as if a child had scrawled them on, with drawings on his arms and chest, a star on his shoulder. And a beautiful girl with shining yellow hair. And there was music – loud, loud music that made his ears hurt.

But that was a long time ago – wasn't it? *Or only yesterday.*

And then the pictures were gone, popped like a soap bubble, because suddenly his eyes were open, his senses tingling. Something was coming.

He began to run uphill, his sure feet following the old wall. Up to his left, through the stooping trees he saw the old black gate. Crouching again, he crept forward, his breath sending little clouds into the air. Ahead of him was an overgrown path and – there! – lying in the centre was a dark shape. A body. Human, still moving. Still alive.

'Isabelle?' he whispered. *Isabelle?* The name had just come to him, appeared in his head like a subtitle. *But I don't know anyone called Isabelle. Do I?*

His nostrils flared; there was something else here. Blood, a lot more blood. And something *bad*. Not a Bleeder, masking their scent with those sickly artificial flowers, but something like him. One who smelled of death.

He tensed again as there was a screech, like a cry of pain – then another. Foxes? Rats? He couldn't tell. His senses were dulling, the darkness seemed to be growing around him, soaking up the light like fog.

'Hello? Is anyone there?' said a voice and he could see the figure framed against an open gate, backlit by the hissing streetlight. A girl: he could smell that much. But not just any girl – it was *her*.

Oh God, he thought, *it's coming*. The thing. The thing with the eyes.

He jumped to his feet and ran towards her, effortlessly lifting the girl from her feet. Up and out onto the road.

'Go, quickly!' he hissed.

The dark-haired girl looked up, the moon catching her face.

She's beautiful, he thought. *Beautiful and . . .*

'Get out of here!' he cried. 'GO!'

Then he turned back to the darkness. And it swallowed him whole.

Chapter One

It was a bright day as April stepped off the train. The sun was pushing through the paper-white cloud but it did nothing to raise the temperature. *Late spring in England*, she thought. *Isn't it supposed to be sunshine and roses by now?* Her breath puffed in front of her and she shivered as she followed the signs off the platform and down through the black iron gates into the cemetery.

April's best friend Fiona had been very excited when she had heard that Miss Holden was being buried at Brookwood. 'It's the biggest cemetery in Europe. It's like a city of death!' she had enthused.

'And that's supposed to be a good thing?'

The last thing April wanted in her life was more death – there had been plenty of that over the past few months. And she certainly wasn't in the mood to get excited about going to the funeral of her teacher.

'Come on, April, it'll be fascinating,' said Fiona. 'Brookwood was built to deal with London's population boom in the nineteenth century. There were so many burials every day, the cemetery had their own train station in London.'

April had actually been pleased to find that the spookily named 'Necropolis Station' at Waterloo was long gone – bombed in the war, the man in the ticket booth had told her – but Brookwood still had its own station out in the leafy Surrey countryside.

Beyond that, however, the cemetery was a disappointment. Fee's description had made April think it would be one of those grand old Victorian cemeteries like Highgate, with ornate gates and tombs, but April thought it looked more like a neglected farm. Just a load of empty fields and rusting signs reading 'No photography'.

April walked along a gravel path towards the cemetery chapel, past a huge rusting conveyor belt machine, its long neck pointing up towards the sky.

Perhaps I've been spoilt by Highgate, she thought. Highgate Cemetery was crammed with beautiful statues of angels and pillars and tombs, all of it magnificently overgrown and wilfully spooky. But then Highgate was not only full of bodies – Highgate was full of vampires.

It had sounded such a sleepy place when her dad had described where they were moving from Edinburgh the previous autumn. She could still remember driving into the little north London village for the first time, and despairing at how boring it looked. She couldn't have been more wrong.

But back then, April had thought that horror movies were stupid, just a load of people running around in rubber masks, spraying fake blood everywhere. But now she knew those 'masks' could be real, and that the monsters inside were real-life vicious killers.

Well, not all of them, thought April. *Not Gabriel.*

Her heart gave a little leap as she thought of her boyfriend: his dark eyes, the upturn at the corner of his mouth when he smiled at her. And the way he had looked that night Miss Holden had been killed, standing on the roof of Mr Sheldon's burning house, surrounded by flames as he'd taken her hand and jumped off the edge. He'd looked so ... vulnerable, but still sexy. Was that possible?

April snorted to herself. Anything was possible these days. Her school – posh Ravenwood school on Highgate Hill – was riddled with vampires. It was a front for a giant global blood-sucking conspiracy and – oh yeah – it turned out that April herself was a 'Fury', some sort of ass-kicking vamp-slayer whose blood was just about the only thing that could make the undead dead again.

Reaching a fork in the path, April looked around nervously. She didn't want to find herself wandering into some grisly cul-de-sac, surrounded by unfamiliar graves; she had enough of the familiar kind to worry about. She turned at footsteps behind her.

'You looking for the funeral? Annabel Holden?' asked a man in a long black overcoat.

'Uncle Peter!' cried April. 'What are you doing here?'

'Heavens, April,' said the man, obviously startled. 'I didn't recognise you from behind. Have you just come in on the London train too?'

He took off his glasses and ran a hand through his white hair; he looked flustered, distracted.

'Yes, just arrived,' said April. 'Are you okay?'

'Oh yes,' said the man, rubbing at his lenses with the end of his tie. 'Just a little … I'm really not looking forward to this funeral, if I'm honest.'

Tell me about it, thought April. She herself wasn't exactly keen to face Miss Holden's relatives, not when she was so weighed down with guilt. But at least now she had a friendly face beside her. Peter Noble was a newspaper editor who'd been close to her father and – now she thought about it – one of the few nice people she had met at his funeral only a few months ago. *God, has Daddy only been dead six months?* It felt a lifetime since she had found him lying there in a pool of his own blood.

'Do you know where the funeral is?' she asked. 'I'm a bit lost.'

Peter forced a smile. 'Easily done here. This place is about five miles end to end – but it's this way, I think.'

He led her down the left-hand fork, past the overgrown graves, an awkward silence accompanying them. How could you make small talk on the way to the funeral of a woman who had been tortured and killed by a half-crazed vampire?

'Do you know why there are so few graves here?' said

April, looking at the open fields on either side of the narrow path. 'I thought it would be packed.'

'Well, it *is* packed, actually,' said Peter. 'There are something like a hundred and fifty thousand people buried here. If you look, you can see lots of indentations – those are the graves. If you stripped the soil off, you'd see all of the bones and skulls still there.'

April shivered and looked down at her feet – was she walking over some poor soul right now? She should be less easily disturbed; she had been visiting her father's grave in Highgate Cemetery for months. However, in Highgate April always felt that William Dunne was the only man buried on that high hill.

'But why don't they have headstones?'

Peter shrugged. 'They have been removed.'

'Removed?'

He nodded. 'When you're buried, you're really only renting the space. When your time runs out, they make way for someone else. It's a business like any other.'

'Eww, so they're all getting buried on top of one another?'

'An unpleasant thought, I know, but it's always been that way. Even when we lived in villages, where everyone would be buried in the little churchyard, there eventually wasn't room for individual plots.'

'How do you know so much about it?'

'You get to my age, April, you spend a lot of time at funerals.'

April nodded. She had already been to too many herself. They walked in silence until finally they turned a corner and saw the squat redbrick chapel at the end of the path, surrounded by people dressed in black. April hesitated. She didn't want to go down there.

'So, why are you here, Uncle Peter?' she said, desperate to delay walking into that church, seeing all the accusing stares. 'I mean, I didn't know you knew her.'

'I knew her father actually. They were from around these

parts; that's why she's being buried out here. Annabel became my go-to woman whenever I was writing anything about history. She knew so much. It's a sad loss.'

April looked towards the chapel. 'Yes, it is.'

Peter put his hand on her arm. 'I imagine this is pretty hard for you. You don't *have* to go in, you know.'

'Oh, I do. I mean, I didn't really see eye to eye with Miss Holden a lot of the time, but she was nice to me. Well, as nice as she could be.'

Peter chuckled. 'She could be a little abrupt, that's true. You find that with academics; they're used to dealing with names and dates and places, things written in books. Living people tend to be more of a challenge for them.'

'But she tried to help me, that's the thing. She stuck her neck out when she knew it would get her into trouble. And now …' And now April wanted only to turn around and run, get on the train and never look back.

'Are you worried people are going to stare at you?' asked Peter gently.

'No, I'm worried they're all going to *blame* me.'

Peter put his hand on her arm. 'Listen, April, as far as I heard, Annabel Holden was murdered by a deranged student who then set fire to himself with a big can of petrol. How could that have anything to do with you?'

April looked away. He was being nice, of course, just trying to make her feel better. But Peter hadn't been there. He hadn't seen Benjamin's face that night, that horrific moment when he had become infected with the Fury virus – the virus in April's blood.

'But I was there, Peter …'

'But nothing, April. You can't carry on blaming yourself because some crazy boy chose to literally drag you into his insane little world. It's a tragedy Annabel was killed and she will be sorely missed by all the people in that church, but really, it's not your fault. You could no more have changed this than you could change the weather.'

She nodded and walked slowly towards the chapel, taking Peter's arm. It was kind of him, but Uncle Peter was a newspaper editor, used to dealing with the facts of normal life. How could he understand what had happened in that house, how Mr Sheldon, her headmaster at Ravenwood school, had ordered her death, how she herself had killed Benjamin Osbourne, one of her 'Sucker' classmates and, most of all, how could he know how Gabriel had almost given up his life – again – to save her?

'Which ones are her family?' whispered April as they squeezed into a pew at the back.

'Front on the right,' said Peter, patting her hand. 'You don't need to worry, I don't think they have any idea who you are.'

That was hardly any comfort to April. *She* knew who she was – what she had done. Trying to focus on something – anything – else, she looked along the walls of the chapel: names recording notable people of the parish fallen in the 1914–18 war, the 'Great War', the 'War to End All Wars'.

That didn't really pan out too well, did it? thought April, then felt bad for being so flippant about it. All those people listed up there – God, there were so *many* of them – had given their lives fighting to protect their country. Terribly sad in itself, worse was the idea that each of them, cut down by bullets or shells or gas, had left so many who loved them behind: mothers, fathers, sisters, sweethearts. What if she died? Would Caro and Fiona and Gabriel come to her funeral? Would 'April Dunne' ever be written up on a wall along with a record of her gallantry and sacrifice? How could it – no one knew about her struggle. Did it even matter, anyway, after you were dead?

April forced herself to look down the aisle towards Miss Holden's coffin. One thing was certain: there had already been too many violent deaths. From Alix Graves, the singer who had died the night April had arrived in Highgate, and Isabelle Davis, that young girl whose body she had almost stumbled over, to her father, his throat torn out, bleeding to death in her arms. And that had only been the beginning. Milo, Layla, Marcus – crazy Marcus who had tried to kill her twice – then Miss Holden.

The service was short and to the point. A couple of readings from a cousin and an aunt, a brief eulogy from the vicar, who told how Annabel Holden had been a selfless person, a teacher, a sister, a friend, someone you could always rely on. April knew that hadn't always been the case – not for her anyway – but even so, tears began to fill her eyes as the vicar intoned Psalm 23:

Yea, though I walk through the valley of the shadow of death,
I will fear no evil;
For thou art with me;
thy rod and thy staff, they comfort me.

And the pallbearers picked up the coffin, solemnly carrying it through the church and out into a waiting hearse. Peter went to speak to one of the mourners, leaving April on her own, slowly following at the back of the line of people walking towards the grave site.

April was pleased to see Miss Holden was being buried in a quiet corner, although she couldn't help thinking of what Peter had said about the layers of bodies piled up under the ground. Was Miss Holden about to become just another layer? And all the people now standing around the open hole? Were they too going to become a jumble of ribs and shins and skulls, churned up again and again as the digger came to cut a new grave? Funerals were supposed to give you closure, a ritual to make sense of the senseless, but April just felt cheated. One of the few people who had understood what she was going through and had tried to help her was being lowered into a hole. She was alone.

Oh grow up, April.

She smiled: she could almost hear Miss Holden saying it.

Peter was right, Miss Holden had not been terribly hot on social skills, but she had possessed passion and conviction. Annabel Holden had been a Guardian, a member of an ancient sect sworn to fight the vampires. It had been Miss Holden who had explained to April what it meant to be a Fury, how the virus April carried in her body could somehow counteract the vampire's finely balanced grip on life. One kiss from April and it was all over. Excellent for a vampire killer, though not exactly what most boys were looking for in a girlfriend.

But Miss Holden would not have let April wallow in self-pity. She would have told her to 'suck it up'. She didn't *have* to like it. Who would? Given the choice of being some sort of antidote to a fearsome tribe of mythical beasts or being an ordinary A-level student, most people would avoid the strong-chance-of-being-eaten-alive option. April didn't even have that choice – she had a job to do – at the very least, find a way to release Gabriel from the living hell of vampirism. And if she could bring down Ravenwood and find out who killed her father that would be a bonus. Either way, she'd spent far too long standing here, it was time to get back to London.

Just as April turned to head back to the station, a young woman stepped over towards her. Pretty, perhaps late twenties, wearing a black dress, her face was very pale and serious.

'April Dunne?' she queried.

'Yes—'

April felt the sting of the slap before she was even aware the girl had acted. Pain exploded in her cheek and April jerked back, stunned.

'You arrogant bitch,' hissed her attacker. 'How dare you come here?'

April was just beginning to stutter an explanation when a silver-haired old woman wearing a long black coat and fur hat stepped over and put her hands on the girl's shoulders.

'Come away, Samantha,' she said firmly. 'This isn't the time.'

'Isn't it?' yelled the girl. 'She as good as killed Annabel! Has she come to gloat, to see what she has achieved?' She looked up at the older woman. 'Don't you even care?'

'Of course I care, Sam. Of course I do – we all do. But you know as well as I do that Annabel chose the way she lived her life. *She* chose it, no one else.'

'But if she hadn't ...'

'There are a million ifs, Samantha,' said the older woman soothingly. 'And none of them will bring her back. Now, you go back to the car. I'll be along in little while, okay?'

Samantha glared at April again, then nodded and turned away.

The older woman gave April a thin smile. 'I can only apologise,' she said. 'Feelings always run high on these occasions. Everyone's looking for someone to blame.'

'I understand,' said April, touching her cheek which was beginning to sting. 'Honestly, it's not necessary.'

The woman, stylish like a retired actress or even minor royalty, seemed to be examining her. April felt uncomfortable.

'I should have introduced myself,' the woman said, putting her hand out. 'I'm Elizabeth Holden. Annabel's mother. '

April's mouth dropped open. 'Oh God, I'm—I'm really sorry ...' she stuttered as she shook the woman's hand. 'I had no idea, I mean ...'

Mrs Holden smiled kindly and touched April's arm. 'Let's walk, shall we?' she said, indicating the path back towards the chapel. April felt horribly uncomfortable as they slowly returned. Every night since that unreal scene in the Ravenwood headmaster's office, she had relived the death of this woman's daughter, had seen Annabel Holden tied to Mr Sheldon's desk as Benjamin Osbourne, his face a terrible twisted vampire's death mask, tortured her with a guttering flame. At least April had been spared actually seeing Benjamin cut the teacher's throat, but her mind had certainly tried to fill in the blanks – that was usually the point April woke up gasping for air, tears running into her ears.

'You know,' said the woman when they had walked a fair distance from the grave, 'when Annabel was your age, she didn't want anything to do with the vampires either.'

April looked at her sharply.

'Oh yes, I know all about it,' said the woman. 'Why wouldn't I? Our family have been Guardians for generations. I begged Annabel not to join, but … well, I know who's really to blame. Them.'

'The, um …' April was hesitant about saying the word.

'Yes, April, the vampires. That's why I asked that no one from Ravenwood attend the funeral. I didn't want any of them standing there gloating.'

'So why did I get asked?'

Elizabeth Holden gave a soft laugh. 'Because I wanted to meet you, of course,' she said. 'I wanted to see this famous Fury for myself.'

April's heart gave a lurch. 'You know …?'

'Of course I know, April. I try to be aware of everything. Most of all I wanted to know why my daughter had been murdered.'

'Oh God, look I'm so sorry, Mrs Holden, but I …'

'April, it's all right. I don't blame you. What I said to Samantha was true: Annabel was an adult – she was entitled to make her own choices, even if they put her in danger. God knows, I lost my husband to this damn war. I've had plenty of time to make my peace with it.'

She turned and gave a sad smile. 'You, on the other hand, had no choice, rather dragged in kicking and screaming, I imagine.'

'Yes,' said April, relieved. 'Something like that.'

'I wish I could give you some words of comfort, tell you it's all going to turn out fine, but I don't suppose that would sound convincing especially as we're talking at a funeral.'

'No, I suppose not.'

Mrs Holden stopped and turned to April. 'Listen to me, April, what I'm going to say is very important. You must fight them.'

'I— I'll try.'

'That's not good enough. You *must* fight and you *must* win, otherwise all this has been for nothing.' Her face softened. 'I'm sorry to be so hard on you and I know it's not what you want to hear right now. I probably look ancient to you, but I can still remember what it feels like to be your age – or at least some of it – and I know you can't want to be involved. But you are, April. You can't wish it away. And you're special, my dear, very special.'

'I don't feel it.'

'I know, but you will. It will come. You may not want your abilities – God knows, I wouldn't either – but you're stuck with them and you have to rise to the challenge.'

'I want to, but on days like today, it all feels a bit overwhelming.'

Elizabeth Holden smiled ruefully. 'Yes, I can see that. But look –' she reached into her bag and pulled out a card '– I've written my number and address on there. If you ever want to talk about it, or just want to get something off your chest, give me a call, okay? I can't promise I'll have any answers, but at least I'll have a fair idea of what's going on. I imagine that must be the worst thing – having to deal with everything on your own. I know that's how Annabel felt.'

'But she had the Guardians, didn't she?'

Elizabeth Holden's face darkened. April wanted to look away, but didn't think she could. 'Remember one thing, April. Do not trust anyone. Question your friends, your family. And above all, question us.'

'Us?' April frowned. 'Of course, you're a Guardian too?'

'Past tense. Oh, I swore their oaths and swallowed their rhetoric. I was young, newly-wed, in love with my husband and everything he said seemed wonderful. But … there is a darkness there, April. The Guardians hold secrets, and with secrets come both power and deception, two very dangerous elements. They are not everything they seem.'

April didn't know what to make of this woman, but she did know she couldn't fight the vampires alone. 'I need help,' she said simply.

The old lady nodded. 'Then choose your friends carefully, April. Very carefully.'

Chapter Two

April walked back towards the station, feeling even worse than she had earlier. Why did everything have to be so complicated? Why didn't somebody just walk up and say, 'Listen, April, forget all about this Fury nonsense; I'll sort it out for you. You just go home and watch the soaps, have some Toblerone.' Instead, it seemed that everybody wanted something from her, everyone had their own agenda. She sighed. At least with the vampires you knew where you stood. They wanted to recruit you for whatever weird schemes they were cooking up at Ravenwood, or they wanted to drink your blood. Not pleasant, admittedly. But straightforward. She turned a corner and suddenly was aware of a figure standing in the shelter of a tree.

'Gabriel!' she cried, running up and throwing her arms around him. He smelled good; he *felt* good.

'Hey, beautiful.' He grinned, kissing her forehead.

'What are you doing here?'

'Thought you might want an escort.'

'God, you have no idea,' said April. 'You have *no* idea.'

They sat on the train in silence, watching as the countryside whizzed past. William Dunne had always loved trains; April had teased her dad about it, saying he was a trainspotter and ought to wear an anorak, but secretly she had loved those journeys. They would look into people's back gardens and make up stories about who they were: wizards or giants or pop stars, then they would play complicated games of 'I Spy' involving colours and words and sounds.

God, Daddy, why did you have to die?

April blinked back her tears and squeezed Gabriel's hand a little tighter – she didn't want to cry, not now. Not when she felt so safe and close, snuggled up against the man she loved. Maybe Miss Holden's funeral had affected her more than she had thought.

She was certainly going to too many funerals. She thought of what Detective Chief Inspector Johnston had said to her: 'People keep dying around you, April.'

Was it her? Did being a Fury mean that she was going to have to accept death as a close companion, shadowing her every move, picking off people she was close to? She looked up at Gabriel – people like him, perhaps. Another of the little movies that played in her head late at night was of Gabe slumped in that burning house, half-dead, his clothes soaked in petrol, begging her to leave him behind. What if she hadn't pulled him onto the roof? It just didn't bear thinking about.

'Gabriel,' she said. 'Can I ask you something?'

'Sure, anything.'

'What were you doing at Sheldon's house that night?'

He looked surprised. 'The night of the fire, you mean?'

'Of course,' she said, more sharply than she had intended. 'I mean, why did you go to see the Vampire Regent all on your own? Why didn't you tell me you were going?'

He gave a small smile. 'Because you would have told me not to.'

'I wouldn't ...'

'You would. You would have said, "Gabriel. It's too dangerous!" or more likely, "Gabriel, you have to take me with you." And I couldn't do that, not without putting you in danger. Besides, I wasn't planning on getting grabbed and tied to a chair – I thought I was going there to meet the Regent, do some sort of deal. But it turned out he knew who I was all along.'

April nodded thoughtfully. 'But what happened when you got there? I mean, how did you end up tied to that chair?'

It was something that had been bothering April for a while. Yes, Benjamin had lured him there, but how had they overpowered a fully fledged Sucker so easily? Especially one who was so massively pissed off.

Gabriel frowned, as if he were trying to remember. 'I … I'm not sure,' he said. 'I suppose I must have knocked my head coming off the roof. It's all a bit of a blur.' He turned to her and held both her hands. His eyes were dark, intense. 'Look, April, I'm sorry to be so vague and I know I've been unreliable over the last few months, but as of now I'm all yours – one hundred per cent. When the Regent dragged you away in that burning house, I thought I had lost you. I couldn't stand feeling that again. I never want to be away from you. Okay?'

April felt lightheaded, her heart doing back flips. 'That's fine by me.' She grinned.

He kissed her, on her face, on her neck. April hated the fact that he couldn't kiss her properly – on the lips – but if he did the Fury virus would consume him slowly from within. *I'll just have to make do with this instead,* she thought as Gabriel slipped his hands around her. God knew she could do with Gabriel's protection – she wasn't exactly doing a great job looking after herself. Either way, whenever she was with him, April felt that everything was right. Well, not *everything*, obviously – the world was full of monsters who wanted to burn her alive – but that small detail aside, when April felt his hand in hers, she wouldn't change anything.

'So, where are we going?' asked Gabriel. 'Shall I escort you back to Covent Garden?'

'No, I want to go to Highgate, the cemetery. I haven't seen Dad in a week.'

'Of course, I should have thought,' he said, opening the carriage door and then leading her down towards the tube. Despite the creepiness of Highgate Cemetery, April still loved going to see her dad. Sometimes it felt as if he was the only one who really understood what was going on. Crazy, of course. William Dunne was dead – no one knew that better than her – but April still liked going to sit by his graveside, chatting to him, telling him her news, imagining what he would say, what advice he would give. Today he would probably tell her not to worry so much about Gabriel – and certainly not to worry about going back to school tomorrow. In life, William Dunne had always given her great advice. Was there any reason he should stop now?

At Archway, they cut through the housing estate below the hospital, skirting around the bottom of the cemetery. Seeing all those headstones through the black iron bars still made April feel uncomfortable, even after all this time. It wasn't so much that her father was buried in the cemetery, it was more the reminder of that night when Gabriel had pulled her out, the night Isabelle had been murdered.

'Gabriel, you remember that night? The first night we met?'

'In the square?'

She looked at him sharply. 'That was you? I was never sure.'

Gabriel smiled, his eyes twinkling. 'It was the first time I ever saw you,' he said, touching her face, stroking her hair back. 'I didn't think I'd ever seen anyone so beautiful.'

April felt butterflies within her take flight. God, she wanted to kiss him so badly.

'So why did you suddenly disappear?'

He laughed. 'Your mother turned up, remember? I had a hunch she wouldn't approve of some strange boy lurking around in the shadows outside her house. Turned out I was right.'

'Oh, I think she's warmed to you now. All those times you've saved my life probably helped.'

Sadly April's relationship with her mother was rather less warm these days. Since Silvia's confession of an affair with Robert Sheldon, April had scarcely been able to be in the same room as her mother and had moved out to live with her grandfather in Covent Garden. It wasn't exactly ideal, but then what was in her life right now?

'Anyway, I wasn't talking about then – I meant that night you pulled me out of the cemetery, the night Isabelle died,' said April as they turned up Swain's Lane. 'What happened? You never really told me.'

His expression darkened. 'I don't know.'

April knew she should probably drop it, but there was something about that night which had never quite felt right – and it didn't help that Gabriel seemed reluctant to talk about it. 'It's just that when we were at Sheldon's house, Benjamin seemed to be saying that you were involved in Isabelle's death.'

'I tried to *help* her, April,' said Gabriel, a note of exasperation in his voice. 'But there was something horrible in that cemetery, something evil. I tried to drag her away like I did with you. But there was a darkness there, something bad, black at its heart. I've never felt anything like that before.'

'But what about what Sheldon was saying ...'

'This darkness...' said Gabriel quietly, almost as if he was talking to himself. 'It was like a blanket, a fog. I couldn't get through, and it was pressing down on me. I felt almost powerless. If I hadn't got you out of there, I don't know what would have happened. And even now, it feels as if ...'

April held up a finger to silence him. 'Sorry, Gabe! Look!'

Up the road near the cemetery, there was a large white police van parked half on the pavement, with a police car right next to it, their lights still flashing.

'What are they doing there?' she said, starting to run. 'Come on!'

At the gates, April could see a uniformed police officer standing in the doorway to the miniature Gothic chapel that served as a cemetery office. He was talking to Miss Leicester, the sour-faced old woman in charge. Miss Leicester always had a frown on her face, but today she actually looked angry.

'Excuse me,' said April. 'What's going on? Has something happened here?'

'Nothing to see here, darling,' said the officer, walking towards her. 'The cemetery is closed. Keep moving along, please.'

'Miss Leicester?' called April over his shoulder. 'What's happened?'

The old woman whispered in the policeman's ear and they exchanged a look.

'I'd better call the boss,' said the officer, stepping to one side and clicking on his radio.

Miss Leicester stepped forward, a look of sympathy on her face. Now April was really worried; Miss Leicester was not the kind of woman who gave the impression of caring that much for other people. She only seemed concerned with the well-being of her beloved graveyard. Sympathy from her was bad. Very bad.

'There's been an incident,' said Miss Leicester, her mouth pinched. The way she said the word 'incident', it was clear she actually meant 'another one of those incidents that keep happening around you, April Dunne'. April couldn't really blame her for that.

'What is it? What's happened?' asked Gabriel.

'There's been some vandalism in the cemetery. All rather unpleasant.'

April looked at her, her eyes wide. 'Is it something to do with my dad? It is, isn't it?'

Miss Leicester looked over at the policeman. 'I think you'd probably better wait until the officer ...'

But April wasn't listening. She pushed past the woman and into the courtyard beyond. Already running, she took the stairs three at a time, ignoring the calls to come back. *What had happened?* she thought as she ran up the path towards the tomb high on the hill. What sort of vandalism? Had someone defaced her dad's grave? As she turned the corner towards the Vladescu family vault, April almost ran headlong into a man wearing a raincoat.

'Mr Reece!' panted April. 'What are you doing here?

What's happened? Miss Leicester said there had been some vandalism. Is it something to do with …'

'All right, all right, calm down,' said the detective inspector soothingly. 'Catch your breath and let's try to be as steady as we can, okay?'

She felt Gabriel come up behind her and put his arms around her shoulders. She looked up at him; his face was grim, serious. 'Please, Mr Reece, tell me,' she said.

The policeman breathed deeply. 'Okay. Maybe it's best if I show you,' he said, leading them along the pathway towards the tall grey stone building. There was another policeman standing by the tomb's iron doorway – it was open. *No!* thought April. It shouldn't be open. Only her grandfather and Miss Leicester had keys, so how could it be open? April moved forward, but DI Reece caught her.

'There's nothing to see, April,' he said. 'You can't do anything now.'

'What do you mean? What's happened to him?'

April threw herself forward, breaking free of the policeman's grip, and ran to the doorway. 'Daddy!' she cried. The stone around the door was broken, the iron portal dented, as if a huge weight had been thrown against it. Sprayed in red paint over the word 'Vladescu' was something else – a foreign language – Latin? 'Omnes fures mori' – what the hell? Inside, the small room was empty. Where was his coffin?

DI Reece stepped inside, his face ashen.

'W – where is he? Where is my father?' stammered April.

'He's gone, April,' said Reece. 'Your father's body has gone.'

Chapter Three

Detective Inspector Reece looked like death warmed up – one of her dad's pet phrases, April remembered. Perhaps not the best choice today. Reece never exactly looked great, but today, seated in the Dunne family kitchen, he looked haggard and unkempt, as if he'd slept in his clothes. Perhaps he had.

'We've had reports of vandalism in the cemetery over the past few weeks,' said the inspector, stirring his coffee. 'Some statues kicked over, slogans sprayed on headstones, that sort of thing,' he added. 'I'll be honest; we hadn't really taken it seriously.'

He looked up, his gaze moving from April to her mother and back again, taking in Silvia's glare and April's discomfort. April hadn't been back to Pond Square since that confrontation with her mother the morning after the fire. Reflecting, April realised she hadn't even spoken to Silvia since that morning, but DI Reece had insisted on talking to her and her mother together. So it was that April stood hovering in the doorway, arms folded, avoiding her mother's gaze, willing Reece to get on with it.

'You hadn't taken it seriously,' repeated Silvia, her voice cold.

April knew the look on her mother's face well: she was furious. And for once, April couldn't really blame her.

'What exactly would you class as "serious", inspector?' said Silvia. 'I suppose there would have to be a killing for it to be treated as serious? Or should I say *another* killing? Is that how the police operate nowadays? Just wait until somebody is dead before you investigate?'

Silvia Dunne's voice sounded calm and even, but April knew her mother was like a grenade with the pin out – she could explode any minute. Perhaps sensing this, the inspector attempted a soothing tone.

'I understand how it looks, Mrs Dunne, but we've had a lot more serious incidents to deal with in recent weeks. You're quite right – people *have* been killed, and it is to those investigations we have devoted the most manpower.'

'Oh really?' said Silvia. 'And how are *those investigations* getting along? Have you found out who killed my husband? Have you managed to prevent any more attacks on my family? Because to me, it doesn't look as if the Metropolitan police are doing anything to deal with what's happening in Highgate.'

In normal circumstances, April would have been sympathetic to the look of helplessness on DI Reece's face. After all, the police inspector had always been good to her, but tonight April was just as angry with the police's incompetence as her mother.

'How could you let this happen, Mr Reece?' said April. 'It's my dad! How could you let someone just *take* him? It's bad enough I had to ...' she trailed off. *Bad enough I had to watch him die.* She turned away, hating herself for getting so emotional in front of her mother. *Bad enough I had to get his blood all over my hands, bad enough he was torn from my grasp* – and now it felt like she was losing him all over again.

'Unfortunately, in this case, April, the local police who dealt with the vandalism neglected to pass it on to CID,' said Reece. 'They assumed it was just drunk kids messing around.'

'Just *kids*?' snapped Silvia. 'Is that what you think —'

Reece held up his hands to stop her, but Silvia was in full flight.

'Kids my arse!' shouted Silvia. 'I'm sorry, inspector, but that's just pure crap. I saw that door. It was solid iron but there were huge dents in it. There's no way that was the work of a bunch of drunken kids.'

'I agree,' said Reece, standing up. He reached into a briefcase by his feet and pulled out a folder, then spread a number of photographs on the counter. April and her mother stepped forward. 'Luckily, Miss Leicester had the presence of mind to take pictures of the damage to the gravestones,' said Reece. 'And … well, as you can see, there's a ritualistic element to this.'

April's eyes opened wide. There were symbols painted on the tombs, slogans scratched into the ground, even what looked like … 'Is that *blood*?' said April, pointing to a dark stain on one of the broken stones.

'I'm afraid so,' said Reece. 'I don't want to alarm you, but I think that's strong evidence that there was some sort of sacrifice going on.'

'Sacrifice?' gasped April. 'Human sacrifice?'

'No, April,' said Reece, 'animal – we found a number of dead foxes at the scene.'

April's heart gave a lurch. There had been a dead fox that first night in the cemetery when Isabelle Davis was killed, hadn't there? Silvia had obviously registered April's stricken expression.

'A few dead animals hardly make this *The Exorcist*, inspector,' said Silvia.

'No, but we have to take everything into consideration.'

He pulled out another photo, a shot of the slogan daubed on the Vladescu tomb. 'These words written above the door – "omnes fures mori" – do they mean anything to you? The words translate as "all thieves die". Does that ring a bell with either of you?'

April shook her head, looking at the floor. Her heart was beating so hard she felt sure that the policeman would hear it. Of course it rang a bell. *Fures, furem, fury*: it was *her*. 'Fury' came from the Latin, dreamt up by angry vampires in the time of the Roman conquest. Marcus Brent had told her this as his horrible bony claws had closed around her neck that night in Waterlow Park. It was a term of disgust and loathing, an accusation that Furies like her were nothing more than cowardly thieves sent to steal the vampire's dark 'light'. Something like that, anyway. She had been too busy fighting for her life to ask for a more detailed history lesson.

Reece examined April's face. 'You sure?'

'Of course she's sure,' said Silvia. 'Don't you think we'd tell you everything, inspector? We want my husband's remains back.'

The policeman nodded and stood up. 'Yes, quite. And I assure you we're doing everything we can to trace your husband's body and return it to its rightful place.'

'Assure me?' said Silvia. 'You don't seriously think anything you say is going to carry any weight with me, inspector?'

'Mum ...'

'No, it's quite all right,' the inspector told April. 'I realise neither of you has much reason to trust the police, but we *will* find your husband's body, Mrs Dunne. It is a priority, because I believe that all of these incidents are linked –' he was looking at April now '– the attacks, the deaths – even this vandalism – I think it's all connected. And we *will* get to the bottom of it.'

'Sooner rather than later would be good, inspector. Do I need to remind you that my family have been attacked repeatedly?'

'No, Mrs Dunne, you do not. Thank you. I will see myself out.'

April listened to the front door close, then picked up her coat, turning to follow the policeman. She didn't feel comfortable being in this house.

'Please stay,' said Silvia, walking to her. 'We need to talk.'

'There's nothing to talk about,' said April.

'Your father's body has been stolen,' said Silvia. 'Don't you have anything to say about that?'

'Of course I do! It's horrible, disgusting, heartbreaking, but it doesn't change anything, Mum. You still did what you did and I still feel the same way about it.'

Did Silvia really think she was going to break down and throw herself into her mother's arms? Maybe a year, even six months ago, perhaps she would have, but too much had changed in that time; April had changed too much.

'Please, April, this is serious.' Silvia paused for a moment. 'Please?'

April sighed and dropped her coat on a chair. 'Five minutes,' she said, reluctantly sitting on a stool and watching as her mother filled the kettle again. If you had no idea about the horrific circumstances, you might think this was a normal everyday domestic scene: mother and daughter sitting down to have a chat over a cup of tea. But that was long gone for them, a relic of the world she had known before she discovered that her ordinary boring old life was filled with hideous creatures with long teeth and claws. April suddenly felt a crushing sadness as she realised that nothing her mother could say or do could bring the old certainties of a normal family life back.

'I do miss you, you know,' began Silvia. 'Please come back; your old room is ready for you.'

'Oh no,' said April, 'we are not having that discussion. If you want to talk about what's happened to Dad's body, fine, but let's not get into this. You know very well why I'm not living here any more.'

'No, April, I don't,' said Silvia, turning to look directly at her. 'I really don't understand it.'

April was surprised how angry she felt. 'Because you *lied* to me,' she cried. 'Because you lied to *Dad*, because you lied about your affair with a man who tried to kill me. Is that enough?'

'All right,' said Silvia. 'Perhaps I'm not the model mother ...'

'The *model* mother? You've barely even tried to be a mother. When did you ever act like a mother? I can't remember one instance of you making me a packed lunch, helping me with my homework, even tucking me in at night.'

'But I did!'

'No – Dad did everything like that. You never even came to see me in school plays.'

Silvia frowned. 'I'm sure I remember seeing a nativity play. Weren't you Mary?'

'That was your friend Amanda's daughter Sophie,' said April, tight-lipped. 'You went to *her* play because it was at some swanky public school where you might meet important people over cocktails.'

'Fine. I'm a terrible parent,' said Silvia, crossing her arms. 'It's clear you've made up your mind about that. But however much you hate me, it won't change the way I feel about you, April. I love you. And I want you to be safe.'

'How are you planning to achieve that exactly? Move me back in here? It wasn't exactly safe for Dad, was it?'

'That's not fair,' said Silvia.

'Isn't it? You said it to the policeman yourself – they haven't got a clue what's going on in Highgate and they've no way of protecting me – of protecting *any* of us. So what makes you think you can protect me here either?'

'I'd never let anyone hurt you,' said Silvia, her eyes fierce.

'Really? You've done a pretty good job of that on your own.' April regretted the words as soon as they came out of her mouth. Her mother flinched as if she'd been slapped.

'Look ... I didn't mean it like that,' April said, but Silvia had turned away shaking her head.

Great. Now I'm *the bad guy*, thought April.

The odd thing was, April had never really minded that Silvia wasn't a conventional Barbies-and-baking sort of mother. That was just the way she was – self-absorbed and irresponsible. It certainly wasn't Silvia's failings as a mother which had pushed April away – it was her lies.

'If only you could understand how hard it has been for me,' said Silvia, dabbing at her eyes with a tissue.

'Hard for you?' said April. 'You brought this on yourself, Mum – be honest.'

The last thing April wanted right now was to get into a war of words about the ins and outs of her mother's infidelity, but ever since that night in Sheldon's house, April had been haunted by his words: 'Your mother came crawling after me like a dog on heat.'

Silvia had always maintained that moving to London was William's idea, that she was only here under sufferance, yet Sheldon had laughed at that, said Silvia had talked her father into it, then begged Sheldon to start a relationship. April wanted to know the truth even though nothing could bring her father back.

'Look, I think I'd better go,' said April, reaching for her coat. 'Besides, Grandad will be worrying.'

'April, can't we talk about it like adults?' said Silvia, turning back to her, a note of pleading in her voice. 'I want you to understand what happened with your father and what happened with Robert and ...'

'No, Mum!' shouted April. 'I won't discuss this. I didn't come here to help you work through your issues. I came to hear what Inspector Reece had to say. Seriously, I'm done with this.'

'And you're done with me too?' said Silvia quietly. April's heart sank as she watched her mother's face crumple. Silvia covered her face with her hands and April could only watch as her shoulders heaved with sobs. Suddenly she felt horribly guilty: she had left Silvia to stew, probably drinking herself to sleep every night – and there was no question she deserved it – but Silvia wasn't exactly surrounded by a support network. What friends she had in Highgate were from her snooty dinner party circuit, and hardly the sort who rallied around when tragedy entered your life.

'No, Mum, I'm not done with you,' she said, walking over and putting her hands on Silvia's shoulders. 'It's just that I need a bit of time alone. You can see that, surely?'

Silvia sniffled. 'I suppose... it's just that I'm so worried about you being so far away. I want to ...' she let out another sob. 'Oh God, how can they take him a second time?'

April rubbed her mother's arm. 'We'll get him back, I promise,' said April.

Silvia pulled away and grabbed a tissue, loudly blowing her nose. 'Sorry, darling. It's just I feel so alone in this big house at night, all the noises, the creaking. And I keep seeing people looking in the windows . . .' She shook her head. 'No, that's stupid.'

April looked at her sharply. 'People at the windows? Why didn't you tell Inspector Reece?'

'Oh, it's probably nothing, just paranoia. It's probably just people in the square walking their dogs or whatever. Being on your own, it makes you see things.'

Was Silvia imagining it, or was the house being watched? Was her mother a target? Again April felt a pang of guilt. She was angry with Silvia, yes, but not so angry that she wanted her dead. The very thought made her feel sick – April had lost enough already.

'Listen, Mum, this is getting us nowhere. I'm fine at Gramps's place – he can look after me. Just give me some space, okay?'

'Space to be with your boyfriend, I suppose?' Silvia said bitterly.

April glared at her. 'See? This is why I need to get away. Gabriel is a good man, you know that. He's looked after me. I thought you appreciated that.'

Silvia looked at her. 'All men are after something, and I should know.'

'Maybe the men you chase after aren't the same as Gabriel.'

Just as April had been softening, thinking that she might actually move back into the house, Silvia went and showed her true colours again.

April realised as she snatched up her coat that perhaps she was getting this the wrong way around. If the Suckers were searching for the Fury – and much as she hated to admit it, if Benjamin and Marcus had worked out her identity, it was only a matter of time before someone else joined the dots – her presence in Highgate was only putting Silvia in more danger. Her mother could be ferocious when roused, but – seriously – what could a sharp-tongued widow do against the army of darkness gathering outside her door? However fearsome Silvia Dunne could be, however strong her instinct to protect her only child, the vampires would squash her like a fly.

'Look, Mum, I've got to get back.'

'You go then,' said Silvia, waving her hand dramatically. 'I'll be fine.'

'You know what? I think you will.'

Chapter Four

April went out through the front door, slamming it behind her. *That's getting to be a habit too*, she thought as she pushed past the creaky gate and across the square.

April was so wrapped up in her thoughts, she didn't notice the slight figure sitting on a bench facing away from the road.

'Hello,' she said, stopping April in her tracks. Davina Osbourne. Queen of the Ravenwood mean girls, top dog in the school Suckers and head of the vampire recruitment team. What was she doing sitting outside her house?

'God, Davina, you frightened the life out of me.'

'Sorry,' the girl said, but there was something odd about the way she said it. April looked at her more closely and was shocked by what she saw: Davina's usual super-groomed poise was gone. She looked crumpled, exhausted, her normally blemish-free skin was mottled and there were frown lines on her forehead. If she hadn't felt it was impossible, she would have said Davina had forgotten to wash her hair.

'I heard about your dad,' said Davina, wiping her nose with a rag of tissue. 'Must be pretty freaky.'

April just nodded. She had no idea how to react. Davina looked up and April could see her eyes were bloodshot and red-rimmed. 'Want to go for a coffee?'

Davina smiled. 'Thanks, that'd be nice.'

Sitting across from April at a table in the Americano coffee bar, trapped under the unforgiving fluorescent lighting, Davina looked even worse. She looked as you'd expect someone to whose close relative had recently died: washed out, raw and broken. Somehow you didn't expect vampires to react in the same way as 'real' people.

'So … how was the funeral?' asked Davina, running a nail around the rim of her mocha.

'You knew about it?'

Davina nodded and looked up at April. 'I wanted to go, you know.'

'Really?' said April, taken aback. 'I thought you hated Miss Holden.'

Davina gave a ghost of a smile. 'Hate is a strong word. She did annoy me, that's true, but I … well, I didn't want anything bad to happen to her. Not the way it did, anyway …' she finished lamely.

Was that true? Did vampires like Davina Osbourne actually regret things? Did Davina really care that her little brother had tortured and killed their teacher? Then again, Davina was not naturally the caring, sharing type – her idea of intimacy was air-kissing – so perhaps her crying meant she was genuinely in pain. Yes, Davina was a Sucker, and yes, her brother had been a psychotic killer – but he had still been her brother. She had to be hurting right now.

'Listen, Davina, no one blames you for what happened,' said April.

'It's kind of you to say so, but that's bullshit. Everyone blames me. I can see it on their faces. Our family has some faults, God knows, and I know the things people say about us, but we're not all … killers.' She began to sob.

'Come on,' said April, glancing around the café. 'Let's get away from here.'

Davina wasn't herself at all. The girl April had known up till now, and was surely only lurking a few millimetres under the surface, would rather die than be spotted weeping in a coffee shop. They walked out of Americano and crossed the road into Waterlow Park.

'How's your mum doing?' asked April.

'It's hit Mummy and Daddy pretty hard. This sort of thing just doesn't happen to us.'

Did she mean vampires weren't supposed to die and therefore it was more of a shock when they did? Davina saw April's confused expression.

'I mean, a death in the family is something that happens on TV shows or to other people, isn't it? My mum barely managed when Milo died. God knows how she's going to cope with this.'

They stopped at the edge of the lake. They were alone apart from a pair of ducks which began to paddle over, presumably hoping for some bread from the nice humans.

'And how are you doing?'

'Oh, I'm okay,' said Davina, waving a hand airily. 'People keep asking me that and the thing is ... they just have no idea what it's like.'

'I do.'

She stopped and grabbed April's hand. 'Oh God, I'm so sorry. That police inspector, what's his name? Reece? He told us what Ben tried to do to you. You probably don't want to hear this, do you?'

'It's okay. Honestly.'

Davina pulled some berries off a bush and began to throw them to the uninterested mallards. 'It's funny,' she said quietly. 'You take your family for granted, don't you? Most of the time you're living under the same roof, and they're just so annoying. "Do this"; "do that"; "clear up your bedroom" – it's a nightmare.'

April smiled inwardly. She had seen Davina's bedroom – it wouldn't have looked out of place in the interiors section of *Vogue*, all spotless white carpets and beautiful furniture – and she couldn't imagine anyone complaining about Davina leaving wet towels on the bathroom floor.

'But even so, you just assume they're always going to be there, don't you? Ben was always teasing me, calling me an airhead or a diva, all those things little brothers say to you – and the number of times I told him that I wished he'd just drop dead . . .' She gulped back a sob, pulling out another tissue. 'And then he did.' She turned to April, tears in her eyes. 'And then he *did* drop dead.'

April could only nod and embrace her awkwardly. Davina had no idea that it had been April's blood which had killed her brother. She hoped to God Davina would *never* know.

Davina took a long deep breath and they began to walk again. 'I hear you're not living with your mum.'

'No, I've moved in with my grandad.'

'Well, that big house in Covent Garden's far more glamorous than that poky place in Pond Square.'

It was exactly the sort of thing Davina always said: thoughtless, shallow, judgemental. But the way she said it, April could tell her heart wasn't in it any more. She looked bleak, sagging, no trace of vampire arrogance left. If she was putting it on to get April's sympathy, Davina was a damn good actor.

'Don't be too hard on her, though,' said Davina. 'Your mum, I mean. It can't be easy being one thing and then having to pretend you're . . .' She trailed off.

April frowned. '"Being one thing?" What do you mean?'

Davina shook her head quickly. 'Oh, I just mean you should hold onto what you've got, I suppose. She might drive you mental, but at least she's still there, you know? And it can't have been easy losing her husband.'

'Twice,' said April, without thinking.

'God, yes. I hadn't thought of that.'

April had to admit she hadn't either. She had been so wrapped up with her own problems, she hadn't really considered how her mother would feel about her husband's remains being snatched away in the night. *God, I'm such a spoilt brat*, she thought. Presumably Silvia was struggling with her own guilt – the fact the recycling bin was always overflowing with wine bottles was a strong clue she was finding it hard to cope – maybe she deserved that guilt, but didn't need her nose rubbing in it again and again. April resolved to be a little more charitable towards her mother. As Davina said, at least she was still there.

'You're back in school tomorrow?' asked Davina.

April nodded. She didn't want to go, of course, but she didn't really have an excuse. The hospital had discharged her and she couldn't imagine her grandfather, protective though he was, letting her stay off any longer on the grounds of just being 'stressed out'.

'It's going to be weird,' said April.

'Honey, it already *is* weird.'

'No, but without Miss Holden and Ben and everything.'

'And the new headmaster.'

April turned to look at her. 'What? We're getting a new headmaster already?'

'Didn't you know? Daddy's pleased about that at least. He didn't get on with Mr Sheldon, God rest his soul. This new guy's more in tune with the governors, apparently.'

'What does that mean?'

'I think it means they'll be recruiting more.'

April looked at her intently. '*Recruiting*?'

'You know, getting all the geniuses to do free research for all their chums.'

April gaped at her. She couldn't believe Davina was saying it out loud, as if it were common knowledge. Davina laughed – her bleak mood had clearly lifted.

'Come on, sweetie, you didn't think Ravenwood was gathering all these brain-boxes together for fun, did you?'

'No, I suppose not. In fact I think my dad was investigating Ravenwood before he died.'

'Very possible. That's the sort of thing he used to do, wasn't it? And I can see the papers getting all worked up about using kids as slave labour and all that, but it's not illegal, just a tiny bit immoral. Or at least that's what Daddy says. Ravenwood's a business, sweetie, and the geeks are their biggest asset. I think the idea is to make them work for their keep.'

'But don't we pay Ravenwood to go there?'

Davina sighed dramatically. 'So naïve, honey. I really need to work personally on your education, don't I?'

That's not such a bad idea, thought April. Not a bad idea at all.

Chapter Five

A school assembly was a big event at Ravenwood. Most schools have regular assemblies, but at Ravenwood you were expected to get straight down to work as soon as possible, so assemblies were only used for major announcements. Consequently, as the students filtered into the hall straight after registration, expectation was high, the room twittering with rumour and counter-rumour. Caro, however, had other things on her mind.

'I can't believe you're going to hang out with Davina,' said Caro. 'After all that's happened? Her brother tried to burn you alive, April!'

April glanced around anxiously, shushing her friend. It wasn't as if what had happened in the headmaster's study and at Mr Sheldon's house was secret; the school had been locked down as a crime scene; students and parents had been questioned; and, if they had somehow managed to miss all that, the 'Ravenwood Triple Slaying' had been splashed across the front page of every paper. Even so, April didn't want to draw any more attention to herself.

'I *know* her brother tried to kill me,' whispered April, pulling Caro into a corner out of earshot of any other Ravenwood students, 'but we still need as much information as we can get on the Suckers, don't we? We got rid of the Vampire Regent, but Ravenwood hasn't crumbled, has it?'

'Worst luck,' said Caro grumpily. April followed her gaze over to the other side of the hall where a group of the Faces were settling into a row of chairs, preening and gossiping with, at their centre, Simon, her old friend and major crush.

It couldn't be easy watching him hanging out with a load of half-dead killers. It couldn't help either that Caro suspected those girls of having led her childhood friend Layla to a horrible lonely death in the cemetery catacombs. April could certainly understand her hostility.

'Listen, Davina may be evil, but she's right about one thing,' said April. 'It doesn't matter who's in charge. As long as Ravenwood's still going, they'll be recruiting kids to the Suckers' cause and if we're going to help people like Simon, then sticking close to Davina makes sense.'

'But she must know we know,' said Caro. 'She must suspect that Ben and Sheldon told you everything, mustn't she?'

'Maybe. Almost certainly, in fact. But what are we going to do – transfer to some other school?'

Caro snorted. 'According to the papers, most schools in inner London are more dangerous than Ravenwood.'

Mr Anderson, April's English teacher, walked onto the stage and said that everyone should take their seats. Caro and April moved into an empty row just across from the Faces.

'See that girl next to Ling?' said Caro, looking over at them. 'The one wearing the Prada dress, with the big hair? That's Sunita from my biology class.'

'So?'

'The last time I saw her, she had horn-rimmed glasses, hair all greasy, and was shuffling around in orthopaedic shoes.'

April looked across. The girl's hair was now sleek and backcombed, like a cascading chestnut waterfall – she didn't look comfortable with it though. April could see her hand straying up to touch it every now and then. 'A new recruit? Well, that's who we've got to do it for. The vulnerable ones, those who can't resist the pull of the dark side.'

Caro raised her eyebrows and nodded towards the door. 'Talking of the dark side.'

Davina Osbourne was walking in on four-inch heels, dressed top to toe in black. Students were openly gaping at her.

'Darling, how are you?' she said, stopping next to April.

'I'm fine,' said April, looking up at her. 'More to the point, how are you? Must be strange being back.'

'I've put it all behind me,' declared Davina. 'We have to move forward, don't we?'

To April's amazement, Davina moved into their row and sat down next to them. Caro shot her a startled look. Davina never sat anywhere except with her vamp cronies. To have the head Sucker sit with them was rather like seeing the Prime Minister cross Parliament to sit with the Opposition.

'Um, aren't you sitting with Chessy?' said Caro, nodding her head over to where Davina's second-in-command was sitting with Ling and Simon.

'No,' said Davina simply, but any further discussion was cut short as Mr Andrews clapped his hands, waiting for the chattering to subside.

'Good morning, school,' he said. 'As I'm sure most of you are aware, there were some very unsettling events involving Ravenwood staff and pupils last week, hence our impromptu holiday.'

Many students flicked their eyes towards April – and Davina.

'But, tragic though the events were, Ravenwood pupils are fighters. We won't let that sort of thing stop us being all we can be, will we?'

Caro elbowed April and made gagging motions.

'Anyway, the school governors have acted swiftly,' continued Mr Andrews, 'and I am delighted to announce that as of today, Ravenwood has a new headmaster.'

There was a murmur of anticipation, people craning their necks towards the teachers, wondering if they could spot the mystery man.

'I know you'll give a big Ravenwood welcome to our new headmaster – Dr Charles Tame.'

April's mouth dropped open. She looked at Caro and saw an equally stunned expression on her face.

'Christ, no,' April whispered. 'Anyone but him.'

Charles Tame was the controversial academic the increasingly desperate police had drafted in to help them with the Highgate murders, using his questionable interview techniques on witnesses – or suspects – such as April. He was ruthless, ambitious and very creepy. April vaguely remembered Fiona telling her that he'd been a headmaster of some private school before, but he was about the last person she would have expected to take over at Ravenwood. Mr Andrews led the school in a round of applause, as Tame walked slowly out, a half-smile on his face, his strange pale eyes scanning the hall. April could barely believe that Tame had now taken charge of the school. *How?* She shivered as she remembered him coming to her house under the guise of 'asking a few questions', then forcing her to the floor on the very spot where her father had died. Dr Tame was a man who seemed to have no qualms about pushing the boundaries of professionalism or decency to get what he wanted. Maybe that's why they had chosen him.

'Good morning, everyone,' said Tame. 'I'm very glad and excited to be here, and extremely grateful to the governors for putting their faith in me. I feel sure that, together, we can make Ravenwood an even greater school than it was under my predecessor.' He paused as the slightly bemused students dutifully clapped again. 'I knew Mr Sheldon personally and losing him is a genuine tragedy. He was a wise and caring man.'

Yeah, so caring, he tried to slit my throat, thought April.

'And let's not forget Miss Holden, a valued and well-loved teacher, another terrible loss. Our thoughts are with her family ... But –' Tame paused meaningfully. 'But whatever rumours you have heard, please do not let your imaginations run away with you. I have spoken to the police and the fire chief in charge of the investigation and I can assure you that the regrettable incidents here and at Mr Sheldon's house were nothing more than a series of tragic accidents. Upsetting though they were, we must all put them behind us and move on.'

'Hear, hear!' said Mr Andrews and Dr Tame smiled.

'There has been a lot of disruption and uncertainty around the school for the last few months – I know some of you have lost friends. It has been a dark time, but many of you may know that I've been working very closely with the police and I can assure you that those dark times are over. Things are different now. Although I still expect you all to get As.' This was clearly Tame's idea of a joke and the teachers forced out a few polite chuckles. 'So, as of today, I intend to introduce a new approach to teaching. The old-fashioned methods we've used for so many years just aren't working. I believe in freeing students from the shackles of conventional schooling. Ravenwood pupils are more intelligent and more mature than your average student and I intend to capitalise on that by giving you the freedom to study what you want, when you want.'

April saw a group of girls in front of her exchange looks of surprise – but also of interest. Suddenly, this didn't feel like just an ordinary 'meet the new teacher' assembly.

Tame clearly sensed the mood and a smug little smile crept onto his face. 'First, I'm doing away with learning from dusty old textbooks – what do they know, right?' His smile widened as he heard the gasps coming from the assembly. 'Some of you actually know more than the people standing in front of the class, am I correct? I don't want obsolete student-teacher structures holding you back. I want you to set the pace.'

April saw people nodding all around her. He certainly knew how to work a crowd, that was for sure.

'In so many areas,' he continued, 'Ravenwood pupils are already in advance of university students, so I'm proposing that we teach you like university students – seminars, one-to-one tutorials and open-ended workshops where you set your own goals and choose your own working methods. Oh,' he paused. 'And I'm doing away with homework.'

There was a sudden spontaneous cheer from the crowd – as Tame must have anticipated.

'Oh yes, people,' he said with feeling, 'Ravenwood is the greatest school in the country. The pupils here are remarkable in every way. I feel so proud and honoured to be part of the Ravenwood story – and make no mistake, that story is going to be one you're going to tell your children.'

Caro looked over at April and mouthed the word 'loony'.

'I truly believe that we're making history here. People will gasp when you tell them that you studied at Ravenwood. You are the elite, the vanguard of something new and special. Ladies and gentlemen, we going to change the world – whether the world is ready or not.'

To April's surprise, the hall erupted in applause and cheering. She looked around her in dismay – were they really buying this rubbish? Clearly they were – she saw people looking up at their new headmaster as if he were a pop star. As the assembly broke up, she could hear the twitter of anticipation, groups talking excitedly about what they had just seen.

April looked around for Davina, but the girl had already disappeared.

'Jesus, it's like he's the messiah or something,' Caro said with disgust as they joined the crowds shuffling from the hall. 'Don't they realise he's a headcase?'

April shrugged. 'To them he's just another teacher. They haven't seen Dr Tame up close like we have.'

'Well, if he makes the school in his own image, I can imagine things are going to get a bit weird around here,' said Caro.

'Oh, I wouldn't say that.'

They both turned around to find Dr Tame standing right behind them. Caro's face froze, aware that the new headmaster must have heard everything she had said. 'Headcase' in particular.

'Things will be a little *different* perhaps, Caro,' said Tame with a sickly smile. 'But I think you'll find it an improvement. I find the, uh, more unconventional students really respond to these methods.'

'You're saying unconventional as if it's a bad thing, Dr Tame,' said Caro, quickly recovering her poise.

'On the contrary, Caroline, I think this school needs as many original thinkers as it can get.'

'Oh, you can count on me for original thinking,' Caro smiled. 'Original I can do.'

'I'm very glad to hear that,' he said. 'Disruption, however, I will not tolerate. Is that clear?'

'Crystal, chief,' said Caro, giving him a mock salute. 'Never dream of it.'

Tame turned to April. 'And you, Miss Dunne. I wonder if you'd mind stepping into my office?'

April looked at Caro. 'Why? Is something the matter?'

Tame gave a laugh. 'Relax, April. I just wanted to have a little chat, that's all.'

She reluctantly followed him up the stairs, her feet dragging as they approached the office marked with the neat sign reading 'Headmaster'. She wasn't all that surprised that Dr Tame had decided to take over Mr Sheldon's old office – it was exactly the sort of thing that would appeal to his macabre sense of humour – but April wasn't looking forward to going inside. The last time she'd been here, she'd been forced to watch Benjamin Osbourne burning Miss Holden with his lighter.

'Come in, come in,' said Tame impatiently, holding the door open for her. Feeling she had no choice, April walked in. She was slightly surprised to find the office as it had always been, a rather shabby and cluttered workspace with overflowing filing cabinets. He might have had a spring clean, at the very least.

'Take a seat,' said Tame, walking behind the desk and sitting down. It was only then that April's eyes widened and her heart began to hammer as she realised that the desk was the same one. The *same one*! The desk Miss Holden had been tied to, the one on which her throat had been cut. How could he? How could Tame sit down so calmly behind that desk, as if nothing had happened?

But of course, that was why Dr Tame had invited her up here, wasn't it? April knew she shouldn't – *couldn't* – forget that the police had employed Charles Tame for his unorthodox methods of questioning a suspect. Tame's psychological techniques had caused more than one hardened criminal to crack and April had no doubt that pressure was being applied right now. He wanted her to know that he didn't mind sitting there inches from the spot where her mentor was brutally killed, and he wanted her to know exactly what lengths he was prepared to go to achieve his ends. He had already shown her that when he had visited her at home. She knew he was a monster, perhaps even more so than the vampires. And given Ravenwood's purpose, she had no doubt that the governors had chosen their new headmaster well.

'I suppose this is something of a surprise for you,' said Tame with a smile. Did he mean the desk or his appointment? wondered April. She didn't think it really mattered to him. The idea was to get her off balance – and she certainly had no intention of playing his game.

'Not such a surprise, actually,' said April as calmly as she could. 'I seem to remember you had been a teacher, maybe even a headmaster before?'

Tame nodded. 'Well remembered – "know your enemy" and all that, I suppose. And that is actually why I asked you here. I'll get straight to the point: April, you're a liability.'

April swallowed. 'A liability?'

'Come now, April, let's not be coy. You know very well what I'm getting at. Far too many of Ravenwood's pupils seem to be turning up dead, and you have been present or involved with every death.' He ticked the names off on his long fingers. 'Isabelle Davis, you found the body. Layla? – you found her too. And you were involved with both Milo and Marcus.'

'I was not!'

Tame continued, ignoring her protests. 'Then there was the unfortunate tragedy with your father, of course. And now we have the situation with two of your teachers and poor Benjamin Osbourne – the situation which brings me here.' He smiled, but there was no humour in it. 'So what am I to do? If I expel you, it reflects badly on the institution. Given your father's connections in Fleet Street, we could well expect headlines like "Elite School Abandons Grieving Child" – and that wouldn't be helpful, especially at this delicate time. On the other hand, I can't do nothing. That would look weak – and I'm not a weak man, April. Not at all.'

April looked at him, unsure if she was supposed to respond.

Tame steepled his fingers in front of his face. 'I'll get straight to the point – I would like you to be the new Head Girl at Ravenwood. I think the challenge will keep you busy.'

April was so surprised she actually laughed, but the laughter quickly trailed off as she realised he wasn't joking. 'Me? You want *me* to be Head Girl?'

'Why not? You're smart, well liked and – most importantly – it deals with the PR problem rather neatly, don't you think?'

With a sinking feeling, April could see that he was right. Instead of shunning her and thereby accusing her of being involved with the many 'inconvenient' deaths of Ravenwood's pupils, this way it would appear the school was embracing her, supporting her in her hour of need. It would seem sensitive and forward-looking – and Tame knew that refusing the offer could make April look ungrateful. He gave one of his trademark smug smiles – he knew he had her.

April sat there bewildered. 'I ... I don't know if ...'

'I'll take that as a yes, then,' Tame said, standing and thrusting his hand out across the desk towards her. 'Super to have you on board, April. I know you will be a credit to the school.'

Chapter Six

'Clever,' said Caro, when April told her what had happened in the headmaster's office. 'Very, very clever.'

'You sound as if you respect him,' said April. It was lunchtime and they had arranged a rendezvous in the little-used ladies' toilets by the library. Caro was sitting on the sink, her back to the mirrors, painting her nails a vivid shade of green.

'Oh, it's not *respect* respect,' she said, 'I still think Charles Tame is the spawn of Satan, but it's a very smart move, you've got to give him that. It's a classic politician's trick: spin a positive out of the disaster, turn the focus onto the bright pretty girl rising above the tragedy – don't dwell on the torture and the mound of bodies.'

'Caro!' said April. She had already checked that the cubicles were all empty, but April was still worried someone would overhear and accuse them of making light of the situation. April knew Caro was only joking to keep their spirits up – other people might not understand. Caro rolled her eyes.

'What? You don't like me to point out that eight people have died – no, nine if you count Alix Graves. And that's not including all the times the Suckers have tried to kill you.'

'Yes, I know,' said April urgently. 'But some people at Ravenwood are cousins and friends of the people who died and we don't need any more enemies than we already have.'

'Fair enough.' Caro shrugged, blowing on her nails. 'Anyway, the bottom line is that you seem to have taken the Big Doc's offer. Actually, he knew you couldn't turn it down. Which is all part of his evil genius.'

'What do you mean?'

'With the best will in the world, A, you need all the help you can get on your university application forms, don't you?'

'Unlike you, you mean?' said April sulkily.

'Well, yes actually. Like Simon, like Ling. We're all brain-boxes; why fight it?' said Caro matter-of-factly. 'Face facts, April, you're going to be up against people like us if you want to get into one of the super swanky unis, so why not use all the leverage you can?'

'Uni?' said April with a laugh. 'If I'm still alive when I'm eighteen, I'll worry about it then. My CV isn't really a priority right now.'

'Yeah, well Herr Doktor has outmanoeuvred you on that one too,' said Caro. 'He probably guessed you wouldn't give a monkey's about it, but knows you could never go home to Grampa Thomas and tell him that you turned down Head Girl. Your grandad would blow a gasket.'

April groaned – she hadn't considered that aspect of it, and she wouldn't put it past Charles Tame to call her grandfather and tell him the news. Caro was right: she had been completely outflanked. She had underestimated Dr Tame. She mustn't make that mistake again. 'So now I'm trapped – is that it? Now I'm part of the Ravenwood machine?'

'But it's brilliant, don't you see?' said Caro. 'They've played right into our hands and they don't even know it. Tame thinks he's keeping you where he can see you, under control as his little lapdog. But he doesn't know we *want* to get on the inside, we want to be part of the Establishment. Now you're the face of Ravenwood, maybe they'll let you in on their secrets. We don't know how deeply our new leader is involved, but you've got to guess he's pretty connected to get this job. And, at the very least, you'll probably get to meet the governors.'

'Yes, but ...'

'No buts about it, April,' said Caro firmly. 'You've *got* to do it, especially after this morning.'

'What do you mean?'

'What do I *mean*? – the hero-worship of Dr Tame. It was as if the whole assembly had been brainwashed.'

'It's not that bad yet – is it?'

'God, April, sometimes I wonder if you walk around with your eyes closed. Not only have they replaced the headmaster, we have three new teachers, all of whom look decidedly vampy, especially Miss Holden's replacement.'

'They've replaced her already?'

Caro nodded. 'Miss Marsh. Pale skin, gorgeous black hair, knee-high leather boots, like a walking Sucker cliché. But that's not the half of it.'

She crooked a finger towards April as she jumped down off the sink. 'Come on, it's better if I show you.'

April followed Caro back into the main school building. As they walked along the corridor, April was aware that people were turning to look at her. She was used to that, of course; they had been gawking at her since her first day. But this time, it did seem different. Girls were standing in little huddles talking, and the glances they threw towards April and Caro as they walked past weren't the usual gossipy 'hey look, that's the girl who found a dead body' whispers. Now they seemed to be having their own secret conversations, exchanges they didn't want April and Caro to hear, as if they regarded the two girls as outsiders.

'They're like little witches' covens, aren't they?' murmured Caro. 'They've already bought into Tame's "new world order" bullshit. It's like he's invented electricity or something.'

'That was damn quick,' said April.

'Yeah, well – it's not just Tame,' said Caro. 'Remember I was telling you about Miss Holden's replacement? Come and see.'

Caro led April towards the refectory and, halfway down the corridor, they turned the corner and saw a group of students gathered around a classroom door. Joining the group at the back, April craned her neck to see what they were looking at. Inside the classroom Miss Marsh – it had to be her from

Caro's vivid description – was sitting on the edge of the desk holding court.

'… and I think it's been the same, throughout history,' said the teacher. 'There's always been an assumption that the older generation knows better. This means we must have missed out on so many ideas, limited so much potential – just because the person involved was young. This is ridiculous – we must acknowledge that because young people are unburdened by all the "received wisdom" that adults fill their heads with, they have a greater chance to make genuine discoveries. Adults can't risk making you too self-reliant – otherwise we'd be out of a job.'

There was a ripple of laughter, and in the pause the woman's eyes flicked up and met April's. 'That's why I'm so envious of you. You have a huge opportunity here, to be leaders, to show the rest of the world just what you can do.'

April felt the hairs stand up on the back of her neck. Was this woman addressing all the pupils, or talking directly to her?

Caro pulled on April's sleeve, and they moved away from the door.

'See?' said Caro. 'It's like one of those evangelical TV shows from American cable. "Be all you can be", "shoot for the moon", I wouldn't be at all surprised if they started playing "Simply the Best" over the school tannoy.'

They walked into the refectory and joined the queue for food.

'I can't believe they're buying this,' said April, picking up a tray.

'You've got to remember, these kids are frightened,' said Caro. 'They're geeks, their idea of a hobby is chess, not kung fu. They see people are dying in Highgate, and they're scared to go out after dark. So along comes Dr Tame, who's worked with the police, tells them they're all special – suddenly they're listening. Then he says he's going to treat them like adults? It's a slam-dunk. The guy's a rock star.'

Suddenly April didn't feel like eating. And anyway, she had spotted something – or rather, someone – on the other side of the hall. 'Look, see you at the table,' she called to Caro and threaded her way over to the lonely figure sitting on her own.

'Hi, Davina,' said April, sitting down next to her. At the back of the refectory, the rest of the Faces were laughing and joking in their usual place at the top table. Normally Davina would – should – have been right up there in the centre of things, surrounded by clucking, fawning admirers. But instead, she was here, on her own. It was *weird.*

'Is everything okay?'

'Of course,' said Davina, her back stiff. 'Why wouldn't it be?'

'Well, it's just that …'

'Just that I've been ostracised? Sent to social Siberia – is that what you mean?'

'Something like that, yes,' said April, glancing back at the Suckers.

'I am *persona non grata,*' said Davina, sticking her fork into a lettuce leaf. 'Apparently, it doesn't do to have a brother who brings Ravenwood into disrepute. We couldn't have the school's reputation suffering, could we?'

'Who said that? Chessy?'

Davina let out a bitter laugh. 'As if! That airhead could never have come up with something so intellectual. No, it's our new leader, Dr Tame. My guess is that he's passed the word to his supporters that I'm not to be trusted or listened to. Presumably he thinks, as I was so close to his predecessor, I might stage a coup or something.'

April put her hand on Davina's arm. 'Oh, honey, I'm so sorry.'

'Don't worry,' she said, glaring over towards Chessy, 'they haven't seen the last of me yet.'

April's heart sank as she saw Ling and Simon get up and approach their table. Simon was wearing all black, with thick make-up around his eyes. He didn't look much like the Simon who had befriended April back in the autumn; he seemed harder, more edgy. Ling, meanwhile, was wearing a tight mini-dress and looked as if she had made the complete transformation from geek loser to fully-fledged Sucker. Had she really made the final step and been turned?

'Now then, who do we have here?' challenged Ling, leaning on Simon's shoulder. 'Is it the Face of Ravenwood?'

'Listen, Ling, if you've just come to . . .' began Davina, but Simon stepped forward.

'She wasn't talking to you,' he said with disdain. 'She was talking to the new Head Girl.'

'Head Girl?' said Davina, her eyes flicking to April.

'Dr Tame asked me this morning after assembly,' April said sheepishly. 'I couldn't very well turn him down.'

'And why should she?' said Ling, looking contemptuously at Davina. 'She's the perfect girl for the job.'

Davina looked as if she'd been punched in the stomach. She had always been top dog at the school, undisputed queen of the Faces and, all in the space of a few days, she had been demoted and marginalised. April saw the hurt in Davina's eyes, but could also understand why Ling was so gleefully twisting the knife. Davina had never exactly made her followers feel as if they had any significance; rather she treated them as if they were just minions she would graciously allow to bask in her reflected glory. The truth was, Davina really could be a grade-A bitch, but even so, April couldn't stand to see her squirm.

'Thanks, guys,' said April quickly, 'but I think there are better candidates. I just think the headmaster's trying to help me out a bit. You know, after all that's happened?'

'Oh yes, I heard about your dad's grave,' said Ling. 'So *creepy*. You're so brave to come in to school after all that.'

The truly 'creepy' thing was how much Ling sounded like the old Davina, how effortlessly she had adopted her mentor's techniques of offering up compliments that were actually barbed put-downs. Davina, for her part, looked as if she was trying to sink through the cracks in the tiles.

'I just wanted to come over and see that you were okay,' said Ling. 'Hey, why don't you come and sit with us? You can bring your … friend if you like.'

'No, that's okay,' said April. 'I'm fine here.'

Caro walked over carrying a tray laden with food. 'Hi,' she said shyly to Simon.

April watched Simon's reaction – she was sure his smile was genuine. Maybe Ling saw it too, because she slid an arm around his waist.

'God, Caro, are you going to eat all that?' said Ling, laughing. 'If I even looked at those chips, I'd blow up like a tyre.'

'I guess you and me are different, then, huh?' replied Caro, jamming a doughnut into her mouth.

'Thank God for that,' sneered Ling, dragging Simon away, waggling her fingers in the air by way of a goodbye.

'Yeah, thank God for that,' said Davina quietly. April almost shivered at the look on her face: pure, undisguised hatred, and something else. Hunger.

Jeez, if looks could kill, she thought.

But at Ravenwood, it wasn't the looks you had to worry about, was it?

Chapter Seven

April slid her key into the lock and pushed open the front door. 'Gramps?' she called, her voice echoing around the marble entrance hall.

'Your grandfather is in the kitchen, Miss April.'

April jumped as she saw Stanton, Thomas Hamilton's butler, standing in the shadows. *What the hell is he doing hiding there?* she wondered. *Does he spend all day just lurking in the hall waiting for someone to come in?*

Nodding her thanks, she headed down the stairs towards the basement kitchen, letting out a long breath. The butler wasn't the only reason April was finding her move to her grandfather's Covent Garden house difficult. For one thing, it was about ten times the size of her old place in Highgate, filled with narrow passages and dark corners. The other was the feeling of being watched, not just by the skeletal Stanton, but also by her grandfather. Ever since she had arrived with her little suitcase, Gramps had been unusually attentive, fussing around, making sure she had everything she needed. Of course she knew that he meant well, but what April needed right now was some space, to be left alone to sort things out in her head. There were so many unanswered questions buzzing about inside, she felt as if she might explode. Still, it made a change from living with Silvia, she reflected. At least here she felt she was wanted.

'Here she is!' shouted Thomas as April reached the bottom of the stairs. 'My princess has come home.'

April had tried unsuccessfully to get her grandfather to stop calling her 'Princess'. She had pointed out she was no longer a little girl who dressed up in fairy-tale costumes, but she might as well have saved her breath. To Grampa Thomas, April was a cute little pink-cheeked four-year-old and she always would be. Secretly, April quite liked it. In the tangled mess of her life right now, it was nice to have some sort of certainty and she knew that this giant bear of a man would do anything he could to keep his adored granddaughter from harm.

'So come on, sit down. I've just made tea,' said her grandfather, pulling out a chair for her at the wooden kitchen table and reaching for another mug. 'Now, tell me all about your first day back at school.'

April pulled a face. 'We met the new headmaster,' she said, as he poured milk into her tea.

'You didn't like him?'

April shrugged. She knew she had to be careful, as Grampa Thomas was connected somehow with the Ravenwood hierarchy – the main reason she had got into the school in the first place was because of him. 'Well, he seemed to like me. He wants me to be Head Girl.'

'Head Girl? Oh, darling, that is marvellous!' he boomed, scooping her up into a huge hug. 'I am so proud of you. See? Things are starting to turn around. I told you they would.'

She nodded sadly, staring into her cup. 'Sorry, Gramps, I knew you'd be pleased, but it's kind of hard to get all worked up about it at the moment.'

'Yes, Dr Tame said that this might happen.'

She looked at him sharply. 'You've spoken to Dr Tame?'

'Don't be angry, Prilly. He was only worried about your welfare. After you were rescued from that fire, he called to warn me about the possible long-term trauma – he is a psychologist, after all. He said you might be suffering from PTD or PTS, something like that. He said the shock waves would keep coming, especially after all your other troubles.'

Damn, thought April. She truly *had* underestimated Dr Tame. Had he had been planning to take over Ravenwood all along? Maybe he'd even been in league with Benjamin – some plan to remove Mr Sheldon as headmaster ... no, that was just paranoid – and she reminded herself that this was Dr Tame's speciality – planting doubts in your mind, keeping you off balance.

'Maybe he's right, Gramps.' She sighed. 'But I'm doing my best.'

'That's the spirit.' Thomas smiled. 'You're a strong girl; you get knocked down – you get straight back up again. It's the Hamilton way.'

She didn't feel strong, she never really had. But there was something about her grandfather, a solidness, a stability that she trusted. April knew she didn't have to pretend when she was around him.

'There's one thing I can't seem to get past, though,' said April quietly, 'I keep closing my eyes and seeing the tomb, you know, with the door open.' She felt tears beginning to well up and wiped them away. 'Sorry, it's silly isn't it? I've been strangled and almost roasted alive, but the one thing I seem to be bothered about is somebody breaking into Dad's grave.'

'It's not silly,' said Thomas firmly, squeezing her hand. 'Someone has stolen your father's body; anyone would be upset by that. And believe me, I will move heaven and earth to get it back – and I will make sure whoever did it is punished.'

He put his arms around her and held her tightly. April hugged him back, but was dismayed that she could feel his ribs. She pulled away from him and looked into his craggy face. He still seemed the same man – huge head, overlong wavy grey hair, bushy eyebrows and deep laughter lines around his mouth – same old Gramps, but were there deeper bags underneath his eyes perhaps? A slight paling of the skin? Or was that only her nervous imagination?

'But you're okay, aren't you, Gramps?' she asked.

'Of course,' said Thomas, banging his chest. 'Strong as bear.'

Not 'strong as *a* bear', noted April with an inner smile – her grandfather had integrated well into British society, but occasionally his mask slipped and his Eastern roots showed through a little.

'It's just it feels like you've lost weight.'

Thomas laughed. 'Ah, you females and your obsession with weight. You complain when we're too fat, complain when we're too thin; you're never happy. Your mother? She's always telling me I eat the wrong things and that I should join a gym. I tell her "I get enough exercise running around after my girls."'

April giggled, but then looked at him. 'I just don't want anything to happen to you … I've already lost Dad.'

'I'm not going anywhere,' said Thomas. 'I fully intend to live until I am one thousand years old. And even then, St Peter will have to bring a team of horses to drag me through the pearly gates.'

'Sorry.' April smiled. 'I just get worried.'

Thomas nodded and patted April's hand. 'I understand. Worries can be good, worries can keep you safe. If no one worried about falling off cliffs, the human race might never have made it out of the caves. But you can't let worries rule your life. You are young, you should be going out into the world, enjoying yourself –' he nudged her with his elbow '– kissing this boy Gabriel, eh?'

April felt herself blush. 'Gramps!'

'Hey, I know you young girls, you think of nothing but boys, boys, boys. Your mother was the same.'

April twisted her mouth. 'I don't think *she's* quite grown out of it.'

Thomas's smiled faded a little. 'No, and I don't condone what your mother has done. It was a bad thing, a very bad thing. One thing I value above all others is family, and Silvia?' He shook his head. 'She has turned her back on it. But still, I love her, and I think you do too.'

'Of course I do, but that doesn't mean I want to be around her at the moment.'

Thomas tipped his head to one side and looked at her shrewdly. 'But I think you're worried about her too, yes?'

April shrugged. 'I suppose. I mean, she's up there in Highgate all on her own and there's still some maniac on the loose. I don't want anything to happen to her.'

'She will be fine, Prilly. I know you laugh at me for saying that Hamilton women are strong, but it is true. I had a sister, did you know that?'

April shook her head. Thomas paid constant lip-service to the importance and strength of the family unit, but beyond her mother, father and grandfather, with rare visits from Uncle Luke, April hadn't got the foggiest idea who any of her extended family were. She had a vague idea that there was a tangled family tree of cousins, half-siblings and uncles three times removed back 'in the old country', but no one had ever taken her to a family gathering or talked to her about family history. April had always assumed there was some sort of family feud going on that no one wished to acknowledge. Not that April had any particular desire to go to dull family parties where she'd have to make small talk with strange old ladies and eat weird pickled fish, but even so, she had always been curious about the strange dark portraits hanging in Thomas's hallway.

'Your mum's Aunt Katrine – she was your great-aunt, I suppose,' began Thomas, a smile drifting onto his lips as if he was picturing her. 'God, she was a feisty child, but her mind was always on other things. Once our mother scolded her for something – letting the milk boil over, not feeding the goat, something like that. Well, Katrine ran out of the house, went to the forest and, using a forked stick, picked up a bee's nest and dropped it through the shutters of our cottage.'

'No way!' gasped April. 'What happened?'

Thomas shook his head. 'I was only a baby at the time, but they tell me I was stung all over my body. In the confusion, my father kicked over a lantern and almost burnt the house to the ground.' He chuckled softly. 'That is what I mean when I say strong. We have fire in our bellies. Back in the old country, they used to say that the first head of our family was half man, half dragon.'

April looked at him wide-eyed, then Thomas cracked up laughing.

'That kind of bullshit was one of the reasons I left the country. They believe all that crap over there, I swear.'

April laughed along, but inside she was thinking that maybe being a Fury wasn't so unusual after all. Maybe it ran in the family.

Settled in her bedroom, April curled up on her bed and picked up her mobile. It had been a terrible day by anybody's standards and she was desperate to speak to Gabriel about it all. She had only just persuaded him to join the twenty-first century and get a mobile, but it went straight to voicemail.

'Hey, babes, just wanted to hear your voice,' she said. 'Been a crazy day at Ravenwood. Or should I say *another* crazy day. Call me, huh? Kiss.'

She dropped the phone and looked up at the ceiling, wondering how often her mother had lain in this very spot, looking up at the same ceiling; had she ever felt the same way?

April's room, if she could really call it that, was a rather grand bedroom on the first floor overlooking the street. It was the same room which had once belonged to her mother. April smiled as she imagined Silvia growing up here and in equally grand houses in Belgravia and St James's. With that sort of upbringing and Gramps's endless declarations about how she was his 'special princess' how could she have failed to turn out like she did: arrogant, snobbish and rude? Oh, and explosive, don't forget that one. Around April Grandpa Thomas was sweet and gentle, but when he and Silvia got together, it was like a match had been tossed into a box of fireworks.

April giggled: were those cracks in the ceiling the result

of endless shouting and throwing of ornaments? But the smile quickly faded; thinking about her mother only made April feel sad. She felt a horrible sense of guilt at having abandoned her in Highgate, but what else could she have done? Shrug and say her mother's actions were okay? April knew taking a stand had been right, but that didn't make it any easier. The truth was: April was lonely too. However useless Silvia was as a mother, at least she was there – most of the time anyway. Increasingly, April felt that she was getting further and further away from a place of safety. It was as if she had fallen overboard in the middle of the night and was watching the boat sailing into the distance without her. April hadn't even realised she was crying until she felt the warm tears trickling down her cheeks.

'Sod this,' she muttered, wiping her face. She grabbed the phone and scrolled down to 'Fee' and pressed 'Call'.

There was a long pause, and just as April was thinking about hanging up, she heard her best friend answer.

'Sorry, babe,' said Fiona. 'Just playing high-stakes poker on the net. Had two pair – didn't want to miss the bet.'

April laughed and immediately felt better. The world could be falling apart and you could always rely on Fee to be thinking about something else.

'How are you doing?'

'Oh, about a mil and a half up. Loads of idiots in Slovenia who don't know a flush from a straight. Not real money, unfortunately, but one of these days when someone lets me have a credit card, I'll buy an island in the Caribbean and we can all move there.'

'Knowing my luck, it'll be full of zombies.'

'Ah, do I detect my favourite vampire hunter is feeling a bit down?'

April smiled. 'You could say that. Sometimes it all just feels a bit too … much.'

Fee clucked her tongue. 'That's only a natural reaction, hon. It *is* all a bit too much. You've basically got the weight of the world on your shoulders – if you don't sort this crap out, we're all going to hell in a hand basket.'

'Oh, thanks for the uplifting pep talk,' said April sarcastically.

'Sorry, but if your best friend can't tell you the truth, who can? It's serious, babe. I really don't need to tell you that. People keep trying to hurt you, and, unlike my game, the stakes are as real as it's possible to get. But even so, you can't let it overwhelm you; let's be logical here. Start with what's most important to you.'

April thought about it for a moment. 'Gabriel,' she said, blushing a little as she said it. 'I – I'm worried about him, Fee.'

'Worried? What about? I thought you were all loved-up together now.'

'We are – at least I think we are. But he's been acting strange. He couldn't remember what happened at Sheldon's house that night. I can't put my finger on why it bothers me, but it's odd.'

Fiona paused. 'Well ... the night of the fire was traumatic for him too, you know. He got set on fire, then had to fight the head of a vampire clan. It's a lot to deal with.'

'Maybe, but I'm still desperate to get him out of this dark hole he's in. I—I just want him back.'

'Okay, let's work out how to do that.'

April shook her head. 'It all just seems so impossible, like I'm weighed down by everything.'

'I know, I know. But just take it one step at a time. What's the first thing you need to do? To get Gabriel back, I mean?'

April looked down, thinking about Gabriel, seeing his face. And to her surprise, she didn't think of the sleek, polished Gabriel, the dashing young man in the dinner jacket at the Spring Fundraiser – she thought of him as he had been that morning, sitting at the top of Primrose Hill: ill, grey-skinned, in pain. That was the real Gabriel. Yes, though frail and sickly, at the same time he'd been so real, so alive, someone who could register pain and cold and the passing of the hours. And she knew she had to do everything she could to get him – the real Gabriel – back.

'We need to find the King Vampire,' she said finally. 'I mean, that's the only way we can release Gabe from this curse.'

'Good,' said Fiona. 'Then at least we know what our goal is.'

'But how do we …' began April.

'It doesn't matter how,' said Fiona firmly. 'You don't need to have all the answers. Right now, Gabriel just needs to know that you're fighting his corner and that you're doing all you can to save his life. Okay, so it's going to be difficult, but the best way to get him out of that hole is to show him the way, isn't it?'

Suddenly April felt much better – having it all laid out in such a straightforward manner really did put it all in perspective. And only in speaking about it had she realised how worried she had been about Gabriel.

'Thanks, Fee,' she said. 'Seriously, thanks.'

April loved that, despite being separated by hundreds of miles, her best friend still knew her better than anyone and could cut straight to the heart of what she was feeling. More importantly, April could see that Fiona's no-nonsense approach might answer some of the other things weighing heavily on her too. Find the King Vampire and there was a good chance she might find out who had killed her father. And if they could stop the King, they might stop the vampires once and for all.

'Of course,' said Fiona, 'there are a few *tiny* problems with your plan.'

'My plan?' April smiled. 'I thought it was your plan.'

'Well, if it works, it was all me. If not …' Fiona didn't need to finish that sentence. If it didn't work, there was a good chance there wouldn't be anyone left to take the blame. 'Either way, we do have the small problem of tracking down a man who has remained hidden for centuries, and who is probably surrounded by some of the most bloodthirsty killers to ever walk the face of the earth. Could be a tricky one.'

'Maybe not that tricky,' said April thoughtfully. 'I think I might have an idea.'

April hung up and walked over to the little dressing table. She pulled back her hair to look at the star birthmark behind her ear. She was a Fury, there was no point pretending otherwise. It was time to do like Fee – bet heavily. There wasn't really an alternative.

Chapter Eight

April banged on the door yet again, her palm beginning to hurt now.

'Come on, come on,' she whispered to herself, stepping back and looking up at the windows above the little bookshop. There was no movement, no twitching curtains; it could just be a store room for all she knew. Maybe Jessica didn't even live here. April didn't actually know very much about Jessica. No, that wasn't true: April knew Jessica was a vampire and that Gabriel had turned her; she also knew Jessica was some kind of witch who knew about secret potions and hidden subterranean libraries. And she knew Jessica would understand her urgent need to locate the Vampire King. The one thing she didn't know about Jessica was how she would react to being woken up at quarter to eight in the morning – if indeed she was even in the building.

Maybe she'll turn me into a frog, she thought, peering through the shop's little window with its dangling 'Closed' sign.

'April?' She whirled around to find Jessica standing there holding a takeaway coffee in one hand and a supermarket shopping bag in the other. 'You know we don't open until ten?' she said with a slight smirk.

'Oh, ah. Yes, but I thought you might be in.' She gestured up towards the windows above the shop. 'I thought you might live here.'

'I do,' said Jessica, stepping past her with a set of jangling keys. 'Just been out for some breakfast stuff. Is there something urgent you wanted to see me about?'

She pushed the door open and April followed her in.

'Not urgent really, I just wanted to …' Actually, now she was face to face with the woman, she wasn't entirely sure what she did want. Redfearne's Bookshop was only five minutes' walk from Grandfather's house – if she was so desperate for these answers, why hadn't she come before?

Because you're frightened what you might find, dummy.

After all, here was Jessica, beautiful and sophisticated, the owner of a mysterious shop filled with weird skulls and books on magic – and who knew way more about April's boyfriend than she did. It was enough to make the most confident teenager insecure.

Jessica was looking at her quizzically.

'Ah, I'm actually living with my grandfather now, just around the corner,' said April. 'So I thought I'd pop in and say hello.'

Jessica nodded, but her smile said that she didn't believe this for a moment. You didn't come and hammer on someone's door at eight a.m. if you just fancied a chat.

'Do you have time for a cup of tea?' she asked, gesturing towards the back of the shop. 'Have a perch by my desk.'

April sat awkwardly, clutching her bag on her knee, silently rehearsing what she would say as Jessica clanked around in the shop's back room. What *was* she going to say? 'So Jessica, you know all about the vampires. Can you give me the address of the King?' or 'Can you tell why my boyfriend's acting weird?' What was the etiquette here? Could you even go up to your partner's ex and start asking about his behaviour? April didn't have much experience in this area, but she suspected not.

Jessica came back out and handed April her tea in a bone china mug illustrated with a storybook picture of a fairy, then sat down behind her desk which was piled high with letters and packages.

'You don't mind if I open the morning's post as we chat, do you? Very dull, I know, but paying the bills is all part of keeping this place afloat.'

April watched as the woman began opening envelopes and arranging the contents – usually books, no big surprise there – into piles.

'So how are you feeling?'

'Feeling?'

'After the fire,' said Jessica. She inclined her head towards the shop. 'My customers make sure I hear about everything even slightly unusual. I couldn't have missed hearing about it if I'd tried.' She blew on her tea. 'They do have some strange theories about what happened.'

'Really?'

'The wildest one was that it was a battle between opposing clans of vampires.'

April almost choked on her tea and Jessica laughed. 'Don't worry. I heard a rumour about dragons being kept in the dungeons at the Tower of London last week. The laws of averages mean that they'll get it right once in a while.'

'You knew?' said April, her eyes wide.

Jessica shook her head. 'No, not at all. I guessed Robert Sheldon might have another agenda beyond Ravenwood, but … no, I had no idea that was going to happen to you – or to poor Annabel Holden.'

'But if you thought something was happening with Mr Sheldon, why didn't you say?'

Jessica slid a gold letter opener into another envelope and slit it open. 'I have known – or rather, known of – Robert Sheldon for many years. He was always scheming, manoeuvring, always on the edge of something, but to be honest, I didn't think he was dangerous. Or rather, no more dangerous than the rest of them. Clearly I was wrong.'

'Did you know about Mr Sheldon through Isabelle?'

'Isabelle?' said Jessica, looking up.

'Isabelle Davis. She went to Ravenwood, didn't she? I thought she worked here too.'

Jessica gave a gentle laugh. 'It's funny how history seems to repeat itself over and over again. No, Isabelle didn't work here, but she came to see me – or rather, she came to the shop asking about the *Albus Libre*, as you did.'

April almost gasped. 'So what did you tell her? Did you send her to the library as well?'

'No,' said Jessica, her expression turning serious. 'Isabelle wasn't like you. I told her I couldn't help her and that she had to find it her own way.'

'So why did you help me and not her?'

'Because you were trying to help someone else; you were prepared to take a big risk in order to save someone you cared about and I thought that should be rewarded. And ...' she paused. 'I imagine that's why you've come to see me again, isn't it? To talk about Gabriel?'

'Am I that transparent?'

Jessica smiled. 'He's the one thing we have in common, isn't he?'

April looked down at the mug, absently examining the faded picture on the side. 'It's just that I'm worried about Gabe,' she said. 'He's acting strange and ...'

'You wanted to know whether it was normal, right? Is Gabriel being a vamp or is he just being a man?'

April gaped at her. *Could she read minds?*

'I know,' said Jessica, smiling thinly. 'Sometimes it's hard to tell them apart, isn't it – a psycho killer or a thick-headed idiot?'

She shuffled her letters into neater piles and smoothed them down on the desk. 'Listen, April, men are men whether they drink blood or not. All those love spells you read about in fairy tales –' she shook her head ruefully '– they don't work, not on men anyway. They're too self-absorbed by half.' Then she looked up, her eyes meeting April's. 'Is he starting to get blackouts again?'

'Yes! How did you ...?'

'Never mind. How much time has he lost?'

'He can't remember much of the evening we went to Sheldon's house – not the bit before I arrived, anyway.' April had a sudden sick feeling in her stomach. 'And now I think of it, he said he couldn't remember much about the night Isabelle died, that night he saved me from the killer.'

Jessica looked at April for a long moment, then carefully put her letter opener down. 'It's happened before. Not for a long time – at least, not that I know of.'

From Jessica's expression, April could tell this wasn't good news.

'What happened? I mean, the other times he forgot stuff?'

Jessica paused for a beat. 'People died, April.'

April tried to draw a breath and found she couldn't. 'Do you think Gabriel was involved?'

'Listen to me carefully, April,' said Jessica, sitting forward. 'I know you love Gabriel, but you have to understand who he is, what he is. He's a vampire, he's a born killer. Or at least he's been turned into one and when he's in the grip of the thirst, when he absolutely has to feed, nothing on earth should get in his way.'

April could feel all the blood draining from her face. She was frightened for Gabriel, for what he was going through, but she was frightened for herself too. Was Gabriel truly a killer? Was he out of control like Marcus had been? Like Benjamin? She had seen that up close, and April wasn't sure she could stand it if Gabriel turned into a monster like that.

She flinched as she felt Jessica's hand on top of hers.

'Hey,' said the woman softly, kneeling down next to April's chair. 'Gabriel's one of the good ones, remember? And so are you – and you wouldn't have fallen in love with anyone bad, would you? But he *is* a vampire and I'm sure you've seen enough of that to understand what he's going through.'

April nodded. She could still close her eyes and see his face that morning at the top of Primrose Hill, just after he'd taken the Dragon's Breath and changed back into a vampire – his eyes red slits, his lips pulled back like a snarling dog's. He wasn't human at that moment, he wasn't Gabriel, not the man she knew. But somehow ... he *had* been. Inside, he was still the man she loved.

'Jessica, please,' she said, 'what's happening to him?'

'I wish I could tell you, April. All I know is that when he starts forgetting things, it always happens at times of increased darkness, times when the vampires are on the rise again. It could be coincidence, but I suppose that's something you're going to have to find out.'

'But you're worried, aren't you?'

'Yes, I am. Not for his physical self – he's about as tough as they come.' She smiled sadly. 'No, I'm worried about what it does to Gabriel's mind. I've known him a long time, April, and he's too sensitive – too fragile emotionally. He may not be able to remember, but he suspects what he might have done and it's been eating away at him. That might be why he pulls away from you at times. He scared of who he is.'

April wanted to cry, but knew she mustn't. Gabriel was the one in pain and he needed her support. 'Can't we help him? I mean, if it's happened before, you must know what to do.' She hated the desperation in her own voice, but that was how she felt. She would do anything to help him, anything.

'People have to want to be helped, April,' said Jessica. 'Gabriel's too proud, that's always been his problem. He's a lone wolf – thinks he has to do it all himself.' She gave a smile. 'That's men for you. They'd rather plough into the sea than ask for directions. But the same applies to you too.'

'Me?'

'You can't do this on your own either,' said Jessica. 'Yes, you're a Fury, and yes, I imagine it feels like a huge burden, but remember that you're not on your own. You have people you can talk to – friends you can trust – so lean on them. That's what they're there for.'

April looked at her. 'Why do I feel there's a "but"?'

'But ... be careful whom you choose as your friends. What you have inside you is incredibly powerful. Don't underestimate it. A lot of people would love to be able to control what you have. Question everyone, question their motives – even question mine.'

'Yours? But I came to you. And what would you want the Fury thing for anyway?'

'Everyone loves power, April, everyone, even if they think they do not. That's why I didn't tell Isabelle about the White Book.'

'I don't understand.'

'Isabelle didn't want the *Albus Libre* for someone else, as you did. She wanted it for herself.'

Suddenly, April understood why Benjamin had wanted the Dragon's Breath that night at Ravenwood, and why Sheldon had tried to drain her blood. If someone had control of both the disease and the cure, they could create an army of vampires at will – and destroy any other nests or clans who might try to question their authority. You'd be a vampire super-power with the power of life and death over everyone.

'So Isabelle was … she was working for the other side?'

Jessica's smile was ironic. 'I don't know who she was working for, or whether it was all her own idea, but that's what I mean about power. It can corrupt, April. You are frightened of your power and that's the best way to be – because you will agonise over your choices, wondering if you're doing the right thing. For Isabelle, I think the answers were all too clear – whatever was best for Isabelle.'

April couldn't think what to say. She felt knotted up with questions, none of which had easy answers. April had always assumed Isabelle was like her, someone struggling with her 'gift', stumbling around in the dark, looking for clues. But April supposed whatever she had in her blood was as random as any disease – cancer didn't only go for bad people, it took plenty of good people too – and there was no reason why a Fury couldn't be as ambitious and self-serving as a vampire.

'So what happened to her? Was she involved in something that got her killed?' April suddenly felt sick again. 'Was it something to do with Gabriel? I mean, he was there the night she died – and he doesn't seem to be able to remember it.'

Jessica shook her head. 'Don't go jumping to conclusions – and no, before you ask, I don't know what happened to Isabelle. But if Gabriel has suppressed his memories of that night, pushed it to the back of his mind for some reason, that suggests to me that it was traumatic in some way, though I can't say for sure. I think that's something you're going to have to take up with him. If he'll open up to anyone, it's you.'

'Thanks, Jessica,' said April, getting up. 'I actually thought I was going to get a telling-off coming in here.'

'Well you have, sort of. It's time to stop pretending all this isn't happening. When you're lost in the darkness, the only way out is to keep moving forward. It's a bitch, but there's no way back now. You can't put the genie back in the bottle.'

April nodded and picked up her bag. 'Sorry for disturbing you so early.'

Jessica shrugged and pointed towards the desk. 'You were only keeping me from my admin. Talking of which, I'd better get back to it.'

April winced at the light as she closed the shop's little purple door. She looked down at her phone: still only eight-thirty. She sighed and turned towards the tube. She didn't feel much like going to school, but Jessica was right – she needed to keep moving forward.

'April!'

She turned; Jessica was standing in the doorway of the shop, beckoning. 'I think you'd better come and see this,' she said, her face serious.

Back inside the shop, Jessica carefully locked the door, then led April back to the desk and picked up a white padded envelope from the pile of post.

'What is it?'

'Tip it out onto the desk.'

From the expression on Jessica's face, April immediately knew that she didn't really want to see what was inside.

Gingerly, she took the envelope by one corner and upturned it.

'Eww!' she cried, as a small wet thing plopped onto the desk. Like a slug or a piece of meat. 'What the hell is that?'

'It's a tongue,' said Jessica simply. 'Someone ripped it from an animal.'

'God!' said April, taking a step back. 'But why?'

'It's a message, April. Someone doesn't want me talking.'

'To *me*? They don't want you talking to me?'

'That'd be my guess.'

'But it's too late,' she said, looking towards the door.

Jessica gave a grim smile. 'Then let's hope no one sends you *my* tongue.'

Chapter Nine

The lesson was sending April to sleep. Something about the metaphysical poets and their role in … God, *something*, April wasn't sure what. Not only was it deathly dull, it was made all the more turgid because Amy Philips was taking the lesson. Amy was one of the biggest know-it-alls in Ravenwood – and there were certainly a lot of candidates for the role.

'Andrew Marvell's poem "To His Coy Mistress" makes an almost self-conscious allusion to the poetic tradition,' said Amy, clearly loving being right at the front of the class. 'But in reality his was a wholly new approach to lyricism, with an emphasis on the freedom of expression.'

'God, she's boring,' whispered Caro, 'I really didn't think anyone was going to take Dr Death's idea of empowering the students so seriously.'

April stifled a giggle, drawing a glare from Amy. In actual fact, April had been in three lessons this week where the students had taken over the lecture. She didn't mind a bit of healthy debate, but the problem was that the only people who wanted to stand at the front and drone on tended to be the creepiest spods in the school. It wasn't until you had to listen to people like Amy Philips that you began to appreciate how hard it was to make dry subjects such as poetry sound interesting.

It wasn't only the change to the school routine that was unsettling. There seemed to be new staff being brought in every day, plus an almost daily procession of men in white coats trooping down to the 'Special Projects' laboratories on the lower levels of Ravenwood.

April flipped a new page over on her notepad and wrote:

What's going on in the basement?

She knew Caro had been invited to a 'special lecture' on biological development or something equally unfathomable. Caro had been particularly excited, not by the subject matter, but because Simon was also something of a brain-box in biology, and it meant that they could sit together, like they had done before the Suckers and Ling got hold of him. Caro picked up April's pen and replied:

Molecular models, some weird stuff about the effect of TV on the brain, loads of 'practical' science.

She drew an arrow towards the word 'practical' and added:

Meaning 'makes money for RW'.

April wrote another note:

And what about Simon?

With an impish smile, she drew a love heart next to his name. Caro shook her head and scribbled out the heart.

Gone total Sucker. Like he's joined a cult.

April squeezed Caro's hand sympathetically. 'Sorry,' she mouthed.

The bell rang to indicate the end of the lesson and April heaved a sigh of relief. Amy Philips was still glaring at them as they filed out and Caro stuck her tongue out at the girl.

'Very mature,' said Amy. 'No wonder no one's talking to you any more, Caro Jackson.'

'What do you mean? April's talking to me.'

'Yes, but that's because both of you are ...'

'We're what?'

'Weird.'

Caro burst out laughing. '*You're* calling *us* weird?' she spluttered.

Amy put her hands on her hips. 'It's about time you grew up and realised that Charles Tame is ...'

'Oh, it's Charles now, is it?' interrupted Caro. 'Has he been offering you *special* tuition?'

Amy's pale face turned bright red and April knew Caro

had hit the bullseye; the girl had a crush on Ravenwood's new leader. Bizarre – how anyone could find him anything other than repellent was beyond her.

'Just because you can't see how important his work is ...' pouted Amy. 'Just because you don't have the imagination.'

'Oh, I think I know exactly how important his work is, Amy,' said Caro. 'And it's you who lacks the imagination. How about I fill you in on exactly what's going on at Ravenwood, huh?'

April grabbed Caro's arm and pulled her out of the classroom. 'Shhh!' she said urgently. 'What the hell are you doing?'

'Well, that stuck up little cow annoyed me. They all think they're so ...'

She trailed off as they turned into the corridor. Written on the wall in fat black marker, letters a foot high, was a slogan:

EMBRACE THE DARK

'What the hell?' whispered Caro in her turn, and the two girls exchanged a look.

'Isn't it wonderful?'

They turned to see Dr Tame watching them, his eyes shining.

'Wonderful?' said April. 'Shouldn't you be getting the caretaker to scrub it off?'

'Yeah, and tracking down the vandals?'

Tame shook his head. 'Girls, your thinking is adorably old-fashioned. What we're looking at here isn't vandalism, it's *creativity*. Free-thinking minds expressing themselves to their fullest. This shows that what I have been saying is getting through – there are no boundaries at Ravenwood any more.'

'So, if I wrote "Screw Ravenwood" on the front door, I'd get a pat on the back?'

'No, Caro, that would be different,' said Tame, 'because

you wouldn't be entering into the spirit of the new times. As I said to you before – open minds yes, negativity, no.'

'And there's nothing negative about "embracing the dark"?' said April.

'Nothing whatsoever, April, in fact I believe it is the only way to progress. We need both light and shade, do we not?'

Jesus, he really is off his rocker, thought April.

Tame stepped forward and grabbed April's arm, squeezing hard and steering her back along the corridor. 'Actually, I'm glad I've bumped into you, Miss Dunne,' he said, seemingly oblivious to the squeak of pain which came from April. 'I wanted to talk to you about your new role.'

April looked over her shoulder at Caro, but her friend merely gave her a shrug before Tame dragged her out of sight.

'Now then, April,' said the headmaster. 'How did your grandfather react to the news of your elevation to Head Girl?'

'Pleased,' said April. *He was over the moon, as you very well know*, she thought.

'Hmm, that's good. Very good.'

April gave him a sideways look. Why was Tame so interested in Grandpa Thomas all of a sudden? And then it hit her. April almost slapped herself on the forehead. How could she have been so naïve? Gramps was well connected with the school governors, not to mention all manner of politicians and businessmen in the city – Dr Tame had given April this so-called honour to impress her grandad. The annoying part was – it had worked.

They turned down a passage that led towards the front of the school and April noticed two boys loitering outside the entrance to the toilet. On seeing Tame, one of the boys immediately slipped inside the door. It was clear to April that the boys were lookouts. Dr Tame hadn't missed it either. He released April and pushed the door open.

'Gentlemen,' he said, 'is there a problem here?'

April didn't want to follow him into the toilet, but over

Tame's shoulder, she could see two boys – from the dark eyes and casual swagger, she immediately had them pegged as Suckers – coming out of a cubicle, quickly followed by another smaller boy with a frightened look on his face. April noticed that he was fiddling with the cuff of his shirt. Had they been *feeding*? Here in the school?

'No problem, sir,' said one of the Suckers, a half-smile on his face. 'Just, uh, preparing for our next seminar.'

'Well, don't skulk around in the shadows, Calvin,' said Tame. 'What have I told you about hiding your light under a bushel? Stand up straight and show the world, hmm?'

'Whatever you say, sir.' Calvin smiled.

April gaped – was the headmaster just going to let them off? He must have known what they were doing, or at the very least known they were up to no good. And yet, instead of giving them detention, he appeared to be giving them a pep talk and a thumbs-up. Tame set off again, the matter clearly having been dealt with to his satisfaction.

'Sir? Aren't you going to do anything?' said April as she trotted to keep up. 'I mean, weren't they doing something wrong?'

'Oh, come now, April, boys will be boys,' said Tame, waving a hand in the air. 'Young Calvin is very popular with the other boys, not to mention something of a talent on the sports field – giving him lines will hardly motivate him to success. I want the students at Ravenwood to know that I support them in whatever endeavour they choose, as long as they deliver. Results are everything to me.'

They stopped at an empty classroom and Tame ushered April inside.

'Which brings us to you, Miss Dunne,' he said, shutting the door behind him. 'As Head Girl at Ravenwood, I want you to set an example to the other students.'

'An example?' said April, glancing at the door. She was feeling very uncomfortable being alone with Tame, especially as he now seemed to be saying that vampirism was fine on school premises – what else would he find acceptable?

'An example, Miss Dunne,' he repeated. 'You need to be someone Ravenwood students can look up to, someone they can aspire to be. Of course, there are brighter students at the school, Ravenwood being one of the top academic schools in the country, so you can't hope to be competing with them.'

Oh, cheers, thought April, *thanks for the words of encouragement.*

'No, what I would like you to be is a leader, someone who embodies everything that's good about Ravenwood, the poster girl if you like.'

'I'm not sure I'm exactly the right person ...'

'Nonsense. With a visit to the hairdressers, perhaps a little fashion advice, you could be quite presentable. But that's only part of the role. I want to see our new Head Girl out there waving the flag for the school, telling the world. So I've arranged a little interview with the local paper.'

'For me? You want me to talk to the newspapers?'

'Of course, April,' he said, his weird pale eyes boring into her. 'Nothing too scary, just a little Q&A. We need to get the message out about what a fantastic new approach we have here at Ravenwood. That's not a problem, is it?'

'No, I ... I just wouldn't know what to say.'

'Don't you worry your pretty little head about that; I'll be writing it for you. Ravenwood is the best school on the planet, blah blah, incredibly supportive to me, all the usual. You just need to pose for the pictures.'

He leant forward and pressed a button on an intercom.

'Mrs Bagly, could you send him through?'

April gaped at him.

'You want to take photographs *now*?'

'No time like the present, hmm?'

God, thought April as she sat there nervously watching the photographer set up, *Caro is right: Tame is good at this*. By getting April to appear in public, saying how happy she was at the school, it would neutralise the 'Headmaster Dies In

Suspicious Circumstances' headlines the tabloids had been printing.

Mercifully, the photographer seemed in a hurry and only wanted to take a few shots of her sitting at a desk pretending to write, before disappearing as quickly as he had arrived.

'So can I go now?' asked April. She was keen to be out of this office as soon as possible.

Tame pursed his lips.

'Soon. But first I do have one other little favour to ask.'

Uh-oh, thought April. She had a horrible feeling she wasn't going to like this.

'As you're mixing with the pupils, I would like you to keep an eye out for anyone who might be, how shall I put this? Who might be a *problem*. Perhaps they're struggling with their studies, perhaps they're not quite fitting in with the other students. Or perhaps they're doing well and just looking for guidance. Either way, I'd like you to tell me about it.'

Unbelievable. Tame was actually asking her to recruit for him. He wanted her to weed out all the undesirables – people like Caro, people like *her* – and presumably he also wanted April to identify the students who might be more open to his special brand of indoctrination.

'Is all that clear?' said Tame.

'Yes, but I don't see ...'

'Yes, you do, April,' he said, standing up. 'I think you understand very well. Let's not spell it out any more than we have to. If you want your grandfather to carry on being proud of you, if you want to carry on attending this school, then you'll do as I ask.'

'And if I say no?'

Tame's mouth split into a wide grin. 'But that's just silly, isn't it? You won't say no. Because if you don't do exactly as I ask, we shall cease to be friends. And you want to be friends with me, don't you, April?'

What April wanted to do was to start choking his scrawny

neck. She didn't want to have anything to do with Dr Charles Tame and his 'new regime'. But once again, he was correct. She *couldn't* say no; she couldn't risk getting thrown out of Ravenwood, not when she was getting so close to the truth. No, she had to play along – play dumb, in fact. Which gave her an idea.

'All right, just one thing though,' said April.

'Hmm?'

'What you were saying the other day? About banishing homework? Well, if I'm doing this extracurricular work for the school it might help if you could have a word with my teachers. Maybe ask them to give a little boost to my marks? It would take the pressure off.'

April saw the look of delight spread across Tame's face, just as she had known it would. Dishonesty, manipulation, these were things he could work with. If April was prepared to cheat her way to qualifications, then the headmaster knew he could manipulate her any way he chose.

'I think that can be arranged,' said Tame, holding the door open. 'One last thing,' he said, reaching into his pocket and pulling something out. 'You'll be needing this. So everyone can see.'

He held it out to her and April took it. It was a brass and enamel badge reading 'Head Girl'.

Chapter Ten

'Hey, baby girl,' said Ling, her hand on one hip. 'Looking good.'

April groaned inwardly. She had been trying to slip out of the main entrance without being seen. The last thing she wanted after her confrontation with Dr Death was to spar with Ling and the Suckers. Not that she had much choice: on one side of Ling was Chessy, on the other Simon, and behind them a handful of Faces wannabes. The only way to the gate was to walk through them.

'Oh, hi, Ling, how're you?' said April, trying to force a smile.

'Just peachy, honey pie. Much like yourself.'

April was unsettled by the way Ling was looking at her and wondered again if the girl had been turned. No, as she looked closer, April could see that Ling was made over to within an inch of her life: pleated micro-mini, crisp white shirt with the top buttons undone and patent black stilettos. But under all the artfully applied eyeliner and blusher, April could still see a rash of acne. *Vampires don't have acne*, she thought.

Chessy stepped forward. 'So where's your little friend Davina today?' she asked, just a hint of sarcasm in her voice.

April shrugged, feigning indifference. Clearly, Davina was no longer part of the gang and if April was going to fit in, as Tame had ordered, she had to follow their lead.

'Her?' she said. 'Not seen her.'

'Maybe she's sick, eh girls?' said Chessy, to snorts of appreciative laughter.

'I'm sick of her, that's for sure,' said Ling. 'And it looks as though we have a new leader, doesn't it, pookie?'

She turned to Simon who reached out and touched April's 'Head Girl' pin. 'Love the badge, April,' he said slowly.

As he moved closer, April could see that Simon's eyes were glassy and unfocused. Oh God, he couldn't have got into drugs, could he? Simon had always seemed so sensible, so down to earth, but April supposed that if his head could be turned by a bunch of glamorous vampires, then there was no saying what he might do. She really didn't know him any more.

'So our boy Cal says you've been hanging out with Dr T,' said Chessy. 'He seems to have taken you under his wing.'

'I wonder what you offered,' said Simon with a sneer.

April glared at him. It was one thing for Simon to want to hang out with the Faces; it was another to adopt their bitchy sarcasm.

'No, she wouldn't – she's got the gorgeous Gabriel to take care of that department, haven't you, babe?' said Ling.

'I can't blame you for that,' said Chessy. 'Sometimes I wish I still had him visiting me in the middle of the night.'

Gabriel and Chessy? thought April with horror. It couldn't be, Chessy was just trying to wind her up – wasn't she? But then she remembered how, at her birthday party at Davina's house, Chessy had disappeared upstairs with Gabriel. The very thought made her feel physically ill – and deep down, she had to admit to herself that she was jealous. After all, April couldn't exactly fulfil her role as a girlfriend very well, given that a single smooch could kill Gabriel stone dead. But there was nothing to stop Chessy and Gabriel kissing – or doing anything else – and on that level, April simply couldn't compete.

'What are you doing on Saturday?' asked Ling.

'Uh, no plans ... I don't think so, anyway,' stuttered April, unsure where this was leading.

Ling and Chessy exchanged smiles.

'That's such good news,' said Ling, 'because it just so happens that I'm having a little get together chez nous, and I was wondering if you'd like to come along.'

'Bring Gabriel too,' said Chessy, practically purring as she said his name. 'I'd love to see *him* again.'

'And bring Caro,' said Simon, drawing a glare from Ling.

'Sure, why not?' Chessy smiled, clearly enjoying the tension between Simon and Ling. 'Maybe she can bring some of those cheesy nibbles of hers.'

April nodded, not sure what to say. 'I'll see you then,' she said, edging around them and out onto the road.

'Can't wait,' said Chessy in a sing-song voice.

April stomped up the hill, smarting. She had the distinct feeling that she was the butt of an elaborate joke. Clearly, the plan to integrate with the Suckers was a dismal failure. Dr Tame might have adopted her as some sort of performing monkey, but it was evidently going to take more than the headmaster's seal of approval to win over the Faces. She thought of that cold afternoon when Ling had come to her and they had talked in the church. The girl had seemed frightened by what was going on at Ravenwood, even disgusted by it. But now? It seemed as though Ling had replaced Davina as queen bee in the Ravenwood honey trap. She might not be a vamp, but that made Ling all the more dangerous, because she had been so utterly seduced.

'Dammit,' muttered April. She had been so flustered by the Faces, she had followed her feet and found herself back in Pond Square. *You don't live here any more, numbskull,* she scolded herself and turned down Swain's Lane towards the tube. To April it seemed as though she couldn't do anything right at the moment. She was failing to help Gabriel, she was being outplayed by Dr Tame and she couldn't even convince the Suckers to be her friends. She couldn't really blame them. Gabriel was always saying vampires were suspicious by nature and April must be deeply suspect to them. She had emerged from Mr Sheldon's bonfire unscathed – either that meant she was very lucky, or she had something going on that they didn't know about. And vampires didn't like uncertainty, she knew that much. They would be watching her closely – very closely.

As she came to the black wrought iron of the cemetery's North Gate, she stopped to peer through. It was hard to pass it without thinking about her first experience of the cemetery, that night with Isabelle and Gabriel and the unseen force with the dark eyes. Now it looked so peaceful, with the sun breaking through the canopy of trees here and there, the dust and the insects whirling in the light. What was the darkness which had descended on this peaceful place? Was there real evil here? Was there even such a thing as 'real evil'? Just then a movement caught her eye and she froze. Standing at the end of the pathway, perhaps two hundred yards ahead of her, was a man – and she immediately recognised him: the caretaker she had met on her ill-fated tour of the cemetery.

'Hey!' she shouted. 'Over here! It's me, April Dunne!'

The man turned and their eyes met, just for a moment. 'Oh my God, it *is* him,' she whispered to herself. So much weird stuff had happened to April since that encounter, she had almost managed to convince herself that he had been a figment of her imagination, some sort of spook conjured up by her grieving mind. 'Please!' she shouted. 'I need to talk to you!'

He had to have heard her – she *knew* he had seen her – but the man turned and moved off down into the trees.

'Hey, no, come back!' she shouted again. 'NO! Don't go!'

April quickly looked up, thinking that perhaps she could climb over the gate, but there were spikes at the top and she wasn't at all sure she would be able to make it in her school skirt.

'Bugger this,' she said and ran down the hill, keeping the cemetery's high brick wall to her right, hoping she was following the caretaker's path, and maybe could even cut him off. Her feet pounded against the road, then skidded as she stopped by the cemetery's entrance. She grasped the black bars, pushing her face into the gap, desperate to catch sight of the man. *Where was he?* If he had continued down the hill, he should have come to this open courtyard.

'PLEASE!' she shouted desperately. She knew she probably looked utterly mad, but something told her that this man could tell her something about her father's disappearance. 'I look after the graves' – isn't that what he had said the first time she'd seen him? She turned and ran to the main gate, rattling it against the lock. *Dammit*, she thought, knocking on the window of the cemetery office.

'Miss Leicester!' she cried. 'It's April, April Dunne! Can you let me in?'

There was a pause, then the old woman appeared. Her face had none of the sympathy April had seen at their last meeting. Her mouth was a fixed line; she looked annoyed at having been disturbed.

'What is it, Miss Dunne?' she said, unlocking the gate, but keeping it half-closed, her body blocking the way.

'Please, Miss Leicester, I need to get in. It's important.'

The woman pursed her lips. 'I'm not sure it's appropriate, April,' she said.

April shook her head, confused. 'What? What do you mean?'

'Access to the cemetery is for the relatives of people interred here.'

'That's me, isn't it?' April said impatiently, craning her neck to look behind the old woman. Why was she stalling?

'No, April, that isn't you – not any more. I don't wish to seem indelicate, but your father is no longer here. You're no longer an *official* relative, are you?'

April looked at her. 'You're kidding me, right?'

'I'm afraid not. If you took the time to look at the regulations we send out to every mourner, it clearly states ...'

'Look, I haven't got time for this,' snapped April. 'I don't even want to go to my dad's grave, I just want to get inside to talk to your caretaker.'

The woman's eyes narrowed. 'Caretaker? What caretaker?' she said.

'I can't remember his name – I met him once and I've just seen him at the North Gate; I think he might know something about my dad's disappearance.'

Miss Leicester gave her a strange look. 'April, I really don't think there's anyone here who can help you. The police interviewed all of the staff – if anyone had any information, they would have passed it on in the proper way.'

'Oh, Jesus Christ, you old witch, will you just let me in?' April shouted.

'April? What's going on?'

She jumped as she felt a hand on her shoulder.

'Mr Gordon,' said April, relieved to see the vicar. 'Thank God you're here. *Please* can you tell Miss Leicester to let me in? I need to speak to someone I saw inside. It's very important.'

She saw the vicar exchange a look with Miss Leicester. Mr Gordon was a kind man, but she knew that look – 'humour the loony in case she goes nuts'.

April closed her eyes and let her shoulders sag. She knew it was too late; she had missed her opportunity. The caretaker – or whoever he was – clearly hadn't wanted to speak to her, and by now he could be anywhere in the cemetery. If someone wanted to hide, the cemetery was the ideal place. Besides, calling Miss Leicester an 'old witch' probably hadn't been a great move. Silently cursing herself, she turned back to the woman, whose face was now a vivid pink.

'I'm sorry,' she said. 'Really, I shouldn't have said any of those things. It's just I thought I saw something, I didn't mean … I suppose I'm not at my best at the moment.'

'Let's just forget all about it, shall we?' said Miss Leicester tightly. 'Perhaps it's better if you come back later, hmm? I'm sure we could arrange a scheduled supervised visit to the tomb if that's what you'd like? Perhaps with your mother?'

April gave a thin smile. 'Yes, thank you. That's nice of you.'

The last thing she wanted to do was visit the cemetery with Silvia, but she nodded gratefully. At least the horrid old bat wasn't banning her outright. The woman pointedly closed the gate with a clang.

'Would you like me to walk you back?' said the vicar once Miss Leicester had gone.

'No, I'm heading to the tube. I'm living with my grandad in London now. My mum and I … we're not really speaking at the moment.'

'Oh, I'm sorry to hear that. Anything I can do? Talk to her, perhaps?'

'That's kind, but I don't think that'll make much difference.'

'Well, do you mind if I accompany you to the station?' asked the vicar, falling into step beside her as she walked down the hill. 'I need to take some leaflets down to the library anyway.'

April nodded mutely and they walked a little way together in silence. April knew she had screwed up badly, but somehow the caretaker – or whoever he was – had felt like a direct link to her father. She realised in a rush that was why she had become so emotional – over the past few weeks, since his remains had disappeared, she had been losing her connection to her dad. Before the tomb had been opened, April had been visiting her father on a regular basis, talking to him, giving him her news, acting as though he was still there. But now? All trace of him was gone. And it hurt. It really hurt.

After a while, April glanced over at the vicar. 'What do you think happened, Mr Gordon?' she asked.

'Happened?'

'You know, the vandalism, the stuff in the cemetery – Inspector Reece said there had even been sacrifices.'

The vicar was quiet for a moment. 'I don't know. But it's not good, April,' he said. 'I hardly need to tell *you* that. But it's not just the cemetery – they attacked the church as well.'

'Really? What happened?'

'Oh, nothing anywhere near as serious as the terrible thing with your father. Just slogans daubed on the walls, a few things left outside the back door, kids stuff really, but I'm worried that it … that it might get worse.' He looked at her and his expression was bleak. 'It's a dark time, April.'

She nodded. She certainly wasn't going to argue about that. She thought about telling him about the animal tongue she had seen at Jessica's, but that made her think of something more important. 'Mr Gordon, can I ask you something?'

'Of course.'

'I was wondering about Isabelle. Isabelle Davis. Remember you told me she had come to you looking for a book?'

When April had visited St Michael's looking for the *Albus Libre*, the vicar had delivered the disquieting news that Isabelle had been there before her, seeking the same thing.

'Isabelle … yes, of course. Poor girl. What about her?'

'I went to the bookshop you told me about and spoke to the owner there. She said she thought Isabelle was a bad sort.'

Mr Gordon paused, frowning. 'Isabelle was a troubled girl, there's no doubt about that, and I was certainly worried that she had fallen in with a bad crowd. I had the sense that somebody was – not using her, that's not quite the right phrase, but that she was under the influence of somebody, maybe a man she was in a relationship with?'

April shrugged. It was possible. She didn't really know much about Isabelle beyond the few snippets she had picked up from Jessica. 'What do you think she was up to? You know, with this book and everything?'

'The occult,' he said matter-of-factly.

'The occult? Like devil worshipping?'

The vicar shook his head slightly. 'No, more like she had filled her head with a load of silly ideas about spells and potions. I think she truly believed they would work. I think she also believed that they were her tickets to wealth and power.'

'And you don't believe in that?'

He gave a wry smile. 'There are more things in heaven and earth, Horatio, than are dreamt of in your philosophy.'

'That's from *Hamlet*, right?' said April. 'We studied that last term.'

Mr Gordon smiled. 'The point is, I believe there are plenty of things out there we can't understand – your father and I agreed on that much at least – but if there is magic in the world, then surely it affects all of us, not just the privileged few.'

April nodded. He was right – vampires did exist and, while there were only a few of them compared to the billions of humans alive, their very existence threatened all of those people. It wasn't just about the Suckers, it was about what the Suckers could do, how they could upset the balance. And he was right, even with all she knew, there were things out there that not even she could understand or explain away. Like the caretaker.

'Mr Gordon, you've spent a lot of time in the cemetery. Have you ever seen anyone inside? Like, someone who shouldn't be there?'

'The vandals you mean?'

'No, not them. I mean more like *things* that shouldn't be there.'

He gave a nervous chuckle. 'Like ghosts?'

'Sort of. That sort of thing, but … not. Like this caretaker guy I saw.'

The vicar stopped walking and looked straight at April. 'Of course,' he said quietly. 'Ghosts, spirits, whatever people might like to call them, but certainly things that defy explanation.'

'Really? You have?'

The vicar gave a soft laugh. 'It's not just me, April. Look it up on the Internet; people have been seeing things in the cemetery for decades. All that nonsense about the Highgate vampire, for example. That all began because somebody saw a spectral presence lurking in the cemetery one night. No doubt many of those sightings are optical illusions, wishful thinking, or something to do with the fact that we're on a direct route from the Gatehouse and the Rose and Crown.'

'But what have *you* seen, Mr Gordon? Why do you believe me, when nobody else does?'

'Because I've seen far too much, April. I'd be a fool to deny it.'

April felt relief washing over her. For a moment she had believed that she was losing her mind. It was ridiculous, of course; April knew for a fact that vampires – legendary creatures from the depths of human imagination – lived among them, sitting next to her in the school canteen and queuing behind her for carrot cake in Americano. But there was something *real* about the vampires. Perhaps scientists hadn't been able to explain it yet, but to April, the vampires were not supernatural, they were simply human – with all the humanity taken out. The caretaker, on the other hand, he seemed to be something else again, something that went beyond what she could see, or hear, or understand. There was no evidence for it – after all, he could just be some old bloke who'd hopped over the fence; it wasn't like he was levitating or anything, but he just felt ... wrong somehow.

'There are things going on in that cemetery I can't explain,' said Mr Gordon, 'either as a rational modern man or as a spiritual man. I can't say I've seen your caretaker, but I've seen people or "things", as you put it, that shouldn't exist.' He smiled at her. 'I suppose it's kind of funny; after all, things you can't see are sort of my job, aren't they? The church is always asking people to have faith, to believe in things beyond the ordinary, to put themselves into the hands of the God they can neither see nor even, in most cases, understand. But when I'm actually confronted with something like that, it still freaks me out.'

April laughed despite herself. It was good to hear somebody like the vicar admit to feeling the same way.

'So what do you think it is? What is going on in the cemetery?'

He shook his head. 'I don't know, but I can say for certain that something is wrong in Highgate. A darkness.'

'A darkness?' repeated April, thinking about the graffiti she had seen in the school only that afternoon.

'It's only a feeling, April, but I've noticed that feeling getting stronger over the last few months.'

'Since I got here, you mean?'

The vicar took a deep breath. 'To be frank with you, yes. I think it does have something to do with you and your family. Your dad had a theory that there was some sort of badness, some sort of evil, under the ground – that it was somehow leaking up through the cemetery. I don't know whether that was right, but too much has happened around you and your family to deny that you're involved.'

For a moment, April thought about telling him everything, about how she was a Fury, about how she was in love with a vampire, about how she was involved in some kind of holy war between the undead and – who? With a jolt April realised she didn't even know who she was fighting for. But April was painfully aware of the fact that virtually everybody she had confided in over the past few months had either ended up dead or in danger. Mr Gordon was a good man, and she had no desire to see him hurt.

'What should I do? How can I stop this darkness?'

'Fight, April. I'm sure my bishop would throw a fit if he heard me giving you such advice. But I don't see how you have any choice. Sometimes you have to choose a side.'

'What about turning the other cheek?'

'What if somebody tears that cheek off? I can't tell you what to do, but if it was me, I would take the fight to them.' A smile played on the vicar's lips. 'Kick 'em in the balls, April. It's what Jesus would have done.'

April burst out laughing and Mr Gordon joined in.

'Sorry, I shouldn't have said that. Of course the Lamb of God would have chosen a more peaceful route – but Jesus wasn't above getting physical to make a point. Overturning the moneylenders' tables in the temple, sticking Doubting Thomas's fingers into his wound, that sort of thing.'

April frowned – perhaps she hadn't been listening hard enough in RE. The idea of Jesus as some ass-kicking ninja didn't really fit into her Sunday school picture-book notion of what he looked like. 'Didn't he tell off one of his disciples for slicing off some Roman guard's ear?'

'Yes, that's true, but that's because he wanted to be crucified.'

'He *wanted* to be crucified?'

'I know it sounds strange – but it's actually the whole basis of Christianity. Jesus allowed himself to be captured and crucified to expose the hypocrisy of the Romans and the Jews. He was making a point about dying for our sins, yes; but on a social level, he was also showing his followers how far they had to go to win.'

They stopped in front of a church and Mr Gordon pointed up at the carvings of Christ on the cross. 'See? Our religion was built on the blood of martyrs – you've heard about Christians being fed to the lions in the Roman arena? – but death often has more power than life in the minds of the living. If Jesus hadn't understood the power of an idea backed up by action, Christianity might well have stayed as some backwater cult.'

'You're saying I need to sacrifice myself?'

'No, I'm saying you need to make a choice. I know I sound like some sort of mad preacher, but making a choice was all Jesus did. Bad things were happening to the people around him, so he stood up and said "enough". He gave people an alternative, set a personal example they could aspire to, even if they couldn't follow him up onto the cross.'

April suddenly thought about Dr Tame and his little pep talk about the Head Girl being someone who sets the example. What if she could set the example in a way Dr Tame hadn't thought of, use her new platform to subtly change the message Dr Tame was broadcasting? She wasn't exactly sure how she could do it, but the idea made her feel energised, hopeful. They had reached the concrete ramp to Archway tube now, the library was on their right.

'I'm going this way,' said April. 'Thank you for listening to me. I can see why my dad confided in you.'

'William Dunne was a very clever man and I think he raised a very clever girl too.' Mr Gordon reached over and gave April's hand a squeeze. 'You'll do the right thing – I know you will.'

April hoped he was right. She really did.

Chapter Eleven

Caro was clearly enjoying herself. 'So, this is like a council of war?' she said eagerly, nibbling on some Twiglets. April suspected her friend would have preferred to be meeting in a bunker somewhere rather than in April's bedroom.

'It *is* a council of war,' said April, looking from Caro to Gabriel, then across to Fiona who was patched in via the laptop. 'It's time for us to fight back – that's why we're all here. It's time to take the battle to the Suckers, not wait around for them to jump out at us. We've had enough of that already.'

After her discussion with the vicar, April was anxious to get moving, stop talking and do something. So she had called Gabriel, for once getting hold of him straight away, sent a taxi for Caro and got Fee to video-call her so she could join them in the room. April kept thinking about what Mr Gordon had said. If Jesus was prepared to get his hands dirty, why shouldn't they? Not that she was putting herself in the same boat by any stretch of the imagination – she couldn't even scrape together twelve followers – but she liked what the vicar had said about using an idea as a weapon.

April looked around the room at glum faces. Fiona was the first to speak.

'We're with you, April,' said Fiona. 'Of course we are. But you can see how depressing it is. They've got the best minds of their generation, unlimited funds, probably half the government and the police force in their pockets – and that's not to mention the massed forces of darkness waiting outside our houses. Whereas what do we have? Three of you down there in your mum's dingy old bedroom and me stuck up here in Scotland. The odds aren't good.'

'Screw the odds!' shouted April, anger bursting from her. 'Listen, we don't have a choice. We have to stop them. *Have* to, otherwise countless people will die. Gabriel – tell them!'

Gabriel closed his eyes, then nodded. 'You're right. Of course you are.'

April looked at her friends, making sure it was sinking in.

'I know it's scary, but there's no more time to scrape around picking up clues here and there. We have to find the head of the vamps and kill him right now. It's that simple.'

'Simple – ha!' said Caro sarcastically, but April turned on her.

'Yes, Caro – simple, really simple. Look around you, look at what's happening at the school – we're running out of time. If we don't move, if we don't do something, right now, we're going to lose. Everyone's going to lose – your family, your friends, everyone is going to be swallowed by this.'

'All right, so what do we do?' said Fiona.

April looked over at the computer screen – her best friend's face was sympathetic, but she could see the scepticism there. Even Fiona, her most practical and reliably 'can-do' friend doubted her. 'We take them on, Fee,' she said quietly. 'Yes, you're right. There's only the four of us, and thousands of them. But at least we have the element of surprise.'

'And we've got you, too,' said Gabriel.

He saw Caro pull a face.

'Hey, I'm not being soppy,' he said defensively.

'Yes, you are,' grinned Caro.

'Okay, maybe a bit. But the point is – April is a Fury. She is our secret weapon – hopefully secret, anyway. In her we have the power to kill any vampire, born or made. But it's bigger than that, because a Fury is the only thing on earth that a vampire fears. If we can make the vampires feel vulnerable, we have a slim advantage and slim is better than nothing.'

Gabriel was sitting forward now, his eyes bright, hands

animated, and April could see he was excited. For the first time that night, she really began to think they might be able to pull it off.

'Actually, that's something Sheldon said on that night of the fire.' She nodded. 'He said the power of the Fury "goes deeper than blood". That's why he wanted to cut my throat and collect my blood in the sink – it was like having a nuclear bomb. He didn't actually need to set it off – it was enough to have the threat of it.'

April could hardly believe that she was talking about herself in such a way, that her blood, the very stuff inside her veins, had become this weapon of war. But she knew she had to use everything at their disposal, however uncomfortable it made her feel.

'What about the Guardians?' said Caro. 'Aren't they supposed to be protecting the Fury? Shouldn't they have some ideas about what to do?'

April shook her head and glanced over at Gabriel; she could tell he wasn't comfortable with it. The Guardians were sworn to destroy all vampires, they didn't differentiate between 'good' and 'bad' vampires, plus April was fairly sure he didn't trust them. Also, from what Elizabeth Holden had said, they could not be relied upon – perhaps Annabel Holden had been the last Guardian willing to help.

'All right, I'm in,' said Fiona decisively. 'What do you want me to do?'

April felt a wave of relief. For a few minutes, she had been thinking that she was going to have to undertake this alone. But she had made up her mind: even if she were alone, she was going to fight. What she had said was true – she didn't really have any choice. She could never have lived with herself if, knowing about the threat, she had just sat by watching it happen – not when she had the power to do something about it.

'Okay, first things first. We need to find the King Vampire – we have to assume he's behind Ravenwood and orchestrating the bigger conspiracy. Get *him*, we get all of them. Or at the very least, if we remove the leader, there's a good chance we'll make the rest of them scuttle away.'

'Plus we get Gabriel back,' said Caro.

'And hopefully we'll get everyone else back too,' said April, holding Caro's gaze. They both knew she meant Simon, although after her encounter with him at the school gates April hoped they hadn't left it too late. He'd looked sick, but not just from the booze or the drugs or whatever he'd been lured into, he'd looked like he'd given up on life. All the more reason to get moving.

'Hey, I've just had a thought,' said Fiona. 'If the King is persuading these greedy fat cats to come over to his cause, he must be revealing who he is and what his plans are. And that means the King is more vulnerable now than he has been for years, maybe even centuries. Which is another advantage to us.'

April felt a rush of love for her friends. They all knew that the vampires were a real threat; they knew involvement could get them all a quick trip to the morgue, and yet they were still here, offering their support with enthusiasm. And what made her heart ache was that they were doing it for her. Yes, maybe they believed in the cause; yes, they all wanted to help annoying geeks like Amy Philips from English who were ignorant of the terrible danger they were in; but they weren't doing it for that – they were doing it because April had asked them to. It was amazing and brilliant and tragic and terrifying all at the same time. *I'd better get it right*, she thought. She pulled out her school notepad and flipped it to a clean page.

'All right, so who *is* the King?' she said. 'I mean, anyone got any ideas – or any ideas on who might know?'

'How about Dr bloody Tame? He's like a Ravenwood cheerleader,' said Caro. 'Surely he must know. And he was working with the police too, remember?'

'Maybe,' said Gabriel thoughtfully. 'He's the sort of man

who would do anything to be introduced to the leader. That's why he's so gung-ho about it all – he wants the King to hear about what a good job he's doing. We mustn't underestimate him.'

'I agree,' said Caro, a smile creeping over her face. 'I think he's a good way in. The Head Girl is probably the best person to be questioning him.'

April's heart sank. She followed the logic of this, but with no desire to spend any more time in Dr Tame's creepy presence. *It's a dirty job* ... she thought to herself, writing down 'Tame' with an arrow pointing to him and 'April' beside it.

'All right, so who else can we try?' she said. 'The King has got to be somebody in authority, somebody who has influence, like a politician, somebody who can actually make changes.'

'David Harper,' offered Fiona.

They all turned towards the screen.

'David who?' said Caro.

'Don't you people read the papers?' she said. 'He's your MP.' When they looked at her blankly, Fiona tutted loudly. 'Elected six months ago? That by-election after the bloke with the red face died? He's all anybody's talking about in politics at the moment – he's like a rock star or something. He's not a minister yet, but he's already being touted as a possible future leader of the party.'

'So how come we haven't heard of him?'

'Anyone heard of David Cameron or Tony Blair before they got on TV? Harper's suddenly this go-to quote machine. Plus he's good-looking and actually seems to have a sense of humour, rare enough in politicians. The press love him.'

'I'm confused, Fee,' said April, frowning. 'You're saying this David Harper might be the King Vamp?'

'Nah, he's hardly going to be able to go around kissing babies and having his photo taken for the local paper, is he?' interjected Caro.

'No, my point is David Harper's your local MP, and it

shouldn't be too difficult for you to see him. Head Girl of the top local school – he's not going to turn down that photo opportunity, is he? And if you can get him talking about politics, maybe you can find something out.'

Gabriel was nodding. 'Actually, he'd be perfect for the vamps. All politicians need financial backing and political support. They could give him that, then he could use his influence in the vampires' favour once he's in power.'

'All right, he's on the list,' said April, scribbling his name. 'Who else?'

'Your grandad is well connected, isn't he?' said Caro. 'He's got friends in the police and business – why don't we ask him?'

April felt her stomach clench. It was one thing meeting a local politician or sucking up to the headmaster, but it felt wrong involving her grandad. He had been so supportive these last few months it would feel like she was betraying his trust. Besides – he'd almost certainly dismiss talk of corruption, let alone vampires, as a consequence of her recent experiences.

'I can't,' she said. 'Dr Tame's already got to him – talked about me having post-traumatic stress disorder. He'll never take me seriously. In fact, he'd probably send me to a shrink. But I *will* take advantage of this Head Girl thing, and see what I can find out about Dr Death.'

April saw the excitement on her friends' faces. For the first time since the disaster of the fire at Sheldon's house, she felt they were back in the saddle – moving forward, getting somewhere. And, if she was honest, April liked the fact that people were deferring to her, asking her what to do. Maybe there was something in this Head Girl thing, after all. Now all she had to do was lead them into battle. *Simple*, she thought to herself with a wry smile.

'Okay, Fee, see what you can find out about David Harper's background,' she said. 'Maybe look around other politicians who might be open to an approach from the vamps. Caro, you concentrate on the science part. Speak to the teachers in the school labs, see if you can find out how close the links with Agropharm are, maybe volunteer to help out with research. I'll go with Tame and see if his mania for publicity will get me into David Harper's office.'

Caro gave a mock salute. 'Okay, boss,' she said, but nobody smiled. They knew what they were facing was deadly serious. The time for joking was over.

'So what do you want *me* to do?' said Gabriel, smoothing April's hair back and kissing her neck.

'I just want you to keep doing that.' She smiled.

Caro had taken a taxi home and Fiona had disappeared into cyberspace, leaving Gabriel alone with April. She felt the almost forbidden excitement of being here, in her bedroom, with the man she loved. There were definitely some advantages to living in a house with a butler, she thought. Grampa Thomas seemed to regard Stanton as some sort of old-fashioned chaperone; as long as he was in the house, her grandfather was fine about Gabriel coming over to visit. April glanced towards the door, gripped by the uncomfortable feeling that Stanton might be peering in through the keyhole.

'You know, it's good to see.'

'What's good to see?' asked April.

'You, taking charge. I'm proud of you.'

'I haven't got much choice, have I?'

'No, you always have a choice, and yet you're still doing the right thing. Whether it comes off or not.'

She squinted up at him. 'You mean, even if it gets me killed?'

'I will never let anyone hurt you,' said Gabriel, his eyes fierce. *That's what my mum said too*, thought April.

'I know,' she said softly. 'But that's the funny thing; for some reason, the risk of it doesn't bother me. All I care about is having you back. The one thing I couldn't stand would be not ever being able to kiss you.'

He grinned. 'Oh, you can kiss me all right, just not on the lips.'

'Seriously, you know what I mean.' April sat up and pushed herself back against the headboard. 'Listen, Gabe, I didn't want to say anything in front of the others, but ...'

'I'm looking terrible?'

She was glad she hadn't had to say it. Gabriel was fully vamped-up, his hair was sleek, dark and immaculate, his skin flawless, just like a vampire's should be, but even so, he still looked ill. There were bruised lines under his eyes and while his irises were their usual dark blue, they looked flat, with none of the usual sparkle.

'It feels like I haven't slept in days,' he said quietly. 'Or rather, whenever I close my eyes ...'

'Bad dreams?' she guessed, reaching out to stroke his cheek.

He nodded. 'And they're getting worse. It's almost as if ...'

'What, honey? You can tell me. You can tell me anything, you know that.'

He sighed heavily. His eyes were focused on some point across the room. 'It's like they're not dreams at all.'

Gabriel's expression was so bleak April wanted to gather him in her arms.

'Then what are they?'

'It's like they're memories.'

April swallowed. She wasn't sure if she wanted to hear the answer, but she had to ask.

'Memories of what?'

'Bad things. Blood, death.'

Her stomach felt as if it was full of glass. She knew what he was suggesting – it was exactly as Jessica had said. He was racked with guilt about her, about Isabelle, about all the deaths he hadn't been able to prevent and now he was torturing himself over what might have been, wondering about what had happened in the blackouts. Wondering if he had killed and couldn't remember. Her heart thudded with anxiety.

'You don't know they are memories, Gabe,' she said, hating the note of desperation creeping into her voice.

'Maybe …' he said. 'Maybe they're just dreams.'

She put her arms around his neck and pulled him close. 'They're just bad dreams,' she whispered, wishing she truly believed it. 'Believe me. They're just bad dreams.'

Chapter Twelve

She ran down the corridor towards the front of the building, hoping that she wasn't too late.

Bloody Miss bloody Marsh, she thought as she ran, *why do teachers always have to mess everything up?*

Skidding around a corner, April ran straight into a girl coming the other way. They both fell to the floor in a tangle of limbs, the other girl spilling an armful of books across the corridor.

'Sorry!' said April, clambering to her feet and heading off towards the main entrance. 'In a hurry – Head Girl stuff.'

April's plan had been simple enough: sit quietly through History, get out of class the second the last bell rang, then try to catch the headmaster as he was getting into his car. She hoped to engage Dr Tame in some witty conversation about the school, flattering him about his brilliant notion of using the Head Girl as PR for Ravenwood, then slip in a suggestion about arranging a meeting with 'a local politician' in such a way that Tame could claim the idea as his own. But of course, that hadn't worked.

Miss Marsh, being a new teacher and, presumably, keen to please the new headmaster, had called her back. April had expected the 'my door is always open' speech but instead, Miss Marsh had looked slightly awkward and said, 'Dr Tame has asked me to give you a little more *assistance* in your lessons.'

April had almost forgotten twisting Dr Tame's arm, by asking for preferential treatment from the teachers. April had nodded, muttered something about needing to do 'an important press thing' and sprinted for the door.

But she was too slow. As she entered the final stretch with the main entrance right ahead of her, her path was blocked by a group of girls, led by Chessy, coming out of the ladies toilets. *Damn.*

'Oh, hi, Head Girl,' Chessy said with a smirk. 'How are you?'

'Fine,' said April, trying not to pant.

'Been running, have we? No one chasing you, I hope.'

April frowned, sensing that something was wrong. The girls behind Chessy all had those sly smiles that said 'we're in the gang and you're not'. And they all looked very pleased with themselves.

'No, no, I'm good,' said April.

'That makes me happy,' said Chessy. 'Because not everyone's feeling so good right now, are they, girls?'

Chessy's gaggle of wannabe Faces – all new recruits, April noted – tittered and followed their leader past April and down the corridor. April began to walk towards the entrance, but then stopped. *Damn, damn, damn*, she thought, turning back. Something was wrong, she could feel it – Dr Death would have to wait. Gingerly, April pushed the toilet door open and peered inside.

'Hello?' she said. 'Anyone in here?'

There was no reply and for a moment, April thought that she had been imagining things. But then she heard the rush of a flushing cistern and a cubicle door opened. At first glance, April barely recognised the girl who emerged.

'Davina?'

Her hair was sticking out, her lip was cut and bleeding, and although she was trying to hide it, there was a livid bruise spreading on her arm, just below the torn sleeve of her shirt.

'What the hell happened?' said April, closing the door.

Davina walked to the sink with as much dignity as she could manage. 'Just a little disagreement,' she said, leaning into the mirror and dabbing at her lip with a paper towel.

‘A disagreement?’ repeated April. *More like you’ve been beaten up*, thought April.

‘I thought I could use the ladies in peace – they disagreed.’

With shaking hands Davina opened her bag, almost spilling her make-up into the sink. She selected an eyeliner and tried unsteadily to apply it.

‘’Vina? Are you all right?’ said April, walking up slowly, as if the girl might bolt like a startled horse.

‘Me?’ she said, closing the liner and shoving it into her bag. ‘Yes, of course. Why wouldn’t I be?’

‘Come on, don’t be silly. We can talk about this. What the hell is going on here?’

Davina kept staring into the mirror, as if she couldn’t bring herself to look directly at April. ‘I should have thought it was obvious. Clearly there’s been a temporary shift in power.’

April put a hand gently on Davina’s shoulder and she flinched. ‘Come on, let’s talk somewhere else. We don’t want any intrusion now, do we?’

Davina took a ragged breath in, then nodded. ‘If we must.’

April led Davina outside into the playground and sat her down on the bench she and Caro considered theirs. Predictably, the cut on Davina’s lip was already healing and April guessed that the bruise would soon be gone too. But surveying her, April could see that the damage on her face hadn’t all come from the attack. If Gabriel looked like he hadn’t slept in days, Davina looked even worse. The queen of the Faces looked as if she’d just crawled ashore from a shipwreck. Her clothes were crumpled, her hair uncombed and – worst of all – her bag didn’t even match her shoes.

‘You don’t mind me sitting here, do you?’

‘No, no, not at all,’ reassured April. ‘It’s good to have you here.’

‘Thank you,’ said Davina, looking down at the table. ‘It helps to know that not everyone hates me.’

‘Why would anyone hate you, Davina?’ asked April.

She gave an ironic laugh. ‘That’s sweet, but we both know

why. I think the word is *schadenfreude*.' Davina smiled as she saw April's raised eyebrows. 'Surprised I know such a *big* word? I believe it's defined as "taking pleasure from someone's misfortune", or "being happy when an enemy gets their just deserts" – something like that, anyway. Let's be frank, there have always been plenty of people who wanted to see me fall on my arse.'

'But why?' asked April.

Davina's face changed in an instant, flipping from self-pity to boiling anger. 'That stupid little brother of mine!' she hissed. 'God, how could he have been so bloody idiotic?' She glanced towards April. 'Sorry, I shouldn't be saying this in front of you, should I? God knows you've reason enough to hate him.'

'It's okay,' said April. 'I ... I feel sorry for him really.'

Feel guilty for having killed him, actually, she thought.

Davina snaked out a hand and squeezed April's arm so hard April almost cried out. 'Thank you,' she said. 'You're the first person who's said a single nice thing about him. And you're the one he tried to hurt.' She shook her head. 'I still can't understand why. Maybe that snake Sheldon talked him into it. Ben worshipped the ground he walked on.'

April had always wondered how much Davina really knew about that night – and now seemed like a good time to ask.

'You think Mr Sheldon was behind it?' she said.

'Why not? It was his house and we all knew that he had some sort of problem with Gabriel.'

'Really? What did he have against Gabriel? '

'That I don't know. I mean he'd call Gabe into his office with the rest of us, give him those ranty talks he was so fond of, telling us we were the new elite, that same crap Dr Tame is spouting now. But when Gabe's back was turned, Sheldon kept going on about how we had to watch him, how he wasn't "one of us". God knows what Hawk thought that entailed – someone who was prepared to burn his house to the ground perhaps.'

'You think that's why he got Ben to lure Gabe there?'

Davina shrugged. 'Maybe that, or maybe it was something to do with your …' she said, suddenly cutting herself off, putting a hand over her mouth. 'Sorry, darling, I shouldn't have said that. It's nothing to do with me.'

'What isn't? What were you going to say?'

But April knew what she was referring to – and she found she had had a strange desire to hear it from someone else. 'About my mum and Mr Sheldon you mean?'

Davina blew her cheeks out. 'I wasn't sure if you knew,' she said. 'I didn't want to be the bearer of bad tidings, not when you've been through so much already.'

Bad tidings. She made Silvia's affair sound like getting caught in a rain shower or forgetting to do your homework. But April knew she would get more out of Davina if she played along.

'Actually, that *was* what I thought,' she said. 'I mean, when Ben took me to Sheldon's house, I assumed it was something to do with their affair. Maybe he thought Gabriel was going to tell me?'

'Oh, I don't think anyone else knew,' said Davina, a touch of the old arrogance seeping back into her voice. 'I saw them together, you see. But I swear I didn't tell anyone else.'

April doubted that. Davina had always been the consummate politician, the sort of creature who believes that 'knowledge is power'. She would never keep a juicy piece of gossip like that secret, not if she felt she could use it to her advantage.

'Where did you see them together?' asked April, feeling sick, but needing to know.

'At the Winter Ball, at our place last Christmas, remember?'

The same Winter Ball where April had been hunted through the grounds of the Osbourne's house by a psychotic vampire? The ball where she had been saved by Gabriel's heroic kiss. No, April was unlikely to ever forget that night.

'I was looking for Benjamin, actually,' said Davina. 'As usual he had disappeared just when I needed him to do something. I thought he had maybe disappeared to a dark corner with some silly girl, so I went across the terrace to look around the side of the house – and that's where I saw them, your mum and Mr Sheldon.'

April's mind jumped back to that night; her mother had looked so beautiful, dressed in a flowing silk dress, her hair pinned up, her elegant neck adorned with jewels. April remembered Silvia raising a cocktail to the memory of William Dunne, the tears glistening in her mother's eyes as she recalled how much her husband would have enjoyed the gathering. And then she had sidled off, found Robert Sheldon, and …

'You saw them … kissing?' she croaked.

A sly smile cracked over Davina's face. 'They did seem very close …'

Oh God, oh God, oh God. April took in a sharp breath, suddenly very sure she was going to be sick. *Come on, April*, she said to herself angrily. It wasn't as if this was news to her – Silvia had as good as admitted the affair, but this was the first time April had actually pictured it, imagined what had been going on behind her back – behind her *father's* back all that time. How could Silvia live with herself? April was so wrapped up in thoughts of disgust and betrayal, it was some moments before she realised Davina was crying.

'Oh, 'Vina, what's the matter?' said April, rather startled. Davina Osbourne, ice queen, crying? April reached over and rubbed her hand up and down Davina's back. 'What's brought this on?'

Davina let out a sob, then wiped her nose on her torn sleeve. Somehow, that was even more unsettling than the tears running down her face. The *old* Davina would never have dreamt of doing such a thing.

'It's just … thinking about that bastard Sheldon and what he's done to me.'

That was more like the old Davina, thought April: what Sheldon had done to *her*. She had almost forgotten that everything in DavinaWorld had to be about Davina.

'I just don't know what to do,' sniffled Davina, looking up at April, her expression pleading, as if April might have the answer. 'I know it sounds conceited, but I've always been in charge – I've always been the one that people look to for the way to do things. You know, fashion, the best clubs, who's in and who's out. And now *I'm* the one who's out.'

April tried to see it from Davina's point of view. In her mind, presumably, she had been unfairly pushed out just because of something her brother had done. In truth, she was the victim of politics – nobody could stay at the top for ever, leadership was always a fluid thing and Davina Osbourne had had more than her fair share of time in the sun. Plus, she hadn't exactly been a benevolent dictator. It was rather hard for April to feel much sympathy, especially when this sniffling girl may well have ordered – or even carried out – numerous killings.

'What do you do? I guess you find yourself some new friends,' said April.

'Yes, well, it's easy for you to say. You've got real friends, people who stand by you and look out for you. I wish I had friends like that.'

April wondered if she was hinting at something, suggesting she could join their side? Could that work? It sounded crazy, but Davina did have intimate first-hand experience of the inner workings of the vampire tribe, much better than Gabriel's, especially if what she was saying about Robert Sheldon was true. And she had a grudge – a desire to make Chessy and the other Faces pay for pushing her out. She could be a formidable ally.

But April had to remind herself who she was dealing with. The Faces were not just a collection of vain schoolyard bullies. They were a front for a vampire revolution. They were clever, underhanded, scheming and murderous. Perhaps Davina was being genuine, perhaps she was in pain, but given previous form, she wasn't exactly someone you could trust.

'So, what are you going to do about Chessy and Ling?'

Davina snorted. 'What do you think? I created those bitches. And I can unmake them too.'

April noticed that Davina was scratching her fingernails into the surface of the picnic table, scoring grooves into the wood as she spoke.

'Chessy? She was nothing before I rescued her from the gutter – *nothing*! I found her down by the canal, living on some old boat, did you know that? She was like an animal. But I took pity on her, talked Hawk into letting her come to Ravenwood, saved her from the rats. And does she remember that? Does she hell. Maybe I will remind her one of these days.'

'If you do,' said April, smiling, 'give me some notice, because I don't want to be anywhere near you when you explode. Seriously.'

Davina laughed. 'Thank you, April,' she sighed. 'It does mean a lot to me that not everybody around here is a horrid cow.'

'I'll take that as a compliment, shall I?'

'You should,' said Davina. 'You really should.'

Chapter Thirteen

April lingered at the school gates and watched Davina walking up the hill towards her home. She shook her head in disbelief. How had a Fury become Agony Aunt to the queen of the Faces? *Miss Holden must be turning in her grave.*

As she turned, something caught her eye and her heart gave a little leap. Dr Tame's car was still there, suggesting he hadn't left yet. Perhaps she could still catch him. But she immediately hesitated. It was one thing casually 'bumping into him' as she left school; it was quite another to be found waiting by his car – she'd look like a stalker. Even so, she couldn't quite drag herself away. She crossed the road and pulled out her phone, trying to look natural. There were two texts from Gabriel:

> Had an idea about our School Project. Call me.
> Love you, G

Another had arrived two minutes later:

> P.S. Can still feel your kisses from last night. Xxx

And there was one from Caro:

> More white coats in the labs today.
> Want cake to catch up? C

April should have felt happy, but instead she felt wretched. Only yesterday, she had given her tiny task force a speech about how they needed to think bigger, act bigger, take the bull by the horns and take the fight to the Suckers. Well, *they* were doing as she asked, while April was standing in the street, hopping from one foot to another, hoping that the headmaster would pop out and obligingly lead her to the Vampire King. It was pathetic. But the most pathetic thing was that she had no other plan. She was trying to set herself up as the real Head Girl, someone worthy to lead the crusade against the spreading darkness, but she genuinely had no idea how to do it.

'Jesus, April, why don't you just bugger off home?' she whispered to herself.

It was then April saw her mother.

'What the ...?'

There was no mistake – it was Silvia Dunne, standing at the door of Ravenwood, her hand on Charles Tame's arm, smiling coquettishly.

What on earth? What was *she* doing here? Was she having an affair with Dr Death now? But April didn't have time to think any more – her mother was getting into her car. April ducked down behind a willow tree just as Silvia turned out of the gate and drove up the hill. April waited until she was out of sight, then began to sprint after her.

Silvia was only just getting out of her car as April arrived, panting, her face pale with the exertion.

'Darling!' said Silvia. 'What are you doing here? I mean, it's lovely to see you of course, but I wasn't expecting you.'

April, leaning against the fence and trying to catch her breath, could only shake her head.

'Why have you been running?' Her mother looked behind her, scanning the square, something like concern on her face. April supposed it wasn't unreasonable to assume that she was being chased – it wasn't as if that hadn't happened before.

'What ...' April gasped, trying to control her breathing. 'What were you doing at the school?'

'Oh, *that*,' Silvia said. 'I was just having a little discussion with the new headmaster. It's wonderful news that you've been made Head Girl. I don't know why you didn't tell me straight away.'

'It's not ... that important,' managed April, finally straightening up.

'Not important? Don't be silly, it's brilliant. Your father would have been so proud.'

'Don't you dare speak about him!' snapped April. 'Don't you *ever* speak about him.'

'What?' said Silvia, taken aback. 'What are you saying? Listen, April, what's this all about?'

'Why were you visiting Dr Tame?'

'If you must know, he called me up to discuss your education.'

'My education?'

Silvia glanced to the side, looking up at the windows of the neighbourhood houses, as if she didn't want to be overheard. 'Apparently,' she said, lowering her voice, 'you're struggling a little bit. That's only to be expected, considering what you've been through over the last few months, and of course, the students at Ravenwood are very academic, but he just wanted to discuss it with me before ...'

'Before what? Is he going to expel me?'

Silvia let out a tinkling laugh. 'Oh, don't be silly, darling. It's not that serious. In fact, Charles has come up with some rather clever solutions to the problem.'

'Charles?' said April. 'It's *Charles* now?'

April's head was immediately filled with the image of her mother and Robert Sheldon 'getting close' in Davina's words, but in April's mind, Hawk's face was replaced by Dr Tame's. She felt sick.

'Don't overreact, April,' said Silvia. 'Surely it is better that I'm on first name terms with these people, especially when he's doing you such a big favour.'

'What big favour? Using me to publicise his brilliant

educational improvements to the school? Don't you remember how horrible he was about Dad's death? Don't you remember what he did to me?'

Silvia began to look impatient. 'Why do you have to turn everything to being about you, April? You're not the centre of the universe, you know. Dr Tame is simply trying to help you – and, actually, I'm hearing very good things about Ravenwood's teaching methods at the moment, especially in science. I was thinking perhaps you should be taking some sort of practical subject too.'

'Oh for God's sake, Mother, can't you see what's going on in front of your nose?'

But, of course, Silvia couldn't. It was like trying to complete an enormous jigsaw puzzle without having any idea what the picture should be. You needed to know the key element – that Ravenwood was full of vampires – before you could ever hope to understand Charles Tame's so-called 'teaching methods'.

'What? What *is* going on under my nose, April?' asked Silvia, clearly exasperated.

'Nothing,' said April. 'Just promise me you'll be careful, okay? Lock all the doors and windows before you go to bed every night, and don't go out wandering about on your own, either, especially not after dark.'

'Is that what all this is about?' said Silvia, looking relieved. 'It's very sweet, darling, but I'll be fine. Honestly.'

'Good,' said April awkwardly. 'Well, I'd better go.'

'I hear you've got another party tomorrow night,' said Silvia, reaching into her bag and pulling out her purse. 'Here, let me give you something for the outfit.'

'No, Mum. I'm not even sure I'm going to go,' said April.

'Of course you're going to go, and you're going to enjoy yourself.' Silvia stuffed some notes into April's hand and looked at her sternly. 'April Dunne, I have visited you in hospital three times in the last six months. Things haven't been easy for any of us, so it's important to go out and enjoy yourself – live life, darling. Don't hide away from it.'

'I'm only going to a barbeque at Ling's house, Mum,' said April, hating the whining tone that slipped into her voice whenever she was talking to her mother.

'All right, but I know how important your friends are to you, so go and have a good time with them. But you be safe too, you hear?'

'Okay, Mum,' April said, taking a step away. It still felt strange not living there and she felt guilty turning her back on her mother when Silvia had no idea she was surrounded by so much danger. But then maybe it was better that way – would you really want to know a tsunami was about to engulf you if you had no way of getting off the beach?

'I'll give your love to Gramps.'

Silvia smiled, but it didn't go all the way to her eyes. 'You do that,' she said.

Chapter Fourteen

The high street was busy at this time of day. People with shopping bags, a mother with a double pushchair, a group of schoolgirls peering in through the window of a jewellery shop. April remembered the first time she'd come up this road, on a rainy Sunday evening, when she had thought that the entire place was filled with geriatrics. It wasn't quite that bad, of course – Highgate *did* have some attractions. Unfortunately they weren't working in April's favour today. Clutching Silvia's money, April had been into the new hairdresser's near the pub, but they hadn't been able to fit her in at such short notice, and the hospice shop across the road from Americano had failed to provide her with a cut-price party dress. Women's magazines were always going on about what a treasure trove charity shops were in affluent areas, but April had never found any of those legendary designer bargains.

What am I going to wear to the party? she wondered. She knew that Ling and Chessy would be pulling out all the stops and that everybody else would be judging her accordingly. God, it was exhausting going to Ravenwood. Half the time you worried that somebody was going to drink your blood, the rest of the time you worried they would laugh at your shoes.

Crossing the high street, April saw a familiar figure approaching, a squat old man walking with a stoop, his white hair sticking out at all angles.

'Mr Gill,' she said.

'Ah, my dear girl,' he replied, with a warm smile. 'Are you

keeping well?' He frowned briefly. 'But now I think about it, you've had another of your little accidents, haven't you?'

April laughed. 'Nothing lasting this time, Mr Gill, just a little bit of smoke damage.'

He gestured towards the doorway of his bookshop. 'Would a cup of tea help in your recuperation? Marjorie has just been out for cake. They will almost certainly be awful boxed things from the Co-op, but her heart is in the right place.'

'Marjorie? The lady from the library? The romance is still going strong, is it?'

Mr Gill, lowered his voice and beckoned her forward. 'Very well, if I'm any judge,' he said. 'Between you and me, I shouldn't be at all surprised if there aren't wedding bells in the near future.'

'Mr Gill!' said April with pleasure. 'You *are* a dark horse.'

She was very fond of the old man and it was good to see him so animated. When she had first entered the bookshop with its dark windows and dusty shelves, the old man had seemed like one of his books: worn away and unloved, not expecting much from life. Now she noted a polka-dot shirt under his usual oatmeal cardigan. Clearly love wasn't just for the young.

Mr Gill held the shop door open and April immediately registered one glaring change. Sitting on Mr Gill's desk was a shiny new state-of-the-art computer.

'Mr Gill!' said April. 'What's happened? You are just about the last person I would have expected to join the tech age.'

The old man's cheeks reddened a little. 'Marjorie's influence, I'm afraid. She's very tech-savvy – I think you call it – could use any computer in the school library. She insisted I get one and, I have to say, it's been a revelation. The amount of information you can store on here,' he said, tapping the top of the screen affectionately. 'I can catalogue the whole shop! And so many libraries are online these days – it's a modern marvel, I tell you.'

April grinned at his boyish enthusiasm.

'Marjorie!' he called, hanging his cardigan on a hook and indicating that April should sit on one of the stools next to the desk. 'We have a visitor.'

'No need to shout, you old fool,' came the reply from the back of the shop. 'I might be senile, but I'm not deaf.'

She appeared carrying a small tray piled up with pastel-coloured Fondant Fancies, looking very pleased with herself. 'They were on offer,' she explained. 'Three for the price of one. Might be past their sell-by date, but then, who isn't around here?' she added with a cackle.

April had met Mrs Townley, in her first week at Ravenwood. Given her grey curly hair and half-moon spectacles, April had guessed that she must be about eighty. The old lady's romance with Mr Gill had not transformed her as much as it had her suitor: she looked exactly the same as she had all those months ago. But April could see from the look on Mr Gill's face as he handed out the tea that Marjorie looked just fine to him.

'So you're the girl from the fire, then?' said Mrs Townley, biting into a bright cake. 'April, isn't it? You *do* keep getting yourself into scrapes, don't you?'

April laughed. 'I suppose I do, yes.'

'So is it the vampires again?'

April almost choked on her tea. 'V – vampires?' She coughed.

'Don't look so surprised, dearie. I remember you coming to the library looking for books on vampires. In a school like Ravenwood? That's a big red flag right there.'

'Marjorie,' said Mr Gill, 'April doesn't want to hear our crackpot theories.'

'Theories? Pish!' said the woman. 'April knows better than anyone they're not theories – she has the scars to prove it, don't you, love?'

April looked from Mr Gill to Mrs Townley. 'What theory are you talking about?'

'Ravenwood being a front for the vampire conspiracy,' said

the old woman with a shrug. 'And how they're preparing for war.'

'Come now,' said Mr Gill, 'we don't *know* anything of the sort. You're just going to frighten the poor girl unnecessarily.'

'All right, all right,' said Mrs Townley, grunting as she pushed herself upright. 'I'll leave you to bury your heads in the sand. Anyway, I have a crossbow to clean.'

They watched as the old woman shuffled off. There was an awkward pause, then the muffled sound of music coming from the back of the shop.

'Don't mind Marjorie,' said Mr Gill when she had gone. 'She likes to speak her mind.'

'I can see that,' said April, setting her tea down on the desk. 'But what she was saying? About a war?'

'As I say, my dear, it's only Marjorie's theory and I'm afraid she has something of a grudge against the school. They forced her into retirement – I think you may well have been in hospital at the time. Apparently, they're thinking of closing down the Chandler Library. The argument seems to be that everybody does their research online these days. Plus they need more space for their research laboratories.'

'But what do you think? Do you think she's right about the war?'

The old man appeared to think for a moment. 'As you're asking me a direct question, I'll give you a direct answer. I believe they are. I've been aware of something growing for many years, since back in the sixties, in fact, but it's most certainly getting worse – I hardly need to tell you that, you have felt the full force of it personally. But as to what's coming next, I certainly think it will get worse before it gets better. In the past, they have stayed hidden, in the shadows, but now? They're almost killing indiscriminately as if they do not care who sees them. That suggests to me that they're planning an all-out assault. And when they do, no one will be able to stop them.' He looked at her ruefully. 'I appreciate that is probably *not* what you wanted to hear.'

Actually, April was glad to hear him say it out loud. She had spent so long creeping around, whispering in corners, scared to talk to the wrong people, it felt good to have it out in the open.

'Thank you for being so frank with me, Mr Gill. Most people … well, most people won't allow themselves to see what's in front of them.'

'I imagine it's quite a heavy burden for you to bear,' said the old man, pouring more tea into April's cup. 'You can take comfort, however – small maybe, but comfort all the same – that this has all happened before.'

'Really? What do you mean?'

'Oh, the darkness has descended before, you can be sure of that. Here, other places in the British Isles, certainly in Eastern Europe – those Hammer Horror films didn't choose Transylvania by chance. There are plenty of well-documented accounts of vampirism going back five hundred years – and they're not all myths and wild stories about men transforming into bats, either.' He leant over and tapped his mouse, bringing the computer to life. 'As you might imagine, the subject has been on my mind rather a lot recently, so I have been reading up on the material.' He rattled at the keyboard, clicking through to a website page featuring a picture of a gloomy castle surrounded by forest. 'This is the first recorded case of a vampire – or Strigon, the local name for a warlock – from 1656. An unfortunate fellow named Jure Grando who lived in Kringa – that's modern-day Croatia – died, but then apparently proceeded to terrorise the village.'

April read an extract:

> One night, a group of brave souls led by priest Father Giorgio went out to the village graveyard and, by lamplight, proceeded to dig up Jure's coffin. Inside, they found a seemingly untouched body – particularly remarkable as Grando had been buried sixteen years previously. Father Giorgio attempted to stake the vampire with a hawthorn

stick, but was unable to pierce Jure's flesh. So another villager took a saw and attempted to decapitate the corpse. The vampire immediately began to scream and blood poured from the wound, filling the grave to the brim.

April wrinkled her nose. 'Pretty gruesome, Mr Gill. Do you think it really happened?'

'There's no doubt that superstition ruled the lives of people in that region and still does to some extent. As to whether there really was a vampire on the loose, there are of course many theories relating to this case and others down the years. Some people think vampirism is simply the manifestation of certain diseases; some people think so-called vampires are just ordinary victims of psychosis.'

'But you don't think so?'

'I think there might be some truth in that, but the problem is that it keeps happening, over and over again. In the past, you might get a sudden rash of murders or unexplained deaths, then it would die away – Dr Crippen, the Brides in the Bath, the Yorkshire Ripper.'

'You think they were all vampires?'

'Perhaps, perhaps not. As I'm sure you know by now, it's very easy for ordinary people to fall under the vampire glamour. But the difference is that in the past, the killings happened, then the killings stopped. This time it is showing no signs of ceasing. And, given the politics involved, it's a potential powder keg.'

'Politics? Like the government?'

'No, I mean internal politics,' said Mr Gill. 'In-fighting, struggles between one faction and another, each of them wanting to be dominant.'

April's eyes were wide. 'More than one? You mean there could be three or four armies of vampires out there?'

The old man shook his head. 'No, and that's the worry April. In the past, the different nests would squabble and fight, like gang warfare – it was a natural safety valve. One leader would rear up and the others would blindly attack him, pushing him back down. Now it appears as though someone has managed to unite these creatures with one common goal – to take over. And unless something is done, I'm worried they may succeed this time.'

Again, April took a strange kind of comfort from the shopkeeper's words. He was only confirming what she already knew: that the King Vampire was preparing for some horrible attack on humanity. *Is that all?* Her mind mocked her. But yes, somehow it seemed better than suddenly learning that there were dozens of different vampire armies surrounding them. At least there was still only one to worry about. Then April recalled something Miss Holden had once said in class.

'You know what you were saying about the murderers – Dr Crippen and all those? Was Jack the Ripper one? I mean, there were – what? Five, six? – murders and then it suddenly stopped?'

Mr Gill smiled.

'What is it?' asked April. 'You look as if you expected me to say that. Why?'

'Just a hunch, my dear.' Mr Gill surveyed her curiously – as though he wanted to say more.

'What is it?'

'If you're after information on our old friend Jack, I think you'd better go straight to a good source. Someone who has personal experience.'

'Who?'

'I believe you know her. She owns a competitor – I'll show you.' He bent over the keyboard again then turned the monitor to face April.

She opened her eyes wide – she immediately recognised the picture of the shop on his screen. It was Redfearne's – Jessica's shop.

Chapter Fifteen

Caro looked amazing. April knew she shouldn't be so surprised; most of the time her friend hid behind a mask of thick eye make-up, distracting hair colour and about three tons of bad attitude, but underneath it all was a very pretty girl with well-defined cheekbones and a curvy figure. Tonight it was accentuated by a stunning, clingy little black dress. With her blow-dried wavy hair – restored for the occasion to her natural chestnut brown – she looked like a sassy supermodel.

'God, I feel like such a loser next to you,' said April as they tottered up the path towards Ling's house. April felt unbalanced on the sky-high heels Caro had chosen for her and uncomfortable in the low-cut purple dress Caro had borrowed from her older cousin's wardrobe. It was flattering, but it was also rather revealing.

'Stop tugging at it,' said Caro, slapping at April's hands. 'If you've got it, flaunt it, baby! And anyway, isn't Mr Lover-Lover going to be there tonight?'

'I believe Gabriel is due to attend,' April said primly, although she was unable to keep a smile from her face.

'Well then, when he gets a load of you, we're going to have to scrape his tongue off the floor.'

'Eww,' said April, suddenly reminded of the tongue she had tipped onto Jessica's desk. After her talk with Mr Gill, April had made a beeline for Jessica's shop, but had been disappointed and a little unsettled to find that Redfearne's was closed, the lights all off. Strange; she would have thought weekends were the busiest time for a shop like that. April pushed the thought away as Caro rang the doorbell. They waited, but no one came. Caro raised her eyebrows. 'The party *is* tonight, isn't it?'

April rolled her eyes. 'Of *course* it's tonight, Caro. As if we could get something like that wrong. Everyone has been talking about it for ages.'

Caro was about to reply, when she held up a finger, cocking her head. 'Ah,' she smiled ironically. 'Maybe worth trying the tradesman's entrance?'

She led the way along a path that curved around the side of the house. As they got closer to the back, the sound of pumping music got louder and April could hear laughter and raised voices. They stepped out onto the decking area and April actually gasped.

'Now *that's* a barbecue,' said Caro, letting out an appreciative whistle.

Right in the centre of Ling's garden was a huge swimming pool, surrounded by a series of red and gold Moroccan-style marquees containing pillow-strewn sun loungers and little tables piled high with what looked like Turkish Delight. The beautiful people milling about on the lawns were being handed exotic-looking cocktails by bare-chested waiters in turbans and harem pants. It looked more like something from a hip-hop video than a garden party in Highgate.

'Jesus, check her out,' said Caro from the side of her mouth.

April followed her gaze to the bar on the far side of the terrace where Ling stood holding court, surrounded by admirers. 'She's certainly thrown herself into the theme, hasn't she?'

Ling looked like a genie: long billowing pants that ended in golden cuffs at her ankle, a sheer, slashed-back vest top and a tall head-dress with a trailing veil, all of it fashioned from almost see-through white silk. She noticed them and waved, pushing her way through the crowd to greet them.

'Girls! So glad you could make it. Isn't it fabulous?'

'It's … very impressive,' said April, and Ling let out a trilling laugh.

'Oh, I know,' she said, 'it's tacky as hell, isn't it? But I thought it'd be amusing. Cost Daddy a fortune, I can tell you, but nothing is good enough for his little girl, that's what he says anyway.'

'Where's the barbecue?' said Caro.

'Oh, no one eats at things like this,' stated Ling airily. 'But help yourself to the cocktails – one of Chessy's secret recipes.'

They watched Ling dance off to greet another group of newcomers. A passing waiter handed them a cocktail each: a balloon glass filled with ice and some dark red liquid. Caro sniffed hers suspiciously. 'What do you think it is?' she said, wrinkling her nose. 'If Chessy thought it up, there's a good chance there's blood in here somewhere.'

April took a tentative sip. 'Blood *orange*, I think. But mainly vodka. I think we're okay.'

'I wouldn't say that,' said Caro, looking around at the crowd. There were a few faces they recognised from Ravenwood, but mostly the partygoers seemed to be older, cooler, like the sort of people you'd find in a VIP enclosure at a festival, only tonight they were wearing sheer dresses and open-neck shirts.

'Do you feel as exposed as I do?' asked Caro.

'*You* feel exposed?' whispered April. 'I'm the one with a dress the size of a bikini.'

'No, I mean being human surrounded by all these Suckers. I feel like a chicken who's wandered into a pit full of foxes. Drunk foxes.'

Don't keep mentioning the foxes, thought April, thinking of the tongue again.

'Hey, I've got an idea,' said Caro. 'Hand me your phone.'

'Why? Are you going to call a taxi?'

'Don't be silly,' said Caro, grabbing the phone and turning so her body hid what she was doing.

'Okay, here we go,' she said, handing the mobile back. 'When in doubt, turn to your handy on-the-spot vampire detection device.'

Frowning, April looked down at the screen – Caro had managed a long shot of the whole party. 'God, I wish you hadn't done that – don't you remember what they did when I was caught taking photos?' said April.

Caro pouted. 'No one saw.'

'Not this time,' said April, her eyebrows raised. They both huddled over the screen and April felt sick at what she saw. In the picture, almost every other person had come out blurred. Where those figures should have been, there was just a blank space as if someone had furiously rubbed them out with a giant marker.

'It's like half the party are vamps,' whispered April.

'Yeah, like *that's* a big surprise,' said Caro, sipping at her drink casually. 'What did you expect? Werewolves?'

Logically, April knew that she should've expected the new head of the Ravenwood Faces to invite a large number of vamps to her party, but it was still disturbing to actually see them there – more shocking because it was more real. She studied the picture again.

'Look, Simon's come out,' she said, tapping the screen. 'That's good news, isn't it?'

Caro just shrugged and looked away. 'I guess.'

'What do you mean, you guess? I was worried they had turned him.'

'It doesn't really make much difference does it? He's as good as one of them already.'

'But don't you see? We can still save him.'

Caro turned to her, with eyes narrowed. 'No, April, we can't. Not if he doesn't want to be saved.' She nodded towards Simon, standing propped up against the bar. He looked drunk, his eyes half-focused, his mouth curled into a sneer. 'Look at him. He might as well be a full-blown Sucker. He's bought into the whole life; he's hooked on it. What are we supposed to do? Throw a bag over his head and kidnap him? What would that achieve if he doesn't have the slightest intention of leaving them? He's *gone*, A.'

April looked across at their old friend and could see that Caro had a point. Simon had always been the life and soul of the party, always ready to see the positive side of things, even if he put his own cynical twist on it. He had loved music and clothes and – yes, April was sure – he had loved Caro too. But now, he looked no more than a shell, burnt out from the inside.

'Admit it, April,' said Caro, 'he's one of them now.'

'Yeah? Screw that,' said April. Striding purposefully, she crossed the deck and pushed her way through the crowd gyrating in front of the DJ's booth.

'Simon!' she called, tugging his sleeve, raising her voice over the pounding music.

Slowly he turned to look at her, his eyes barely focusing. For a moment, it seemed as though he didn't recognise her, but then he broke into a half-smile.

'Hey, April,' he said, reaching a hand out to stroke her face. 'How are you doing? You want a drink? They're free. Least, I think they are. If they're not, I'm buggered.' He began laughing, a wheezy sort of chuckle that quickly trailed off.

'I've got a drink, thanks,' said April, holding up her glass. 'Listen, can we go somewhere to talk?'

Simon squinted across at her, one eye closed. 'Why do you want to move?' he slurred, gesturing vaguely in the air. 'I got everything I need right here. Booze, tunes and … nuts.' He groped towards the bar. 'There were some nuts here …'

'You can come back and find them in a moment. First I've got something to say to you.'

April grabbed hold of Simon's wrist and yanked him away from the bar, ignoring his protests. She pulled him back towards the house and into a passageway that seemed to lead to an outbuilding.

'Hey!' cried Simon, holding up his empty glass. 'What the hell do you think you're doing? You made me spill my drink!'

'Really? Well, why don't you have mine?' said April. And she threw her cocktail into his face.

Simon's hands went up to his eyes, and his glass fell with a crash. Off balance, he reeled backwards, cracking his head hard against a brick wall and sliding down to the floor. 'What did you do that for?' he whined, rubbing the back of his head. 'You've soaked my bloody shirt.'

April knelt down next to him, so her face was on a level with his. 'A wet shirt is going to be the least of your troubles unless you sober up, Simon,' she said, her voice cold, detached.

'I've only had a few,' he mumbled defensively.

'I don't mean the booze, you idiot!' she shouted. 'I mean what you're doing to yourself. Do you really want to end up like Layla?'

At the mention of the dead girl's name, Simon recoiled, seeming to withdraw into himself. He crossed his arms and glared at April. 'I don't know what you mean.'

'Yes, you bloody do. You know exactly what I mean. You will end up dead. *Dead*, Simon.'

Simon's sneer was back. 'Is that really so bad?'

April's hand shot out and she slapped him hard around the face, then seized his shoulder, squeezing hard. 'Don't you ever say that,' she hissed. 'If you ever say anything like that to me again, I will kill you myself.'

Simon stared at her, his eyes wide, frightened. If she had wanted him to sober up, it looked as if it had worked, and all of a sudden she didn't feel angry any more – she just felt sorry for him. April let out a long breath and sat down on the floor, tugging her dress over her thighs.

'My dad died in my arms,' she said quietly. 'I was there when Miss Holden was killed. And Benjamin too. I know a little bit about death, Simon. It's ugly and brutal and there's not the slightest hint of romance in any of it. It's not poetic or noble or cool. It's just horrible.' She glanced over at him. 'You know what else it is? Death is selfish. People say all these heroic things when they're facing a firing squad, or they're about to throw themselves on a grenade or something. "Save yourselves, I'll hold them off" – all that crap. But that's it for them, game over – and that's the easy part. Dying's not the hardest, Simon. Going on afterwards, that's hard, bloody hard. All those people you leave behind, whose hearts you've broken, who spend every day at night wondering whether they could have done something differently – they're the ones who have to endure the pain.'

'So? Why should I worry about them?' said Simon. 'They never worried about me.'

'Bullshit!' spat April, her anger returning. 'Do you want me to slap you again? *I* worried about you. And *Caro* cared for you – if you'd ever taken the time to notice. *We* were your friends, real friends.'

'I don't want friends, I want a purpose,' he said, his eyes glittering. 'I want to be part of something. You must feel it, April – the start of this movement. We've got a chance to be part of an amazing new world.'

'Jesus!' cried April. 'Listen to yourself. You sound like one of those door-to-door religious nuts you used to laugh at.'

She grabbed his wrist and twisted it, seeing the tiny scars on the inside. Feeding scars, the same ones April had seen on Ling that day when she was crying in the school toilets. 'Is this the amazing new world you want to be part of? Even when you know what these people – these creatures – are like?'

'They understand me,' he said sulkily, pulling his arm away. 'They know what I want. They *give* me what I want.'

'And what's that?' said April. 'Booze? Drugs? Sex?'

Simon gave her a nasty smile. 'For starters.'

'Christ, Simon, is that really enough for you?'

'It's all I . . .' he began, and then April understood. *It's all I deserve*, was what he was going to say. God, the vampires were clever – horribly clever. Like any predator they knew how to separate the weak ones from the herd. They preyed on their insecurities: loneliness, doubt, greed, and with Simon, they had found an ideal candidate, a super-sharp brain with one flaw: a lack of self-worth. He must have known how much Caro cared for him, yet didn't feel he deserved such strong unconditional love. April didn't know Simon quite well enough to guess why and she supposed it didn't really matter. However they had done it, the Suckers had managed to get their hooks into him and had dragged him down to their level.

'Simon,' said April, fixing him with a steady gaze. 'You *are* loved. You *do* have friends. I think, deep down inside, you know that. And I think you also know how you'll end up if you keep on –' she gestured towards his scars '– like this.'

She clambered to her feet – no easy task in those high heels – and brushed off the back of her dress. 'But you can always come back. We'll be here, whatever happens. And I think you know that too.'

She walked away, knowing she couldn't say any more.

'What was all that about?' said Caro, falling into step beside her as April walked through the party and down to the swimming pool. 'What did you say to him?'

April pulled a face. 'I got a bit Fury on him, then I told him the facts of life about the Suckers and then told him you were in love with him.'

Caro's mouth dropped open. 'You *didn't*?'

April smiled. 'Not quite, but maybe I should've done. Sorry, Caro, I wanted to shake a bit of sense into him, snap him out of this trance he seems to be walking around in. I'm not exactly sure I managed it.'

Caro touched her arm. 'But you tried,' she said. 'That's the main thing. Thanks, A. You're a good friend.'

April turned to look back at the bar – Simon was again propping it up. 'I'm not sure that's going to be enough.'

They each took a bottle of beer from a cooler by the pool and sat down on some cushions by the edge, staring into the water. The music was still hammering and the air was thick with shouts and laughter, but the girls sat in silence, both lost in their thoughts.

'Hey, why so glum?'

April twisted around, a smile on her face. 'Gabriel!' she said. 'When did you get here?'

'Just arrived,' he answered, sitting down next to her, kissing her shoulder. 'But it looks as if I've come to the wrong place. I thought this was supposed to be a party, not a wake.'

'Sorry, hon,' said April, 'I've just had a run-in with Simon. Tried to get him to see sense, but …'

'But the idiot is too far gone,' finished Caro, looking back towards the bar.

'Ah, I see,' said Gabriel. 'All the more reason to keep going, isn't it? If we find the King and eliminate him, there's a good chance …'

'This isn't some bloody fairy tale, Gabriel!' snapped Caro. 'It's not like killing the evil witch. It won't break the spell and make everyone wake up and live happily ever after. We have absolutely zero idea what will happen even if we find the King Vampire and cut off his head. Even if you drink his blood, we don't know if it's going to cure you, do we?'

'Caro, it's not his fault,' April intervened.

'I know!' Caro cried, then shook her head. 'I know. Sorry, Gabe. Didn't mean to bite your head off.'

'It's okay, and you're right. We saw this happen with the Regent, didn't we? Sheldon died in the fire, but if anything the vampires got stronger. Yes, we could kill the King, but maybe there will always be another vamp waiting to take over. God knows, kids are always going to be drawn to this –' he gestured towards the bar '– because it's cooler than ping pong at a church youth club.'

'It's more than that,' said April, remembering what Simon had said. 'All this stuff Dr Tame has been spouting at school about his new world order – though we make fun of it, some people are taking it seriously. The fact that they can be in at the start of something, in on the secret before everybody else, that's going to be attractive, isn't it?'

They went quiet, all feeling deflated. 'So what should we…' Gabriel was interrupted by the sound of breaking glass and a loud cheer. It was followed by more smashing glass and another cheer.

'I'm going to see what's happening,' said April. She turned to Gabriel. 'Can you get me a drink? And while you're at the bar, see if you can talk some sense into Simon?'

She walked back towards the house and saw that a crowd had gathered. Another smash followed by a cheer. April elbowed her way to the front to see two boys, both stripped to the waist. April recognised one – his name was Calvin, wasn't it? – the boy she'd seen in the toilets in Ravenwood, the one Tame had let off scot-free. Calvin was standing there with a beer bottle balanced on his head, while the other boy was holding what looked like a child's cricket bat. As she watched, the boy with the bat took a run up and swung it at the bottle, shattering it, showering Calvin with broken glass. A whoop of excitement went up.

'What the hell are they doing?' April said to one of the bystanders. The boy's eyes were wide, clearly in awe of these mad creatures.

'Calvin bet the other one – Danny, I think his name is – he couldn't stand still while he smashed the bottle. Now they're taking it in turns. Crazy!'

'Yes,' said April. 'Yes, it is.'

She could see that Calvin was bleeding from a number of cuts on his shoulders and chest, but he didn't seem to feel it. In fact, as she watched, he ran a finger through the blood and licked it off, laughing as he did so. She wondered if these were boys who had come out as the dark blurs on her photo, or whether, like Simon, they had just been caught up in the twisted glamour of it all. As she stepped away from the crowd, April was suddenly very aware that the buoyant circus atmosphere of Ling's party theme had evaporated and been replaced by a darker undertone. An uncomfortable tension now seemed to grip the party. The flare of a match made April turn towards the alleyway where she had talked to Simon. A group of figures stood there in a tight circle doing – what?

Smoking something? She didn't know and wasn't about to ask. And that couple up against the wall ... Suddenly April just wanted to find her friends and had turned towards the bar, when she walked straight into Chessy.

Her long hair had been pulled back into a plait and she was wearing a one-shoulder Grecian dress in bottle green. *If she hadn't been radiating spite from every pore, Chessy might have been genuinely beautiful*, thought April.

'Head Girl,' she mocked, 'we must stop meeting like this. You all on your lonesome, or is Gorgeous Gabe with you?'

'He's here,' said April, attempting to move away. 'I'd better go, I think he's got my drink ...'

But Chessy blocked her way. 'And where's your other little friend? Davina, I think her name was.'

'I don't think she's coming,' said April, reminding herself that she was supposed to be joining in with the 'bash Davina' consensus – at least when she was talking to the Suckers.

'Not surprised.' Chessy smiled. 'I think it will be a while before she wants to be seen out in public.'

April looked towards the bar again, hoping to see Caro or Gabriel, all the time feeling Chessy's eyes burning into her.

'Why *you*, Head Girl?' she said.

'Why me what?'

'Why did Tame choose you as his pet? Does he have some special plans for you? Have you played the same trick on him you played on Sheldon?'

April looked at Chessy, wondering what she knew, what she was trying to imply, but all she saw in that face was malice. She wondered why Chessy had suddenly turned against her. It wasn't so long ago that they had been out on the town in London, getting their nails done together and sharing in-jokes. *She's a vampire, remember*, she thought to herself. *She'll do or say anything to get what she wants.*

'What trick would that be?' said April as casually as she could.

'That's what I want to know, Head Girl. That's what I'd like to know.'

Chessy moved closer to April, invading her personal space, making her skin prickle. 'What was it Sheldon thought you had? What did he want from you? And why did poor little Benjamin go off the deep end that night? Why did he try to burn you?'

April forced herself to meet Chessy's icy gaze. 'Because he had fallen in love with me,' she said. 'And who can blame him?'

Chessy threw her head back and laughed. 'Oh, you're good,' she said, pointing a wagging finger at April. 'You're very good. I'm really going to have to watch you.'

As Chessy walked off, April let out a long breath. She supposed it was inevitable that the Suckers would be suspicious of her, especially after the mysterious blaze at Hawk's house, but she was surprised that any of them would bring it up directly. Maybe Gabriel had been right – perhaps their greatest weapon against the vampires was to make them feel uncertain, off balance. They had to be thinking that if vamps like Sheldon and Benjamin could be killed, then perhaps none of them were as invulnerable as they thought.

Caro came running up. 'A – we have a situation,' she said, taking April's hand and leading her towards the swimming pool.

'What is it?'

'Ling. I saw her going into the tents with a guy and I think she's bitten off more than she can chew.'

As they approached the pool, April could immediately see what was happening. Each of the Moroccan tents next to the pool had their canvas doors tied back with gold ropes revealing their cushion-filled interiors – all except one. The last tent had its flaps firmly closed and there was a boy standing outside, as if on guard. Inside, April could hear muffled voices, one of which sounded like Ling, her voice raised in protest.

April and Caro exchanged glances.

'What's going on?' said April, walking up to the guard.

'None of your business.' The boy smiled. He had a shaved head and one gold stud in his ear. He was also about three stone overweight. 'Not unless you want to *make* it my business, sweetness, know what I'm sayin'? There's plenty of room in one of these tents for you and your friend.'

He sucked his teeth and raised his eyebrows in what he clearly imagined was an appealing way.

'Yeah, in your dreams,' said Caro. 'Now why don't you get out of our way. Our friend is in there and she doesn't sound very happy.'

Gold Stud stepped forward. 'Yeah, but she's making Cal happy, and when he's finished, she's gonna do the same for me.'

'Why don't I show you what makes me happy, huh?' said Caro, moving over to the boy.

'I knew you wanted some of this.' He grinned, but his smile froze then turned to a look of comic surprise as Caro brought her knee up, slamming into his groin. He doubled over and crumpled to the floor, groaning.

April stepped past him and pulled the tent's curtain back to find Ling sprawled on the floor, her genie costume torn and spotted with blood. There were wounds on her wrist and her neck, her face twisted with misery and terror. Standing over her was Calvin, the boy from the sideshow by the house, the one who had licked the blood from his own wounds. He looked at them and grinned – and April knew without a shadow of a doubt that he was a vampire.

'Evening, ladies,' he said. 'Is there a problem?'

April looked down at a cowering Ling, then back at Calvin. 'Yes, there's a problem,' she said. 'And it's you.'

The boy tilted his head to one side. 'I know you from school, don't I?' he said. 'You were at the witch's shop, weren't you?'

April's heart jumped as a million questions ran through

her head – *how did he know about that? Had he been watching her? Was he something to do with Jessica?*

'I think you've got me confused with someone else,' said April as smoothly as she could. 'Someone who tolerates rapists.'

'"Tolerates"?' he repeated, mocking her. 'Now that's a very big word for a little girl.'

'How about "sod off",' said Caro, who had come in behind April. 'Short enough for you?'

She leant over to offer a hand to Ling, but Calvin jumped forward, grabbing Caro's hair and yanking her up. 'Oh no you don't, I don't think I've quite finished with her,' he hissed, twisting her hair even tighter. 'But when I've done everything I want to do to her, I'm going to think of a whole load more things I'm going to do with you.'

All Caro could do was let out a little squeak.

'Hey, Calvin,' said April coolly.

As he glanced up, she swung a beer bottle straight at his head, making contact with a satisfying clunk. Falling backwards from the force of the blow, he released Caro and toppled over the low table, his arms pin-wheeling, hands grabbing the sides of the tent, pulling it down on top of him.

'Come on, Ling, let's move,' said April urgently, bending to help Ling to her feet. April had a sneaking suspicion that when Calvin untangled himself, he would not be in the best of moods.

'Caro, you okay?' she checked, as Caro took Ling's other arm.

'Yeah, fine,' she said between gritted teeth as they began moving back towards the house. But they didn't get far: Calvin sprang up in front of them. There was a trickle of blood coming from his temple and a snarl on his lip.

'Get out of my way,' April yelled, feeling the Fury surge up in her. At the back of her mind, a little voice seemed to be telling her "not here, not now", but she couldn't help herself. She was angry, too angry to stop.

'No way,' said Calvin, shaking his head, 'Calvin's not going anywhere. He's thirsty – needs a drink.'

But even before April could do anything, she saw a blur move in from her left – and suddenly there was a space where the vampire had been.

'Gabriel!' gasped Caro. April whirled around to see the man she loved grab Calvin by the throat then hoist him into the air.

'Thirsty are you?' he said, and threw Calvin sideways, his body crashing against the concrete surround of the pool. Calvin twisted on the floor, trying to regain his feet, but he was too slow – Gabriel was on top of him in an instant. He grabbed the boy's hair and plunged his head into the water.

The crowd that had gathered raised a nervous cheer as they saw Calvin go under. 'Dunk him! Dunk him!' they began to chant. 'Dunk ...' the cheers died off as they saw that Gabriel wasn't dunking him – he was holding the struggling boy's head under the water. Calvin was twisting desperately, his legs thrashing, his hands fruitlessly trying to reach Gabriel.

'Gabriel! No!' shouted April, but still he held the boy under. The vampire's struggles weakened, his legs scissoring, his hands thrashing feebly at the pool's edge.

April fell to her knees next to Gabriel, catching at his arm. 'Please, Gabriel, don't,' she begged. 'Let him go.'

Gabriel turned to her a stony, emotionless face. It had the fixed concentration of someone involved in no more than a simple DIY task like putting up a shelf or unblocking a sink. The vampire needed killing and he needed to do it.

'Gabriel, for me,' she whispered. 'Please.'

There was a pause, a heartbeat, then Gabriel gave a tiny nod. He hauled Calvin out of the pool in an arc of spray, tossing him onto the grass as if he were discarding an apple core.

The crowd was silent now, the only thing that could be heard above the still-pumping music being the gasps and retching of the man sprawled on the grass.

'Come on,' said April, taking Gabriel's hand. 'I think we'd better go.'

Caro followed, helping the now sobbing Ling. Briefly, April turned to look back and was appalled to see Calvin staring after her, fury and spite in his glittering eyes.

'Witch girl!' he shouted. 'I know who you are and I know where you live! This isn't over, not by a long way!'

Gabriel turned, but April clung to his arm. 'Please, can you get me home?' she said. 'I just want to go home.'

Chapter Sixteen

The doors of the train hissed closed and April sighed with relief, finally allowing herself to relax. The carriage was virtually empty: at the far end, a loud group of girls in party dresses were passing a bottle, but otherwise they were alone.

Looking straight ahead, April could see her face reflected in the train window opposite. Gabriel's too, strange though that was. He couldn't be seen in photographs or on video, but mirrors seemed to work just fine. April normally liked the way the bright overhead lighting and slightly concave glass of tube trains had the strange effect of hollowing out the eyes, accentuating the cheekbones; it was slimming, flattering even. But tonight it made them both look like corpses. Perhaps that's what they were, just dead bodies in waiting.

'Can we talk about it now?' she said, glancing up at Gabriel. He had been virtually silent since the fight by the pool. They had all hobbled back to Caro's house where Mrs Jackson immediately went into crisis mode, rallying around with hot sweet tea, carrot cake. She had found a change of clothes for Ling, who did a decent job of not looking too horrified at the floral prints. Caro's dad got onto his contacts in the police – April had forgotten that Caro had once said her family were all either villains or coppers – and had waited till they had broken up the 'festivities' before taking Ling back and making sure the house was secure. All that time, Gabriel had sat in a corner, silent, lost in his own world. Even when they had been dropped off at the tube, Gabriel refused to talk to April, meeting her questions with a sullen glare.

Then, finally, 'What do you want me to say?'

'I don't *want* you to say anything, Gabe. Just tell me what happened back there.'

'What do you think, April? I was protecting you.'

'You can't wriggle out of it that way,' she said, turning in her seat to face him. 'Caro and I were managing without you. That was something else.'

'Tell me what, then. You seem to have all the answers.'

God, she thought. Gabriel might be a hundred years old but he could act like a spoilt teenager. April realised she was going to have to change her approach.

'Listen, Gabe, I'm not accusing you of anything,' she said, taking his hand. 'I'm on your side, remember? It's just that, well, you were trying to kill that boy.'

'He isn't a boy, April. He is a vampire, a stone-cold killer. Fifty, a hundred years old, itching for a thrill, any excuse to make a kill. Don't imagine he would have let you leave that garden unharmed.'

'I know he is bad, I saw what he was doing to Ling. Maybe he's raped other girls, maybe he's killed hundreds of people. But ...'

'But what?'

'I don't know,' said April. 'Maybe all vampires – that kind of vampire anyway – maybe they all need to be destroyed, wiped from the face of the earth, perhaps that's the only way to finally defeat them. But I don't see it as our job now, Gabriel. I think our job is to find the King Vampire, find where the snake is sleeping and cut off its head. And maybe then the rest of them will wither and die. I don't really know. But we're not executioners – and we can't kill them all.'

'But you're the Fury, April!' said Gabriel. 'You're the only one with the ability to take them down.'

She nodded. 'That's what I thought. When you first told me – when you first showed me the birthmark behind my ear, that's what I imagined. I thought I was going to be fighting vampires hand to hand. But not any more. I think being a Fury is more like being the bloke with the flag at the front of a battle, shouting, "Charge!" It's not *just* about special powers, but also about giving everyone else the courage to fight back.'

'The courage to die?'

'Maybe, Gabriel,' she said, irritated now. 'Maybe that's what's going to happen – let's face it, the odds aren't good for me however you look at it. How many times have I been attacked already? But better me than one of those geeky innocents at Ravenwood.'

'So you didn't want to be rescued?'

God, he is maddening! April thought.

'I didn't want you to drown him, no. Push him over, punch him maybe, but Gabe . . .' she looked into his eyes, 'I virtually had to beg to get you to let him live.'

'That's because I'm a killer, April!' he snapped. 'It's what I *am*.' Gabriel's expression combined frustration and sorrow.

April glanced down the carriage at the partying girls, but they were too wrapped up in their own cackling banter to notice what Gabriel had said.

'You say you love me. Well, this is what you've got to love,' he said spreading his hands. 'I *wanted* to kill that – that creature. I wanted to see him struggle, kick; I *wanted* him to die. We're monsters, April. Do you really want to spend your life penned up with an animal like me?'

There were tears in his eyes.

'Yes,' she said simply, reaching out to touch his face. 'Yes, Gabriel, that's exactly what I want. I know who you are, I know what you are, but I also know you're more than that.'

'Am I?' he said, pulling away from her. 'Is that what you think? Or is that what you wish I was like? I'm not this noble savage you can cure with your love. I'm exactly like the rest of them – I want to bathe in human blood.'

This time, the girls at the end of the carriage had heard him. 'Oooh, scary goth bloke!' shouted one, and the rest of the girls cracked up with laughter.

April grabbed his hand and pulled him further along the

train. 'Gabriel, I *know,*' she said. 'God knows, I understand what you're feeling.'

'Really?'

April gave a bleak smile. 'Gabriel, look at tonight. I hit that boy – that thing – over the head with a bottle! When things happen like tonight, I just feel this rage building up; it's like it just rushes in on me and I want to strangle someone, crush their throat in my hands. And it's getting worse and worse.'

'That's because you're a Fury, April. That's to help you fight them. To fight us.'

She laughed. 'Or maybe I'm just getting more crabby. Thing is, I do understand a tiny bit of what you're talking about and, Gabe –' she took his face in her hands and gently kissed him on the cheek '– I love you so much for what you did.'

'What did I do?'

'The Dragon's Breath, Gabe. When you kissed me at the Winter Ball, you were released from that killer instinct. The Fury virus was killing you, eating you away, but I could see the relief on your face. You were happy to die if it meant you were no longer a prisoner of the hunger.' She kissed his cheek again. 'I know how hard it was to give that up, to swallow the Dragon's Breath and step back into the darkness. To become a monster again. I know what you did for me – I'll never ever be able to repay that.'

He turned away. 'I didn't do it just for you. I did it for myself, because I wanted to find my master and free myself from this for ever, but ...'

'But now it's taking you over?'

He looked at her and in the white glare of the strip lights his face was bleak, miserable. 'I don't know what's happening to me. I think I'm losing my mind.'

'The dreams?'

He nodded slowly, glancing down at the girls. 'It's always women,' he said. 'It's like I'm stalking them, hunting them down.'

'Gabe, it's only a dream.'

'No,' he said forcefully. 'No, it's *not*. It's like I've been there; it's like I *am* there.'

'Look, come back to my grampa's,' she said, feeling in her clutch bag for her keys. 'We'll sit down and talk about it.'

Then two things happened almost simultaneously. There was another burst of laughter from the drunken girls, and the lights went out. In the darkness, a girl screamed, high-pitched and hysterical. Then the lights flickered on and off rapidly like a disco strobe and April could see Gabriel on his feet, backing away from her.

'Gabe!' she called, suddenly frightened. His eyes were wide, staring at her, mouth frozen in an 'O'. And then they were flooded in light and the girls were laughing again as if nothing had happened. April moved towards Gabriel, but he backed further down the carriage.

'Gabriel, what's the matter?'

'I love you,' he said. 'Never forget that.'

The train had stopped at a station and Gabriel pulled the door open and leapt from the train.

'Gabe!' April ran down the platform, but Gabriel was too fast. He dashed up the stairs at a speed she could not match. She could only plod after him, knowing the lift would be too slow. Once at the top, she pushed through the barriers, ran through the ticket hall and out into the dark street. But April found herself alone. He had gone.

'Gabriel!' she shouted, looking up and down the street. 'Gabriel, please! Don't leave me here!'

But there was nothing except empty road. April swore under her breath in frustration.

What had just happened? Gabriel had always been flaky and unreliable, disappearing at the most inopportune moments, but this was something different – he had looked frightened, almost sick. Was it the bad dreams? It couldn't just be that, could it? Why had he bolted like that?

'Gabriel!' she shouted again, hopelessly.

It wasn't until she was a hundred yards from the tube

station that April began to feel uncomfortable. Back at the party, she'd started a fight with a vampire, and now she was alone in the dark. Was she being followed by a mightily pissed-off vampire? *Could Calvin have followed them?* she wondered, looking over her shoulder. And he'd called her 'witch girl'. He'd threatened her, hadn't he? Had he been stalking her, like Marcus Brent had done?

Witch girl. April changed direction, turning away down the narrow street towards the little shop with the purple door, but Redfearne's was closed. Not just closed for the night, but *closed* closed, as in 'everything must go'.

'Oh no,' said April. Her stomach sank as she peered through the window. Inside, she could see piles and piles of books stacked on the floor or crammed into packing cases. What the hell was going on?

April saw movement at the back of the shop – Jessica walked into view. April rapped on the window.

'Jessica!' she called. 'It's me! Can you let me in?'

The woman stood there looking at her for a moment, then shook her head and walked hesitantly towards the door. 'What do you want, April?' she said, only opening the door a crack. 'I'm very busy.'

'I wanted to … are you leaving?'

Jessica opened the door further and looked up and down the street. 'Inside, quickly.'

The shop was in chaos. Half of the shelves had been dismantled and the display cabinets had already gone. Books were stacked in teetering piles and the walls had been stripped bare of their pictures and trinkets.

'Where are you going?' said April.

'Does it matter?'

Jessica was standing with her hands on her hips, glaring at April, anger coming off her in waves.

'What? Is this something to do with me?'

'Is it something to do with you?' said the woman. 'I take it you didn't notice the door? Take a look.'

April opened the front door and gasped. There were deep gouges in the wood, as if a massive vicious animal had been trying to claw its way in. Scored into the frame were the words 'witch' and 'traitor'. She felt sick as the image of her father's grave flashed into her mind.

'I cleaned the rest off,' said Jessica, as April stepped back inside and Jessica bolted the door behind her.

'The rest?'

'Blood. They'd smeared it on the step, the windows too. Similar words. Same sentiment, anyway.'

'But who did it?'

'Why don't you tell me, April?' she snapped. 'You seem to be right at the centre of all this.'

April began to object, but then stopped herself. It was true, wasn't it? 'How can you leave, though?' she said. 'You can't let them scare you away.'

'Do you really think it's that simple, April? Do you?'

'Yes, I do! We have to fight back, Jessica. We can't give in. I know you must be frightened, but it's only a door.'

'Only a door?' muttered Jessica in a low voice. She grabbed April's arm and pulled her across the shop, bumping into boxes and scattering books as she went.

'That's not just a door,' she said, pushing April through a doorway into a small kitchen area. April let out a moan. There was a cat lying on the sink. Or rather, it had been a cat. Now, virtually torn in half, its entrails were spilling out like spaghetti, its grey fur stiff with blood, jaws open as if in a scream. And around its neck was a collar, one April had seen somewhere before.

'Is that . . .?' said April, her hand over her mouth.

'Recognise it?' said Jessica. 'I think we're supposed to, April.'

It was Jasper, Miss Holden's Siamese cat, the one which April had stroked and petted while they had been cooking up the Dragon's Breath. If the animal tongue had been a subtle – or not so subtle – hint, there was no doubt in this message. 'Keep helping April Dunne and you will get exactly what Annabel Holden got.'

Jessica turned and marched back to the front of the shop, angrily grabbing books and shoving them into cartons.

'I know it's horrible,' said April, following her, 'but do you really have to run away?'

Jessica slammed a book down. 'I'm not running away, April!' she shouted. 'God, you're so naïve! Can't you see that this is bigger than you and your father's ham-fisted attempts to write a newspaper story?'

April shook her head.

'This is war, April, war! Not some stupid schoolgirl game creeping around in the bushes. *Everything* is at stake here, not just your bloody boyfriend.'

'If it's all so important, why are you going?'

'I don't have any choice. The vampires are coming for *me*.'

'Look, I'm so sorry I brought all this down on you, but …'

Jessica laughed – a hollow, bitter laugh. 'Not *everything* is about you, April. Don't you see? I am a catalyst; not just a vampire.'

April frowned. 'You mean the witches?'

'Finally, she gets it!' said Jessica, throwing up her arms. 'Yes, I mean the witches. The witches took me in, they helped me control my hunger, adopted me as one of their own. As far as the coven is concerned, I am a witch. So if the vampires kill me, the witches will have no choice but to retaliate, and they will be drawn into the war. *That* is what whoever sent this message wants.'

April felt a an unexpected flash of hope. Maybe her little gang weren't so alone after all, not if Jessica's coven were prepared to stand up to the vampires too. She imagined fighting side by side with an army of witches equipped with powerful spells and potions – if they could make elixirs like the Dragon's Breath, then there was no telling what else they could do. At the very least, they could make the vampires think twice, slow them up.

'But that's great,' said April. 'I mean, we can take them on together.'

'No!' yelled Jessica. 'I am leaving the shop and I am leaving the witches and I am getting as far away from here as I can. I won't have people I care about put in danger because of you, April. '

'Look, I'm sorry that you feel you have to go, but …'

'You're sorry? Is that it?' said Jessica, narrowing her eyes. 'You're sorry? I have to leave the protection of the only people who ever cared about me. Because of you, I have put them in terrible danger. And you're sorry.'

'Gabriel is in danger too, Jessica,' said April desperately. 'He certainly cared about you once. I thought you cared about him too.'

'I do. I *did*. But …'

'No, Jessica,' said April fiercely. 'Either you care about him or you don't. He needs help, he's having more and more of the dreams – he's convinced that the killer he sees in these nightmares is him. He thinks he's remembering some horrible slaughter from his past.'

'Maybe not just his past,' said Jessica.

'What is that supposed to mean?' said April. 'What do you know about this, Jessica? Why can't you just tell me the truth?'

Jessica closed her eyes and turned away.

'Christ!' shouted April, sweeping a pile of books off a stool. 'It's like you're all playing some stupid game! Everyone I speak to says, "Ooh, April, you wouldn't understand", "Ooh April, if I told you the truth it'd blow your mind!" – like I'm too stupid to grasp the rules of your secret little club. Maybe the truth is you don't want your cold war to come to an end because then you'd have to stop pretending you're all so important.'

Jessica glared at her. 'You want to know what's eating Gabriel?' she said, walking over to a box and pulling out a book. 'Here, read this.'

She shoved the book into April's hands. It was a hardback

with a picture of a spooky Dickensian back street under the title: *The Ripper's East End.*

'Here's another one. Take it – they're no use to me any more.' Jessica held out a paperback. 'And this one; you'll like this one too.'

Jessica was throwing books at her now and April had to duck to avoid them.

April looked down at the book she had managed to catch: *Jack the Ripper: The Face Behind the Cloak.*

'What are you trying to tell me? That Gabriel was Jack the Ripper?'

'Work it out for yourself, April!' she shouted. 'I think I've wasted enough time on you. Now if you'll excuse me, I have my own mess to clean up.'

April stood in the doorway, wondering what had just happened, what had made her anger this woman, wishing she could turn back the clock and start again. But she couldn't, could she?

April turned and held up the book. 'I'm not going to like it, am I?' she said.

The anger on Jessica's face faded, replaced by what looked like sadness. 'That's the trouble with the truth, April. Everyone thinks they want it, but no one is ever prepared when it comes.'

April stood in the street, just breathing in the night air. Funny how quiet it could be right in the heart of London, she thought. But then, if you listened hard enough you could always hear it: the low hum of traffic, of chatter, of life. It was always there.

Maybe it was the same with secrets, thought April, glancing down at the book with its artist's impression of the Ripper in his clichéd top hat and cloak. Maybe they just sit there waiting for you to find them. And maybe it would be better not to. She walked from the shop, remembering the claw-marks in the woodwork. She didn't want to wait around for the modern equivalent of Jack the Ripper, whoever that might be. *Gabriel?* She almost laughed. Okay, so he was a vampire and he was certainly capable of violence – she had seen that tonight – but Gabriel was fundamentally… gentle – that was the word. Decent, too. And sensitive, so very sensitive, that the doubts filling his mind were literally tearing him apart.

April opened her bag and pulled out her phone, scrolling to Gabriel's number.

She wasn't surprised when it went straight to voicemail. 'Hi, it's me,' she said after the beep. 'I'm sorry for whatever I said. Just give me a call, okay? I love you.'

Then she scrolled straight to Fiona's number and pressed call. 'Pick up, Fee, pick up,' she whispered.

'Hey, beautiful.' Fiona sounded groggy and a bit muffled.

'God, I didn't wake you, did I?'

'Little bit. I must have dozed off.'

'Sorry, honey, just needed to hear your voice. Things have got a bit strange.'

Instantly Fiona's voice was more alert. 'What's up? Where are you?'

'Cov Garden, just walking home, but it's a bit spooky right now.'

She quickly filled Fiona in on the events at the party.

'Damn. So where's your knight in shining armour?'

'He ran off.'

'Oh. Not good. Lover's tiff?'

'No, more like he's …' April was turning into her grandfather's road now. The terrace was lit by those old-style gas-lamp streetlights the tourists so loved – and there was a man standing there, right in front of Grampa Thomas's house.

'April?' said Fiona. 'What's going on? Have you seen something?'

'There's some bloke waiting outside Gramps' place,' whispered April, pulling back behind a wall.

'Who? Gabriel?' asked Fiona.

'I don't know.' Her grandfather's house was surrounded by black iron railings and there was a tall gate you had to open to get to the front door. She squinted, trying to see in the low light. The man seemed to be standing at the gate, peering through the bars.

What the hell was he doing?

She took a few steps forward. 'Gabriel?' she called softly, her phone still to her ear.

'You're not going over there,' said Fiona. 'April, do *not* go over there. I forbid it!'

But April was already crossing the road. She could now see that the man was holding onto the bars high up, either shaking them or preparing to climb over. Had Gabriel come to find her?

'Gabriel?' she repeated. 'Is that you?'

But now she could see it wasn't him – not tall enough, wrong hair. And the man didn't turn as she approached.

'Hello? What are you doing? Excuse me?' April was only two paces away now. She reached out to touch the man on the shoulder – and the gate swung inwards.

It was then April screamed. Because now she *could* see. His hands were impaled on the spikes at the top of the gate, a dark bloody hole gouged in his neck. Blood was forming a puddle at his feet. And she recognised him – Calvin, the boy from the party.

April screamed again.

Chapter Seventeen

'Look, Mr Reece, I *don't know* where he is. I wish I did.'

April pushed her hair out of her face and looked up at the policeman. *This seems familiar*, she thought. Her grandfather's front room was a new venue, but the set-up was the same: tepid tea in front of her, policeman asking questions. Another murder.

God, another murder. And no ordinary murder either. Her mind flashed back to the previous night, the snapshot frozen in the streetlight, that boy left hanging on the gate – left there, for her to see, blood pooling around her party shoes.

'All right,' said Detective Inspector Reece, pushing himself up from his chair and walking over to the window. 'Let's go back to the party. You say Gabriel and this boy Calvin had a bit of a fight – some pushing and shoving – is that how you'd describe it?'

'Well … Calvin was threatening me and Gabriel tried to protect me – give Calvin a bit of a scare, so he'd back off.'

Reece sighed. 'But, April, I have a dozen witnesses who say that Gabriel threw Calvin to the ground, then proceeded to try to drown him. They thought Gabriel meant to go through with it.'

'He'd never have taken it that far …'

'April,' said Reece, turning to face her, 'stop lying to me. I'm starting to get very tired of it.'

April began to object, but then thought better of it. She had never seen DI Reece angry like this.

'I think I've been very tolerant of you and your friends, April,' he continued. 'Especially after your father died – I could see how hard you were taking it, so I was prepared to cut you some slack.'

'Listen, Mr Reece—'

'No, April, you listen!' he said sharply. 'I am sick of you taking advantage of my good nature. I have protected you, I have given you information I shouldn't have – and I've always tried my best to be straight with you. But it's a one-way street, isn't it? You haven't got the decency to cooperate and give me a straight answer.'

April was taken aback. Mr Reece had always been so gentle and understanding with her; clearly this had pushed him over the edge. And she could hardly be surprised – April had spent the entire time she had known him telling him half-truths, obscuring the facts and, yes, lying to his face. It was less than he deserved, much less.

'All right,' she said quietly. 'What do you want to find out? Ask me anything you like, and I promise I will tell you all I know.'

Reece looked at her, his eyebrows raised.

'Seriously, Mr Reece, I'll tell you everything. But I can't guarantee you're going to like what you hear.'

Reece pouted doubtfully, then nodded. 'Okay, let's start from the top. Did Gabriel kill Calvin Temple?'

'No,' said April. 'He was with me till shortly before I found Calvin.'

'But you don't know for sure.'

April looked down at her tea cup. 'Honestly? No.'

'Do think Gabriel is capable of killing?'

April looked up at him. 'I think everyone is capable of killing, given the right circumstances. Isn't that what people say?'

'No, April,' said Reece impatiently, 'they do not. I happen to know a bit about this subject, so I'd ask you not to be so flippant. This was not some boys' scuffle, however much you might like to portray it as such. This was a cold-blooded, vicious murder carried out by somebody pretty bloody unbalanced, in my professional opinion.' He paused. 'Okay, next question: if Gabriel didn't kill Calvin, do you have any idea who might have done?'

'I don't know. Honestly, I would tell you if I did.'

Reece shook his head with some exasperation. 'This new open policy of yours doesn't seem to be bearing much fruit, does it?'

'I'm sorry, Mr Reece. I just don't know.'

'Maybe you know the answer to this one: why you? Why was Calvin left hanging on your grandfather's gate? If it was just a fight in the street that got out of hand, we would have found him where he fell, but this was clearly premeditated, deliberate. Why leave him for *you* to find?'

April swallowed. Did he really want to hear the truth? Having promised to tell the truth, did she now have any choice?

'I think it was a message.'

Reece frowned. 'A message? What sort of message?'

'Someone's trying to scare me, showing they can get to me any time they like.'

'But who? Who would send such a message?'

She closed her eyes. 'The vampires,' she said quietly.

'The vampires,' he repeated. 'You're telling me that a vampire did this.'

April looked at him. 'Yes.'

'Oh Jesus Christ, April!' Reece yelled, making April jerk backwards in surprise. 'Is that the best you can do? I ask you to be honest with me – after all I've done for you – and that's what you give me? *Vampires*?'

'Mr Reece, I've wanted to tell you all along. I just didn't think . . .'

'Maybe you didn't think I'd believe you? Is that what you were going to say? Well, guess what – I don't. Forgive me, April, but I really don't think I can take that one to the Crown Prosecution Service with much hope of getting a green light. God!' he said, banging his hand against the window frame in frustration. 'And I suppose you want me to believe that Isabelle, Layla and Benjamin were all killed by Dracula and his pals, too?'

'No, Benjamin was a vampire himself,' muttered April, looking down at her hands.

'What was that?' said Reece, bending over and cupping his hand behind his ear. 'Because I don't think I heard it properly. Are you telling me that Benjamin Osbourne killed Annabel Holden because he wanted to drink her blood?'

He turned his face towards the ceiling and barked out an ironic laugh. 'And there I was thinking we had built up some sort of relationship, April. I thought there was some sort of mutual respect between us. Stupid of me really, wasn't it? All along, you've just been taking the mickey, haven't you?'

'No, Mr Reece, honestly. I knew I shouldn't have said anything.'

'I'd have to agree with you on that one, April.'

Just then there was a gentle knock on the door and Stanton appeared, clearing his throat. 'Sorry to interrupt, sir. Telephone call for you – said it was urgent.'

Reece sighed deeply, then nodded wearily. 'Wait here,' he said, pointing at April as he followed Stanton out, 'I haven't finished with you. Not by a long chalk.'

April slumped forward, her head in her hands. 'What have you done now, April?' she moaned to herself. 'Stupid, so very, very stupid.'

She couldn't blame the policeman for his reaction, not one little bit. What had she expected him to do? Say, 'Really? Vampires? Of course! It's the breakthrough I've been waiting for. Now the whole case makes sense.' Why had she been so naïve? All she had done was to undermine her relationship with the policeman, alienating one of the few people she had been able to rely on. And for what? So she could feel better about herself because she had told the truth for once. Well, she didn't feel better, she felt sick.

Reece walked back in. 'I have some good news and some

bad news. The good news – from your point of view, anyway – is that we have CCTV footage from Covent Garden tube station. Seems Gabriel left you and shot off in the opposite direction. There's no evidence he went anywhere near this house.'

She nodded and waited for the bad news.

'The bad news is that I have this from Detective Chief Inspector Johnston – I'm sure you remember him? He's not at all happy about last night's murder.'

'But, Mr Reece—'

The policeman held up a hand. 'I haven't finished, April,' he said. 'Would you like to know why DCI Johnston is unhappy? Because this murder is in Covent Garden and – I don't know if you've looked out of your window this morning – both ends of the street are completely jammed with camera crews: Sky News, BBC, even CN-bloody-N's out there. Highgate is one thing, but this is right in the middle of London's billion-pound tourism industry. We're not going to be able to sweep this under the carpet, not now it's been sent around the world on a million bloody iPhones.'

He walked over to the window and looked out, as if to make his point. 'DCI Johnston is feeling the pressure from every single political party with an axe to grind against the police – and that would be all of them – not to mention the Met's top brass and the Mayor's office. They all want this solved yesterday.'

April sat there, not wanting to speak, wishing she could disappear.

'All of which adds up to one thing, April. If I don't crack this quick smart, my career is down the toilet. More important, there will still be a murderer on the loose – more people might die. Is this making you feel bad?'

She nodded, still not looking up.

'Good. Then maybe you'll realise this isn't some stupid role-play game for you and your friends. A boy had his throat cut last night.'

'I know, Mr Reece. I saw him.'

'Keep that image in your mind, April. Remember it, and remember that's what keeping secrets looks like.' He stared down at her. 'So, is there anything else you want to tell me?'

She shook her head.

'Right,' he said. 'Right then. That's just fine.'

'I'm so sorry if I upset you, Mr Reece. I honestly didn't mean to.'

'That's fine, April,' he said, picking up his coat. 'Just promise me one thing, okay?'

'Anything.'

'For God's sake, don't breathe a word of your stupid bloody vampire nonsense to that pack of jackals out there on the street. That would be the final nail in my coffin – and yes, pun intended.'

'Honestly, I wish you could ...'

Reece held up another hand and reached for the door. 'I think I've made myself clear, April. If you change your mind, you know where to find me.'

April watched him close the door behind him, then put her head in her hands again and began to cry.

Chapter Eighteen

April pulled the curtain back and peeked out. *God, they're still there.* Well, that wasn't quite true: the TV vans with their satellite dishes had gone, but the photographers and reporters were still there. She counted eight of them camped out on either side of the road, chatting and smoking, waiting. Waiting for her.

'They obviously know I'm going to have leave for school,' she said into the phone.

'You can't really blame them,' replied Fiona, the line a little crackly. 'It's not often you get a mutilated body strung up only ten minutes from the newspapers' offices.'

'Thanks for that,' said April. 'Like I needed reminding.'

'Sorry. Doesn't your grandpa's house have a back entrance?'

'Annoyingly, no. Anyway, unless it had a secret tunnel linking it to Buckingham Palace or something, they could just wait for me at the back door, couldn't they?' She sighed. 'I feel like a criminal.'

'Don't take it so hard, sweetie,' said Fiona. 'It's not your fault.'

But April wasn't so sure. Her stomach churned as she thought of Calvin hanging on the gate, his head rolled back, his neck torn open. *Jesus.* She had to stop and take a long breath. No, she hadn't killed Calvin and she had no idea who had, but the facts remained – someone *had* killed him, and whoever it was, they had wanted her to see the grisly outcome.

'I just wish I knew what it was all about,' she said. 'I mean, it's one thing killing Calvin, it's another leaving him here.

I can understand why Mr Reece was so angry yesterday; it doesn't look good for me. Why would someone leave him hanging outside my home?'

'I know what you mean, but if it was a message, I'm not getting it,' said Fiona. 'Is it a threat?'

'Yeah, that did cross my mind. That and a million other things, none of which make sense.'

April had spent the entire previous day turning it over in her mind, not to mention answering endless questions asked by various police officers. Her grandfather hadn't exactly been over the moon to find a corpse impaled outside his house either. He had grilled April about the events at the party, insisting she tell him every detail, then had spent hours on the phone haranguing everyone from the police commissioner to the headmaster at Ravenwood.

'What kind of children do you allow at your school?' he had yelled at the no-doubt apologetic Dr Tame. 'I am paying you a small fortune and this is the kind of student my granddaughter is mixing with?' Such had been Thomas's onslaught, April had even managed, briefly, to feel sorry for the headmaster. But only briefly.

'They must have been trying to frame Gabriel – or me?' she put to Fiona.

'Doubt it. It'd be a pretty poor way to achieve that,' replied her friend. 'I mean, I'm no criminal mastermind, but if I wanted to frame someone for murder, I'd go a bit more low-key. You know: hide the murder weapon at their house, plant some DNA evidence on their clothes or something.'

'Really? Remind me never to get on your wrong side.' April drew back from the window as she saw a paparazzo look up. 'I just wish I'd been able to ask Gabriel about it.'

'Still no word?'

'I guess I should be getting used to it by now. It's not like he hasn't disappeared before, but never like this. I'm just so worried about him, Fee. There's something going on inside his head. He really seemed in pain and, after everything Jessica said, I've been imagining all sorts of scenarios.'

She had read the Ripper book Jessica had hurled at her from cover to cover, looking for the truth Jessica claimed was inside. But all April had found were endless theories on who the Ripper was – a butcher, a surgeon, a member of the royal family – and sketchy accounts of the rather depressing lives of his victims. April had been expecting some blinding revelation, but instead she was simply more confused. Could the sick-minded individual who had threatened Jessica also be the one who had left Calvin's mutilated body for her?

April had, of course, brought this up with the police. But by the time they had made it to Redfearne's, Jessica had disappeared, the 'Closed' sign firmly in place. Neighbours said she had gone away on holiday, not expected back for a couple of weeks.

'I know this may seem weird,' said Fiona, 'but this isn't sounding like vampires to me. Aren't they all just killing machines? Isn't that what they do best? I didn't think the Suckers were very big on subtle threats.'

'Not exactly subtle,' said April bleakly. From where she was standing, she could see the top of the gate. She didn't want to think about what she had seen down there the night before last.

'No, but if some mad killer wanted to get to you, why not just tear your heart out or something?'

'I'm not sure you're helping all that much, Fee.'

'Sorry. Anyway, I did ring for a reason. I've been doing some digging about those politicians we were talking about the other night.'

'David Harper?'

April had actually seen quite a lot of the MP over the past day. She had kept the twenty-four-hour TV news stations on constantly to see what they were saying about the 'gruesome Covent Garden slaying', as they were calling it, and Fiona had been right on two counts: one, David Harper was everywhere, seeming to pop up on every other news item with a well-judged sound bite; and two, he was very handsome. No wonder people were taking notice of him.

'What did you dig up?'

'Well, you know how MPs have to declare any financial interests, like businesses they are involved with? Guess what business David Harper is connected to?'

'Ravenwood?'

'Close. The Right Hon. David Harper MP was a non-executive director of Agropharm International until he resigned six months ago, just after he won his by-election.'

'No way! So he *is* part of the conspiracy?'

'Woah there,' said Fiona. 'Not so fast. It's tempting to jump to that conclusion, I admit. But Agropharm is enormous. It's a publicly listed company: there are something like a hundred thousand shareholders and literally hundreds of directors on the various local boards. It's not at all unusual for a branch of Agropharm to have a few politicians or councillors on board to help sway planning issues and the like.'

'But?'

'It does at least tell us that David Harper is moving in similar circles to the likes of Nicholas Osbourne, plus he sounds like the sort of man who might well be open to a spot of conspiracy – if there is enough money in it for him.'

'Or power,' said April.

'Exactly,' said Fiona, 'or power.'

As April came down the stairs, she could already hear her grandfather shouting into the phone in his study.

'What do you mean? Aren't I entitled to the protection of the law?' he was yelling. 'I hope I don't need to remind you that I am the victim here!'

Thinking it best to avoid Gramps while he was in attack dog mode, she turned towards the smells of coffee and toast which were wafting up from the kitchen. As she was passing through the entrance hall, she was startled when the doorbell rang in her ear. She heard her grandfather swear and slam the phone down, then his pounding footsteps as he stalked through.

'Ah, Prilly,' he said as he saw her, 'it's probably best if you stay out of sight. If I see one of those damned TV people, I swear I might take his camera and shove it …' he trailed off as he opened the door, his scowl softening. 'Peter, my friend,' he said, 'please, please do come in.'

April was surprised to see Peter Noble stepping into the hallway.

'Uncle Peter? I didn't know you were coming.'

Peter glanced over at Thomas and her grandfather looked sheepish.

'Sorry, Princess,' he said, 'I called Peter, asked him to come over. I …'

'I think I'm what they call a lesser evil,' said Peter. 'Your grandfather realised that you'd need to talk to somebody in the press, otherwise they'd never leave you alone. So he called me, suggested we have a chat on your way to school. How's that sound?'

April thought it sounded horrible. She didn't want to talk to anyone about Calvin Temple ever again and she certainly didn't want whatever she said to be read by tens of thousands of people over their cornflakes.

'Don't worry.' Peter smiled. 'I'll be sympathetic. And besides, I've got a plan to get you out of here.'

Peter's plan actually worked quite well. Having parked his car outside, he went out to talk to the paparazzi and hacks on the pavement. Presumably when the editor of a national newspaper hints there is a better line of enquiry, even the most hardened media vultures listen. When April nervously stepped out onto the pavement – trying not to look at the gate as she passed – and quickly climbed into Peter's car, the street was empty.

'What did you say to them?' asked April, turning to look out of the rear window as Peter drove them away.

'You don't need many skills to be a newspaper man, but

being able to tell a lie with a straight face is one of them.'

They sat in silence as Peter negotiated the traffic through the clogged rush-hour streets. April had never been driven to school before and it totally different up here on the surface. Commuting to north London on the tube was hot, cramped and often claustrophobic, but it was comparatively quiet. No one spoke on the tube at that time of day and, apart from the tannoy announcements and the rushing air of the trains coming into the platform, everything was muted, just the sound of the carriages rattling along the tracks and the swishing of doors. Up here on the roads there was a constant barrage of sound: honking horns, grinding gears, angry shouts, the revving of a hundred engines. To April, it was like lifting up a rock and suddenly seeing hundreds of beetles and earwigs scurrying away.

'So, how are you doing?' asked Peter finally.

'Okay, I suppose. It's not like it's the first dead body I've seen.' As the words came out of her mouth, April turned to look at Peter. 'Oh no, you're not going to quote me on that are you? That sounded horrible.'

Peter laughed. 'No, April, the idea is to make you sound good, remember? So speak freely – I won't put in anything you don't want me to, I promise.'

The funny thing was, her comment about the body was correct. Most ordinary people could get through their lives without ever seeing a dead body, not a real one, anyway. And yet at seventeen, April had seen – how many? Three? Four? God, she didn't even know. Somehow, that was even worse.

'Why don't you tell me what happened?'

Slowly, April recounted the whole evening: the party, Calvin's attack on Ling and the rescue – an edited version, with Gabriel removed – then her journey home and finding the body outside the house.

'Maybe don't put in the bit about Calvin and Ling in the tent,' she said when she had finished. 'I'm not sure Ling would like that very much.'

'Nor would Calvin's parents, I suspect,' said Peter. 'Anyway, I want this to be more about you, April.'

'Me? It was Calvin who was murdered.'

'Yes, and that's tragic of course, but we want to turn the focus away from the crime, make it a human interest story. The girl who's survived one trauma after another but always manages to rise above it, that sort of thing. That way, people will ask fewer questions about what happened with the fire in the East End.'

That was certainly something April wanted. She had actually been wondering if Peter had somehow used his influence to stop such a story appearing so far. After all, if a reporter did enough digging, what came out could look very bad for her: April Dunne had discovered three dead bodies, watched her father die and been seriously attacked twice, one attack ending in a fatality. And that was before she had been kidnapped at the school where her teacher Miss Holden had been tortured and murdered in front of her, then taken to Mr Sheldon's Shoreditch house where both he and Benjamin had also died, apparently in that house fire. Put all that together, it looked – at best – as if April was some sort of jinx. At worst, she was almost a walking example of 'no smoke without fire' and she shuddered to think how the tabloids might handle that.

'You know,' said April, 'your idea is almost exactly the same as the one Dr Tame had. Different reason for it, of course – he was only concerned with making the school look good.'

'I'd hope that's the only similarity between us.' Peter smiled, keeping his eyes on the road. 'I spoke to that man a few times when he was working with the police. Seemed to me he was one of those guys who's just a little bit too convinced of his own genius.'

April giggled. 'You're a good judge of character, Uncle Peter.' She looked at him sideways. 'Talking of which, you spend a lot of time talking to politicians, don't you?'

Peter rolled his eyes. 'Too much. After a while, you even start to think of them as human.'

'Have you met David Harper?'

'Of course, he's the master of the sound bite at the moment. Tomorrow I'm going to some reception he'll be at. Why do you ask?'

'Only that I heard he was connected to Ravenwood.'

Peter pulled up at some traffic lights and turned to face April. 'You think he might be involved in this thing your dad was investigating?'

He might just be 'cuddly, reliable friend-of-the-family Uncle Peter', but he was sharp, thought April. She nodded.

'You're right – after a fashion. As you know, I have been following up on your dad's hunch about Ravenwood, about how they were exploiting the students, using their ideas without payment?'

'Yes, since Dr Tame has taken over, it's become a big thing at school,' said April. 'They're quite open about it actually.'

Peter nodded thoughtfully as the lights changed and they drove off again. 'I've had it looked into and, unfortunately, it's not actually illegal. It's difficult to copyright ideas and in the world of science, whoever publishes their findings first is seen as the owner. Also, a place of work or study can make a claim on whatever work is done in their labs, so if Ravenwood nicks some brilliant student's brainwave, that's all seen as fine and dandy.'

'But it's so unfair!' said April. 'Dr Tame even has people from Agropharm sitting in Ravenwood's laboratories taking notes – how can that be right?'

'It's not right, April. Legal, yes. Right, no. But that's where the great British free press comes in; public opinion is a powerful force and I'm fairly sure our readers will agree that it's immoral to steal from children. However, before I accuse anyone of anything, we need evidence about what's happening, otherwise they will simply deny it.' He sighed. 'Unfortunately, Agropharm categorically denies being involved with Ravenwood in any way, beyond donating some laboratory supplies. So due to the libel laws, I need hard facts, and at the moment, all I have is a few reports that Agropharm is ripping off ideas. Presumably the teachers or scientists involved would claim the ideas were theirs all along – very hard to prove who came up with the original spark.'

Leaving Kentish Town, Peter turned off into Dartmouth Park, driving past the mansions cowering behind gates and high walls.

April craned her neck, trying to spot where Alix Graves had died. She had meant to come down and see his house on her first day in Highgate, but she had never got around to it. Alix's death had been the first, hadn't it? What if he hadn't died? she wondered. What if the singer had agreed to be a figurehead for the conspiracy? Maybe Ravenwood wouldn't be such a big part of the vamps' plan. Using Alix's influence, they might have been able to recruit on a massive scale – persuade a whole generation of kids that they should 'Embrace the Dark', as it had said on the wall at Ravenwood. *Not a bad title for an album, that,* thought April wryly.

Finally, they pulled up outside Ravenwood and April watched as the other students filed in, chatting to one another as if they hadn't a care in the world. Maybe they hadn't, beyond worrying if they'd got another A in astrophysics. She wondered how many of these kids had watched the news yesterday. Probably all of them: this *was* Ravenwood; they'd be tuning in anyway – to monitor the situation in the Middle East and check out the FTSE. Besides, even without satellite news stations, the school's grapevine was second to none. They would all be aware that their new Head Girl had been involved with a fight at Ling's party and that 'popular', 'sporty' Calvin had turned up dead on her doorstep. April shrank down in the seat a little.

'Is it okay if we just wait here until everyone else has gone in?'

'Of course,' said Peter. 'I understand. In fact, I rather

expected there to be film crews here this morning. Perhaps you're already old news.'

Or perhaps someone inside Ravenwood has pulled a few strings, thought April. The last thing the governors would want were snaps of the school on TV above a headline reading 'Murdered Boy's School'. Which gave April a thought.

'You told me about how your paper is looking into the school, but you never said how David Harper was involved?'

'Only very slightly.' Peter shrugged. 'Like a lot of career politicians, David Harper started out in local politics and he was on the planning committee which allowed Agropharm to build their testing lab in Baston Water; you probably heard about that?'

She had heard the name. There had been some hoo-hah about the lab a few years before, something to do with vivisection and animal rights. April remembered that a load of rabbits had been released which then destroyed like a billion pounds worth of carrots on local farms, somewhat undermining the Animal Libbers' message.

'Anyway, there are some people who think that Baston Water was David Harper's big break. Because he scratched Agropharm's back, they scratched his, or at least the investors behind the company did – and that's why he's been so successful in landing contracts from the government, getting a factory built in his constituency, that sort of thing. And now he's being tipped for a Cabinet seat as Minister of Education, which means he'll be in a perfect position to help out with whatever Ravenwood requires.' Peter raised his eyebrows meaningfully. 'That's the theory, anyway. As I say, no hard evidence of any corruption.'

'Maybe I could help,' said April. 'What sort of evidence would you need?'

Peter laughed. 'Hey, this interview is supposed to be about you. No, if there's anything to find, you rest assured we'll dig it out. I have some of the best investigative reporters in the country on my payroll – let them earn their money.'

April could hear the bell ringing inside school, calling for registration. Peter reached over and opened the door for her.

'Seriously, April,' he said. 'Don't get involved. You don't want to be on the wrong side of these people.'

It's a bit late for that, thought April.

Chapter Nineteen

Ravenwood had never been a very welcoming place. The building itself was creepy: dark corridors, creaking floorboards, high echoing ceilings. Despite a few modern additions like the refectory and the library, it had always reminded April of the orphanage in *Oliver Twist*. On top of that, she had started at the school as the weird new girl and that outsider status had been compounded by the fact that, in her first week, she had found herself mixed up in a murder. So it was all the more unsettling to walk into school today and find herself suddenly the toast of Ravenwood. Yes, people were looking at her – the sly glances, the whispers to their friends were still there. But today was different. Today, they were looking at her in awe, as if she were a visiting celebrity.

'Hi, April,' said one girl as she passed, 'how's it going?'

'Hey, love the shoes,' said another. Where before they had dropped their eyes when April looked up, now they met her gaze, smiled, sometimes even waved. Suddenly, April Dunne was cool.

'Hey, don't knock it,' advised Caro at lunchtime as they sat down at their table in the refectory. 'It's what all teenagers dream about, isn't it? We're all desperate to be accepted. Or that's what they say in all those American teen dramas.'

But Caro clearly didn't feel any desire to fit in. Her hair had been sleek and shiny for Ling's party, but now it was back to standard Jackson: a streak of blue running down one side matching her glittery nail polish.

'I'm only cool because they all think I *killed* someone.'

'Not just "killed",' said Caro, framing the words with

imaginary quotation marks. 'They think you mutilated Calvin. I read all about it in the papers yesterday. *Everyone* did.'

April winced. She had seen the reports, of course. That was before Grampa Thomas had torn them into pieces and burnt them in the fireplace.

'Do you remember when the police came to school to question me over Isabel Davis's murder? Everyone treated me like I was some kind of pariah. Now everyone wants to be friends with a killer.'

Caro shook her head and jabbed a straw into her smoothie carton. 'Just shows how quickly things have changed, doesn't it? Those Yank college shows are right about one thing: everybody wants to fit in, so they go with the current consensus. If everybody is wearing black trainers, no one's going to wear white ones, are they? So now it's cool to go over to the dark side; everyone wants to be one of Dr Death's chosen few.'

'Suddenly it's okay to be a murderer?'

'No, but it's cool. The millions of kids who bought Alix Graves's records didn't necessarily want to get into hardcore drugs or occult-based orgies, but they still thought he was cool for doing it – same thing.'

April gave a twisted smile. 'I'm a doomed rock star?'

'Duh!' said Caro. 'No, they heard you kicked Calvin's butt at the party and now they think you finished him off. Nerds and Suckers alike.'

'So why aren't you cool? You kicked his mate in the nuts.'

'Yeah, but no one hung him up on a gate on Sky News, did they? I saw Chessy earlier and you could tell she thought that was a particularly nice touch.'

April turned towards her. 'Hang on, even the *Suckers* think I killed him?'

Caro shrugged. 'Ling and Chessy were full of it, like you'd passed an initiation or something.'

April was dumbfounded. She put down her spoon. 'Why would they think . . . ?'

'Come on, A, it's only logical.' Caro ticked off the names

on her fingers. 'Isabelle, Marcus, Miss Holden, Benjamin – you've been there when they all shuffled off this mortal coil. Now *we* know you didn't do it, but for everyone else? No smoke without fire.'

April put her head in her hands, and Caro touched her on the arm. 'Hey, sweetie, it's okay. Look at it this way – the more the Suckers believe you're one of them, the more they're going to open up to you and let you into their little club.'

April looked up. 'Listen, we're beyond that now. *Way* beyond it. You said it yourself: *we* know I didn't kill Calvin.'

'So?'

'So *we* know he was killed by a vampire. Which means someone in their little club tore his throat out and dumped him on my doorstep, right?'

'I guess.'

'So someone in that group knows it wasn't me. They must be laughing at Sky News, Caro, seeing they are the real killers. Besides, we don't have time to mess about trying to infiltrate the Suckers; things are starting to move. Can't you feel it? I think that's why Gabriel's having all these nightmares: he can feel something coming.'

'What's coming?' said Caro.

'The darkness, the war? I don't know. But I *do* know the time for looking for clues is over. We have to start getting answers.' She stood up. 'And I think I know who to ask.'

Chapter Twenty

For once, April had a plan. Not a particularly good one, but a plan all the same. She was going to save Gabriel. Yes, she needed to find the King Vampire; yes, she needed to somehow avenge her father. All that went without saying. But the only thing she really, truly cared about right now was saving the man who made her heart do cartwheels every time he walked into the room.

April strode purposefully up Swain's Lane and cut across the park, glancing briefly at the pathway where Marcus had sunk his claws into her. For a long while, it had unnerved her walking this way, but not now. April hadn't been exaggerating when she had told Caro she could feel the darkness coming; it was almost as if she could smell it in the air, like you sometimes inexplicably know that summer has turned to autumn. And to her surprise, April felt stronger. For so long, she had been living with fear and uncertainty, but now it all seemed to have boiled down to one simple choice: either give in or fight. And there was no way she was going to let the vampires win. Smiling to herself, April pulled out her mobile and began to tap out a message to Gabriel.

> Don't know where you are, but I'm thinking of you right now.
> Please come back to me soon, we can face this together.
> Love you loads xx A

She had no idea if it would have any effect, but it couldn't do any harm, could it? She was sure of one thing – Gabriel was hurting right now. Maybe the dreams he was having *were* memories – it didn't matter to April. She knew deep in her heart the *real* him. Yes, he'd lied to her, let her down, and now he was running away from something April would gladly have faced with him, but her feelings hadn't changed for him, not one bit. She was going to help him, even if it brought risks. *Risks like this*, she thought, taking a deep breath.

She pressed the intercom and waited. Nothing. She stepped up to the iron gates and peered through. The lights were on in the house, so she pressed the button again.

'What the hell is it?' came a fuzzy male voice at last.

'It's April Dunne. I've come to see Davina, is she in?'

'Davina! It's for—' she heard the man shout, then the sound cut off.

Maybe I could have chosen a better time, thought April as the gate buzzed open and she picked her way along the rain-sodden gravel driveway. *I could have chosen some better shoes, too*, she thought as she jumped another puddle.

Davina was waiting for her at the front door, a grim look on her face. Even from the outside, April could hear the sounds of a heated argument coming from within.

'Sorry, Mum and Dad are having a bit of a domestic,' she said. 'Let's sneak up the stairs to my room.'

But even before April could step inside, Nicholas Osbourne appeared behind Davina.

'Ah, April,' he said, '*do* come in and join the fun. We're having a little family discussion – perhaps you can give us some perspective.' April noticed that he had trouble pronouncing the word 'perspective' and that he was holding a tumbler of some golden liquid.

'April doesn't want to get involved with your argument, Dad,' said Davina. 'Leave her alone.'

'Leave her alone? I wouldn't dream of it,' said Nicholas Osbourne, taking April's arm and pulling her through to the living room. 'What kind of host would I be if I *didn't* involve her? It would be the height of rudeness.'

The house was a mess. Not just your ordinary lived-in family messiness, but the sort of disarray that suggested it hadn't been cleaned or tidied in weeks. There were papers and food wrappers strewn on the floor, plates and cups left on side tables, their contents congealed or, in a few cases, growing mould. April could see a coffee mug lying on the cream carpet – no one had bothered to clean up the dark stain. Worse than that, there were signs of a more recent disturbance. A dining chair was upended, the curtain torn – and most obviously, the mantelpiece had been forcefully swept clear, broken pieces of a clock and glass from a photo-frame lying in the hearth as evidence.

'So, April,' said Mr Osbourne, 'what do you think of our humble abode?'

'It's very ... nice.'

'It's a shit-hole,' replied the man. 'Come on, don't be shy, you can say it. My beloved wife is attempting to run it into the ground – a little interior design project of hers.'

'Nick, please,' appealed Davina's mother. 'She's nothing to do with this.' Barbara Osbourne had been sitting so quietly in an armchair, April hadn't even noticed her. Her usually immaculate up-do was slightly off centre and she had clearly been crying. She, too, was nursing a large drink.

'April? Nothing to do with this? Oh, I wouldn't say that,' said Mr Osbourne. 'After all, Davina's nice little friend almost bled to death on our lawn, or have you forgotten about that?' Nicholas turned towards April. 'You'll have to excuse my wife. She likes to push violent episodes like that under the carpet.'

'Dad, don't!' said Davina.

'April doesn't mind, do you, April?' he continued, with a nasty look. 'After all, April was there when Benjamin died. Almost family, aren't you? United in death, just like the rest of us.'

Davina glared at him, but didn't speak.

'I'm so sorry for your loss, Mr Osbourne,' muttered April.

'Are you? Well you'll be the first. Nobody else seems to be in the slightest bit bothered about his passing.'

'Nick!' snapped Barbara.

'What? You don't agree?' shouted her husband, slopping his drink as he turned towards her. 'How many people came to his funeral? What was it, four? All those friends of his – they all seemed to melt away, didn't they? Now why is that, do you think?'

April felt trapped. She couldn't walk out without appearing rude and yet she felt horribly awkward standing there, obliged to watch this man's terrible grief unfolding. Little wonder the Osbournes had let their once-pristine house degenerate like this. April knew only too well from her own experience that in the stark face of a violent family death, trivial things like spilt coffee seemed unimportant.

'We adopted them, did you know that?' slurred Nicholas, waving his glass at a painting on the wall near the stairs. April hadn't noticed it before, an oil portrait of Davina and Benjamin, presumably painted quite recently.

'Dad, we don't need to go into all this now. April came to see me, remember?'

'But who can I tell if I can't tell April?' said Mr Osbourne. 'Your mother? You? Neither of you want me to talk about him any more.'

Mr Osbourne moved over to April and put his arm around her shoulders. She could smell the whisky on his breath and it took a conscious effort not to pull away from him.

'He was so good-looking, April, they both were,' he said, seemingly unaware of April's discomfort. 'And we were so happy, weren't we, Barbara? We couldn't have a family of our own, you see. Two perfect children sent to us who sprinkled fairy dust on everything: the Agropharm job, the house, this lifestyle, who could ask for more? But it was all built on quicksand, wasn't it? And it's sucked us all down, every one of us.'

Davina strode over and pulled April's arm. 'Come on,

April, you don't need to put up with this. I'm taking you up to my room.'

But Nicholas pulled back, gripping April's shoulders tighter. 'No, I think April wants to hear about this, don't you, April? You've always shown an interest in our family, haven't you? I remember you and your friend Caro asking about Agropharm at the Winter Ball; perhaps you'd like me to tell you a little more now?'

April felt Davina stop tugging.

'Dad, I'm warning you,' she said.

'Warning me?' He laughed. 'What on earth do you imagine you could threaten me with? What more can you take away from me? I have nothing left. *Nothing*.'

He leant in close to April, his tone friendly, one pal to another. 'You see, April, I've been fired. They're calling it redundancy, the old "golden handshake", but the upshot is: I'm surplus to requirements. I don't fit in, not the right sort, can you believe that?'

'Darling, please,' said Barbara, standing up, 'I think you've said enough.'

'Enough? Rubbish! April wants to hear about Agropharm, don't you? She's just like her father – she has that inquisitive mind. You may not trust me, April. I know your friend Caro doesn't – she's a smart girl, that one; I like her. But you can believe this much: I was only ever interested in all this –' he swept his hand around the living room, spilling most of his drink onto an expensive-looking sofa '– I was in it for the money, isn't that right, Barbara? We wanted all the nice things, the big cars and the first-class tickets and, God forgive me, we got it in spades. But them?'

He pointed towards the television which was playing on a news channel with the sound off.

'They were only interested in control. That's what drives them, not the cash or the trinkets – they just want complete power. And now they have it over us, don't they, daughter, dear?'

'All right, that's *enough*,' hissed Davina. She picked up a bottle of Scotch from the coffee table and shoved it at her father. Mr Osbourne clutched at it in surprise.

'There, you've got what you need,' said Davina. 'Now let go of my friend.'

Nicholas looked down at the half-empty bottle as Davina pulled April back towards the front door. 'Just remember one thing, April,' he shouted after her. 'When you think you've hit rock bottom, there's always further to fall. Always.'

Davina slammed the door and followed April out onto the driveway. 'I'm sorry you had to see that, April,' she said, crossing her arms. 'Dad just hasn't been the same since Ben died, you know?'

'Really, there's no need to explain,' said April. 'I completely understand, I imagine I'd feel the same way if I'd had a son, and he had ...' She felt a sickness in the pit of her stomach, knowing that she had been – however unwillingly – responsible for Mr Osbourne's pain.

'It's kind of you,' said Davina, 'but I'm not sure Daddy's one hundred per cent in control at the moment. So don't listen to anything he says, okay? It was the booze talking.'

'Has he really lost his job?'

'Yes, that was another blow for him, but I can't imagine he'll find it too hard to get a new one, not with his connections. It's all just getting a little bit on top of him at the moment. Both of them, actually. Mummy is using it as an excuse to drown herself in Pinot Noir.

April smiled. 'You don't need to tell me about that sort of thing, my mum isn't exactly a stranger to the off-licence either.'

They picked their way through the puddles and out to the gate.

'So were you coming for something in particular?' said Davina as they walked.

Yes, I was going to ask you to use your father to get me in to see the top brass at Agropharm in the hope that one of them was the

King Vampire, thought April. *There goes another brilliant plan.*

'No, just wanted to bitch about boys.'

'Not heard from Gabriel?' asked Davina.

April raised her eyebrows. How did Davina know he had pulled his disappearing act again?

Davina smiled. 'Just because I wasn't invited to Ling's party doesn't mean I didn't hear about it. Not all of those little clones following Chessy about are *hers*, if you take my meaning. I haven't completely lost my touch.'

April smiled ruefully. 'Yes, Gabriel has fallen off the map, and no, I haven't heard from him. If I'm honest, I have no idea where to start looking.'

Davina looked awkward. 'It's probably not what you want to hear,' she said, 'but if it were me, I would try the cemetery.'

'The cemetery?' said April. 'Why there?'

'Well, you do know that Gabriel used to have another girlfriend.'

April swallowed. 'Chessy?'

Davina tipped her head back and laughed. 'She wishes. No, the one who died.'

April was taken aback. 'You mean Lily?'

Davina nodded. 'Like I said, no girl wants her boyfriend to run off to another girl, even if she's dead. But I do know that he used to visit her grave quite often. Maybe he's been there again, and maybe people around the cemetery have seen him. At least that way you might find out if he's okay.'

April could have explained that she wasn't exactly the most popular person at Highgate Cemetery right now; she certainly couldn't imagine Miss Leicester giving her a rundown of the comings and goings at the graveyard, not that Gabriel would have used the main entrance anyway. But Davina's mention of Lily had given her an idea. *Damn!* – why hadn't she thought of it before? April leant over and kissed Davina on the cheek.

'Thanks, 'Vina,' she said, heading for the gate. 'You're a genius.'

'What?' called Davina after her. 'What did I say?'

But April was already through the gate and halfway up the hill.

Chapter Twenty-One

Just for a moment, as she slotted her key into the yellow front door at Pond Square, April had an uncomfortable feeling that perhaps she wasn't welcome at the place she had once called home. What if she turned the key and discovered that her mother had changed the locks? *God*, what if Silvia was in there with a man? What if she found Dr Tame lounging in the kitchen again? Steeling herself, she twisted and the door clicked open.

'Mum?' she called. 'Mum, are you there?'

She closed the door and stood in the silent rather narrow passageway, sniffing the air as she had that first time, a lifetime ago, when they had all piled out of the family car to inspect their new home.

'Mum?' she tried again, popping her head around the living room door. There was always the chance that Silvia would be sprawled face down on the sofa, one shoe hanging off, house keys still clutched in her hand. April had seen her mother in that undignified position far too often.

April racked her brains, trying to remember if Silvia had told her where she would be tonight. She had, of course, been on the phone on and off all day yesterday, checking on April's 'emotional state' after Grandpa Thomas had refused to let her come to the house. 'She's upset enough, Silvie,' he had said. Good old Gramps.

Hooking her bag on the banister – force of habit – April sprinted up the stairs to check her mum's bedroom. No, the bed was empty – unmade of course, but at least that meant Silvia had been there; the house was starting to feel a little lonely, even abandoned. April looked up the dark stairwell towards her room – or what *had* been her room. For all she knew, Silvia could have let it out to a lodger. But April knew she was only making excuses – she had to go up, however much she was dreading it.

'Come on, April,' she urged. 'What are you scared of? Vampires?'

Breathing out, she climbed the narrow staircase and opened the door, starting when it creaked. *Why didn't I ever get that oiled?* she wondered. *Like I needed to make my life any more like a teen slasher movie.*

She looked around her room. Just a normal everyday bedroom at the top of a little Victorian terrace. Nothing special, a little cramped and dusty. But still, it felt strange being here, like revisiting something she had left behind.

April walked over to her old desk and ran a finger along it, coming back with a smudge of grey dust. April snorted. She really shouldn't have worried; Silvia clearly hadn't set foot in here in weeks. But, truthfully, April couldn't ever remember seeing her mother with a can of Pledge in her hand.

All right, enough moping, she thought, *time to do what you came to do.* She crossed to her bed, knelt down and felt around underneath, hoping not to disturb any creepy crawlies. Her fingers caught the handle and April slid the suitcase out and heaved it onto the bed with a bump.

'Sorry, spiders,' she said, popping it open. The suitcase was crammed with papers, newspaper cuttings and books – her Ravenwood treasure trove – all the notes and material she had been able to find about her father's investigation after sorting through his things in the cellar.

'All right, where is it?' she mumbled, beginning to rummage through the case. Her fingers stopped as she came across familiar items: a packet of family photos, her mother's birth certificate, her dad's diary and notebook. April cast an eye over each, then carefully put them all to one side.

'There,' she said finally. An envelope containing a handful

of slightly faded Post-it notes. These little square notes had been tacked up all over her dad's study the day he had died. The police had originally taken them away for examination, presumably to use in evidence when they found the killer. *Not that they'd ever been needed, had they?* thought April bitterly. Still, at least they'd returned them – presumably there were copies of everything here in some police file somewhere, an idea that made her feel like someone was looking over her shoulder.

She flipped through the notes, looking for one in particular. And then there it was, scrawled in her dad's handwriting: '23.11.88 – 14.02.93'

That particular note had stuck in her mind because the second date was her birthday – but now it was the other one she was interested in. Reaching over to her bedside table, she tore the corner off a page of a magazine and scribbled the date down.

Putting everything back into the suitcase, April pushed it back under her bed and ran downstairs clutching the paper. In the kitchen – a mess, obviously, the sink piled high with unwashed dishes – she picked up the local directory from by the telephone and quickly leafed to the right page, running her finger down the black print, then picking up the receiver.

'Mr Gordon?' she said breathlessly as the call connected.

'Speaking?'

'It's April, April Dunne.'

'Ah, April, how are you?' began the vicar, but April hadn't rung for small talk.

'Mr Gordon, you know how you said you were friendly with Isabelle Davis – she was in choir at the church and stuff?'

'Yes, that's true ... why do you ask?'

'I wondered if you had been asked to do the funeral?'

'No, I'm afraid not,' he said, his voice wary. 'Her family are from the area, but I think seeing as she ... well, considering the manner of her passing, they weren't too keen to have her buried in the same location. I believe she was cremated up at Golders Green. I know Reverend Brice up there, if that's any help?'

'No, that's okay,' said April, disappointed.

'What was it you wanted to know?'

'Oh, I thought you might have a record of her date of birth. You know, because you'd have to put it on the headstone, that sort of thing.'

There was a pause. 'Just hold the line a moment …' said the vicar. April was just about to give up when Mr Gordon came back on.

'Twenty-third of November, 1988,' he said.

April looked down at her scrap of paper, her heart pounding. It was same as the date on her dad's note!

'How do you know?' she asked. 'I mean, how did you find that out so quickly?'

The vicar chuckled. 'Computers, April, marvellous things aren't they? We have everything on a digital database these days.'

'But why do you have Isabelle's date of birth on your computer?'

'A few years ago, the diocese put the parish records online. Partly because the bishop is something of a progressive sort, partly because of that annoying TV show, you know the one where celebrities trace their family trees? We were getting swamped with requests to go through the records and it was taking up far too much of our time to have people poring over the ledgers and records, so we had the lot transferred online.'

'And Isabelle's on there because she died nearby?'

'No, because she was born in the parish.'

Of course! And suddenly April had another idea. She was filled with both excitement and dread. It was something Robert Sheldon had said to her that night of flame and blood, something about a coincidence.

'How far do the records go back, Mr Gordon?' she asked, her heart beginning to beat faster.

'Oh, all the way back. We had a team come over from America to do it all,' he said proudly. 'Went right through the vaults, parchment scrolls, everything.'

'Could you look something else up for me? Another name, a burial in the cemetery that happened in 1887?' April remembered that date vividly, the year Gabriel had been turned.

'Of course, if you can tell me what this is all about?'

'Not really, Mr Gordon, but it could be important. Very important.'

He paused. 'All right, you'd better give me the name.'

'It's Lily … Oh.' It was only then that April realised she didn't know Lily's surname. There was little hope of the vicar tracing her with only the first name. Then she had a sudden thought. 'Try Lily Swift.'

April could hear the rattle of the keys as the vicar typed it in.

'March 15th, 1887.'

It *was* her! 1887 was the year Gabriel had told her Lily had died, the year he had become turned himself in a desperate attempt to keep Lily with him. And Gabriel had used his name, of course he had. They were engaged to be married, after all. It was Gabriel's way of linking them together even in death. Perhaps a way of reminding himself of the promise he had made to her on her death bed, the promise that he would never take a human life, that he would stay strong for her. If she hadn't been slightly jealous, April knew she would have found it romantic.

Concentrate, April, she said to herself, *concentrate on what it all means.*

What it meant was that Sheldon had been right. He had sneered when Gabriel had said he was in the cemetery for Lily's anniversary on the night of Isabelle's death. Gabriel *hadn't* been there for Lily. So why *had* he been there? And more importantly, why didn't he remember?

'Are you all right, my dear?' asked the vicar.

'Yes, just …' April turned as she heard the front door

open. 'Sorry, Mr Gordon,' she said quickly. 'I'll explain later, my mum's here, I've got to go.'

She hung up the phone just as Silvia walked in staggering under the weight of a number of clanking grocery bags. *Mainly liquid groceries by the sound*, thought April.

'Darling!' she beamed, dropping the bags and coming across to embrace April. 'How are you? Tell me the truth – I've been so worried.'

April wriggled from her grip. 'I'm fine, Mum, don't fuss. It's nothing.'

'Nothing? I watched the news. The way they've been describing it, it wasn't nothing. That poor boy! And right in front of the house too – so horrible.'

'*That poor boy*,' thought April. It was amazing how sudden death could wipe away all your sins. Calvin had been described in the press as 'a wonderful son, gentle and loving' and 'world-class athlete cut down in his prime'. There had been nothing about drinking the blood of vulnerable school children or forcing himself on weeping girls.

'The only reason I didn't come straight over was because your grandfather said I'd give the paparazzi another picture to keep the story going.'

Yeah, that and your busy social calendar, thought April.

'There was no need anyway, Mum,' she said. 'I've seen much worse.'

Silvia looked at her, her expression serious. 'Yes, and that's what I wanted to talk to you about. I'm glad you've visited, because we need to have a serious chat.'

Oh God, not another woman-to-woman discussion, thought April. These things always turned into a lecture about how evil men were, and how they couldn't be trusted and if she wasn't careful, April would end up pregnant on crack in a council flat. Silvia was not a great motivational speaker. Even so, April could see she wasn't going to escape this one easily, so she sighed and reluctantly sat down.

'Now, I know things haven't been very easy for you since we moved here,' began Silvia.

'That is the understatement of the year,' said April.

'Exactly,' said Silvia, missing the irony in April's tone. 'Your father and I made the decision to move to Highgate, and clearly ... well, clearly it was the wrong decision. Having said that, I've been so proud of you, April – the way you have coped with this – but the truth of the matter is, I – your father and I – made a terrible mistake coming here.' She paused. 'That's why we're moving back.'

April could feel her mouth drop open. 'Back? To Edinburgh?'

Silvia nodded. 'With your father's insurance coming through, we'll be able to afford something very nice in Merchiston. I've already had a look at a few things online, but of course it's a joint decision.'

April could feel her anger rising. She couldn't believe Silvia was actually suggesting this. 'Instead of listening to me a year ago, you wait until our family is torn apart, my father is dead and you're exposed as an adulterer? *Then* you decide to leave?'

It was a low blow and April knew it, but she was too furious to hold back. How *dare* she? How dare Silvia make decisions – life-changing decisions – without even consulting her? Yes, April had already moved out, but that wasn't the point, was it? Her mother was still trying to push her around, with no thought for April's own feelings.

'Of course you're upset about how things have worked out, April,' said Silvia, 'but I think cutting our losses and moving back to Scotland is the best solution for everyone.'

'Best solution for you, you mean! What about me? I've made friends here; I have responsibilities. I've made a *life* here!'

'I know you've bonded nicely with some girls – Gabriel too. I understand you don't want to leave him, I'm not completely insensitive. But you'll be off to university next year anyway, darling, and you'll make a whole load of new friends then.'

'That's not the point!' cried April. 'You can't just play around with my life like this, Mother! You made me leave everything behind in Edinburgh and now you've decided to run back on a bloody whim?'

'No, April,' said Silvia, 'not on a whim. A boy was killed outside your grandfather's house – that's a serious matter. Clearly you're not safe here.'

'Oh, and you're just working that out now? How is some stranger getting killed in the street "a serious matter" and my father being slaughtered in front of me isn't? Why didn't you suggest going back then? What about the three or four times people have tried to *kill* me? Seriously, how come none of that made you think it's not safe here?'

'Clearly in hindsight, I should have—'

'Hindsight? Jesus, Mother! Listen to yourself. A man actually tried to set me on fire, remember? Another one tried to kill me – twice! Why didn't this miraculous "hindsight" kick in then?'

And suddenly April realised *this* was why she was so angry with her mother. It wasn't that she was a useless mother, it wasn't that she was aloof and absent, it wasn't even that she had let them all down with her affair – she was angry because her mother *hadn't* taken her away. That was what mothers were supposed to do, wasn't it? Surely, even rubbish mothers did what they could to protect their children? Now April could see that this was what she had been yearning for – for her mother to wake up one morning and say, "We're leaving; you're more important than anything here. We're off to Scotland, or the Channel Islands, or France, or Jamaica, anywhere that isn't this village of death."' But she hadn't. She *hadn't*.

Silvia opened her mouth, then closed it again. The look of misery on her face almost made April relent. 'I … I tried,' Silvia stammered. 'I just didn't …' She looked up, her eyes wide. 'I just didn't know what to do.'

Oh God, thought April. Another horrible, unwelcome

revelation. Silvia hadn't taken her away because she just wasn't capable of it. Too selfish, too fundamentally lacking in maternal instincts. You always assumed that your parents were the strong ones, those superhuman beings who knew how to do everything and how to cope with everything, but it turned out that actually they were pretty crap.

'Your father always made the big decisions,' said Silvia. 'He was the strong one. People laughed at him, said he was under the thumb, but he was always in charge. And when he was gone, I just didn't have anyone to ...' She looked down at her hands and let out a sob. 'I didn't have anyone to talk to.'

'Oh, Mum,' said April, stepping forward and putting her arms around her. 'Don't be so bloody silly. You've got me, you've got Gramps, Luke, about a zillion friends.'

Only that wasn't true, was it? thought April, not for her, anyway. She hadn't been there for her mother, in fact she had been selfish and mean. Okay, so Silvia had deserved some of it, but April knew deep down she'd been a pretty poor daughter.

'I know,' said Silvia. 'But the thing is I couldn't talk to any of you, not really talk like I used to talk to your dad. I know you think we just argued all the time, but ... but that's why I couldn't leave Highgate. I just didn't want to leave Will. God knows, I'd let him down enough in life, I couldn't leave him behind here on his own.'

'Mum, I do love you, you know,' said April.

'But you're not leaving, are you?'

'No, I can't. I know you probably don't understand, but I have too much here to just up and go. People are depending on me. I'm not sure I can make much of a difference, but I have to try.'

'You're talking about Gabriel.'

It wasn't a question, it was a statement of fact.

'Partly Gabriel, yes. I love him. And before you say it, it's not just puppy love.'

Silvia held up a hand. 'I may not be able to boil an egg or

remember the date of your parent-teacher evenings, but one thing I do understand is what goes on inside a girl's heart. I know it's real to you.'

April was about to protest, but Silvia carried on. 'That's not to belittle it. I just mean all love affairs *always* feel right, they feel perfect – until that horrible moment they don't and you realise how wrong you've been about a man. But that's the tragedy of love. Every single relationship you have is wrong until you find the one that's right. It's that old cliché about how you have to keep kissing the frogs, otherwise you'll never find your prince.'

'Gabriel *is* right for me, Mum,' said April.

'I hope so. For all the right reasons, I truly hope so. But ...'

'But what?

'You asked "why now?" – why I left it until this boy Calvin was killed to get you out of here?'

The serious look on her mother's face told April she wasn't going to like what was coming.

'Two nights ago, you found a boy strung up on a gate, his blood in a puddle on the floor. And look at you, you're fine.'

April laughed nervously. 'I'm not *fine* ...'

'Yes, April, you are. And I can't tell you how much that terrifies me. If any other seventeen-year-old girl had bumped into a corpse, they'd be blubbering in a corner, having nightmares and screaming fits; they'd need a lifetime of therapy. But with you, it's like water off a duck's back, straight back to school, not a care in the world.'

'When you've been attacked as many times as I have ...'

'Exactly. And that's why I thought – I *knew* – we had to get away from here. This village, everything that's happened here, it's changed you.'

April knew she was right, but what could she do? Did she want to be a Fury? No. Did she want to know about the vampires? No, of course not. Who would want to know they were surrounded by undead killers? But you couldn't go back, she couldn't become innocent April Dunne again. It *had* changed her, *of course* it had changed her, but she was stuck with it, for better or worse.

'So what are you going to do now?' April held her breath at the question. She wasn't sure she could stand it if her mother said she was going back to Scotland.

'Don't worry, I'm not going anywhere. If you're staying, so am I. It's not the sensible choice, but when did I ever choose the sensible route? I suppose I had to face the fact that you were going to grow up and start making your own decisions sooner or later – after all you do have your father's stubborn streak.'

'I do?' said April, unable to hide her pleasure.

'God, the two of you were like a couple of mules. Remember that time we went up to Loch Ness? You insisted on going out on the water in that horrid old rickety rowing boat looking for the monster. I tried reasoning with you, bribing you with candy floss and Barbies and God knows what else, but you stamped your little foot. You just *had* to see Nessy.'

'I don't remember that.'

Silvia put a hand up to stroke April's face. '*So* like your father. I guess I'll just have to find someone else to fuss around. Your grandfather probably. He's not as well as he used to be; he could do with a bit of TLC.'

'Gramps? What's wrong?' said April, but she knew. He hadn't been looking well – and the stress of the last few days certainly wouldn't have helped.

Silvia laughed. 'Don't worry, your grampa can still wrestle a grizzly bear. We just need to get him to slow down a bit. He is very old, after all.'

April was about to say something else when her mobile rang. She looked down at the screen. Davina.

Silvia waved both hands at her. 'You take it. I've got to put this shopping away.'

April stepped into the hallway as her mother began rummaging in her bags, pulling out variously shaped wine bottles.

'Hey, 'Vina, what's up?' she said.

The moment Davina began speaking, April knew something was wrong. Badly wrong.

'April ...' she said, her voice almost a whisper. 'It's my dad.'

'Your dad? What's the matter?'

'He, he ...' she choked off into a sob. 'He and Mummy were arguing and then he jumped in the car and drove off. Oh God!'

'What?' said April, but she had guessed.

'He's dead, April. Daddy's dead.'

Chapter Twenty-Two

Silvia drove April straight down to the hospital where a police woman in reception filled them in. Nicholas had not let up on his drinking, and his bickering with Barbara had escalated into a screaming row. At the height of it, he had taken a phone call which had sent him into a rage. He had thrown the handset through a mirror, jumped into his car and skidded out of the drive, down Highgate Hill. As he approached the roundabout at Archway, he had lost control and flipped the car over. The policewoman said it was a miracle no one else had been hurt.

After a brief battle of wills with the staff nurse, Silvia and April had been allowed through to see Barbara, who was lying in a curtained cubicle, comatose through a mixture of alcohol, shock and sedation. Davina was sitting by her mother's bedside, staring with mild interest at the sink.

'Davina?' said April gently, crouching down next to her. 'They're keeping your mum in overnight for observation, okay? She's in the best place here. Why don't you come home with us?'

'Home?' said Davina absently.

'Our house on Pond Square,' said April, glancing up at Silvia, who nodded.

Silvia whispered, 'I'll square it with the police. I'll go to the commissioner if I have to.'

April put her hand over Davina's.

'Come on, there's no point you staying here,' said April. 'We'll see if we can get some sleep.'

Davina just nodded. 'Okay,' she said.

It felt so strange to be comforting the queen of the Faces, a cold-hearted monster, someone who April felt sure had killed time and time again, possibly even slaughtered people she knew. But if this was vampire manipulation, then Davina Osbourne was an outstanding actress, worthy of Hollywood. Davina went to bed in April's room. The girl was pliant and meek, like a woman sleepwalking. It was surprisingly poignant to see this self-confident, arrogant girl reduced to a shell by grief, made all the more disturbing by the fact that she *shouldn't* be this way. Vampires should be as one with death, shouldn't they? But what did April really know about vampires? Only what Miss Holden had told her, what she had read in Mr Gill's dusty books and what she had seen in Gabriel. It wasn't exactly a thorough education, was it? April left Davina curled up, her head turned to the wall, her eyes wide open.

'Try to sleep, okay?' she said as she gently closed the door, wincing at the creak.

April had intended to sleep on the sofa, but Silvia insisted she share her bed. 'It's quite big enough for both of us,' she had said and April hadn't argued too hard. The truth was, she welcomed her mother's closeness and when Silvia casually threw an arm over her, April didn't resist. She was asleep almost immediately.

April couldn't tell what time it was. For a moment, she didn't even know where she was. She turned her head on the pillow and was suddenly aware that someone was standing over her. April let out a squeak of surprise.

'Shh, it's me.'

It was Davina, wearing the old Minnie Mouse T-shirt April had given her to sleep in.

'What is it?' whispered April, sitting up and glancing across to Silvia who was still sound asleep.

Davina put a finger to her lips and beckoned her. Rubbing her eyes, April swung her feet out, careful not to wake her mother. She followed Davina down the stairs and into the kitchen.

'Couldn't sleep, do you think your mum will mind?' she said, gesturing towards the half-empty bottle sitting on the counter top. She had evidently been up for a while. 'Do you want one?'

April shook her head. 'I think I'll have some toast,' she said, reaching for the bread.

She popped it into the toaster then looked around for a clean plate and knife.

'So how did you manage it?' said Davina quietly.

'Manage what?'

'When your dad died. How did you carry on? I mean, what's the point?'

Davina was slurring her words a little. Perhaps that wasn't her first bottle. April could hardly blame her – her brother and her father dying within weeks of each other – it was enough to send anyone to drink.

'There's always a point, Davina,' said April. 'There's always someone to go on for.'

'Who? My mother?' Davina laughed. 'I doubt she could motivate anyone to soldier on.'

'She needs you, Davina. She might not say as much, but you're going to need to lean on each other.'

'What? Like you and Silvia have been leaning on each other, just one little happy nuclear unit?'

Ah, this is more like the Davina Osbourne I know, thought April as she began to spread Marmite on her toast.

'That's different, Davina. You know it is.'

Davina waved a hand in the air. 'Sorry, sorry. Shouldn't have said that. You're being good to us – more than can be said for any of the others.'

'I suppose it was hard for people when Ben died,' said April. 'I mean, they probably didn't know what to say, none of the usual clichés applied, did they?'

'Ah, cut the crap,' snapped Davina. 'My so-called friends?

They loved the fact that little baby Benjamin went crazy. It gave them a perfect opportunity to push me out. That and the fact that my cheerleader at Ravenwood – Robert bloody Sheldon – was burnt to a crisp next to him. Chessy and Ling must have been doing cartwheels.'

April didn't reply. She cut her toast in half and sat down opposite Davina.

'Okay, so you're finding out who your real friends are,' she said. 'That's good isn't it?'

Davina snorted. 'I suppose I can't complain. It'd be like a tiger moaning when one of the other tigers in the enclosure bit them. When you're dealing with the undead, you can't complain that they're suddenly a tiny bit mean.'

April was just taking a bite of her toast and she stopped, her eyes wide. 'Un-undead?'

'Yes, April.' Davina smiled. 'Vampires. We are vampires; I am a vampire. There's no point in pretending any more, is there?'

'But … but I don't understand.'

Casually Davina picked up April's knife and, placing it against her open palm, sliced the skin open. April jumped backwards, knocking her stool over as dark blood welled along the deep cut and dripped onto the table.

'Jesus, Davina, what are you doing?'

'Making a point. Sorry, possibly overly dramatic. Can you throw me that kitchen roll?'

Mutely, April handed it to her and watched as Davina wrapped her hand in the paper and wiped up the pool of blood.

'You knew, April,' said Davina, in a matter-of-fact way. 'You've known for months. How could you be dating Gabriel and not know? And I know you and Caro have been trying to work out what's going on at Ravenwood too.'

April's heart was beating wildly. Not only from Davina's display, but also from the fear – how much did she know? *Does she know I'm a Fury?* What would her next trick be? To reach out and cut April's throat?

'Relax, babe.' Davina smiled. 'I'm on your side. At least, I think I am.'

'What side is that?'

'I'm just guessing here, but I'm assuming you've been trying to find out who killed your dad, right?'

April nodded. 'Do you know?'

Davina took a sip of her wine. 'Afraid not. The truth is it's all gone bat-shit here over the last few months. Nothing has been working according to the rules and there are a million different factions fighting for control. Besides, I'm only a foot soldier, no one tells me anything. Not any more anyway.'

April's struggled to gather her thoughts, but her mind was reeling – right here in front of her was a vampire, casually confessing to her true nature. Never in her wildest dreams had April imagined anything like this would happen. But now it had, she found herself at a loss what to say, what to ask.

'So, you're like, really … dead?'

'Not really, no,' said Davina. 'It's pretty simple, actually. An infection is killing us, but super-charging our metabolism at the same time. It's like we're being constantly remade. That's why we don't seem to age, and how we can do this.'

She watched, transfixed, as Davina unwrapped the wet kitchen towel from her hand and held it, palm out, towards April. The wound was already closed – just an angry raised scar where the skin was knitting back together.

'Weird, huh?' Davina smiled. 'Bet you didn't think you'd be seeing a conjuring trick like that tonight.'

'No, not really.'

'So when did you twig?' asked Davina. 'About the vamps, I mean.'

April frowned – when was it? She had seen the signs everywhere for weeks, months, but each time she had shaken her head and thought, *No, that's stupid, it can't be.* Even after her father's blood had painted the hall, she still hadn't seen it.

'The night of my dad's funeral,' she said. 'I stabbed Gabriel.'

Davina's eyes grew wide, then she threw her head back and laughed. 'You *stabbed* him? Where?'

'By Cleopatra's Needle.'

'No, I mean where on his body?'

Anyone else would have asked, '*Why* did you stab him?' April pointed to her abdomen.

'Oof, I bet that hurt,' Davina smiled. But the smile quickly faded from her face and April knew she was thinking about her adoptive father. Nicholas Osbourne was no vampire; he could not spontaneously heal; he had no miraculous immortality. Humans were fragile.

'You're so weak,' said Davina bitterly. 'You see why we loathe you? It's like walking through a flock of sheep; stupid frail animals, half out of your wits with fear most of the time, yet you have no idea just how much real danger you are in, that the wolves are all around you.'

'We're not all weak,' said April, annoyed by Davina's arrogance. *Don't be so bloody stupid, April*, she scolded herself. *What are you going to do, tell her you're a Fury next?*

'No, I guess not,' said Davina, raising her glass in a mock salute. 'Here's to April Dunne, the heroic little girl who cheats death.'

April didn't rise to the bait this time. Instead, she stood up and took a glass from the cupboard above her. 'Actually, I think I *will* have that drink,' she said.

'That's the spirit.' Davina smiled, filling the glass and watching as April took a swallow. 'Okay, what I want to know – what we all want to know, April Dunne – why is death so interested in you? Hmm? Why does he keep grasping at your throat?'

'Maybe I just have very bad luck.'

'No, I don't think so,' said Davina. 'Quite the opposite in fact. When you find yourself in a burning building with two – no, three – vampires, and come out the other side smiling, that's something special.'

April took another drink, partly because her nerves were

jangling, partly to hide her face. Davina Osbourne had always seemed to know everything – who had been seen with whom, who had said what to whom, all the hottest gossip, almost before it happened – so April had no idea how much she knew about the night of the fire. But she couldn't know about Ben, could she? She couldn't know that April had killed him, boiled him alive in his own blood – she *couldn't,* could she?

'Look, Davina,' she said quietly. 'I'm so sorry about Ben.'

Davina pulled a face. 'Don't be. He just got greedy, that's all. Ben wanted power and he wasn't prepared to wait. That's why he hero-worshipped Sheldon. He was convinced Hawk was going to be the new vamp leader. I think Sheldon agreed with him, actually.'

April knew she couldn't reveal to Davina the full extent of her knowledge – not yet, anyway. She had to act as if all this was news to her.

'So you're saying Sheldon wasn't the leader? There's someone else?'

Davina gave a thin smile, as if she was deciding whether to tell her something. 'Yes, there's someone higher up the tree,' she said. 'But Sheldon was arrogant, thought it was time he got rid of the old guard, thought he was better suited to the job and he used Ben as his loyal little soldier.' Her words were bitter and angry, but also sad. She looked down at the table, running a fingernail through a droplet of blood she had missed.

'He wasn't my brother, of course.'

'What? Ben?'

Davina shook her head sadly.

'I'm surprised you hadn't worked that out. No, we are – were – made vampires. But Sheldon was born and you could tell. Arrogant and impatient, you tend to get that with born vamps. But Ben and I, we chose this. We asked to be turned.'

'How long have you been . . . when were you turned?'

'Does it matter? Far too long ago. I'm a classic case; I wanted the glamour, the eternal youth. I wanted to be at my prime for ever.' She gave a bitter laugh and poured out the rest of the bottle into her glass. 'Everyone does. You see the soft skin, the silky hair and the late nights and assume this life is one long party.'

She sat forward and grabbed April's hand.

'It. Is. Hell,' she said, enunciating each word. 'We live in the shadows, constantly on the run, cowering like animals, risking our lives every time we feed, having to live from hand to mouth, stealing, lying ... worse. Much worse.'

'I thought you all lived a glamorous life.'

'How?' spat Davina, the anger sparkling in her eyes. 'I mean, think about it: where can you live? A sixteen-year-old schoolgirl on her own? How do you pay your way? You can't hold down a full-time job – you're too young, too many questions. And who can you trust? Not other vampires – they have their own problems. Not Feeders – that's what we call the humans we tap for a little blood every now and then, the ones who shelter us, pretend to be boyfriends, husbands, families – the ones who hide us.'

'Why can't you trust Feeders? Don't they help you?'

Davina's lip curled. 'They always want something from you – sometimes the most vile things. That's why we haunt the clubs and the streets; we don't have anywhere else to go.' She looked up, her eyes full of pain now. 'It's the loneliest life imaginable.' She sighed. 'So, along comes Robert Sheldon and offers you a Get Out of Jail Free card. Two years without having to worry about where you're going to live, what your cover story is, who you can talk to. Ravenwood was bliss. Utter, utter bliss. Hawk set us up in a lovely home, gave us freedom, security, status and all he asked in return was a few souls; just convince the unsuspecting Ravenwood egg-heads that playing with the vamps was the coolest thing ever. Not exactly hard, darling.'

'So if your mum and dad aren't ... who are they?'

'Recruits. It's not just students at Ravenwood who are dazzled by "The Life". There are always plenty of adults who want to be a part of it. What's not to like? Daddy – Nicholas, I suppose I should call him – got a high-powered position in a vamp-owned company. Agropharm is a real-life billion-dollar powerhouse, but it just happens to be owned by us. Not hard to see how it became so big – aggression and ruthlessness is what makes Wall Street and the City tick and no one intimidates a vampire, do they? On top of this almost unlimited wealth and the beautiful house in Highgate, Mummy and Daddy got connections and the mother of all guard dogs. All you have to do is turn a blind eye to where your "children" go at night.'

She gave a short laugh. 'You can imagine the dynamics of that family unit when the doors were closed. Dysfunctional doesn't even begin to cover it.

'But Ravenwood made up for it all. Suddenly I had a purpose – we all did. It was fun, building up Sheldon's little robot army, picking out which of the brains and the geeks to promote, who to turn. But it couldn't last, could it?'

'So what happened?'

She twisted her mouth into a smile. '*You* happened, darling.'

'What?' said April, her heart hammering.

Davina waved a hand at the ceiling. 'All this because of your family. Before you arrived, it was all going swimmingly, but I fear the *great* William Dunne's investigation into Ravenwood put the cat among the pigeons. '

'Really? It was my dad?'

'Overnight, Robert Sheldon's whole attitude seemed to change. It's only a guess – Hawk didn't exactly include me in his planning meetings – but I think the governors were worried about getting exposed too soon. Vampires like to stay hidden at the best of times, but it was especially important as your dad was poking about. They were planning a big move, you see.'

'What big move?'

'To take control, of course,' said Davina casually. 'Isn't

that obvious? They had already spun a spider's web over business, finance, banking and so on, now they were going to move into government. Slowly and subtly, of course, no big revolution, just greasing the right palms, whispering in the right ears, one little corruption after the next until they had control of all the people they needed in Downing Street, the Mayor's office, the Met, wherever anyone had real power.'

April knew this, or had at least suspected it, but it still felt strange to hear a vampire say it out loud. *Play dumb, April, don't let on how much you know,* she reminded herself.

'I thought it was just Ravenwood.'

'Ravenwood*s*, plural,' said Davina. 'They were going to open them all around the country. But it obviously wasn't happening fast enough for some people.'

'Who? The money men?'

Davina shook her head. 'For Benjamin. He worshipped Sheldon – for the same reason I did, I guess. Sheldon had found Ben feeding on foxes in the cemetery. Do you know how low you'd have to be to eat fox?'

'What do you mean?'

Davina curled her lip in disgust. 'Don't you find those overgrown rats revolting? I don't know what it is, but the vamps have always loathed foxes – it's a bit like Bleeders and spiders. Can't abide them, they make my flesh crawl.' She shivered at the thought. 'Anyway, after that, Ben would have done anything for Hawk. *Anything*. But Ben was impetuous – he didn't want to wait for someone to hand him power, he wanted it right now. God, we used to argue about it, but there was no talking to him. "Robert Sheldon should be leading us," he would say, with this crazy light in his eyes. I think Ben's adoration made Sheldon even more ambitious, actually. Clearly they both got a little too ambitious in the end.'

Davina looked down at her empty glass, her face sad and tired. 'I do miss him. I know it sounds crazy, but we *were* like a family. I mean, I know it was completely artificial, everyone thrown together for what were basically selfish reasons, but you can't live together like mother and father, brother and sister without having some of that bond rub off. Ben was obviously the craziest of all of us, but … he was the closest thing I ever had to family. Does that sound stupid?'

April shook her head. In many ways, it was one of the easiest parts of this whole situation to understand. Why shouldn't the Osbournes have come to care for each other? There were a lot of 'real' families with less in common.

'So what now?' asked April.

Davina threw up her hands. 'You tell me. No job, no family, back to square one. But there's something I need to do first. A few things, actually.'

'What?'

'Revenge, sweetie. Revenge. No one screws with me and gets away with it. They have *no* idea how pissed off I am.'

'But who are "they"? Whoever's giving Dr Tame his orders?'

Davina grinned and wagged a finger at April. 'Are you fishing for information, April Dunne? You *are* your father's daughter, aren't you?'

'Well, why not?' said April. 'If the men behind Ravenwood were worried about my dad's investigation, then I have to assume they killed him.'

'Fair enough.' Davina shrugged. 'That's why I said we're on the same side now. You want to find out who killed your father, I want to find out who destroyed my family.'

'The King?'

'You *have* been doing your homework, haven't you?' said Davina, with a crooked smile.

'Do you know who he is?'

'If I did, believe me, I would already have killed him.'

The look on her face as she spoke made April shiver.

'No, no one's ever met him,' Davina continued. 'Not at my level, anyway. There are all sorts of rumours: he's in the Cabinet, he owns an airline, he's a member of the royal family, but one thing's for sure – he has managed to stay hidden, while simultaneously organising a large-scale vampire takeover. That's pretty impressive, no?'

'You admire him.'

Davina sat forward, her eyes narrowed, nostrils flared. 'No, April Dunne, I do not,' she hissed. 'I hate him for what he did to Ben and Nicholas, and I will make him pay. But never underestimate him. He's clever, resourceful and he's pure vampire through and through.'

Davina picked up April's knife and ran her thumb over the blade.

'But born or turned, they all die when you cut off their heads.' With a movement so swift it was a blur, Davina flipped the knife over and stabbed it into the table. It stood there, slowly rocking.

'Oh God,' said April. 'Silvia's going to go berserk.'

Chapter Twenty-Three

She watched as the chink of sunlight slowly crept across the ceiling, willing it to stop. But still it moved, inch by inch. They were never going away, were they? They were just going to keep coming. Until someone stopped them. *If* anyone could stop them.

After Davina had gone back to bed, April had slid back in with her mother, but her mind was so full of new information and the endless, endless questions, she hadn't been able to close her eyes, let alone sleep. So instead she lay staring up at the ceiling, trying to make sense of everything she had heard.

Could she trust Davina? No, of course not. But it was tempting. Davina had inside information and more importantly, she was motivated and snarlingly angry. She wanted to find the King just as much as April, and that could be a powerful incentive. The trouble was, Davina was a vampire. Who would be stupid enough to trust a vampire?

She felt her mother stir and groan.

'What time is it?' she mumbled. 'God, is that sunshine? Any chance of a cup of tea, darling?'

April smiled to herself. It hadn't taken Silvia long to get used to having April back at home, had it? April hadn't even told her mother she was coming back – officially she was only staying in Pond Square as long as Davina needed a place to stay and a shoulder to cry on – but privately April had liked being here, close to Silvia and to whatever passed for normality in the Dunne family. April clambered out of bed and padded downstairs to find Davina already there, fully dressed, her hair immaculate.

'You haven't been there all night, have you?' said April, self-consciously trying to smooth her own hair down.

'No, that last bottle of Silvia's did the trick,' said Davina, holding up a cup of coffee. 'Out like a light as soon as I got back to your bed.'

'I'm glad you're so perky, I feel like I need another five hours,' said April.

There was a double thunk from the passage behind her – the morning paper.

'I'll get it,' said April. 'Could you pour me some of that coffee? Make it strong.'

She stooped to pick up the paper – and froze.

'HIGH SPEED SMASH HORROR' read the headline over a picture of a mangled overturned car.

> Nicholas Osbourne, prominent businessman and chairman of Agropharm, the international chemicals producer, was killed yesterday when the car he was driving ploughed into a north London landmark. Mr Osbourne was driving his Maserati sports car at speed through Highgate yesterday evening when he overturned the vehicle on the Archway roundabout. Medical staff from the nearby Whittington hospital battled to save him, but he was pronounced dead at the scene. Mr Osbourne was reported to be intoxicated and weaving wildly across the road before the crash.
>
> There had been rumours that he had been removed from his £1.5 million a year position as head of development at Agropharm. The controversial British-based chemicals giant published record profits last year, despite repeated claims that it was 'poisoning a generation' with its aggressive marketing of over-the-counter drugs.

Davina was waiting as she walked back into the kitchen.

'Let me see,' she said, her hand outstretched.

'I don't think that's a good idea, 'Vina,' said April, pulling the paper away. 'You're already upset enough.'

'Oh, I'm nowhere near as upset as I'm going to be, believe me.'

Reluctantly, April handed the paper over. She watched as Davina read it, scouring the report silently, her face impassive.

'Remember what I said last night?' she asked, without looking up.

'Davina, you were drunk last night.'

'Drunk, sober, I'm going to get even with them, whatever it takes,' she said. 'Now are you going to help me?'

April didn't immediately respond.

'Oh, maybe you don't care as much about your dad now he's gone.'

'That's not fair,' said April, her face turning red.

'Isn't it? Either you want to nail the bastards who tore his throat out or you don't. Which is it?'

'Davina ...'

'Which is it?' Her eyes were blazing.

April felt trapped. No, she didn't want to trust this girl, but had she any choice? As Fiona had so painfully pointed out, there were so few of them. They were fighting and they were losing. She looked at Davina for a long moment, then she made a decision. 'All right, where do we start?'

Davina stabbed at the paper. 'Here.'

The Crichton Club stood at the foot of Haymarket on the edge of Mayfair, only a stone's throw from Whitehall, Parliament and the Mall. A tall white Georgian townhouse, it had a grand entrance hall with a huge Union flag hanging over the street. If it had been a haunted bat cave, April couldn't have been more intimidated. 'But what am I supposed to say?'

Davina put a reassuring hand on April's knee as their car pulled up at the kerb. 'Just be yourself. You don't need to be Sherlock Holmes, just keep your eyes open. Try to remember who's there.'

Davina had spotted a news item in the morning paper about a fund-raising lunch being held at the Crichton

Club, a well-known haunt of right-leaning politicians and high-powered business types. According to the piece, the lunch was being held for various government bodies to honour 'Outstanding Contributions to Education', but Davina had immediately known it for what it really was: a gathering of vampire sympathisers. 'Sheldon used to take me along to these things,' she had said. 'All those crusty old men loved to see the pretty girl from Ravenwood.'

As Davina had said it, April had felt sick, knowing that Davina was going to suggest gate-crashing the event. And now, sitting in the Osbournes' Mercedes outside the building, she felt even worse, especially as she was going in alone.

'Are you sure you can't come in, just for a bit?'

Davina shook her head. 'I'm in mourning, remember? Every man in there will have known Nicholas Osbourne one way or another, and my presence will draw far too much attention.'

'And I'll fit right in, I suppose?'

'Relax, April, you're Head Girl of one of the top schools in the country. Why wouldn't they invite you? Besides, you're not gate-crashing, you have an official invitation.'

Ignoring April's objections, Davina had picked up Silvia's kitchen phone and called the Parliamentary Under-Secretary for Education – or someone like that – April was still a little fuzzy from sleep – and, putting on a plummy accent, pretended to be the PA to the Head of Investment for 'Ravenwood Corp'. She had explained that their student representative, Davina Osbourne, was no longer able to attend the Crichton Club lunch – 'Her father was killed last night. I don't know if you read about it in *The Times*? All very tragic …' – so could they add April Dunne to the guest list in her stead? The combination of Ravenwood, dead fathers and Davina's take-no-prisoners approach had worked, the Under-Secretary assuring her that Miss Dunne had only to announce herself at the reception desk where a name tag would be waiting.

'Chop-chop,' said Davina, opening the car's door and giving April an encouraging shove. 'You'll miss the canapés.'

A woman with a clipboard and a fixed grin took April down a long corridor and stopped outside some double doors. 'Professor Young has almost finished his address, I'm afraid,' she said, consulting her watch.

April frowned and nodded, as if she knew exactly who Professor Young was and was very sad to have missed most of his talk.

'A buffet lunch will be served at one.' With that, the woman turned on her heel and disappeared.

April gingerly opened the door and slipped inside. It was a large room with dark wood panelling and ornate paintings of gods and cherubs in gold frames – it had once been a ballroom, she guessed. Mercifully, the fifty or so people in the room were all facing the other way, towards a man speaking on a raised platform at the far end. April found a space at the back and tried to blend in.

'Of course, this is a radical approach,' the speaker was saying, 'and historically, we have all resisted the radical. But if we are to build a stronger, more focused generation, we need to be bold. We need to believe in what we're doing, and do it quickly and decisively. No half measures, no apologies, it's finally time for us all to act.'

God, is he talking about running a school or planning a war? April glanced up at the faces of the assembled crowd – they were nearly all men, apart from a smattering of frumpy-looking women in over-long skirts – and saw they all had the same expressions: excitement and expectation, the sort of look you see on a six-year-old girl sitting under the Christmas tree clutching a Barbie-shaped parcel. Davina had been right – it was a rally for the converted. Professor Young wasn't talking about education at all, he was talking about 'us', the Vampire Nation, the Chosen Ones and all their new BFFs, and how they were getting ready to send the troops over the top.

Suddenly the room erupted into applause, along with a few shouts of 'Hear, hear!' No wonder the woman with the clipboard was worried she had missed the talk – it was clearly the headline act. As the professor left the stage, the crowd broke up into groups and the hum of chatter filled the room. A waiter offered April a silver tray of wine glasses, but she carefully picked up a glass of orange juice. Wouldn't do to have the Head Girl getting sozzled at lunchtime, however much April felt like a little Dutch courage.

'So what did you think of the professor's speech?'

April had been so busy taking it all in, she hadn't noticed the man standing in front of her. Dark hair and brown eyes, he was mid-forties, she guessed, and actually quite handsome.

'Sorry, I got here late,' she stammered. 'Only heard the last few minutes.'

'You didn't miss much. The old duffer always says the same thing.' He leant forward, a half-smile on his mouth. 'Bores me stiff, if I'm honest,' he whispered.

April smiled into her juice and relaxed a little. At least someone was friendly.

'So what brings you to our little gathering, April? Can't be the buffet.'

April froze for a moment at the mention of her name, before remembering that she was wearing a name badge. The man caught her searching for his and tapped his chest.

'Sorry, I don't have one.' He smiled. 'I'm afraid the secretary believes everyone should know who I am by now.' He put out his hand. 'David, David Harper.'

April was so surprised she almost snorted her juice down her nose.

'Gosh, that bad?' Harper laughed, pulling a handkerchief from his pocket. 'Seems you have heard of me after all.'

'No, sorry,' spluttered April, feeling her cheeks flush. 'It's just you're my MP, I think.'

'Ah-ha, so you'll be the new girl from Ravenwood,' said Harper. 'How's it going with the new regime?'

New regime? thought April, *does he mean the academic regime or the pro-vamp regime?* So far David Harper seemed very human, but she reminded herself there was a good chance – especially given the present company – that he was a human with his own pro-vamp leanings.

'Dr Tame has some very strong ideas,' said April tactfully.

'Yes, he does, doesn't he?' said Harper, a distinct gleam in his eye. Or perhaps David Harper was just another politician, happy to agree to any political movement as long as it served his purpose – furthering David Harper's career.

'You must let me know if there's anything I can do to help you over there at the school,' he said. 'I have a real passion for education, and I think the students at Ravenwood in particular hold the keys to the nation's future.'

Yeah, you would say that, thought April, *especially as you obviously think your friends the vampires are going to be in charge.*

'Listen, I need to mingle,' he said, 'but it's been fascinating meeting you, April. Don't overdo the orange juice, okay?'

She watched him move back into the crowd, shaking hands and slapping backs, the consummate politician working the room, and suddenly April was filled with an intense anger, a loathing for David Harper and all his kind. Oh, he was charming all right, in a superficial slightly condescending way, but that was just a mask, wasn't it? Looking at all these men and women with their red faces and bad suits, she couldn't believe they were motivated by ideology, or that they believed wholeheartedly in the vampire cause. They had simply aligned themselves with the Suckers to further their careers and feather their nests. They had chosen to back the vampires because they believed the Suckers would give them money and power – it was as simple and depressing as that.

Yeah, yeah. But how are you going to stop it? mocked the voice in her head.

April knew what she wanted to do – she wanted to jump up on that stage and grab the microphone. She wanted to scream at them, tell them exactly what they were doing.

They weren't just making a sound business move, they were opening the gates of hell. If these people truly thought that the vampires would treat them gently, more favourably when they finally seized power, they were very much mistaken. The vampires would slaughter them like pigs.

She pulled out her mobile and sent a text to Davina.

Met David Harper, horrible. Can I leave now?

The reply came back in seconds.

Names, remember?

She cursed under her breath and flipped her phone to camera mode and shot off a few snaps as casually as she could, reasoning that if anyone saw the token teenager holding up a mobile, they would assume she was tweeting or doing something equally alien. At least this way, she might be able to read a few name tags or perhaps Fiona could identify them from news pictures. April glanced down at the screen. No, no vampires, these were all humans. Somehow that was all the more sickening.

Looking up, April suddenly saw a familiar face, or rather his back. Still, she would recognise Uncle Peter anywhere. She resisted the urge to shout out to him, and instead began to work her way across, skirting two groups of loud, guffawing men. She was within ten feet of Peter when she stopped. She could now see that he was deep in conversation with someone she wasn't sure she wanted to see again: David Harper. *Damn.*

It was only then that April remembered Peter saying that he was going to a reception with David Harper. April hung back, watching. They seemed to be involved in some sort of argument. Peter was gesturing, banging his fist into his palm to make a point, while Harper was nodding.

'I agree, of course,' she heard Harper say. 'Let's just hope you can persuade everyone else.' Curious about what they were discussing, but not wanting to be caught eavesdropping, April stepped back into the crowd and almost walked straight into Dr Charles Tame.

Oh God, oh God, she thought, quickly turning her back, 'Please God, don't let him see me,' she whispered to herself as she quickly searched for the exit.

'Miss Dunne?'

Oh God.

'Dr Tame,' she said, swivelling around. 'I didn't know you were coming too.'

A frown flickered across his face and April felt a chink of hope. Maybe she could bluff this out after all. 'Such a good idea of yours, I have to say.'

'My idea?' he said suspiciously.

'Yes, you know how you said I should get out and start spreading the word about Ravenwood? Well, I sat down with my grandad, and we drew up a list of ways I could do that. Turns out he knows quite a few people. Don't worry, I've arranged for someone to take my notes at school.'

Tame blinked at her and April knew she had him – the mention of her grandad had been the clincher.

'Oh,' said Tame, 'yes … Full marks for initiative, April. Glad you're taking it seriously. Did you enjoy the professor's speech?'

'Inspirational stuff. Will you be speaking today?'

Everyone had a weakness and clearly Dr Tame's was pride. She watched him puff up like a peacock at the notion.

'No, perhaps next time,' he said. 'If we keep getting good results from Ravenwood.'

'Exams you mean?'

Tame gave a superior smile. 'No, no, mere qualifications are a thing of the past, April. Soon our schools and universities will be filled with students producing real work, not just empty theories copied from a book and scribbled down on an exam paper. Why wait five, six, even ten years to tap the potential of young people? Why not use our nation's greatest resource right away?'

The fervour of his words lit up his face and April saw that she had underestimated him once again. Perhaps the other men and women in this room were in it for the money, but April could see that Charles Tame was a genuine convert – he believed all the promises the vampires had given him, truly believed that they were going to use their power to aid society. Or maybe he was coming up with a way to justify his actions – because April had no doubt that Charles Tame, of all the people in this room, knew what the vampires were capable of.

'Gosh, I wish they had let you speak today,' said April. 'You put things so much better than Professor Young.'

'It's gratifying to hear you say that, April,' said Tame, unable to hide his pleasure. 'You know, I'll admit I wasn't sure about you when I offered you the position of Head Girl, but I'm very pleased to see that you're rising to the challenge.'

April was about to make her excuses and slip away when they were interrupted.

'What's this, a Ravenwood convention?'

April groaned inwardly as Detective Inspector Johnston stepped out of the crowd, with a familiar figure on his arm. Chessy. It was as if someone was sending her the people she most loathed in the world all at once. If she was really lucky, Marcus Brent would come back from the dead and try to strangle her again.

'April!' cried Chessy, disentangling herself from the policeman long enough to come over to air-kiss her. 'Why didn't you tell me you were coming?'

Because you were about the last person I wanted to know I was here, thought April, wondering how Chessy had managed to wangle an invitation – had she got her claws into the detective or merely latched onto him when she got here?

'You giving the girls an impromptu lesson, Tame?'

The headmaster gave the detective an oily smile. 'We're

merely exchanging views,' he said. 'That's the sort of thing we value at Ravenwood.'

Johnston raised his eyebrows. 'As long as they agree with you, presumably.' Ignoring Tame's glare, Johnston turned to April. 'Did you bring Gabriel Swift with you?' he said. 'I'd very much like to speak to that young man.'

'We don't speak much any more,' said April.

'Lover's tiff, eh?' He nodded, as if that was information he already had. *From Chessy?* Suddenly April felt a rush of paranoia. Chessy had dropped heavy hints about some long-past relationship with Gabriel – could he have been in touch with her during his disappearance? No, that was just silly, wasn't it?

DI Johnston continued, 'I hear you have Davina Osbourne staying at your house?'

April looked at Chessy; now *that* information had to have come from her. 'My mother's house, yes.'

'Such a horrible thing – her dad's crash,' said Chessy.

'Yes, she's taking it pretty hard.'

Johnston nodded. 'Even so, perhaps you could pass on the message that she should come along to the station as soon as possible.'

'Is the girl in any trouble?' asked Tame, his tone of voice suggesting he was more concerned by the potential for bad publicity for the school than Davina's well-being.

The inspector sighed. 'I don't suppose it will do any harm telling you – it's all over the news channels already. Seems that they've dug up eyewitnesses who saw another vehicle chasing Nicholas Osbourne's car moments before the crash – there's been a suggestion that it wasn't an accident after all.' His eyes locked with April's. 'Looks like we might have another murder on our hands.'

Chapter Twenty-Four

There was laughter coming from the kitchen as April opened the door. She tiptoed in and peeked through the crack in the door: Davina and Silvia, sitting at the counter, a bottle between them.

'I know, you should have seen his face,' giggled Davina. 'He thought he was in for a frisky night, the dirty old sod, he genuinely had no idea that—'

'Mother?'

Davina stopped dead in the middle of her sentence and both women looked up, their faces slightly guilty, the lipstick-smeared glasses in front of them telling their own story.

'April, we didn't expect you back from your lunch so soon.'

'Looks like you've been having your own little picnic,' April replied.

'Just a glass, darling. We've been down to see Barbara – still under sedation poor thing – and I thought Davina could do with a little pick-me-up.'

'I saw Chief Inspector Johnston at the lunch,' April said carefully.

Davina nodded, her smile sagging. *So she had heard.* 'The police came to the house. It's going to be all over the papers again. The last thing Mum needs.'

''Vina tells me you met that dishy David Harper,' said Silvia, clearly trying to change the subject. 'Is he lovely?'

Dishy? What century was she from? Why did grown-ups always insist on slipping into their old-fashioned slang when they were talking to young people? She'd be saying things were 'groovy' and 'far out' next.

'He was horrible, Mum. They all were – just a load of old men only interested in money.'

'That's not all they're interested in, by the sounds of it,' giggled Silvia, nudging Davina, who broke up laughing.

God, they really are drunk.

'I think I'll go up to my room,' said April. 'Leave you two to your picnic.'

If Davina were hiding inside a bottle, April couldn't really blame her. April could vividly remember how wretched she felt after her own father's death; she would've welcomed anything that could have masked the pain, even for a moment. Anything was better than that horrible helpless feeling, like falling through space, seeing the ground rushing towards you, knowing it was going to slam into you, unable to stop.

Up in her room, April sat on the window ledge, looking out across Pond Square, remembering that night when she had first seen Gabriel.

Where are you, Gabriel? She checked her phone for the hundredth time that day. Why hadn't he called? Why hadn't he come back? DCI Johnston had said he was 'keen to talk' to Gabriel, but that didn't mean he was in trouble – after Calvin's murder, she doubted the police would be very interested in pursuing the fight between him and Gabriel – so there was really no reason to hide. So where was he?

Surely he hadn't contacted Chessy – no, that was just stupid. But he *had* gone off with her at that Valentine's party at Davina's, hadn't he? *Come on, April, get a grip.*

Actually, a more likely scenario, and a more worrying one, was that he had gone off in search of the King. What if he found him? Gabriel could already be dead for all she knew. It was so hard not knowing. April heard the door creak and Davina put her head around.

'Knock knock,' she said with a weak smile.

'It's okay, come in. I thought you were bonding with my mother.'

Davina shook her head. 'She's having a little lie-down. I think it's gone to her head.'

'And you're okay?'

April hadn't meant to sound disapproving, but it came out that way. *God, April, she's entitled to let off a little steam*, she reminded herself. However, Davina didn't seem to have noticed; she just sat down on the bed and looked at her hands.

'So I guess DI Johnston told you the latest about my dad?'

'Not much, just that there was another car.'

Davina nodded. 'Rammed him from behind, sent him into a skid which flipped his car over. Apparently forensics found paint from the other car on the wreck.'

'So you think he was deliberately killed? But why?'

'Why not? He knew just about everything there was to know about Agropharm – and in a company that size, there are always plenty of secrets they want to keep.'

'But what about Ravenwood? Was that involved?'

Davina turned to face her, her eyes blazing. 'Oh, grow up, April – of course it was! What do you think has been going on there for the last year? It's one big hot-house: brainy kids for industry, rich kids to be used as influence over their parents. Ravenwood was fundamental. If they couldn't persuade the Establishment to come over to their side, they'd always have the option of holding their kids to ransom. By any means necessary, remember?'

April thought of the gathering in the Crichton Club and wondered if such a thing would be necessary. It certainly didn't look as if the Establishment would require much persuasion to join the vampires. Just a matter of dangling the right carrot.

April reached over for her bag and pulled out a folded sheet of paper. 'Here, I think this is what you wanted,' she said. 'A list of everyone attending the lunch.'

Davina looked up, a surprised smile on her face. 'Wow, good work, Sherlock. How did you get this?'

'No special detective skills, I just asked the lady on reception. Said I wanted it for the school paper.'

She sat down next to Davina as she looked over the list. 'So, is the King Vampire on there?'

Davina shrugged. 'I doubt it. Why would he expose himself? That place is far too public. But I think at least a handful of these people know where to find him.'

'David Harper, maybe?'

'Perhaps. Rumour is that he is being lined up for a new Cabinet post. I doubt he would have got that far without being part of the inner circle.'

'He *was* very smug,' said April, wrinkling her nose.

'Well, they all are until they feel teeth on their jugular.'

'Davina! My dad, remember?'

'Oh, yeah. Sorry.'

'You really think the vampires killed Nicholas because he knew too much?'

'Who knows? But humans are expendable to the vampires. Like this David Harper. He plays his cards right, it's possible he might even make it to prime minister. But he won't have any real power; he'll be doing exactly what the King says. And if he gets out of line – whoosh! – he'll be straight off to landfill.'

April gave Davina a sideways look.

'What?' she asked. 'Why are you looking at me funny?'

'I just don't understand how you can be so blasé about death and yet be so upset about your father and brother.'

'Because Benjamin and Nicholas were mine,' she said with feeling. 'Maybe they weren't a real family, but however unorthodox my home there was, it's the only one I can ever remember. They protected me, looked after me, and whoever took them away from me is going to pay. You of all people can understand that, surely?'

April nodded.

'But these people?' said Davina, tapping the list. 'These people are here because of one thing – greed. They think it's a smart move, making friends with the wolves before they overrun the village, but they'll find you can't make deals with wild animals. When the time comes, they will all be herded into the fields with the rest. Everybody dies, April.'

'Even her?' April pointed to *Francesca Bryne, Ravenwood.*

'Chessy?' spat Davina. 'Ha, I'm not at all surprised she was there. What's that phrase – "Would you jump into my grave as fast?"'

April told her about her encounter with the girl and her suspiciously cosy friendship with DCI Johnston. Davina shrugged as if it was only what she had expected.

'She's just aligning herself with the most useful people. Or thinks she is. She will soon see that she has chosen the wrong side. In fact, it will be the last thing she ever sees. '

A shiver ran up April's neck. It was chilling to listen to her.

'Does that shock you?' said Davina. 'Perhaps it should. Because that's exactly what their plan is. Vampires have no morals, no standards of decency. They will kill everyone in their way, and we have to play by the same rules.'

April nodded slowly. She knew Davina was right and that the time for half-measures had passed. She had stood in the Crichton Club and seen just how high the conspiracy went, and how ready all those people were to move.

'We have stop them,' said April.

Davina looked at her and put out her hand. 'So you're in?'

This time, April didn't have to think about it. 'I'm in,' she said.

Chapter Twenty-Five

The clouds above Swain's Lane were plump and grey; you could smell the rain in the air, but even so April was glad to get out of the house. April needed to be alone, to think and to plan her next move. But it was so hard to think. She badly needed to talk about Davina with someone, but she wasn't sure Caro and Fiona would understand that April had decided to collaborate – was that the word? – with a vampire. And a *bad* vampire at that.

Maybe Gabriel would get it: that she had to do whatever was necessary to bring this to an end; that there was too little time and too much at stake to waste more time worrying about the right way of doing things. But still Gabriel was nowhere to be found. April knew that was why she was drifting down the lane towards the cemetery, hoping he might be there as on that first night.

That first night. What *had* happened to Isabelle that night? April ran over it in her mind. Walking down Swain's Lane, spotting the cemetery gates open and hearing a cry from inside. Creeping into the darkness and finding the ground wet with blood, then Gabriel appearing from nowhere and telling her to run for her life. It had been Isabelle lying on that cold pathway, April knew that now. But she didn't know why Isabelle was there or who had killed her. Had Isabelle got in over her head? Had she tried to outmanoeuvre the vampires? Sheldon had said something about that, and about how she had been punished for it – April wished she could remember every detail of that night, but it had become fuzzy and unclear, just a jumble of images and sounds. You'd think someone pouring petrol over you would focus the mind, wouldn't you?

April slowed as she neared the cemetery gates – for once, they were open. Inside the courtyard, a gang of men were unloading scaffolding poles and crates from a large black lorry. *Strange.* The cemetery was still being used for funerals, of course – perhaps someone was holding the wake in the grounds too. April dismissed a brief urge to investigate. She couldn't face a confrontation with Miss Leicester right now – and besides, why would she want to go in there anyway? In actual fact, Miss Leicester had been right; her dad wasn't even there, so what business did she have in the West Cemetery any more?

Instead, April turned to the left and joined a small queue of tourists shuffling into the East Cemetery just across Swain's Lane. She paid the entrance fee and picked up the photocopied map. Most of the visitors were heading straight along the main path down to the famous sculpture of Karl Marx, but April turned the other way, following the path that ran parallel to the lane. As she walked, April noticed something she had never seen from the other side of the fence. The closer the graves were to Swain's Lane, the better kept they were: weeded, free of leaves, the names easy to read. But wander closer to the centre of the graveyard and the headstones teetered and lolled, overgrown by moss and choked by ivy. It was an island of forgotten names, the soil rutted and overrun by plants, the trees stooping down over the dirt paths, sucking away the light and the warmth. April walked that way, letting her feet choose a path, often finding her way blocked by an uprooted slab or a tree growing straight across a now-abandoned path. Finally she found an old bench, itself covered in green lichen. She sat down and pulled out her phone.

Flipping to her messages, she quickly tapped:

Hey, it's me, sitting in the cemetery (East! Cost me £3!) and thinking of you. Hope you're okay. Call me when you can, okay? Ax

She felt sure it would be ignored – like the other fifty texts she had sent to Gabriel since that night of the party. But even if it was completely one-sided, it still felt as though she was keeping up a dialogue with him. That was something, wasn't it?

Sighing, April dropped the phone into her lap, and looked up through the branches of the tree above her bench. The leaves were starting to turn red and brown already – global warming? April snorted and shook her head. If Davina was right, she doubted whether anyone would give two hoots about the environment soon. They would all be too busy fighting for their lives.

Not so long ago, April had assumed that the vampire conspiracy had centred on Ravenwood and that the students were their main focus – converting them to the cause or using their intellect and influence. But now April could see that the conspiracy went far beyond the walls of the school and that it was happening *now*. She didn't have years to solve this puzzle, she had months, weeks, perhaps not even that. Perhaps it was already too late. Important, influential men and women – politicians, media people, wealthy investors – were already working on the inside towards one goal: bringing the vampires out into the light.

And April had what? A handful of friends? One rogue vampire – *at best*.

'So, what do you need, genius?' she whispered to herself.

She grabbed the mobile, found the number and pressed 'Call' before she could be paralysed with indecision.

'Hello? Who is this?' Elizabeth Holden's voice was both guarded and irritated, and April almost hung up.

'It's April, April Dunne. We met at Miss ... uh, Annabel's funeral.'

A pause.

'I know who you are, April,' said Mrs Holden.

'You said I could call if I needed to talk.'

'It's happening, isn't it?'

April almost said, 'What's happening?' but the time for playing games was over. Besides, she had called Elizabeth Holden because she was the one person to whom she could speak freely, to whom she wouldn't have to explain the situation, who wouldn't say, 'Vampires? Are you mental?'

'Yes, it is,' sighed April, 'I thought it was all happening at Ravenwood, but it's way bigger, Mrs Holden. Politicians and businessmen – they're all involved.'

'I'm surprised it's taken so long,' said Elizabeth Holden. 'I'm guessing you want to know what to do?'

'Yes, I mean, I know what to do – I just don't know how.'

'Sorry, April, but that's bullshit. Let me simplify things. The vampires are about to take over, right?'

'Yes.'

'So, whose plan is this? Who's in charge of the vampires?'

'The King,' said April. 'The King Vampire.'

'Right. So what do *you* have to do?'

'I have to stop the King, but ...'

'No, April – you have to *kill* the King Vampire. Nothing else is going to stop them. And no one else has the power to destroy him.'

'But I don't even know who the bloody King is!' shouted April, before glancing around, hoping no one else was in this part of the cemetery. She lowered her voice. 'Even if I did, how can I get to him? I need help, Mrs Holden. I need the Guardians.'

There was a long pause at the other end of the phone.

'April, listen to me. The Guardians are not the answer. My daughter was, perhaps, the last one worthy of the name. None of the others want to take the risk.'

'Why not?' April said, a note of desperation creeping into her voice. 'I thought the Guardians were sworn to help me? You know, help the Fury?' she added, lowering her voice.

'In theory, yes. But I'm not sure that swearing an oath carries as much weight as it used to, not in the modern world. I find that people tend to do whatever they feel is in their best interest, don't you?'

That certainly fitted the people gazing up at the stage in the Crichton Club. It was depressing to think that people on both sides might think exactly the same way.

'So what do I do? How do I find the King?'

'Oh, it's not a case of finding him,' said Elizabeth. 'It's a matter of *identifying* him. I'm pretty sure you've already met.'

'*What*?' gasped April.

Mrs Holden chuckled softly. 'Vampires don't hide in castles in Transylvania, April. They hide in plain sight. They sit next to you at school, they masquerade as teachers, policemen, doctors. You could have passed him in the street this morning and never known it.'

'How do I spot him? I mean, it's not like he's going to wear a crown, is it?'

'Something my husband always used to say: "They can hide, but you just have to turn over the right stone." Keep looking, April. Eventually, you'll step on the worm.'

April walked back up through the tangled thicket, emerging out onto the main path just below Karl Marx's tomb. She stopped to look up at the huge carved head for a moment. He was just an old man with a beard, really. Quite grumpy-looking too; he reminded her of her grandfather whenever he was arguing with her mother. Which, of course, was most of the time. There was a gold-painted inscription chiselled into the marble:

Workers of All Lands Unite.

The philosophers have only interpreted the world
in various ways; the point is to change it.

April walked on back towards the entrance, thinking about it. He had a point, old Karl. It didn't matter how much you thought about things, or wished they could be different, there was no substitute for action.

Another lesson she needed to learn – people would go to any lengths if they truly believed in something, even if it was something as insubstantial as an ideal. She thought of Charles Tame – yes, he was ambitious, but she was convinced he believed in whatever lies the vampires were feeding him. The rest of them? They only believed in money and power, but that was enough for a lot of people. She remembered that Luke had said something similar about her grandfather: he would deal with businessmen and court politicians because it helped him make money. You might not like them, but that was how it worked. In fact, April was in the same situation herself with Davina. She would rather not have to trust a self-confessed vampire, but she needed Davina. She needed anyone she could get right now.

'Right,' she whispered to herself, pulling her phone out again and thumbing to the number she wanted.

'Caro?' she said. 'I need you.'

When she had finished talking, April walked out of the cemetery and turned right into Waterlow Park, following the path up the hill. It was time to stop worrying. Karl was right: it was time for action. If anyone wanted to help her, they were in – it was that simple. She couldn't fight a war without troops, so Caro and Davina would have to make nice. April was so deep in thought, she didn't see the man standing in the shadow of the overhanging trees until she was almost on top of him.

'Gabriel!' she cried, running towards him. She jumped in the air and threw herself around him, squeezing him, smelling him, feeling his warmth. He was *here*, he was alive.

'I was so worried – I thought you'd gone off and decided to take on the Vampire King on your own.'

'No baby, not yet,' he said, kissing her neck. April rolled

her head back, savouring the feel of his lips on her tingling skin, then stopped and looked at him.

'Not *yet*?' she said, stepping back to look at him.

He gave her a weary smile. 'It's on my to-do list.'

'No,' said April firmly. 'Gabriel Swift, you are not going off to do anything on your own, particularly not fighting full-blood vampires. If you're going to take on the vampire nation, I'm bloody coming too.'

He laughed and pulled her close again, lifting her off her feet. 'That's why I love you, April Dunne.' He grinned. 'You're fearless.'

'Don't go,' she said, more softly, brushing his hair back from his face. 'Please? I've got a bad feeling about what's happening. And seriously, Gabe, you're not looking well.'

It was true. His eyes were slits, bloodshot and hooded, as if he hadn't slept for days. She held his hands; they were filthy, his fingernails crusted with dirt.

'Yeah, I know it's not a good look,' he said, running a hand through his hair. 'But I *feel* good. It's like I can see clearly for the first time in years.'

'What can you see clearly?' April didn't like the way he was talking. He seemed spaced out somehow, detached, his smile slightly too wide.

'Where have you been, Gabe? Why did you run off like that?'

She had been over that evening hundreds of times and she had never been able to work out the trigger which had sent him charging from the train. Had he seen someone? Was it some vampire sense thing?

'I don't know.' He shook his head. 'I was there on the tube with you, then it was like I was flickering in and out. The next thing I knew I was jerking awake to find myself standing in the street, no idea how I got there. One moment I was in Spitalfields, the next I was in Trafalgar Square, holding my phone. I ... I got your messages, but I didn't trust myself to see you.'

'Why, Gabe?' she said softly, although her heart was pounding. 'Is it the dreams? The things you've been seeing?'

He nodded, his eyes half-focused, as if he were trying hard to remember. 'I'm hunting,' he said, his voice barely a whisper. 'Stalking the streets like a wolf. It's like … like I'm looking through the eyes of some terrible creature that only knows hunger. All I want to do is kill and feed and kill again.'

April forced herself to keep watching his face, although she could barely stand it. The words he was saying were terrible, but as he spoke his face lit up, his eyes almost glowing, as if what he was seeing gave him pleasure.

'They're only dreams, Gabriel.'

'Are they?' he said, staring at her, his tone harder. 'Are you absolutely sure about that, April? Because I can see the doubt in your face; I can smell the fear on you.'

'Yes, I'm scared,' she cried. 'Of course I'm bloody scared, because I can see what it's doing to you! But I'm not scared of you, I know who you are and what you're capable of. Yes, you're a vampire, but so bloody what? You're not like *them*.'

'But that's just it, don't you see?' he said. 'I thought I was different from all the others, but now I know. I too am a killer.'

She grabbed his jacket, pulling him closer. 'No, Gabriel,' she said fiercely. 'You are so much more than that. You *are* different, you *are*. I wouldn't love you otherwise, don't you know that?' April could feel tears rolling down her face. All she wanted was to keep him safe, but she could feel him slipping away from her.

'Please, Gabe, whatever's happened, we can overcome it. Whatever's wrong, we can fix it.'

'Not us, not you,' he said, gently pulling her hands away from him. 'This time, I have to fix it. That's why I came here – to tell you I know how to make the dreams stop. I know where they're coming from.'

'Where? Where are you going?'

'To the King, April. The King did this to me. And I know who he is.'

'Who? Who is he?'

Gabriel just shook his head sadly, stepping away from her.

'Please, Gabriel!' shouted April, feeling almost hysterical. Gabriel was walking straight into the jaws of the lion and she couldn't stop him. 'Tell me, let me help!'

'Not this time, Fury.' He smiled, retreating from her up the path. 'This I have to do on my own.'

'Why?' she cried.

'You must trust me. Just one more time?'

He pressed two fingers to his lips and kissed them, throwing the kiss to her as he turned and began to run.

'Gabriel! Please!' she shouted, sprinting after him, her feet pounding up the path, watching in despair as the man she loved moved further and further away.

By the time she had reached the gate, he was out of sight.

Chapter Twenty-Six

April burst through the front door.

'Davina!' she shouted. 'Are you here?'

She heard a noise in the kitchen and rushed through. Davina was slumped at the breakfast bar, her head on the counter, an empty glass by her ear.

'Wake up!' snapped April, shaking her shoulder. 'I need to speak to you.'

'Wurr?' said Davina, raising her head and opening one eye. 'Why are you making all that noise?' She clutched her forehead. 'God, what time is it?'

'Here,' said April, grabbing a bottle from the counter and pouring wine into Davina's glass. 'Drink up. We need to talk, right now.'

Davina tipped back her head and emptied the glass, then set it down for April to refill.

'All right,' she said. 'Now, what's so important you have to interrupt a dream about Bear Grylls and a waterbed?'

April pulled up the stool next to Davina. 'I need you to tell me who the King is,' she said.

Davina began a laugh, which turned into a cough as the wine caught in her throat. 'What makes you think I know?' she said. 'I'm out of the gang, remember?'

'I've just seen Gabriel and he says he knows.'

Davina looked up, her eyes suddenly focused and sharp. 'What did he say?'

'Nothing, as usual. He wouldn't give me a name, wouldn't tell me where he was going either.'

Davina nodded. 'I'm not surprised,' she said distractedly, as if she was thinking of something else.

'What's that mean?' said April, putting her hands on the counter and leaning towards her. 'Tell me! Who is the King? Where has Gabriel gone?'

'I don't know.'

'Please, Davina,' said April, softening her tone. 'I'm terrified Gabe's gone off on one of his mad hero missions, trying to take on the King single-handedly.'

'Yes, that sounds like Gabriel,' said Davina bitterly. 'Always thought he was something special.'

'Dammit, Davina!' shouted April, slamming her hand down on the table. 'I'm sick of all these bloody riddles – just tell me what you know.'

'You don't want to know,' said Davina, lifting her glass. 'Believe me, you *don't*.'

April backhanded Davina's glass across the kitchen, shattering it against the fridge.

'YES!' she yelled. 'Yes, I *do*. Now are you going to tell me or do I have to drag it out of you?'

Davina looked at April, her smile changing to something more unpleasant. 'Gabriel's a killer, April.'

'I know that.'

'No, you don't,' said Davina. 'Because you don't want to believe it. You want him to be your version of a vampire, some neutered, scrubbed-clean version who never gets his hands dirty. But look at the facts: your precious lover-boy has been drinking human blood for a hundred years. Do you seriously believe he's never killed anyone in that time?'

April began to protest, but the words stuck in her throat. *Did* she really believe it? After all those dreams, all those visions of the past plaguing Gabriel? What if he really had been stalking those women? What then? Could she really live with that, could she look at him the same way?

'He made a promise ...' said April, and Davina laughed.

'That promise he made to Lily, his poor, dead, pox-ridden

girlfriend? How he'd never, ever take another life? You really bought that crap? Jesus, think about it. Put yourself in Gabriel's size twelves. He's become a vampire for the sake of his one true love, but his master refuses to save her, so Gabriel's forced to watch Lily die. How do you think he would react? Do you really think he shrugged his shoulders, then went into hiding for fifty years? *Bullshit*, April. He went on a killing spree and he didn't stop until he was knee-deep in bodies.'

April tried to take a breath, but found she couldn't. Davina was vicious and spiteful, but her logic was persuasive. Would he really have taken it lying down? No, he would have wanted revenge – bloody, violent revenge. God, *had* he killed before? More importantly, once he had, did he ever stop? April turned to Davina, looking straight into her eyes. 'Did Gabriel kill Isabelle?'

She tried to remember all the things Gabriel had said about that night, what he said he had seen, how he had struggled to protect Isabelle from a powerful vampire seized with a terrible blood-lust. Could he have been talking about himself?

'No,' said Davina finally.

'But how do you know for sure? How do you know Gabriel didn't kill Isabelle?'

'Because *I* killed her.'

April's eyes opened wide. 'What? No! How could you?'

'How could I?' snapped Davina. 'I was doing the world a favour! It was like putting down a rabid dog. Do you know what she was? A *Fury*.' Her voice dripped with disgust, as if she was describing a revolting breed of snake. 'She was diseased. You heard what happened to Milo? His skin rotted off the bone and he bled from his eyes. That was who Isabelle Davis was and she *had* to be destroyed.'

April's heart was in her mouth now, her head pounding. How could she have allowed Davina to suck her in, make her believe that she was half-human, that she was capable of pain and remorse? All vampires were the same, nothing more than killing machines. She realised just as suddenly how much danger Gabriel was in. He had gone to take on the most powerful, most ruthless of all the vampires stalking the city. April's eyes searched Davina's. 'Who else have you killed, Davina? How many?'

The girl's face twisted with spite. 'You mean did I kill your father? I wouldn't have dirtied my hands.'

April's fingers were around Davina's throat before she knew what she was doing. She squeezed as hard as she could, seized by a terrible desire to kill this girl – this disgusting creature from the darkest pit. She wasn't human, she was unnatural – she didn't deserve to live. Everything in April's vision reduced to a single point, where her thumbs were pressing on Davina's windpipe – all the rest was a red haze. Then she felt herself yanked backwards. Losing her footing, she crashed into the fridge and she felt hands grabbing her, holding her in place.

'April, stop!'

She could hear the voice, but she couldn't recognise it. She struggled to get back to Davina, every nerve and sinew desperate to hurt her, to sink her nails into the girl's eyes.

'April, it's Caro,' said the voice, frightened but firm. 'Look at me.'

Finally, April tore her gaze away from the vampire across the room and looked at her friend. Caro's face was white, her brow furrowed with concern.

'That's it, now take a deep breath. Good. Here, sit down,' she said, scooping up the stool April had knocked over.

Davina was still squashed up against the kitchen counter where April had pushed her. For a moment, April thought she was choking, but she was laughing.

'Damn girl,' said Davina, rubbing her throat. 'That's some grip you've got. Was it something I said?'

April lunged at her, but Caro jumped between them again.

'STOP IT! Come on, what the hell is going on here?' she

said, looking from April to Davina. 'Will someone explain to me why I found the front door open and you two in the middle of a catfight?'

Davina sneered, waving a hand at April. 'Your little friend can't take a joke.'

'A joke?' spat April. 'You call that a joke?'

'What joke?' said Caro.

'Oh, I'll explain the hilarity, shall I?' said April. 'Davina here is a vampire, a killer, a cold-blooded murderer.'

Caro didn't even blink. 'Yes, and?'

Davina began a slow handclap. 'At least someone gets it. Well done, Caro Jackson. You win the "staring you in the face" prize.'

'Oh shut up,' said April, turning back to Caro. 'On top of being a vampire, she freely admits that she killed Isabelle Davis and God knows how many other innocent people.'

'Isabelle Davis was no innocent,' said Davina. 'She was greedy and stupid. She was quite happy to sell her people out – all of you Bleeders – in order to get herself a position in the Regent's cabinet. When that didn't work, she tried blackmailing us – thought the fact that she had some foul disease meant that she should be treated like a superhero.' Davina made a mocking sad face. 'She got that one wrong.'

'All right,' said Caro, raising her eyebrows meaningfully towards April at the mention of the Fury. 'So Davina's a horrible murderer, I get that. But why were you trying to throttle her when I came in?'

'She's worried about poor little Gabe,' said Davina. 'Thinks I know where he's run off to. Which I don't. I mean, if he was *my* boyfriend, there's no way he would have left me all alone.'

Caro put up her hands to stop April launching at Davina again. 'Okay, let's start at the beginning, tell me everything – both of you. Then I'll decide who needs strangling.'

Glaring at Davina, April told Caro about Gabriel's revelation in the park and then what Davina had said about

Gabriel and a killing spree. When April had finished, Caro looked over at Davina, her face serious.

'Oh bugger,' she said.

Davina nodded. 'See? Caro gets it.'

'Gets what?' said April impatiently. 'Gets *what*?'

'Look, A, I know you're worried that Gabe's going to run off after the King and get his neck snapped,' said Caro.

'I could have done without the detail, but yes.'

'Well ...' She pulled a face. 'Don't you see? We might have more of a problem than that.'

April looked from one to the other. 'What? Tell me!'

'It's not just the danger he's in from the King, is it? If Gabriel has remembered who the King is, then there's a good chance he will remember *everything*. Gabe's a sensitive guy, isn't he? He's certainly spent the last hundred years convinced he's kept his hands clean because of that promise he made on Lily's deathbed. Now, all of a sudden, he starts to think he's Jack the Ripper? What do you think that's going to do to him?'

Oh God, thought April. *It's going to tear him apart*. She remembered the terror and remorse on his face when he had admitted to her about having turned Jessica. He'd worn that regret like a crown of thorns for decades – what would the sudden realisation that he was a multiple murderer do to him? April made another grab for Davina, but she dodged out of the way.

'You knew about this! Why didn't you help him?'

'Oh, yes,' said Davina, tutting. 'Blame the vampire. People in glass houses shouldn't throw stones, April Dunne. Haven't you ever heard that one?'

'What are you talking about?'

'Do I have to paint you a picture, April? What has caused this change in Gabriel? He's been blissfully unaware of his true nature for a hundred years. Then you waltz into his life and the sky falls in.'

'This is *my* fault?'

'I think what Davina is trying to say,' said Caro, glaring at Davina, 'is that you have unlocked him emotionally. Your love has made him want to live again.'

Oh God, thought April. *This is all my fault.*

'If he wants to live, he's gone to the wrong place,' said Davina. 'The King is a *true* vampire, ten times as strong as a turned vamp like Gabriel.'

'Not helping,' said Caro. 'Do you know where he is?'

'No,' said Davina.

'She does!' cried April. 'She must do.'

Davina put up a hand. 'If you'd just let me finish,' she said, standing up and smoothing her creased shirt. 'I was going to say that no, I don't know where he is, but I know someone who might. Get your coats.'

'Where are we going?'

'We're going to a party.'

Chapter Twenty-Seven

They could hear it all the way up Swain's Lane. The thudding 'boom, boom' of the bass coming from a powerful sound system – it was like walking past the back of a music venue when a band were on stage. As the three girls approached the gates of the cemetery, they could see two burly security guys dressed in standard issue black, one holding a clipboard – there was even a little velvet rope stretched between two silver poles.

'A party in the cemetery? How the hell did they get permission for this?' said April.

'The cemetery is owned by a trust, presumably they want to make a few quid,' said Caro.

Davina shook her head. 'More likely the trust has been infiltrated by vampire-sympathisers and they voted "Yes" for a party.' She gave April a sarcastic smile. 'We do love a good party.'

April tried to imagine Miss Leicester's face when she was told there was going to be a load of teenagers dancing to loud music in the cemetery, but she couldn't. For all her possessiveness towards Highgate's graveyard, Miss Leicester was just an employee who would have to do what she was told.

'There's no way they're going to let us in there,' whispered April.

'You forget who you're with,' said Davina. 'I've never been turned away from a party in my life.'

April and Caro hung back as Davina walked confidently up to the doorman with the clipboard. She leant in and whispered something in his ear, simultaneously touching his arm with one finger. The bouncer's stony face broke into a grudging smile, then a wolfish grin. While they were alone, Caro turned to April. 'Listen, what's going on? How come we're talking to a vampire all of a sudden – and this one in particular?'

'I don't like it either, Caro, but we've gone past the point of picking and choosing our allies. If Davina's angry enough to help us get in the door, we have to take advantage of this opportunity. We're running out of options. And if Gabriel's really found the King, we're out of time too.'

Caro paused for a moment, then nodded. 'Fair enough. But what was all that stuff about Isabelle and her "disease"? Do you think she knows you're a Fury?'

'God knows, but if she wanted to kill me, she could have come into my room and done it while I was asleep.'

'Nice thought. Okay, we'll play along, but remember whose side she's on.'

'And you remember that I'm only here to find Gabriel, okay?'

Across the road, Davina and the security guards were laughing and chatting like old friends. The first man nodded and beckoned to April and Caro.

'In you go, girls,' he said. 'Behave yourselves, yeah?'

'Until later, anyway,' said Davina, as the guard unhooked the velvet rope and allowed them all inside.

'What did you say to him?' whispered April as they crossed the courtyard and up the stone steps.

'Oh, just a little bit of harmless flirtation. Muscles and his friend think they're going to cop a feel in the bushes later.'

She glanced at April. 'Oh, don't look so shocked, Little Miss Prim. Don't tell me you and Gabriel haven't rustled a few leaves in this cemetery. Besides, I did that meathead guard a favour. If they go into the bushes with anyone else here, there's a good chance they're not going to come out again.'

They walked up the steep pathway and April couldn't help casting a glance down towards her father's tomb.

Watch over me, Daddy, she thought, *wherever you are.*

The music was getting louder now and, between the trees, they could see flashing lights.

'Where the hell are we going?' whispered Caro.

'Isn't it obvious?' said Davina. 'We're going right to the heart of the darkness, as William Dunne so eloquently put it.'

April grabbed her arm. 'What do you know about my father?'

Davina brushed April's fingers off disdainfully. 'And they call *us* arrogant,' she said. 'Do you really think you're the only ones who can use a computer? University of Strathclyde, February, two years ago. Your father gave a talk called "The Devil's Disease". There's a transcription of it on the university's website.'

She saw April's blank expression and rolled her eyes. 'Your father hypothesised that all large-scale violent crime – riots, serial killers, even wars – could be down to a certain strain of disease. He thought it was all coming from underground. And if he's right, then …' They walked around a corner and Davina gestured dramatically. '*This* is where it's coming from.'

'Bloody hell!' gasped Caro. They had come to the gates of the Egyptian Avenue. The carved stone gateway was grand enough during the day, but tonight, next to the pillars either side of the opening, there were flaming torches, the inside of the sloping passageway lit with a glowing red light.

'It looks like the mouth of hell,' said Caro.

'Could be right, darling,' said Davina, leading the way inside. Exchanging nervous looks, April and Caro followed her. The passage was filled with smoke and there were dark figures hanging about in the swirling red-lit mist, drinking, necking, swaying to the music. April was relieved that they paid no attention to them as they passed.

'What *is* this place?' whispered Caro.

'This corridor is a series of burial vaults,' said April, nodding towards the iron doors lining the alleyway on either side of them.

'It's making me claustrophobic,' said Caro nervously.

'Don't worry, it opens out at the end.'

'Behold! The Circle of Lebanon,' said Davina, raising her voice to be heard over the now pounding music.

'Wow!' said Caro as they stepped out. The walls curved off on either side, open to the sky, but packed with undulating bodies – they were clearly using the circle as the party's dance floor. The girls threaded their way through, half-hidden by the billowing dry ice and the flashing lights set over the circle on scaffolding – presumably that was what April had seen being unloaded earlier. Davina led them to a set of stone steps; from the top they could see down into the circle. It really did look like one of those medieval paintings of the underworld – the dancers' hands reaching up out of the flames and smoke. They walked away from the pit, towards a makeshift bar piled high with bottles and set up close to the cemetery's catacombs.

April glanced over at Davina. If the girl felt any discomfort being this close to the spot her brother had killed Layla, she didn't show it. April couldn't bring herself to turn that way; when she closed her eyes at night, she could still see Layla's white face, the eyes open, her legs dangling. *Remember it*, she told herself. *Remember what these creatures are capable of.*

She turned up the collar of her coat, suddenly feeling cold. Caro, however, seemed as unconcerned as Davina, returning from the bar with beer for them both.

'This is off the hook,' said Caro, grinning.

'You're not supposed to be enjoying yourself,' snapped April.

'Hey, lighten up, sourpuss,' replied Caro. 'I know you're worried about Gabe, but let's not jump to conclusions until we know exactly what's going on, okay?' Her gaze switched to over April's shoulder. 'Anyway, it looks like we've got problems of our own.'

Chessy. She was striding over, with Ling, Simon and a gang of Suckers trailing behind her like a royal entourage.

Chessy was wearing a tiny red dress and Ling, despite the uneven ground, was in sky-high heels. One look at Chessy's face and April knew she'd made a mistake coming here.

'What are *you* doing here?' demanded Chessy, glaring across at Davina. 'Do I need to teach you another lesson?'

'You can try,' said Davina, stepping forward. 'But I'm not sure it would be such an easy job this time.'

Then she smiled and nodded towards Ling.

'Or maybe you should ask your new girlfriend to try. I mean, after all, little Ling owes Chessy a favour, doesn't she?'

'You shut your mouth!' hissed Chessy.

Ling looked uncertain, her eyes flicking across to Simon.

'What are you talking about?'

'I suppose it was rather sweet really,' said Davina, a smirk on her mouth. 'I mean, that nasty boy Calvin forced himself onto you, so your bestest friend in all the world got him back for you.'

'I'm warning you,' said Chessy in a low voice. April could see that she had curled her hands into claws. What was Davina playing at? She was supposed to be finding out where the King was – where *Gabriel* was – and all she seemed to be doing was settling old scores.

'Oh, come on, Chess, I thought you'd have wanted the whole world to know that it was you who punished that boy. Though it sounds to me like he deserved it.'

Ling turned to Chessy, her eyes wide.

'It was *you*? You killed Calvin?'

Chessy took two steps towards Davina, but Davina stood her ground.

'Hey now, remember the rules,' she said, 'although you weren't exactly following them that night, were you? Dumping the dead boy on April's doorstep. Tut-tut, Chess. I can't imagine that pleased the Big Boss.'

'You shut up!' said Ling. 'What do you know? You're not one of us any more!'

'Oh, it's "us" now is it?' said Davina. 'Has Chess promised to initiate you into this glorious life of ours?'

A smile crept onto Ling's face. 'Yes,' she said, looking over at Chessy with something akin to adoration. 'Tonight.'

'No!' shouted Simon, grabbing Ling's hand and spinning her around. 'You can't, Ling!'

'Why not?' she replied, yanking herself free. 'I'm not like you – I don't need all these weaklings around me.' She looked over at Caro. 'Why don't you just go back to *her* – you know you want to.'

'Ling, don't be stupid,' said Simon uncertainly.

'I've seen the way you look at her. Go on – I don't need you any more. I won't need anyone any more, not after tonight.'

'Ling, you can't,' said April. 'Think about what you're doing.'

'I know exactly what I'm doing, *Bleeder*,' said Ling furiously. 'You think I want to be like you? You think I want to be a goody-goody, a Head Girl? You're all dead already and you don't even know it.'

She laughed and stepped towards Davina. 'Well, if Chessy did kill that bastard, I'm glad. It shows she cares about me.'

'It's not you she cares about, Ling,' said Davina, looking towards Chessy. 'Is it, sweetie? She didn't do it for you.'

Chessy stepped forward and backhanded Davina across the face, sending her sprawling.

April moved to help her, but Caro put a hand on her arm, shaking her head slightly. Davina was on her knees, a string of blood running from the corner of her mouth.

'Now that's not a good look, is it, *darling*?' crowed Chessy, and the surrounding crowd of Suckers let out a titter of nervous laughter.

'I think it's about time you stopped talking about these things as if they concerned you,' continued Chessy. 'I thought we'd made it clear that you and your little family are no longer a part of the plan. Oh,' she said, putting a hand to her mouth, 'I forgot. You don't *have* a family any more.'

April watched as Davina slowly swivelled her head to look up at her adversary, her eyes narrowed, her lips drawn back in a snarl. She could only remember seeing such hate once before – on the face of Marcus Brent, shortly before he tried to tear her limb from limb. *This isn't going to end well*, thought April. She stepped between Davina and Chessy, her hands held up.

'Okay, that's enough,' she said. 'We were just going, anyway.'

'Oh no,' said Chessy. 'You're not going anywhere.'

She casually raised a finger and immediately April and Caro were grabbed, their arms twisted up behind them.

'Him too,' said Chessy, nodding at Simon.

'Hey!' protested Simon as he was seized. 'I'm on your side.'

'Yeah, sure,' said Chessy. 'Hold him. I think he might wriggle.'

She turned to Ling and extended her hand. 'Come to me,' she said. 'It's time.'

'No, Ling!' cried Simon. 'You don't have to do this! Please God, no!'

But Ling, looking as if she were in a trance, stared rapturously into Chessy's eyes. The vampire gently, tenderly, lifted Ling's thin arm.

'You have to want this, you know that?' she whispered.

Ling nodded slowly. 'I want it, please.'

Without warning, Chessy bit into Ling's arm, like a snake striking its prey.

'No!' yelled April as she watched Ling's eyes grow huge, her face registering terror and fear. If she had been expecting her turning to be ethereal and beautiful, she was wrong – dead wrong. It was brutal, violent, horrific. Ling's body bucked, her legs jerking uselessly as Chessy held her in a vice-like grip. April struggled to get to the girl, to help her, but with a vampire on each arm, it was like struggling against quicksand.

Ling's mouth was open now, as if frozen in a scream, her eyelids fluttering, fingers jerking.

'Stop,' said Davina quietly. 'You're killing her.'

Immediately Chessy opened her jaws and dropped Ling. The girl fell to the floor like a bag of sand. Chessy pushed her face inches from Davina's. 'I *know* I'm killing her!' said Chessy, dark blood running from the corners of her mouth. 'That's the *idea*. I have no intention of turning that stupid little airhead. We don't need runts like her any more.'

'Help her!' screamed Caro, looking down at Ling. The girl had flopped on the ground, her body seized by spasms. 'Why are you all standing there? Someone help her!'

Chessy laughed, a dark gurgling laugh. 'No one can help her now,' she said, moving over to April. 'But you know what? She tasted good.'

'You're disgusting,' hissed Caro.

Chessy smiled again, a grotesque, twisted thing. 'Aren't I, though? All right, put them in the vault.'

The vault? thought April, as they were dragged backwards, She couldn't mean the catacombs? She was filled with a black terror at the idea of being shut in that horrific tomb, the very place she had seen Layla's body. She began to struggle, but Chessy snapped her fingers.

'Not her,' she said. 'Give *her* to me.'

Chessy twisted April's arm up her back and pushed her down a path; they were leaving the party behind and April knew she was in deadly danger.

'Where are you taking me?' cried April, trying to struggle, but Chessy was shockingly strong.

'Don't worry,' she said. 'I'm just going to give you a little history lesson.'

She pushed April through a narrow gap in the trees and down a steep track. The ground underfoot was slippery and April stumbled, the stones in the path cutting into her knees. 'Get up, Head Girl,' ordered Chessy impatiently, yanking her up. 'Don't make me drag you by your hair.'

She pushed her out onto a wider path, then shoved April back against the cold stone of a low tomb. The sound from the party was just a dull throb now, and April was horribly aware that she was out here alone in the dark with a creature she had just watched sucking blood. April could see Chessy's outline, but it was too dark to see her expression. She could guess, though.

'You do know we'll be missed, don't you?' said April, trying to sound brave, defiant. 'My mother knows we're here.'

'No, she doesn't,' said Chessy. 'No one knows you're here. What responsible parent would allow their daughter to come to a party in a graveyard?'

'Since when was my mother ever responsible? You'll never get away with this,' April said, knowing how weak it sounded.

'We already have,' said Chessy, moving closer. 'Don't you know what this little gathering is for? It's our coming-out party. We're going overground. It's all happening at Ravenwood tonight.'

April swallowed. *Gabriel* – was that where he was?

'What's happening at Ravenwood?'

'Don't insult my intelligence,' hissed Chessy. 'I know your father was investigating Ravenwood, trying to find out about how we're exploiting the poor students, oh boo-hoo. But it's bigger than that, Head Girl. All those people you saw at the Crichton, all those politicians, all those captains of industry, they are all gathered at the school, meeting the King. We are taking over – tonight.'

April felt her stomach knot. She had left it too late. 'The King is at Ravenwood?'

Chessy laughed. 'You still don't see how hopeless you are, do you? You really think you can stop us. You thought we didn't know about you and your friends trying to worm your way in? We're vampires, April, not morons. Davina was all like "leave her alone, we can't kill her, not after her father's been killed, it will draw too much attention". So we left you. But Davina's not top dog any more. And now none of that matters anyway.'

'Someone will stop you,' said April, hoping she sounded more certain than she felt. She began to inch along the tomb, spreading her hands, feeling for the edge. Maybe if she could just get around the corner she could get away.

'Stop us? What, you mean the Guardians?' sneered Chessy. 'Miss Holden and her stupid herbs? You? Let me show you what you're dealing with.'

Chessy grabbed April by the throat and lifted her. *God, she's strong*. She dragged April across the path, then pushed her to her knees.

'Look at that,' Chessy whispered in April's ear. 'Ah, isn't it beautiful?'

April looked. The cloud had parted and the clear moon was shining down between the trees, throwing its light onto a stone sculpture. It was an angel, but not like any of the other winged figures in the cemetery. This one was lying on a stone bed, apparently in a gentle slumber.

'The Sleeping Angel?' said April. 'Yes, it's ...'

'It's revolting,' Chessy spat. 'Mawkish, sentimental and crass.'

April frowned. 'So if you hate it so much, why have you brought me here?'

'Because that is my grave, April Dunne.'

'Your ... what?'

April turned to glance up at Chessy. She was staring at the tomb, almost as if she were gazing at a loved one, a smile on her face. And it all came flooding back, what the caretaker had said – the one April had seen that day she had run away from the cemetery tour – he had said it was the grave of a girl called Francesca, hadn't he?

'You?'

'Me.'

'But you're ...'

'Walking around? Well spotted – no wonder they made you Head Girl.'

April twisted around, looking at Chessy with wonder. She had no reason to disbelieve what she said, however crazy it sounded.

'Then who are – who *were* you?'

'Francesca Mariana Bryne,' she said with a slight bow. 'Born in County Antrim, brought to London by my parents when the potatoes failed, turned out on the street at eight years old, when my father died of consumption and my mother could not afford to feed five children.'

'How did you survive?'

'Any way I could,' she said. 'Stealing, lying, cheating and eventually taking men into the alleyways – you could say not much changed when I turned.'

'But I still don't understand – how is there a monument to you? I mean, if you died but—'

'I died twice – you should try it.' Chessy's voice became wistful, as if she was an old lady reminiscing about her scandalous youth. Which April supposed she was, in a way. 'I wasn't one of those filthy whores hanging around the street corners making barely enough money for a drink of gin. I had wealthy clients; they came to my rooms, beautiful rooms in St James's. Politicians, gentlemen. But one of those fine upstanding lords and sirs gave me the pox. Syphilis, Head Girl. Kills you slowly. But he was good: he said he'd take care of me. Not to cure me, no. He meant commissioning this monstrosity. He said it was to my memory – and to all fallen women – a monument to his guilt.'

Despite herself, despite the danger she was in, April was fascinated by Chessy's story. 'So what happened?'

'Oh, call me picky, but I wasn't content to just die and become an upper-class bleeding-heart symbol of goodness and hypocrisy. I staggered from my bed to the Bear's Head, a tavern on the South Bank. We all knew they were there, the "Dark Ones" – we called them "Lifers" then. No one used the word vampires, it was all a bit too … foreign. So I struck a deal with them; turn me and I'd provide … well, certain assets they were interested in. Which is how I managed to dodge being pushed into this tomb. As you might imagine, there was no problem providing an alternative body – and his lordship was far too delicate to check.'

'So they buried someone else?' asked April, looking over at the tomb.

Chessy nodded, the moon shining down on her. 'I came to the funeral, of course. Then I followed the lord home and killed his wife.'

She said it almost casually, like she was adding an amusing footnote. Chessy walked across to the sculpture, running her hand over the stone, its contours emphasised by the moonlight. 'For years, I loathed this thing. But now, I see it differently. Don't you think it's become apt, appropriate for our new world? We're all sleeping angels, aren't we? And tonight, we will wake.'

'You're no angel,' said April in a low voice, 'you're a monster.'

Chessy turned and darted towards her. 'Yes, I am,' she said gleefully, pushing her face close to April's. 'We all are, even your precious Gabriel.'

April felt a spasm of fear again: what exactly did Chessy know about Gabriel? And more to the point, how?

'Gabriel is different,' said April, but Chessy laughed, high-pitched and edgy.

'You're so naïve. He is worse than any of us – he's a killing machine. That's why he was so useful to the King.'

April knew she shouldn't listen to this creature. She knew Chessy was just toying with her, playing on her fears, yet even so she had to ask. 'Who *is* the King?'

Chessy shook her head disbelievingly. 'You *really* don't know? After all this time?'

Chessy threw her head back and laughed, mocking her, goading her, enjoying April's confusion and discomfort. 'Why don't I show you?' she said. 'Give me your phone.'

She reached into April's coat pocket and grabbed her mobile, opening the 'Media' folder.

'Now, let's see,' she said. 'What would a teenage girl take

pictures of? Her friends?' Chessy tapped one open – a snap of Fiona and Caro arm in arm. 'Aah,' pouted Chessy. 'Sweet. Would she have a picture of her boyfriend? Uh-uh, not in this case.' She put a finger to her lips. 'Now who else?'

Perhaps it was fear or helplessness, or just the fact that Chessy seemed to enjoy belittling her, but suddenly April was filled with a blind rage.

'Shut UP!' she yelled, launching herself at Chessy in a rugby tackle, throwing her on top of the Sleeping Angel. Not having any other weapon to hand, she grabbed the phone dropped in the struggle and smacked it into Chessy's mouth, splitting her lip. Chessy looked up in surprise, then began to giggle, running her tongue into the blood.

'Is *that* the best you can do?'

Effortlessly, Chessy pushed April off, flipping her over and onto her back. Before she had time to move, Chessy had seized April's hair and dragged her up to her knees.

'Do you think this is what it was like for your father?' said Chessy. 'Do you think he was on his knees? Begging for mercy?'

April tried to scream at her, but Chessy clamped her hand over her face. 'Shh . . .' she said. 'Don't bother asking – there is no mercy. Not for him, not for you. Not for any of you.'

With inhuman strength, Chessy lifted April up and slammed her against a tree, knocking the air out of her lungs. April snatched in a breath, knowing she had to move, had to get out of this monster's reach. But she was too slow. Chessy's hand shot out and grabbed April by the throat, pinning her back against the trunk.

'Do you want to know why we killed him?' she said.

April frowned, her head was swimming, 'My . . . my dad?'

'Yes, April, your nosy father. I bet you think we killed him because he was sniffing around Ravenwood, don't you?' She barked out a laugh, full of malice. 'No, it was *personal*.'

April grabbed hold of Chessy's hand, trying to prise her

fingers off, but it was like trying to pull oak roots from the frozen ground. Chessy began to squeeze.

'We should have turned him,' said the vampire. 'That would have been a hoot, wouldn't it? Then maybe he could have killed you all, one by one as you came home. That's how I would have done it – a nice solution to a lot of problems.'

A cloud crossed Chessy's face, as if she was annoyed about something. 'But that wasn't in his plan.'

'Whose plan?' croaked April. 'The King's?'

Even now, staring death in the face, April wanted to know, wanted answers.

'Of course the King, you little fool. Who else would have dared? He wanted to take care of him personally. Quite Shakespearian actually.'

April struggled to grasp what Chessy was saying, but she was cutting off her oxygen, making her thoughts sluggish. Shakespeare? Was he the King? No. That was stupid. In a detached part of her mind, April knew she had to get away soon, or she would die.

'Help,' she croaked and Chessy actually laughed, amused by the weakling's pathetic attempts to escape.

'Who do you think is going to help you?' she crowed. 'Gabriel? He's *ours*, April. He always has been. And when you're dead, he's going to be *mine*.'

April knew she had to get to him. She *had* to. If she died here, who would help Gabriel fight the King? Summoning all her dwindling strength, she pushed forward, screaming as she went. Chessy's face barely had time to register her surprise before she toppled over backwards. April didn't stop to look back, but sprinted down the path, sending gravel flying, her only thought to get away. She was gulping in air desperately.

Ahead April could see a fork in the pathway and immediately knew where she was – one path went uphill towards the Vladescu vault, the other straight down to the courtyard and, past Davina's burly friends in the penguin suits, led to the way out. *Damn it*, she thought and turned right, up towards the tomb. Yes, downhill was the way to safety, to civilisation, telephones and the police, but April couldn't leave Caro and Simon. She couldn't leave her friends to be slaughtered. She couldn't even abandon Davina, however vile she could be. So April ran on, up the narrow path towards her father's tomb. If she could just get beyond that, there was another path that looped back up the hill and past the east side of the catacombs. April had no real plan beyond that – all she could do was run, expecting to feel Chessy's talons claw her back at any moment. Her feet pounded up the path until the dark shape of the tomb was looming to her right. Just past it, she knew the path turned uphill, and if she could just get to—

April felt a heavy blow to her side and flew through the air, slamming painfully into the corner of the tomb, her face scraping on the gravel. Before she could even raise her head, she felt a crippling kick to her back and she cried out, scrabbling away until she was sitting on the steps of the vault. The metallic tang of blood was in her mouth – *God, I haven't lost a tooth, have I?* – and her arm, never quite right after the mauling she had received at the Winter Ball, felt badly twisted.

'How lovely,' said Chessy, grabbing the front of April's dress and pushing her back against the iron door. 'A little family reunion.'

'Leave me alone,' growled April, still breathless from her run.

'No, I don't think so,' said Chessy. 'Not until I have finished with you, anyway.'

April had just about had enough. 'What do you *want* from me?' she yelled.

'The same thing I've always wanted from you Bleeders, April. I want you to die.'

Oh God, thought April, knowing that she was trapped. She tried to struggle, but this time Chessy's weight was on top of her – there was no chance of escape. The vampire would not fall for the same stupid trick twice. The only thing she could do was play for time, keep her talking and hope for Chessy's guard to slip. *Some hope.*

'Why do you hate me so much?'

Chessy laughed. 'I don't hate you, Head Girl. You barely register in my mind. It's your family I hate.'

'My family?' repeated April, genuinely mystified.

'Don't play dumb – you can't be that stupid. Why do you think I had my fanboys kick in this door,' she said, slamming her hand against it causing a hollow ring.

April's eyes opened wide. '*You* stole my dad's body? *You're* the vandal?'

'Vandal?' laughed Chessy. 'Is that the best explanation you and those half-witted policemen could come up with? There are one hundred and seventy thousand people buried in this cemetery. Didn't it occur to you to ask why these vandals attacked this particular tomb?'

'Because you lack imagination?' said April sarcastically, immediately regretting it as Chessy raised one manicured finger and pressed the nail into April's skin, just below the eye.

'I could blind you in a second, Bleeder. I could tear your throat out like I did that idiot Calvin's. In fact, maybe I will.'

Stall April, stall, she thought desperately.

'But why hang him up on the gate?'

'Because I wanted the King to see that I could get to anyone. I wanted *everyone* to see.' Chessy smiled. 'I got that idea from your boyfriend, actually.'

'Shut up about Gabriel,' April spat. 'You're not fit even to mention his name.'

Chessy raised her fingernail again. 'Do I have to pop your eye? Show some respect.'

'You stole my father's remains,' said April, 'and you expect respect? You're revolting.'

Chessy brought her face closer to April's, moving into a shaft of moonlight. April could still see dried blood around Chessy's mouth. Ling's blood.

'I didn't take your father's foul remains,' hissed Chessy.

'They were never even inside. But I hope whoever has them is using his skull as an ashtray.'

April had never wanted to hurt someone more. But even her Fury rage wasn't enough; she was pinned, unable to move. So she did the only thing she could; she jerked her head forward and spat in Chessy's face.

'You little ...' snarled the vampire, lifting a hand to wipe the spittle away, then smiled. 'Oh, I'm going to make this very slow ... and very painful for you now.'

'I don't think so, darling.'

April looked beyond Chessy and gasped. Standing there, hands on hips, was Davina.

'Back off!' hissed Chessy, letting go of April and twisting around to face Davina. April could only push back up against the iron door as the two vampires slowly circled each other, moving in and out of the moonlight. To April, they looked like two pit bulls about to lunge. Then Davina stopped, her face registering surprise, then delight.

'Oh dear, Chess, what has the nasty girl done to you?' she said, letting out a cackle.

'What? She hasn't done anything,' returned Chessy, her eyes narrowing. 'It's what I'm going to do to you that should be troubling you.'

'Really?' said Davina. 'And you think you're up to it?'

Chessy snorted with derision, but April could see doubt on her face.

'No, seriously,' pressed Davina. 'Are you feeling okay, sweetie? Because you look terrible.'

And then, as Chessy turned into the light, April could see it too. She went cold. Black lines were spreading across Chessy's neck, like ink through water, dark tendrils moving under her pale skin.

'Oh God,' whispered April as she realised what was happening.

'What?' barked Chessy, a hand touching her neck. 'What is it?'

Davina licked a finger and drew an imaginary '1' in the air. 'Well done, Fury. Chalk up another one.'

April looked at her wide-eyed. 'You *knew*?' she gasped.

Davina raised her eyebrows. 'I do now.'

'Fury?' gasped Chessy, putting her hand to her cut lip and looking at the blood on her fingertips. April could see the terror pass over Chessy's face as she realised what had happened. The blood from April's mouth had entered her cut; Chessy had been infected by the Fury virus.

'But the Fury is a myth!' she screamed. 'It's a fairy tale! There's no such thing!'

April was now backed up against the far corner of the tomb. Every nerve, every sinew was desperate to run, to flee, but she couldn't; she was frozen in place, mesmerised as the black lines snaked down Chessy's arms and onto her hands. Chessy held up her fingers in front of her face in disbelief. She let out a shriek of despair and this, April knew, was what Gabriel had been talking about. The vampires felt untouchable, *immortal*. They didn't understand, could not comprehend that they would ever die, but here, right before her eyes, Chessy was dying, the poison spreading through her. Not as quickly, not as spectacularly as with Benjamin, but the same horrific reaction was taking place inside her.

'Help me!' screamed Chessy, falling to her knees, holding out her hands to April. 'Help me, PLEASE!'

'No,' whispered April, shaking her head. 'I can't.'

'Then I'm taking you with me!' Chessy roared, charging at April. April threw up her arms to protect herself, but Chessy never made it that far. Davina shot across in a blur, throwing Chessy back onto the path.

'Run, April,' shouted Davina. 'Go!'

She didn't need telling twice. She sprinted down the gravel, skidded out onto the main path and bolted for the stairs at the bottom. Her feet stung as she leapt into the courtyard and ran for the gate.

'Over here!' called a familiar voice. 'April! This way!'

'Caro!' cried April, throwing her arms around her friend. 'You're alive! Oh thank God, thank God.'

'Thank Davina, actually,' said Caro. 'She was the one who super-vamped the guards and sneaked us out the back.'

'Us?' said April, looking around. Now she could see Simon crouching over another figure slumped on the ground, the smaller security guard doing something behind him, a grim expression on his face.

'Simon, you're okay?' said April, then looked back at Caro. 'Ling?'

Caro reassured her. 'She's alive. Just.'

They could hear the rapid *whoop-whoop* of an ambulance coming from the Archway end of Swain's Lane. But April knew she couldn't wait.

'Look after her,' said April, kissing Caro on the cheek, 'I've got to go.'

'April, no!' said Caro, clinging onto her hand. 'Wait for the police – let them handle it. It's too dangerous – look at Ling, for God's sake!'

April shook her head. 'I'm not going after anyone,' she said, sprinting up the hill. 'I'm going home.'

Chapter Twenty-Eight

The case was still there, under her bed. April yanked it out and turned it upside down, emptying the contents onto the mattress. 'Where is it? Come on, come on,' she whispered urgently. Her fingers rifled through the collection of her father's things, tossing aside cuttings and papers, only interested in finding the one thing she felt sure would tell her what she needed to know.

But you already know, don't you? said a voice inside her head. *You don't need the envelope, you don't need to see what's inside. You know.*

Up by the tomb, Chessy had been goading her about her family. April knew vampires were malicious and twisted – experts at mind games, but what she had said about the pictures on her phone hadn't been a surprise, had it? Not if she was completely honest with herself. It had always been there at the back of April's mind, but she'd been unable or unwilling to face it.

April picked up a photo – the snap of her and her father sitting by Loch Ness, the one which had triggered so many happy memories when she had found it down in the cellar. Today it only unearthed more questions – like why hadn't there been any family photos like this in the Dunne family home? *That* was what Chessy had been getting at when she was going through her phone; she had no photos of her family. Why? More to the point, why wasn't there a single snap of her anywhere in Silvia's house? April had seen them every time she had visited a friend's home, proudly displayed in silver frames, pinned to the fridge, even used as screensavers on the family PC – pictures of boys and girls in party hats, on cute little bicycles, standing in front of the Christmas tree. But not here, not in the Dunne household. Why the hell not? It was weird, really weird. But the question really bothering April, making a cloud of butterflies take flight in her stomach, was this: why hadn't April noticed it before? She had never questioned why her parents had been reluctant to leap up with a camera when the birthday cake was brought out, or when she won a medal for long jump at sports day. Was it because deep down, she had always known?

Known what? asked the voice again. *What exactly is it you think you know?*

April picked up another photo. It was a picture of her, aged eight or nine, the one she had found wedged in a book her father had been reading, the little school photograph he had been using as a bookmark. She looked at her own face beaming back at her. So innocent, so happy. What would she look like now? Weary? Heartbroken? Lonely? She imagined her face in the Ravenwood end of year portraits. She gave a grim smile. *As if.*

And then she saw it, the envelope she had been searching for. She slid it from the pile, then paused, not sure that she wanted to look inside. But she had to know; she hadn't come this far to shy away now. April tipped the contents out: a passport – her dad's, but an old one with the corners snipped off – and a pile of old documents. She picked up the first: it was her birth certificate. Father, William, mother, Silvia, born on Valentine's Day, a baby girl. Nothing unusual there. She looked at the next one, a slightly more yellowed sheet, bearing the title 'Certificate of Birth' and the name, in copperplate writing, 'Silvia Margaret Hamilton, date of birth, 1969 May 24th. Father, Thomas Hamilton.'

So what's wrong with that? the voice in her head questioned. Nothing, nothing at all. Because it was the other document which was wrong. So, terribly, horribly wrong. April's hands shook slightly as she picked it up. This sheet was older, the folds in the paper worn and delicate. It was written in a language April did not understand, but the format was the same: a space for the baby's name: 'Silvia Mariutza Vladescu'. A space for the place of birth 'Vatra Domei, Romania'. And then date of birth. And this swam before her eyes: '24th May *1936*'.

Nineteen *thirty-six*. Could it be another Silvia? Her grandmother, perhaps? Some cultures had a tradition of naming infants after their parents, perhaps … but April knew, she *knew*. Her grandmother had been called Beatrice. This was her mother's certificate. She *knew*.

Almost in a trance, April stood and, holding the documents loosely in her numb fingers, walked out of her bedroom and down the stairs. She could hear movement in Silvia's room, the *psst* of hairspray, the familiar creak as she sat down at her dressing table. April pushed the door open without knocking.

'Oh, hello, darling,' Silvia said, leaning in to the mirror to apply her make-up. 'I didn't hear you come in – drying my hair.'

April stood there, unable to move. What should she say? What *could* she say? It felt as though she was standing on the edge of the world and the earth was crumbling beneath her feet. Noticing her silence, Silvia swivelled around to face her daughter. 'Something wrong?' she said, then seeing the papers in April's hand, she frowned. 'What have you got there?'

April slowly raised her arm and dropped the documents onto the bed. She watched as Silvia's eyes widened.

'Where did you find those …?' she began, but April cut her off.

'Why?' she said. 'Why didn't you tell me? How could you have kept it from me for so long? You and dad … how could you?' April expected tears, but she just felt numb.

For a long moment Silvia said nothing. 'We wanted to protect you,' she said quietly. 'That's all we ever wanted.'

'How?' shouted April. 'How were you protecting me? By making me think I was human? By pretending that the real world –' she gestured towards the certificates '– this world didn't exist?'

'And what then?' said Silvia. 'What if we had told you? Do you think you could have kept it a secret? Could any child?'

'I'm not a child any more!' shouted April, suddenly burning with anger. 'How many times since we came to this village could you have told me what was going on? Don't you think I could have protected myself better if I had known I was the daughter of a vampire?'

Daughter of a vampire.

It was as if the words were echoing around the room, repeating themselves over and over again. And, as she said the words, it was like a thousand pieces of jigsaw all clicking into place at once. The lack of photographs, the reluctance to rise before noon, the short, ferocious temper. *God, she's a vampire*; April's own mother was a *vampire*. It had been there all the time, right under her nose. Then a sudden thought sickened her.

'Does that mean I'm a vampire too?'

'No, darling. We can only be born or turned. But you must know that by now.'

'Don't you dare!' April screamed. 'Don't you dare be so calm about it! You've lied to me all my life!'

'Only to protect you, April. To keep you safe.'

April pulled up her sleeve to show the scar across her arm. 'You call this safe? I've been beaten up, strangled and half torn apart. Is that your idea of protecting me?'

'I couldn't always be there,' said Silvia defensively.

'Oh, I forgot. You were out on your dates.'

Anger flashed across Silvia's face. It was the same age-old irritation and belligerence April had seen every day of her life. Her mother was like that – fierce and uncompromising, always on a short fuse. But it wasn't just some off-beat personality trait. Silvia was spiky and constantly on a hair-trigger because she was a vampire. April had spent her entire life sharing a house with a pure-bred killer.

'Did Dad know?' she asked, but then shook her head at the stupidity of the question. Of *course* he knew, how could he not? And then April felt the full force of what that meant and she dropped down on the bed. It was as if her brain was one of those spinning wheels you got on your computer when the CPU got overloaded, as her mind struggled to rewrite everything she knew about everything.

'Jesus ...' she whispered. All of the screaming rows, all of the upheavals, all of Silvia's 'headaches', now April saw them in a completely new light.

'Did you feed from him?'

'Of course,' said Silvia softly. 'He was a good man.'

April turned away, filled with revulsion at the idea. It was worse than walking in on your parents having sex.

'A good man?' she snapped. 'Then how could you do that to him? You made his life hell!'

Silvia nodded. 'Yes, I suppose I did. But for all that, he seemed ... I know you won't understand it.' She trailed off.

But April did understand; in a sudden terrible rush, it all made perfect, perfect sense. Silvia was aggressive, demanding, constantly arguing, never satisfied – William Dunne might as well have been living in a cage with an alligator. And yet he had stayed, a constant solid presence in April's life, supporting them both, always the peacemaker, always the fixer. He was always there. Always. Despite knowing who – *what* – she was, he stayed.

'He loved you,' whispered April. 'God, he really must have loved you.'

Silvia nodded. 'Yes, he did. It was the one thing I was always sure of. The only thing, actually.'

She looked up at April and her eyes were shining with tears. 'And I loved him back. I really did.'

'So why did you ...' began April, then stopped.

'Oh Jesus,' she whispered. Because it had all suddenly fallen into place. She knew. She knew who the King Vampire was – and she knew exactly where he was too. She looked at her mother. There were a million questions she wanted to ask, but they would all have to wait. Because there was someone she loved who needed her help right now. April jumped to her feet. She had been wasting too much time.

'Where are you going?' said Silvia.

'It's great you've told me all this, but I've got to go.'

'*Now*?'

'Now.'

She turned and ran down the stairs, taking them three at a time.

'April! Come back,' shouted Silvia. But April was already running, sprinting towards the school. Running towards Gabriel.

Chapter Twenty-Nine

Ravenwood was dark. April stood in the shadows across the road, panting, with her hands on her knees. She had run all the way from Pond Square, suddenly filled with a desperate need to find Gabriel – and at the same time, somehow absolutely sure he was here. If Chessy had been telling the truth – that tonight was some sort of audience with the King for the chosen few – then everything April had ever wanted to know about the vampires would be inside that building. But why was it so dark, so lifeless? It just looked like an ordinary school shut up for the night. Maybe the Suckers had just been boasting. But April could almost *feel* their presence – she knew they were there, just knew it.

For a moment, her mind flashed back to her mother's bedroom, the certificates, the photographs. Why had she hidden so much of her own childhood from herself? She could understand why Silvia might need to do it, but why had she, April, suppressed the one thing that she must, *must* have known all along? It was as if she had somehow understood what her mother and father were doing, and colluded.

'Crazy,' she whispered. But it was just one of the questions she would have to find answers for later. Right now, she needed to find Gabriel. Right now, that was all that mattered.

April drew back further into the shadow of a tree as headlights swept around the corner and a car pulled in through the school gates. She watched as the doors of the black Mercedes opened and two men in suits climbed out – she could hear their voices and laughter; they certainly sounded like they were going to a party. Just then Ravenwood's wide front door opened, briefly spilling yellow light across the steps before it closed behind them.

At least I know that something's going on, she thought, taking a deep breath. *Here goes nothing*.

April slipped through the gates and around the side of the school. Keeping the dark building to her left, she ran along the wall, hoping no one was looking out. But then, why would they be? If there was some vampire mass rally going on inside, all eyes would be turned towards the stage or throne or wherever the King Vampire was holding court.

The King Vampire. April stopped, her hand over her mouth. How could she have missed it? *How?* But then she had managed to avoid seeing that her own mother was a bloody vampire, hadn't she? If her reeling mind had refused to accept that, then it was only logical that she could miss the fact that the King, the very person she'd been hunting for so long, had been right under her nose. April shook her head. She couldn't let all that stop her now; if she thought too hard, she'd freeze. And then Gabriel would be lost.

She paused at the corner of the gym and peeked around the wall. At the back, the main hall looked out over the playing fields – light from the windows was flooding across the hockey pitch. *That's where the party is then*, she thought. There was no way to sneak past those windows and besides she needed to get inside. Retracing her steps, she padded down a set of stairs towards one of the side exits: the double doors she and Caro would go through on their way to their favourite picnic bench. Back when all this had been only an idea, when they had just been playing at detectives. But now it was deadly serious, wasn't it?

'Got a light?'

April darted back behind a bush as two men stepped into view. *Please God, don't let them have seen me*, thought April, not daring to breathe. The two stood at the foot of the stairs, smoking. April could smell the rich tobacco in the air: cigars. *Typical*, she thought as a cloud wafted over her. She hated cigars; they made her feel sick. She pulled her coat over her mouth. Now was not a great time to have a coughing fit.

'What are we going to do about the *other* royal family?' said the first man. He had a high-pitched voice and April could see his silhouette: skinny and tall.

The other laughed. 'I've been wondering about that too,' he replied with a deep Scots accent. 'Maybe they'll join up – they wouldn't like the alternative.'

'On that note, we'd better get back. We don't want to be missed.'

They threw their cigars towards April's bush and went back into the building. April let out a silent breath, her pulse racing wildly. She stayed where she was for a count of thirty, then quietly stepped back onto the stairs. *Yes!* The men had left the door slightly ajar; she slipped inside. April felt the familiar thrill of being somewhere she shouldn't, only this time she wasn't just rifling a library for books. This time, if she were caught, the vamps would almost certainly kill her.

Better not let that happen, then, she thought, turning away from the hall and taking the stairs down towards the basement. Logic told her that if Gabriel was here, he had to be captive somewhere and April had seen enough bad horror movies to know that prisoners were usually kept in the basement, rattling at the bars and yelling for their lawyers.

But this isn't a movie, is it? mocked the voice in her head. *It's real.*

'Oh, shut up,' she whispered.

She turned into a dark corridor: the laboratories. Each of the labs had a window cut into their doors and April peered gingerly through the first, labelled 'Chem 104'. Nothing. Just a dark room and a few Bunsen burners. She tried the next and the next; still nothing, just empty rooms and strange equipment. At the end of the corridor, April finally found an unlocked door. *Damn, only a store cupboard.* She was just about to turn back when her phone buzzed in her pocket. April had switched it to vibrate, but it still made her give a little squeak of surprise. Looking around anxiously, she closed the cupboard door behind her and clicked 'Accept'.

'April, thank God,' said Caro breathlessly. 'I'm at the hospital and …'

'Caro, not now,' she hissed. 'I'm … I'm busy.'

'Where are you?' her friend asked suspiciously.

'In the basement of Ravenwood, surrounded by a million vampires, so I can't really chat.'

'The school? What the hell are you doing there?'

'Chessy told me the vamps are making their big move – tonight – and they're having some sort of council of war right now. Here, at Ravenwood.'

'Shit. Is Gabriel with you?'

'I was actually hoping to find him down here.'

Caro was silent for a moment. 'A?'

'What?'

'Don't get caught.'

April pulled a face and hung up, then, easing the door open, she tiptoed across the corridor – another lab, this one labelled 'Audio Vis 108'. It was too dark inside to make out much, but it all looked pretty high-tech. There was a row of computers under the windows and a large whiteboard in the far corner – *hang on, what's that?*

A flurry of moving colours, like a reflection on glass. Squinting, April could make out wires attached to the wall and one of those old-fashioned microphones you see crooners singing into. A radio studio? But there was definitely something flickering in the corner, just out of sight – and a dark shape in the middle.

'What the hell?' she whispered, her nose pressed against the glass. It couldn't be – could it?

She tried the door, but the handle wouldn't move. *Of course not, that would be too easy.*

She turned and went back to the store cupboard looking for a way to get into that room. A broken office chair – *wrong shape*, she thought, *too heavy to pick up anyway*. Behind that was a mop and broom – not heavy enough.

'Bingo,' she said, pulling a long pole from the shadows at the back. It was a roll-up viewing screen, the sort used with projectors. The long heavy metal tube was perfect for what April had in mind.

God, this'd better work, she thought, hoisting it over her shoulder. Steeling herself, April ran towards room 108 and slammed the end of the tube into the window like a battering ram. The centre of the glass cracked into a spider's web, bending inwards, but it held. *Dammit, it must be safety glass.* She glanced up the corridor. The sound of the impact in such an enclosed space was like a pistol going off, but she couldn't stop now. She backed up and tried again, her arms shaking with the effort. This time the tube crashed straight through, taking the frame and the glass with it. April had surely been heard, but she couldn't worry about that now. She hoisted herself up and slithered head first through the hole, landing in a twisted heap.

'Gabriel,' she called, scrambling to her feet. 'Gabriel, are you there?'

And then she stopped, transfixed by the bizarre scene in front of her. Gabriel was strapped to what looked like a dentist's chair. One arm had tubes running to a hospital drip and there were wires attached to his temples. He was staring straight at a large flat-screen TV on which was playing what looked like a home-movie of a dog fight – pit bulls tearing bloody chunks out of each other. But it was Gabriel's face that made April catch her breath. It was blank, literally blank, as if all trace of personality had been removed. His eyes were open, but there was no other sign of life. He looked like a waxwork in Madame Tussauds.

'Gabe,' she said softly, taking a step closer. 'It's me, April. Can you hear me?'

She reached out to touch his hand – and suddenly he moved, grabbing her wrist, squeezing.

'Please, Gabriel,' she said, trying to twist away, 'Gabe, you're hurting me.'

He turned to face her and April recoiled. His eyes were fierce, his lips drawn back, just like the snarling dogs on the screen. It was the same vampire face she had seen that morning on top of Primrose Hill when he took the Dragon's Breath and turned back into a vampire, but this time there was no recognition, no trace at all of the Gabriel she knew. The creature straining against the straps of his chair wanted to kill her.

There was a sudden crash and the room was filled with people, hands pulling her backwards, as a figure in black bent over Gabriel with a large syringe.

'No!' she screamed. 'Leave him alone!'

'I don't think that would be a good idea, April.'

Whoever was constraining April twisted her around and she saw Charles Tame standing in the doorway.

'Bring her,' he said with a malevolent smile. 'There's someone I think will want a word with her.'

April's arm was twisted behind her back and she was frogmarched out of the lab and back along the corridor. As they got to the steps, she looked back and saw Gabriel being hauled from the room, slumped between two men, his head hanging forward, his toes dragging along the floor.

'What have you done to him?' she yelled. 'If you've hurt him, I'll kill you!'

Tame stepped in front of her and grabbed her face. 'No, April, I think not,' he said, his fingers pressing painfully into her cheeks. 'You will do exactly as you are told.'

'Do you know who I am?' she hissed. 'Do you know who the King is?'

Tame laughed. 'Of course I do. I've known since I came to Ravenwood, we've been working side by side, you could say.' He looked over at Gabriel.

'*You* did that to him? What have you done to his head?'

'It's my speciality, April, you knew that. The mind is

a surprisingly simple thing when you know how to re-programme it.'

'What did you do?' screamed April.

Tame stepped forward and slapped her. April's head jerked back, her mind reeling.

'Tonight is too important to let your hysterical teenage nonsense get in the way. Either you cooperate, or your boyfriend has an unpleasant, and fatal, accident. Is that clear?'

Tame's eyes were sparkling in the light, his mouth a fixed grin. *God, he's mad*, she thought.

'Is that clear?' he repeated.

April nodded. *We'll see who has an unpleasant accident*, she thought. Her defiance must have shown on her face, because Tame slowly shook his head.

'Oh no, don't think you'll be getting special treatment,' he said. 'The King has been very clear on that from the beginning. You will see our point of view and fall in line, or you will be joining dear Gabriel in his shallow grave.'

He stood watching her, that grin still there, clearly waiting for a reply. April nodded again.

'Fine, then I think it's time for your reunion.'

In front of her, the double doors to the school hall were opened and April was pushed through. April had been expecting a party, perhaps something along the lines of the reception at the Crichton Club, but this was different. A long wooden table had been placed in the centre of the floor, surrounded by perhaps two dozen high-backed chairs – and sitting in each of them were serious-faced men and women. April didn't have time to recognise any individuals because Tame pushed her elbow, causing her to stumble to her knees at the foot of the table.

'Ladies and gentlemen,' said Tame, 'may I introduce Ravenwood's Head Girl, Miss April Dunne? Miss Dunne, it seems, has been on a rescue mission,' he said. 'And I suspect she was also planning to disrupt our little meeting.'

April had expected an angry shout or at the very least a

hum of discussion, but instead the hall remained silent, as if everyone was waiting for someone to give them a signal.

'Pick her up,' instructed a low voice. April felt hands behind her, and she slowly straightened up, her stomach turning over.

'Hello, Princess.'

April looked up into the face of her grandfather.

'Come, April,' said Thomas, gently lifting her chin with one finger and looking into her eyes. 'You will sit next to me. As you were always meant to.'

But April could not move, she could only look at him, her mouth open. All those months, looking everywhere, searching for clues, she had missed the glaring truth, the thing that had been right in front of her. Her mother, her grandma, Uncle Luke – her whole family were vampires. And Grampa Thomas, her rock, her protector, he was the most dangerous of them all.

'You're the King?' she said. 'The King Vampire?'

She had to ask, had to hear him say it.

Thomas just smiled, not the twisted smile of a tyrant, but the warm smile of a doting grandparent.

'Yes, April, I am the King. Now join me.'

He led her to a chair next to him at the head of the table. April noticed to her horror that all eyes in the room were focused on her. Did they expect her to say something? But instead Grampa Thomas began to speak.

'This, you will have gathered, is my granddaughter, April,' he said.

To April's surprise and bewilderment, the group began to clap. They were all smiling at her!

'This means a minor deviation from the plan, but now I see that fate has brought her to our meeting. April is the last of my line and my natural heir.'

This snapped April out of her daze.

'What? No!' she said. 'Gramps, I can't, I don't …'

He laid his huge hand over hers and bent his mouth to

her ear. 'Don't rush it, Prilly, I know this must be strange for you, but this is the future. Our future.'

Thomas looked down the table with pride. April could now see David Harper, DCI Johnston and a few other faces she thought she recognised from the TV news or perhaps from the meeting at the Crichton Club. They were all looking at her expectantly.

'Are they the governors?' she said.

A twitter of polite laughter ran around the table.

'No, darling. This is the Council of Light.'

'Light? I thought it was all about darkness.'

'This is not a Hammer Horror film, April,' said Thomas. 'Look for yourself, these people are just like you – they're humans not vampires. But they are forward-thinking humans, people who simply want the world to be different, who want society to finally recognise and accept that vampires live among them and wish to share in the government of the land.'

'No! I'm not like any of these people.'

She pushed herself up, away from the table, as if to distance herself from them.

'Don't you realise what you're doing?' she cried. 'Do you realise who you're dealing with?'

'April, please,' began Thomas.

'No, Gramps,' she said. 'Tonight I saw exactly what your people are capable of. I saw an innocent schoolgirl savaged, her blood drained by a monster.'

'We are not monsters, darling,' said Thomas, his demeanour calm, but his eyes betraying annoyance. 'Vampires simply have a different physiological make-up. We need plasma to survive and it is society's inability to accept our difference that has forced some into such desperate acts.'

April laughed incredulously. 'So now you're presenting vampires as some sort of oppressed minority? Crap, Gramps! That Sucker didn't *need* to feed, she did it because she could, because she liked pain and suffering and terror. That's your idea of a bright new future?'

She saw Thomas glance towards the watching faces around the table.

'No, that is my idea of a dark past which we must distance ourselves from and control. We cannot allow that perception of vampires as skeletal ghouls lurking in the shadows to hold us back.'

There were a few more claps.

She shook her head. She still couldn't believe what she was hearing. 'It's not a bloody PR problem!' she shouted towards the people round the table. 'These people are going to destroy your world!'

There were indulgent smiles from the table and Dr Tame sat forward.

'There will be no war, April, no revolution; there is no army waiting to storm the palace gates. This is a peaceful alliance of like-minded individuals who only wish the nation to benefit from our mutual gifts.'

'NO!' shouted April, slamming her hand on the table. Couldn't they see? 'You can't negotiate with them. They will slaughter you like cattle!'

Thomas stood up, raising his hands.

'I think this seems a good point to call for a break,' he said. 'You'll find drinks laid out in the refectory; we'll reconvene at –' he checked the clock above the stage '– shall we say eight?'

It was all so genteel, all so polite and calm, as if they were a group of regional sales managers who'd come for a team-building conference, not some of the most powerful figures in the country here to plan the entire destruction of the society they knew. Dr Tame ushered the council through the double doors and closed them behind him, leaving April and her grandfather alone. April looked at Thomas, then moved towards the doors.

'April, stay. Please.'

'I'm going to find Gabriel,' said April. 'He needs me.'

But Thomas caught her arm. '*I* need you, Prilly,' he said. Something in the way he said it made April stop.

'What do you mean, you need me?'

'I'm dying, April,' he said.

Despite her anger, April's heart lurched. At that moment this wasn't the King Vampire, this was her Gramps, the man who had bounced her on his knee, the solid immovable thing at the centre of her life, the one man she could always rely on.

'You're dying ... What's wrong, Grampa?'

Thomas gave a sad smile.

'I am old, darling, worn out. Even pure-bred vampires age eventually and I am very, very old now. I feel it in my bones. Don't worry, I have time to do what I set out to do, but I need your help.'

April wanted to throw her arms around her grandfather, to hold him and be held, reassured. But she was still too angry, too confused.

'Why didn't you tell me, Gramps?'

'Your mother. She said I should wait. I wanted to tell you about our family and our legacy – I tried – but Silvia insisted she wanted to raise you as a normal child.'

'I am – I *was* – a normal child. Just because you are ...' she gestured helplessly.

'A vampire?' said Thomas. 'Yes, I am a vampire, April. So is your mother, so are *you*, April. We have been the royal line for countless centuries.'

'So all that stuff about the Black Prince? It was true? I thought it was just you trying to make our family look important.'

Thomas chuckled, his back straight with pride.

'You are a true princess, darling. Some believe we ruled in the dark ages, before even the Mayans and the Aztecs, before the others –' his mouth curled in unconscious distaste '– before they bred their way across Europe like rats. And now it is time for us to return to our rightful position, as kings and queens.'

April shook her head. 'You sound like a mad dictator, Gramps.'

'There is nothing mad about it, Prilly,' he countered, bristling. 'It is pure logic that we should rule. We are superior in every way – stronger, faster, more intelligent.'

'*You* might be. I'm one of the cattle, just waiting to be tapped for blood. I'm just one of the Bleeders, remember?'

'No, Princess, you are not. You are of royal blood, you are exceptional.'

'Why not Mum? She's a real vampire. Why not put her on the throne?'

'She turned away from me,' he said, his anger plain. 'When I reached out to her, offered her the crown, she rejected me and told me I was crazy. But I always knew you would come to me.'

He put out his hand to stroke April's hair, but she pushed it away.

'No, Gramps!' she said, turning and running towards the hall's double doors. 'I don't want this. I don't want any of it!' She had to get out of the hall, out of this trap her grandfather had set for her. She needed to find Gabriel, take his hand in hers and run far, far away – anywhere but here, away from all this craziness. She was twisting the door handle when Thomas pushed the door shut.

'Don't turn your back on me, Prilly,' he said. It was a threat. 'I cut your mother off and I can cut you off too.'

April blinked at him, her heart torn. He was her grandfather, her family, and he was sick. But she loved Gabriel too and he needed her help right now.

'I know you need me, Gramps,' she said, 'but what about the people who don't fit into your new world? What about my friends, what about the vampires who don't want to be part of this?'

'You mean this boy, Gabriel, don't you?'

'Yes! I love him, Gramps. I know you can't understand that, but I do.'

Thomas's expression hardened. 'Forget him, Prilly. He is no good for you.'

April felt a rush of anger. She had been lied to, manipulated and pushed around – and now Gabriel was being … what? Experimented on? She had no idea what had been going on in the basement, but it had hurt him badly, she could tell that. And no one hurt the man she loved.

'I will decide who and what is good for me,' she said, holding Thomas's gaze. 'You can forget all about this "Princess April" rubbish until I'm sure he's all right.'

'Very well,' said Thomas. 'If that's your decision.'

He stepped into the corridor and April could hear him speaking with Dr Tame.

There was a pause, then the doors opened and Gabriel was brought in, half-supported by the headmaster. Tame dragged him to one of the high-backed chairs and stood back as Gabriel's head rolled backwards, his eyes fluttering, half open. 'What have you done to him?' said April, kneeling down next to her boyfriend, touching his forehead. His skin was burning hot, as if he was gripped by a fever.

'Tell me!' she shouted at Tame. 'What's wrong with him?'

'Everything.' Tame smiled, looking over at Thomas. 'He is a failure, April. An experiment gone wrong. Gabriel was supposed to be a soldier, but soldiers are supposed to follow orders, aren't they? Your boyfriend – he wouldn't do as he was told.'

April looked up sharply as her mind joined the dots. This was the final part of the puzzle – of course. Grampa Thomas was the King, Gabriel's mysterious master, the one who had turned him from lovelorn student into a creature of the night. As the pieces fell into place, it was as if April had been kicked in the stomach. Because if that were true, it meant that Gabriel would never be free.

'You turned him? You?'

Thomas laughed bitterly. 'He's been a thorn in my side ever since. I should have killed him the moment I set eyes on him.'

'Then why didn't you?'

'Because I wanted an army. I planned to create a battalion of perfect killing machines to take this godforsaken country by force.'

'You used Gabriel as a … *guinea pig*?'

Thomas looked away, as if he was remembering and his voice softened.

'It was a golden time, Prilly. Science was taming the planet. With electricity, navigation and munitions, Victoria had the greatest empire the world has ever seen. With the advances in drugs, surgery, even psychology, I knew we had an opportunity to change the course of history, swing the pendulum back our way.'

'What did you do to him in that basement?'

'Neuroendocrine disassociation,' said Tame proudly. 'I've been working on it for some time. We want to get inside the subject's head, rewire him, take away all fear and remorse. Over the years, your grandfather's so-called advisers have tried everything: hallucinogens, deep hypnosis – and with the greatest respect, none of them worked. In fact, the earliest experiments were a disaster. They turned Whitechapel into a blood bath.'

'Whitechapel?' said April. 'You mean … Gabriel *was* Jack the Ripper?'

Tame let out a high-pitched giggle. 'Not quite. Those murders were carried out by other vampires, early prototypes for the army. They were being field-tested if you like. But your friend there, well …'

'He tried to make a fool of me!' snapped Thomas. 'Some sort of petty revenge for the death of his whore. He killed my soldiers one by one, left the bodies out for everyone to see. That was why I have never let him out of my sight, why I will never let him rest. That is his punishment for defying me.'

'You call *him* petty?' snapped April. 'You have been holding a grudge for a hundred bloody years just because he wouldn't do what you said?'

'I have done worse to people who refused to see my point of view,' said Thomas, his mouth curled into a sneer.

'Like my father?' said April quietly.

It was the one thing she hadn't allowed herself to think about until now. How could she? It was unthinkable. But then it seemed almost everything that had seemed impossible, grotesque and horrific was coming true tonight. Why not face this one too?

'Your father?' For a moment, Thomas' arrogance seemed to desert him.

'Yes, my father. William Dunne. The man whose murder you ordered.'

Thomas shook his head. 'No, Princess, I never ordered his death.'

It was April's turn to sneer. 'And I suppose you never knew anything about it, either? Bullshit, Gramps. You're the King Vampire, who would kill your son-in-law without your say-so?'

'Believe it or not, I did not send anyone to your house,' said Thomas.

'Then why is he dead?' April held her grandfather's gaze, until he finally looked away.

'Yeah, that's what I thought,' said April, turning back to Gabriel.

'Come on, Gabe, I'm taking you out of here,' she said, grabbing his shirt and trying to lift him, but it was hopeless, like trying to lift a dead body.

'Please, Gabe,' she said, looking into his half-closed eyes. 'Help me out here. I can't do it on my own.'

Thomas walked over. 'Gabriel,' he said quietly.

Immediately, Gabriel's eyes opened and he looked towards Thomas.

'Stand up, Gabriel.'

Gabriel jumped to his feet. April could only stare, her mouth open.

'Gramps, what are you doing?' she said, but Thomas ignored her.

'Now lift your hands.'

Gabriel did as he was told.

'Now strangle Dr Tame.'

'What? No!' said the headmaster, but Gabriel's hands were already around his neck, his fingers pressing into the pale flesh. Tame's mouth opened, his tongue protruding, and he began to make sharp gagging noises at the back of his throat.

'Gabriel, stop!' shouted April. She stepped forward and grabbed his hands, but he was too strong. Tame's eyes were rolling up in his head now and April turned to Thomas. She had no great love of Ravenwood's headmaster, but she couldn't stand by and watch him die.

'Stop him!' she shouted at Thomas. 'I'm warning you, Gramps—'

Thomas's hand shot out and grabbed April's arm, twisting.

'You're warning *me*?' he hissed, pulling her face close to his. 'You dare to threaten the King? Just like your mother. Neither of you are fit to wear a crown.'

He threw her to the ground and stood over her. 'Choose,' he said. His voice was hard, cold. Terrifying.

April looked up at him, her eyes wide. 'Choose?'

'Choose between him and me. Between this worthless slave and the glory of ruling over the eternal kingdom. I'll give you three seconds.'

'Gramps, no!' cried April, her heart hammering. He couldn't be serious, could he?

'Two …'

'PLEASE!'

'Three. Very well. If you want him, you can have him.'

He turned to Gabriel. Tame's face was now almost blue.

'Gabriel, strangle April.'

April barely had time to gasp before Gabriel dropped Tame and switched to her, his hands around her throat, squeezing, crushing, closing her windpipe. Her head began to pound, the blood rushing in her ears. She grasped Gabriel's wrists, vainly trying to prise them apart, but she was nowhere near strong enough.

'I'm sorry, Princess,' said Thomas calmly. 'I had such high hopes for you.'

'Stop,' she croaked. 'Gabriel … please. I love … you.'

For a moment April could see the fog clear from Gabriel's eyes and his grip released a little. It was as if he were looking at her from a long way away, trying to recognise someone in a vast crowd.

'April?' he whispered.

'Yes! It's me,' she said, reaching a hand up towards him.

'Yes, Gabriel,' said Thomas, his voice cutting in. 'It's April. Now please continue. I turned you, Gabriel, I am your master. Now do as I command and kill her.'

It was like the jaws of a vice locking on her throat. The words she wanted to say were choked, frozen. She could feel the pain in her chest swelling to the size of a fist. Soon it would spread to the rest of her body. And yet still she was staring into Gabriel's eyes, searching for some sign of recognition, but there was nothing of her boyfriend there, only vampire, pure obedient killer. *It's not your fault, my love*, she thought, her head swimming. *It's not you.*

With the last of her strength April swung her foot sideways, kicking Gabriel's knee as hard as she could. With a cry of surprise, his legs buckled and he fell hard on his left side with a sickening crack. April rolled away, rasping air into her screaming lungs, coughing and retching. There was a terrible pain in her chest, but April forced herself to move. She knew she should probably get up and run, but instead she crawled over to Gabriel.

'Gabe,' she croaked, cradling his face. 'It's April. Don't you recognise me? Please … *please* say yes.'

There were tears running down her face as she looked into his eyes and her heart felt as if it might crack down the middle. If Gabriel had gone, if he had been turned into the killer of his dreams, then she wasn't sure she wanted to live. For a moment, all hope seemed suspended, then she saw something – a movement, a twinkle deep in his dark eyes.

'Hey, baby.' He smiled. 'I think you've broken my elbow.'

April didn't have time to answer. There was a terrible thud and Gabriel flew sideways, out of her grasp. Everything seemed to move in slow motion, as if in the flickering illuminations of a strobe – frozen pictures one after another, the storyboard of a living horror film: she saw her grandfather lifting a chair and the sickening crunch as he brought it down over Gabriel's skull. She saw the splintered wood and the pool of blood spreading across the floor.

'No!' she screamed, snapping back into the present, flying across the room, slamming her grandfather against the wall. Her nails raked against his face, her lips pulled back in a snarl. She looked at Thomas's throat, exposed only inches from her bared teeth and she knew she could kill him. Just sink her jaws into his neck, then sit back and watch as the poison spread through him, its black tendrils bruising the skin just as it had done with Benjamin and Chessy. It would be so easy, so right. And all this would be over.

'Do it,' he hissed.

April looked into her grandfather's face. 'Finish it,' he said. 'Prove you are strong, Princess. Take my life and lift the crown.'

Suddenly April's mind was clear. Through all these months of confusion, tragedy and pain she had struggled with herself, wondering who she was, who she could trust, what she wanted – but now she knew. She was April Dunne, and she had a mind of her own. She bent her head and kissed Thomas on the cheek.

'No,' she said. 'I don't think I will.'

And then she was flying, flung across the hall like a puppet with the strings cut, crashing against the table, sending chairs clattering to the floor.

'NO!' roared Thomas. 'You WILL NOT defy me! I am the KING!'

He reached down and grabbed April by the neck and effortlessly lifted her into the air, throwing her against the stage. The edge slammed into her back and she dropped, groaning, but Thomas picked her up again and pushed her back against the wall. April struggled, but he was so strong. So very strong.

'Is that the best you can do, Fury?' he mocked, smiling with pleasure as the shock registered on her face.

'Oh yes, I knew,' he crowed. 'You think I'm that stupid? You think I didn't know why Silvia ran? A star birthmark behind the ear is a hard thing to hide. I saw it the first time I held you.'

He paused, soaking up her terror, enjoying the impact of his words.

'Fury,' he said, his mouth twisting with disgust. 'Are you really all we have to fear? I thought that you had my blood. I thought we could rule these maggots, enslave them together. But you are weak, just like your father. And that's why I will kill you too.'

Thomas saw the look of disbelief on April's face and laughed.

'You?' she gasped. '*You* killed my father? But you said...'

'No April, I said I didn't *order* his death. Oh, that one was personal, there was no way I was going to let anyone else have the pleasure.'

'Pleasure?' screamed April. 'He was my dad!'

'He was not worthy of this family,' sneered Thomas. 'Your precious father destroyed my dynasty, weakened my blood-line – and then had the arrogance to believe he could deprive me of my war.'

He moved his face closer to April's. His face transformed into a hideous mask – the snarling teeth and wrinkled snout of a wolf, the true face of the vampire.

'He *had* to die,' he whispered.

April's hand lashed out, her nails raking his face. Thomas didn't seem to feel it. He lifted one finger to the cut and held it up to April.

'That is what royal blood looks like, Fury. Take a good look, because it's the last thing you will see.'

His huge clawed hand reached for her throat and April could only watch as it came towards her. *I love you, Gabriel*, she thought. *Sorry I got us both killed*, vaguely wondering if vampires got to go to heaven.

'Put her *down*.'

Thomas whirled around. Over his shoulder, April could see that the double doors of the hall had been thrown open. Standing there – *At last*, thought April, *at last you got it right* – was her mother. Had Silvia heard? Did she know? Did she know that her father had killed her husband, the man she had loved? From the look on Silvia's face, April could see that she did. It was cold, hard, a face of utter fury.

'Perhaps you didn't hear me,' said Silvia, her voice almost a whisper. 'I said: put her *down*.'

Thomas shrugged and dropped April to the floor. As she slid down the wall, April could see the so-called Council of Light standing behind Silvia.

'Oh, so that is how it is going to be?' laughed Thomas. 'You're staging a coup? Stealing my power base? I think it's going to take a lot more—'

Silvia moved with incredible speed, crossing the space between her and Thomas in half the blink of an eye, her jaws closing on his throat before he had even started forming the next word. *Mum, no, please don't*, April thought, but she knew it was too late, much, much too late. She could only stare in horror as the dark red blood bubbled between her grandfather's fingers and he slowly slumped to his knees. *How*? she thought in terror. *Wasn't he the King Vampire? How had Silvia killed him?* And then the spell broke and April screamed.

'No!' she screamed, but then Silvia was there, wrapping

her daughter in her arms, holding her as sobs wracked April's body.

'Look away, darling,' she whispered, stroking April's hair. 'It's all over now. It's all over.'

Chapter Thirty

From the third floor of the hospital, April could see the cemetery, gleaming white in the sun. Funny how they'd built the hospital so close to all those headstones – some town planner with a twisted sense of humour perhaps? Or maybe it was pure convenience. She leant closer to the glass and rubbed her breath away. Once – and it seemed like a long time ago now – she had been chased into that graveyard by a monster with red-rimmed eyes and a manic laugh. It was the sort of story that should have ended in nothing but tragedy, but instead the thought of it filled April with a warmth that spread through her chest. Gabriel had found her that night and he had kissed her as the snowflakes had spiralled down. And he had told her he loved her.

'Why are you smiling?' said Gabriel.

'Just thinking how this makes a nice change,' she said, turning back towards the bed. 'You the patient, me the visitor. I should have brought you some grapes, but I didn't think you'd be able to eat them with your arm in a sling.'

'I can still move it,' said Gabriel grumpily, lifting up a corner of the bandage wrapped around his head. 'This one's almost healed too.'

'I know, but this time we're doing things properly,' said April. '*Normal* people go to hospital when they've been smashed over the head, *normal* people need bandages and slings, and from now on, Gabriel Swift, you're going to be normal, whether you like it or not.'

'But I'm ...' Gabriel lowered his voice. 'I'm not, am I?'

'No, you're not,' she said, leaning over to kiss him on

the shoulder. 'You just have to pretend until the police are satisfied we're not making it up.'

'Which we are.'

April nodded. 'Which we are.'

It wasn't as if they had much choice; who would believe the real story? Who would believe that her mother was a pure-bred creature of the night and that she had killed her father to stop him – and vampires like him – from taking over the world?

April's buoyant mood ebbed away as she thought of that moment. Her grandad lying there in a pool of dark blood, so very still. Had he *really* killed her father? Yes, he had confessed to it – no, he had *boasted* about it, a proud smile on his face. And then he had tried to kill her – she shouldn't forget that either, *couldn't* forget the look in his eyes: the shining madness, the hate and the hunger. Why was it so hard to accept? Why couldn't her mind grasp the idea that her Gramps was the bad guy, the villain in her own dark fairy tale? Because it was crazy, that was why. But, somehow, April knew she had to find a way to deal with it.

Still, one thing at a time, eh? she thought, squeezing Gabriel's hand.

There was a tap at the door and April looked up to see Detective Inspector Reece standing there.

'April?' he said. 'Could I have a word?'

She glanced at Gabriel and nodded.

'I've just been speaking to my boss – my new boss, actually – and you'll be glad to hear that we won't be taking this any further.'

'Really?'

He shrugged. 'We have some excellent witnesses to corroborate your version of events, April. And, given Dr Tame's state of mind, I'd say any further investigation would be a waste of police time, frankly.'

When the police had arrived at Ravenwood, they had found April weeping over Gabriel's unconscious form. Not far away, they had found Thomas Hamilton's body, lying in a pool of dark blood. And next to him, they had found Dr Charles Tame, clutching at Thomas's hand. He was giggling to himself and muttering one phrase over and over again. 'The King is dead, long live the Queen ...' Paramedics had given him a strong sedative and wheeled him off to the secure psychiatric unit at the Whittington Hospital. Which meant he was probably only a few hundred yards away from this spot, thought April, suppressing a shiver.

'What's going to happen now?' said Gabriel. 'About Dr Tame, I mean.'

The policeman raised his eyebrows. 'We'll have to wait and see. Although his throat was badly bruised – I understand you were trying to fight him off, lad? – he still managed to give us his account of the events.'

'And?'

'It seems he believes your grandfather was a vampire, April.'

'A vampire,' she said, looking at Gabriel. He didn't even flinch.

'According to Dr Tame, your grandad was the Vampire King, the figurehead for a giant global conspiracy to enslave mankind. Tame also believed Gabriel was some kind of zombie assassin whom your grandad ordered to strangle him. I'm sorry, April; I know this has been horrible enough for you already, but I felt it was better you heard it from me.'

April looked down at her hands and nodded.

'Thanks, Mr Reece.' She didn't know whether to laugh or cry. 'But he seemed so normal. Why do you think ...?'

'Why did he go crazy? I asked the very same question and apparently a breakdown of this type is not uncommon in high-achievers; an underlying schizophrenia is triggered when the mind fails to cope with the pressure. The most likely scenario is that he became fixated with your grandfather after he asked the police commissioner to remove Dr Tame from his role as a police adviser.'

'Did he? I didn't know that,' said April.

'Something about Dr Tame coming to your house and threatening you? I haven't read the whole report. Anyway, apparently once Dr Tame became convinced your grandad was his enemy it would have been easy for his unbalanced mind to create this strange alternative universe to justify his actions. We'll be looking into the murder of Calvin Temple too.'

'You think that was him too?'

'It would make sense, given his grudge against your grandfather, but I'm not sure we'll ever know. One thing's for sure, I doubt he'll ever get out to hurt anyone again. Not that it's much consolation for you, but . . .'

'No, that is something, Mr Reece.'

April felt bad about letting Charles Tame take the blame for something he hadn't done, but he wasn't exactly innocent either. He had gleefully volunteered to turn hundreds of children into vampires or vampire-slaves and had been overseeing the creation of a zombie army, beginning with his brutal reprogramming of Gabriel in the Ravenwood laboratory. Did he deserve this? April wasn't sure, but she knew that was another thing she would wrestle with later on.

'I'd better be going,' said Reece, walking to the door, 'I hear your friend Ling is better?'

'Yes. I think she's gone home already. I heard her parents were sending her to some rehab unit abroad.'

Ling's injury had easily been explained away as a cry-for-help suicide bid after the ordeal of Calvin's attack and there had been no witnesses to say otherwise. By the time the police arrived, the Suckers had all melted into the darkness, leaving behind the scaffolding poles. It was as if they had never been there.

April walked with Reece down the corridor.

'Can I just ask you one thing?' said the detective as they waited for the lift.

April nodded.

'Why vampires?'

'I'm sorry?'

'That morning in Covent Garden, I asked you to tell me why all this was happening and you said "vampires".'

'Oh, that.' April had been expecting this question, and had prepared a story. It wasn't a good story, she had to admit, but she hoped it would be adequate. 'I suppose your friend the psychologist is right. I guess the mind can only take so much. My dad, Marcus, Layla, then Mr Sheldon – all those people dying, none of it made sense – and then I found another dead body. I suppose I was clutching at straws, trying to find a reason for it all, however crazy it sounded.'

She held her breath as the policeman looked at her for a long moment. 'I know you've been struggling with this since your father's death,' he said. 'But I've seen a lot of death in my job, and sometimes, April, there simply is no reason.'

April breathed out; Reece seemed to have accepted it. But then, why wouldn't he? Who was ever going to believe that vampires were behind all these killings? That really was crazy.

'Maybe you're right, Mr Reece,' she said. 'But you know what? This time I think it's over. I think death has had enough of me for one lifetime.'

Reece gave her a wintry smile as he stepped into the lift. 'I certainly hope you're right, April. I really do.'

Chapter Thirty-One

The bed was covered in photographs: April making sand-castles, April dressed as Wonder Woman, April proudly displaying her missing milk teeth. And there were other mementos and sentimental knick-knacks that were every bit as evocative to April. Her tiny plastic ID bracelet from the hospital, three ticket stubs for a pantomime, even a crumbling daisy chain carefully wrapped in tissue.

'I can't believe you kept all this,' said April, looking up at her mother. 'I thought you didn't care about any of this stuff.'

Silvia shrugged. 'We couldn't have photos around the house – well, none with me in anyway – but that didn't mean I couldn't hold onto the memories.'

She passed April another picture. In this one, April was wearing a leotard and holding up a tiny silver cup. 'You won third prize for trampoline. I was so proud.'

'I don't even remember being there,' said April numbly. It was as if the memory had been wiped. Or perhaps she had simply suppressed everything – if her mind wouldn't – couldn't – accept the things that didn't fit with normality, she had blanked it all out, both the good and the bad. Looking at her mother's photo collection was like being shown someone else's home movies, a record of a life she couldn't remember living. For a moment, April wondered whether she would ever be forced to hoard photos of her children, filing them away in dusty shoeboxes like her mother had done. Silvia seemed to read her troubled expression.

'It's over, darling. Honestly.'

April wished she shared her mother's optimism. Yes,

she believed the vampire conspiracy had died with Thomas Hamilton in the hall at Ravenwood – but that didn't mean there wouldn't be another Vampire King and, if he was vanquished, another after him. And another and another. After all, vampires had a real habit of coming back from the dead, didn't they? Still, at least they could be certain this particular uprising had been put down; her mother had made sure of that.

Having dispatched their leader, blood still dripping from her chin, Silvia had addressed the 'Council of Light'. She had told them to go back to their constituencies, offices or 'whichever hole you've crawled out of' and resign, pack a suitcase and disappear.

'Go to Belgium, go to Bulgaria, I don't care,' she had said. 'If I ever hear of any of you again, I will find you and kill you. Is that clear?'

Not a single one of them said a word, but it was obvious from the speed with which they left the building that Silvia's message had got through. The question, of course, was whether that would be enough; whether it would ever be enough.

'Are you thinking they'll come back?' asked Silvia. 'Is that what's bothering you?'

'They'll definitely come back,' said April quietly. 'Oh, not those particular people. I think you scared them enough that they'll thank their lucky stars every time they swallow. But there will always be vampires and there will always be humans who think they can make a deal with them.'

'That's true,' said Silvia. 'That's always been true. But that was before I was Queen.'

April looked at her sharply, but her mother only laughed.

'I have a plan,' she said, tapping the side of her nose. 'I won't be keeping you in the dark any more, I promise you that. But let's take one thing at a time, hmm?'

April nodded. Silvia had shown plenty of cunning when she had dismissed the Council of Light at Ravenwood, so

April thought it was entirely possible her mother knew what she was doing. She had kept Detective Chief Inspector Johnston and David Harper behind when the others had left and spoon-fed them an alibi: the reason for their presence at Ravenwood that night was indeed a meeting with Thomas Hamilton, however it was to discuss keeping the students safe after the latest outbreak of violence in Highgate. Without warning, Silvia informed them, Dr Tame had attacked Thomas – and Gabriel when he tried to intervene – leading to the tragic outcome. The policeman and the politician were given the same terms as the others: full cooperation with Silvia or a bloody end. They had both managed to look convincingly shaken when the police had arrived. No, Silvia had covered all the bases. All except one thing.

'Mum, can I ask you something?' said April.

Silvia pulled a face. 'Why do I think I'm not going to like this question?'

'You loved Dad, right? That's why you killed Gramps?'

Silvia reached over to squeeze April's hand. 'I'm so sorry, darling. Really I am. I wish—'

'No, I get it,' said April, 'Seriously. Gramps went to our house and –' her voice began to break '– and he knocked on the door and when Dad let him in, he tore his throat out.'

She was sobbing now, her voice thick. 'When he admitted it, when he *boasted* about it, you wanted to kill him, right?'

Silvia's arms were around her now, holding her tight, but April had to finish, had to get it all out.

'But then he tried to kill *me*,' April whispered, choking as she said it. 'He tried to *kill me*, Mum! Why? Why did he do it? Did he hate me so much?'

And this is what April had been holding back, what she had been hiding from. Maybe she had always known there was something wrong about her family – that's why she had never questioned the lack of photos in the house, why she had never followed up all those stupid hints about the Black Prince – and maybe the reason she hadn't confronted it was simple. Because vampires were killers, monsters, ghouls – who could cope with knowing that their grandfather was something from the depths of hell? Yes, Grandpa Thomas had killed her father and that was like a stone weighing on her heart; she would never, ever be able to forgive that. But this man, the big bear of a man who had hugged her, bought her dolls and sweets, and who had been the one solid thing in her life – this man had wanted to rip her throat open. That was breaking her heart.

'Oh, baby,' whispered Silvia, rocking her back and forth, 'it wasn't you, it wasn't your fault.'

'But if I had done as he said? What if I had agreed to it?'

Silvia turned April's chin so she was looking straight into her eyes. 'Listen to me, April, because this is important.' April could almost feel the heat of her mother's fury as she spoke. 'You did nothing wrong. Your grandfather wanted the world to do exactly as he said and if you didn't go along with it, that made you expendable, whoever you were: you, me, Gabriel, your father, anyone. Believe me, April, even if you had done as he asked, there would have come a time when you became inconvenient or surplus to requirements. Like my mother.'

'Grandma?'

Silvia nodded.

'We'll probably never know exactly what happened. Your Uncle Luke spent years over in the old country piecing it together, but in the end it came down to Mother wanting me to live a normal life, to grow up free of Thomas's ambition. She was only trying to protect me, just as I was protecting you, but your grandfather couldn't accept that.'

'So what did he do?'

'He burnt her alive and fed her remains to his dogs.'

'Jesus,' whispered April.

'That is why you must never doubt you made the right choice. You made the only choice you could. I'm so, so proud that you did. Your dad would have expected nothing less.'

April couldn't say how long they sat there crying together. She suspected that Silvia had needed this as much as her. It can't have been easy living with a huge secret your whole life and it can't have been easy seeing that secret devour the people you loved, one by one. But most of all, it can't have been easy to kill your father, however evil he was, however much he deserved it – even if was to protect your own child. *That* truly can't have been easy.

But like all storms, theirs finally passed. Mother and daughter blew their noses, wiped their eyes and Silvia began to gather up the photographs and knick-knacks, carefully putting them back into the boxes, along with a little of the pain. It felt – well, not good exactly, but better. Together they carried the boxes downstairs and put them on the shelves in the study, above William Dunne's old work desk. It felt the right place for them, just as it felt right when Silvia took a handful of pictures and propped them up in the hallway: April as a little girl in her ballet costume, April as a gangly pre-teen sitting on a swing and, best of all, the one of April with her dad, posing by the Loch Ness sign.

'I'll get some frames tomorrow,' said Silvia. 'I'm never going to hide them away again.'

They walked through to the kitchen and Silvia began to fill the kettle, humming a tune that April remembered was one of her dad's favourites. April sat at the breakfast bar and watched her mother. It was almost as if nothing had happened. No vampires, no murders, no blood on the floor. But it *had* happened and April hoped she could learn to live with it, because she was tired of secrets.

'Mum,' she said, 'there's one more thing we haven't talked about. Don't be mad.' Unconsciously, April's hand moved up to touch the star birthmark behind her ear. Silvia caught the gesture and smiled.

'You mean the Fury thing?' Silvia burst out laughing at the look of fear and surprise on April's face. 'Of course I knew, April. I couldn't really miss it: you almost killed me.'

'How?'

'Breastfeeding, honey. Luckily, the Fury part of you didn't fully develop until puberty, but wherever your little mouth touched me as a baby, I came out in a violent rash. I think your dad understood what was happening before I did. You know what he was like – he researched everything to death – so he knew about the Fury legend. We switched to powdered milk pretty quickly.'

'Is that why you never wanted me close?' asked April. 'Why you never kissed me?'

'I so wanted to, baby. But I couldn't.'

'Mum, you could have *hugged* me. You were always so cold.'

'I know … I'm sorry. I think it was self-preservation. You know, if I don't get too close, maybe I thought it wouldn't hurt so much when …'

'When what?'

Silvia sighed and passed April a mug of tea.

'You were always in danger, April. It was just a reality of our lives. That's why we moved around so much when you were little. In the early years, we were almost gypsies, always on the move. Rural Surrey, West Sussex, the Cotswolds, we had a farmhouse in the Wye Valley for a while. It was quite romantic, actually.'

'But why? I mean, why did we have to keep moving?'

Silvia looked serious. 'Because we thought the vampires would find out who you were and try to kill you.'

'And did they? I mean did they find out?'

Silvia hesitated for a moment. 'The truth? I never knew for sure. I suspected your grandfather had worked it out – I was sure he had spies following us – but no one ever made a move. But then the fact that you were part of your grandfather's precious royal line meant that there was always a chance someone might try to eliminate you.'

Eliminate. April felt herself go cold. She had always thought of her childhood as idyllic, hazy days spent playing in woods and fields and streams, climbing trees and messing about making dens. But all the time she was being stalked, hunted. Silvia saw April's troubled expression.

'Don't look so sad,' she said. 'They didn't find us, remember? Or perhaps they just didn't think we were a threat. So we eventually moved up to Edinburgh and your father made a decent career with journalism and the books.'

'Was that why Dad was so obsessed with the yeti and mermaids and stuff? Because he knew they were real?'

Silvia shook her head ruefully. 'They weren't. I can't count the times I told him "just because vampires are flesh and blood, doesn't mean there are unicorns hiding in the Cheshire hills". But I suppose it could have been worse – he could have been into golf.'

'If everything was so sweet in Edinburgh, why did we move down here?'

Silvia looked down at her tea. 'Because of Ravenwood.'

'The school? Why?'

'Your grandfather wasn't the only one with spies. I had always kept my ear to the ground and when I heard about Ravenwood and its links with Agropharm, I just knew that Thomas would be behind it all: he was making his move. And I knew that would put us in terrible danger.'

April frowned.

'But why? Why would Gramps want to harm us?'

A cloud passed over Silvia's face.

'You saw him that night, April. He was paranoid, insane; he wasn't a man you could reason with. And besides, we were in danger from anyone who chose to oppose him: holding his two heirs hostage would be a pretty solid bargaining chip.'

Silvia sighed.

'So I tried to make a move, a pre-emptive strike if you like. I went to your grandfather and told him I wanted to be part of the family again, that I wanted to help him. I wasn't sure if he would believe me, but at least that way we would be under his protection. And if we could get close to your grampa and

Robert Sheldon, find out what they were planning, we'd have a better idea of how to protect you.'

Robert Sheldon. Silvia had finally named the big, fat elephant in the room. April felt her stomach clench. She had come so far with her mother – it was as if Thomas's death had closed the yawning gap that had been between them – and April had no real desire to ruin the mood. And yet still, she had to know.

'Mum, I know you loved Dad, I totally do. But … why did you go off with another man?'

Silvia closed her eyes and let out a long breath.

'I never cheated on him, April. I told you I had because it was easier for you to understand that way. And it was easier if you hated me. But now you know about us, about the vampires, I can tell you the truth.'

April's head was spinning as Silvia got up and left the room. She was pin-balling between relief that her mother had lied about the affair and utter disbelief: *she's a vampire, April*, she reminded herself. *Vampires lie.* A vampire would say anything to get their way. But why would Silvia want April to hate her? How would that make anything easier?

Silvia returned carrying a box file, the sort that opened out like an accordion. She pulled out a large photograph. It was black and white, slightly yellowed at the edges, one of those formal shots of a whole school lined up in rows. In this case, it was a university graduation class, where everyone was wearing long black gowns and those funny flat hats with the tassels. The names of the class were written underneath in tiny writing.

'Recognise anyone on there?' said Silvia. 'Back row, third from the left.'

'It's … it's you,' said April, checking the name against the face. It looked like Silvia, but she was indistinct, her wide hat tilted downwards, casting a shadow over her face. 'But how?'

'Retouching,' said her mother. 'That was the way they did it before Photoshop and digital manipulation. We'd find a friendly snapper and pay him to paint the missing parts back in. You could only do it on long shots like this though. Anyway, I'm not showing it to you for that. Look at the date.'

April's eyes opened wide. It read: '*Trinity College, Oxford, Class of 1957*'.

'But you went to college in the seventies,' she said.

'Fifties, sixties and seventies,' said Silvia. 'I was the perpetual student. We age slowly, remember? It's the perfect cover for a vampire, to start as a freshman at a new university every few years, where everyone accepts you at face value.'

She pulled out a small pamphlet; April could see it had some sort of regal-looking crest on the cover and the name of another university. Silvia turned to a particular page and held it open for her. April frowned as she read: 'Faculty of Classics and Ancient Languages. Lecturer in Greek and Latin: Dr Silvia Hamilton.'

She looked at her mother, eyes wide.

'*Doctor?* You worked at the university? I don't understand.'

'Eventually I began to look too old to be a student, so I changed tack – become a teacher. It was easy enough after all the lectures I'd sat through, not to mention the degrees I'd sailed through. And that's where I met this guy.'

She reached into the file and pulled out another photo, this one of her dad, standing next to a motorbike wearing a beaten-up-looking leather jacket.

'He thought he looked like Marlon Brando in that thing,' said Silvia. 'But God, it stank.'

'You were his lecturer?'

Silvia smiled. 'My little toy boy.'

April shook her head. It was all too much information to take on board at once. She frowned. 'But what's all this got to do with you and Mr Sheldon?'

Silvia pointed down at the staff list again. There at the bottom was listed 'Head of Faculty, Professor Robert Sheldon'.

'It was the beginning and the end for me, I suppose. Sheldon knew who I was, and what I was; he suspected about your grandfather too. This was when he had gone back to the old country, when your grandmother disappeared – I think Robert saw there was a power vacuum and wanted to seize it for himself, using me as a pawn. Unfortunately for him and for his plan, I fell in love with your father.'

'What happened?'

'Robert gave me an ultimatum: either I became his or he would kill your father. I didn't like either of those options, so …' Silvia gave a small smile. 'So we eloped, ran off and got married at a register office, jumped on a bus and headed for the hills. It was so romantic, like Bonnie and Clyde, for a while at least.' The smile slipped from her face. 'Of course, Sheldon tracked us down. I was working in a bar and he seized me as I left one night, repeated his threat, said he would never let me go.' She sighed.

'Why didn't you … you know, kill him?'

Silvia laughed. 'Oh, I wanted to, believe me. But your dad pointed out that we were supposed to be in hiding and that a dead body might attract undue attention. Plus I knew your grandfather would go crazy when he heard I'd married Will, so we just kept moving.' Silvia paused, looking at the picture of her husband. 'Of course, as you grew older, it began to weigh more heavily on us. We knew the fact you were a Fury would come out eventually. We'd heard through friends that Sheldon had set himself up as the Vampire Regent and was running Ravenwood, so I went to see him, pretended our marriage was on the rocks, that I wanted to rekindle the embers of our romance, all that crap.'

'And he agreed to take me as a favour?'

'Oh, that was the idea, but I knew it wouldn't be that simple. Your grandad just had to be involved behind the scenes. It was all one massive chess game.'

She looked weary, tired. April could barely imagine how hard it would have been to play such a game with the people you loved as pawns.

'But I don't understand, if you knew that Highgate was

full of vampires, why would you bring me there?'

'We had no choice, April. It was either that or sit there in Edinburgh waiting for the axe to fall. Coming down here was dangerous, yes, but it was our only move while we found out everything we could about Ravenwood. We thought if your father could expose them in the press, then we could force the conspiracy back underground.'

'But wouldn't they have killed Daddy?'

Silvia smiled.

'He wasn't planning on putting his picture by-line on it, darling. No, that's where your Uncle Peter came in. He had agreed to print the story in his paper if we could get the evidence, there would be no connection to us.'

April's mother shook her head.

'But of course, your grandfather knew all along and…'

April leant over and held her hand.

'"Keep your friends close and your enemies closer", isn't that the phrase? Who would dare harm the granddaughter of the King, or the favoured student of the Regent? That's what we thought. But we got it wrong, darling. So, so wrong.'

'I hated what happened to you when Dad died,' said April.

Silvia nodded. 'It was hard, I won't deny it. Will and I, we'd engineered a few rows to make the move to Highgate believable, but after he died…that was all real. I didn't want to get out of bed, didn't want to live really. The only thing that kept me going was you.'

'But you were never there, Mum,' said April, 'I was hurting too. I needed you and you were out every night.'

Silvia squeezed her daughter's hand.

'I know, darling, but … I was trying to save your life. In order to protect you, I had to find out who had killed your father; that was why I went out every night. I was flirting with Sheldon to get information, then going to the vamp haunts – clubs, drinking dens – trying to find out what I could, all the rumours, any scrap of information I could scrape together.'

April frowned. 'But why did you let me think you'd cheated on Dad? Why did you let me hate you?'

'I knew you'd have to move out and, well, I thought that you'd be safer with your grandad. I knew he was capable of evil, but I never for a moment thought he would ever harm you. Plus, I knew that you'd have Gabriel watching over you.' She gave a rueful smile. 'Got it completely wrong, didn't I?'

'Mum, do you think … I really like Gabriel and …'

Silvia smiled. 'And …?'

April began to blush. She was hearing the deepest secrets, things she had been desperate to know, but she still didn't feel comfortable discussing her boyfriend with her mother. It was icky somehow. But they had talked about life and death and the future and the past, and she felt closer to Silvia than she had perhaps ever. So why couldn't she ask? It was the one question she wanted an answer to above all the others.

'Gramps was messing with Gabriel's head for years – hypnosis, electro shock, pumping him full of drugs. Do you think he could have made him fall for me?'

Silvia laughed. 'Oh, honey, don't be an idiot. Making a vampire kill is one thing, but making them love? That's never going to happen.' She took April's hand in her own. 'This man gave up his own life for you, then he walked back into the darkness because you asked him to. No, I don't think it's all a conjuring trick.' She looked at the photo of William again. 'I've lived longer than most and along the way you learn a few things. One is that true love is rare. Yes, we had our ups and downs, but despite appearances, your father and I were a love match. I've seen the way you look at Gabriel and I know what he did for you at the Winter Ball. Don't ever doubt it, and enjoy it for as long you can.'

April hugged her mother tightly.

'I love you, Mum,' she said. 'Really.'

Silvia threw her head back and laughed.

'Darling, I never doubted it for a moment.'

Chapter Thirty-Two

The cemetery was full of flowers. At least, that's how it seemed to April. The walk from the chapel up to the Vladescu tomb had often felt gloomy and oppressive, with every statue and shadow threatening and treacherous, but today the air was full of the smell of fresh blossom. Yellow bunches of cowslip, the red and purple of prunella, even the tiny blue flowers of speedwell peeping between the buttercups; to April, it was like spring and summer all at once. And it was fitting too that it had been her dad who had taught her the names of the wild flowers. April squeezed Gabriel's hand tighter and smiled up at him. 'I think he's watching us,' she said. 'I can feel my dad – I think he's happy we've come.'

Gabriel looked back as they heard laughter behind them. Silvia was following them up the steps, arm in arm with Davina and they were laughing with Fiona, down from Scotland for the day. 'Sounds like everyone's feeling the same way.'

April nodded. 'Mum and Davina have been thick as thieves for the past few days. Can't help but think they're up to something.'

'Your mum certainly had something up her sleeve with … well, your dad's grave. I wouldn't put anything past her right now.'

At first, April had to admit she had been angry at what her mother had done, but once she had calmed down, she saw the wisdom of it; in fact, she saw it was the only thing Silvia could have done in the circumstances.

She had moved the body. Or rather, in collusion with the

vicar, Mr Gordon, she'd arranged to have William Dunne's remains quietly buried in an unmarked grave near the tomb.

Only Silvia had known who Thomas Hamilton really was and only she had suspected what he was capable of. She certainly wasn't about to let him have access to the remains of a hated enemy. If Thomas could hack his wife's body into hunks of charred meat, there was no telling what else he was capable of. So when Chessy's servants had battered the vault door down, they had found the coffin empty.

'Do you think he ordered Chessy to do it?' asked April as they walked a little further up the path.

'I doubt it,' said Gabriel. 'She confessed to hanging Calvin up on that gate, didn't she? I'm pretty sure it was her twisted attempt to impress the King, get him to notice her, show she was protecting you for him. I'd guess that was what the raid on the tomb was all about too. Trying to win his favour.'

April gave a humourless laugh. 'Knowing what we know now, I imagine it had the opposite effect. Gramps would have gone ballistic – the last thing he wanted when he was about to launch the Council of Light was a hundred TV film crews outside his front door.'

'Still,' said Gabriel. 'It does mean you get to say goodbye properly this time.'

April looked up the path towards the tomb and the grave where her dad still lay; where he had been all the time. She was glad of that. And she was glad of what her mother had done – loved her for it, in fact.

She heard another peel of Silvia's laughter from behind.

'It's good that everyone's happy,' said Gabriel. 'A funeral should be a joyous thing, I think – it should be a celebration of a life well lived.'

April looked at him curiously. She knew he meant it, of course, but there was something else, a sadness she could detect behind his words. She gave his arm a squeeze. 'What's up? You feeling okay?'

'Fine, good,' he said, his smile not quite meeting his eyes. 'Arm's as good as new, anyway.'

'Gabe, come on. You can tell me *anything*, remember? After everything we've been through together, you don't think anything's going to shock me, do you?'

'No, it's just …' He looked away, staring at a stone angel that seemed to be reaching out to them, one arm extended. 'The dreams. They haven't gone away.'

April tried to hide her concern with a bright smile. 'You can't expect it to happen overnight, can you? They were messing with your head for years and years.'

'Yes, but the fear's still there. With your grandfather gone, I'll never know whether those things I see when I close my eyes are real. Whether they are memories or just dreams.'

April stopped and turned to face him. 'Gabriel, listen to me,' she said firmly. 'Whether they are real or not, they are in the past. It's what you do now – who you are *now*, that matters.'

'But, April …'

'No buts. I love you and if I've learned anything, it's how fragile life is and how easily it can be snatched away, so all I want is to be here with you, with my family and my friends. Let's live in the present, okay?'

Gabriel stroked the hair away from her face. 'It's just that …'

'You're still a vampire?'

He gave a sad smile. 'I wish I could kiss you.'

April nodded. It was something she hadn't really wanted to face. All these months they had searched for Gabriel's master, clinging to the hope that the legends had been right; that if Gabriel drank the blood of the vampire who turned him it would release him from the curse and return him to normality, whatever *that* was for an ex-vampire. But Gabriel had been lying on the floor unconscious when Thomas was killed. He could barely breathe, let alone drink blood. That door was closed for ever.

'We'll find a way,' said April. 'We're both alive, and where there's life there's hope, right?'

'You're right,' he said. 'And I can still do this …'

He grabbed her, dipping her back like a tango dancer and kissing her neck.

'Hey! Hey, put me down!' She laughed. 'This is supposed to be a funeral, remember?'

They turned as Silvia, Davina and Fiona had caught up with them. 'Hey April, your mum's just been telling me some very risqué stories about your dad,' said Davina, a faux-shocked look on her face. 'I had no idea.'

April put both hands over her ears. 'No, please! I really don't want to hear.'

Silvia tugged at her arm. 'Come on, Little Miss Prude. We don't want to be late for the funeral, do we?'

When they reached the tomb, April was pleased to see that Mr Gordon was already there, standing chatting with Luke and Peter. Standing a little way off were Caro and Simon. April noted with a smile that they were holding hands.

'Look at you two,' she said. 'Have you been arranging the wedding with the vicar?'

Caro's face turned almost the same shade of red as the streaks in her hair and she tried to pull her hand away, but Simon tugged it back.

'What Caro means to say,' said Simon, 'is that we're both very happy but we're taking things one step at a time.' He leant in to give a loud stage whisper. 'This is actually our first date.'

'This is a date?' said Caro, obviously pleased.

'We *have* been kissing,' said Simon. 'Although not in front of the vicar.'

Caro flushed again. April burst out laughing; she couldn't remember seeing Caro so lost for words – or so happy.

'All right, out of the way,' said April, elbowing Simon. 'We need a girls' group hug.'

Inside the huddle, their heads together, April whispered. 'Listen, ladies, thanks. I couldn't have …'

'Ah, shut up,' interrupted Caro. 'It's what we do.'

'Yeah,' said Fiona. 'Because you're worth it and all that.'

April kept squeezing them until the vicar clapped his hands. 'Now down to business. Are we all here?'

April looked around the little congregation: Caro and Fiona, Gabriel and Simon, Davina and her mother and her two uncles – real and honorary – Luke and Peter. All the people she loved and cared about, all gathered together to celebrate the man she had loved the most.

'If you'd all like to step this way,' said Mr Gordon, leading them to the side of the tomb. April felt her heart leap into her mouth as she saw the headstone. She had already buried him once, of course, but it was still a shock to see the grey slab standing there, as if to say 'it's really over now'. But she was glad to see that his final resting place had been so close to the steps of the tomb. *He must have heard every time I came to talk to him*, she thought. She couldn't help giving a half-smile when she saw the simple inscription.

'William Dunne. He lives on.'

'Your father's idea of a joke,' whispered Silvia. 'But if you think about it, it's pretty apt, isn't it?'

April nodded, feeling the tears welling up and not caring who saw. 'Yes, I think he'll always be here with us. Always.'

Her mother took her hand, holding it tight as Mr Gordon began to speak. There was no need for his prayer book; those words had already been said. Instead, he spoke about the kind of man William Dunne had been; his boundless enthusiasm, his insatiable curiosity about everything – whether it was mermaids or lawnmowers – and how his endlessly positive approach had uplifted everyone around him.

'We should not mourn him,' he said, 'for he is in heaven and in all of us. We should not mourn him because he left us all richer. We should not mourn him because we will all see him again.'

By the end, April's face was wet with tears, but she felt lighter somehow, as if the vicar's words had lifted a weight from her shoulders. Finally, they all turned and began to walk back down the hill and April looked up at her mother. She didn't think Silvia had ever looked more beautiful or more sad.

'He would have liked that,' said April.

'Yes, I think he would.'

'Mum, where's Gramps going to be buried? He's not going to be in the vault is he?'

'No, darling.' She smiled. 'I don't think that would be appropriate. No, I think we'll send him back to the old country. His family can decide how to remember him, if at all.'

April nodded. She couldn't say that she had made her peace with her grandfather, she doubted she would ever be able to forgive him, but at the same time, it did seem somehow right that Thomas Hamilton – or rather Tomas Vladescu – should find a resting place in the dark country he cared most about. Perhaps one day she could go and visit him and speak to him as she had with William Dunne, but not now – and not for a long time yet.

'Sooo … what's this secret plan?' said April.

'Ah, that. I am going to arrange a meeting between all the vampire clans to tell them that it's over.'

'Over?'

'All the wars, all the internal fighting, all the politics, I'm bringing it to an end – at least that's the plan. Luke is going to help. I'm hoping that the vampire nation as a whole has had enough death. I'll offer them a viable alternative: a source of blood, a comfortable life and peace.'

'How are you going to stop them from feeding?' asked April.

'Actually Gabriel's given me a few ideas. With his medical background, he thinks we can run our own blood donation scheme much like the legitimate one; much better than feeding from lowlifes in nightclubs, anyway. In return, the vampires must undertake to live by the rules and, vitally, bring an end to turning. No more new "made-vamps". No more promises to the weak of eternal life.'

'What makes you think they will go along with it?'

'Vampires are very macho and very proud – you may have already spotted that,' said Silvia, looking meaningfully at Gabriel.

April giggled. 'Yes, I had noticed.'

'They don't like to publicise that vampires are like spiders: the female of the species is more deadly than the male. Faster, stronger, smarter, just a natural predator. And as Vampire Queen, I'm more powerful than any of them. I'm hoping the threat of my retribution will be enough.' She let the words hang in the air, her eyes meeting April's. She didn't have to continue. It explained how Silvia had been able to destroy the King Vampire that night in the hall of Ravenwood. How her mother had been able to kill April's grandfather with such terrible ruthlessness. April nodded sadly.

'Having a daughter who's a Fury won't do any harm, I suppose?'

Silvia snorted. 'Vamps are also very superstitious. Young vampires are told stories about the Fury the way Bleeders are told about the big bad wolf. So yes, it will be a strong deterrent.'

There was something else that had been nagging at April. 'So who is the third Fury?'

'Third?'

'Well that's the legend, isn't it? There are three Furies every generation. So there was Isabelle, then me – where's the other one?'

Silvia shook her head slowly.

'Wales? Scotland? Next door? Maybe we'll never know – in fact, I hope we never do. After all, you're only going to find out you're a Fury by coming into contact with a vampire. And that's my plan; the more they're underground, the more they're under my control, the less likely it is to happen.'

April nodded. 'Thanks, Mum.'

'What for?'

'For trusting me. For telling me the truth – finally. Not

knowing what's going on, that's the one thing that's been driving me nuts since we got here.'

'I know, but I couldn't...'

'I understand,' said April. 'But let me know what's happening from now on, okay? I've had enough surprises for one lifetime.'

She looked at her mother awkwardly.

'And there's one other thing,' she began, 'I think what you're doing is brilliant, but I'm not going to get involved.'

'No, darling. I wouldn't ever want that. I want you to have the life I could never have with your dad. I want you to be free of all this.' She looked over at Gabriel, who was laughing with Caro. 'And if that boy is the one for you, then I want you to have him, too.'

Silvia was carrying a large leather tote over her shoulder; April had assumed she thought she would need a lot of tissues, but inside was a parcel, gift-wrapped in red polka-dot paper.

'Here,' said Silvia. 'For you.'

April frowned. There was a feeling of finality about Silvia's gesture, as if this was one last thing she needed to do.

'Mum, you're not going back to Scotland are you?'

Silvia laughed. 'No, darling. I'm not going anywhere. And neither, I hope, are you – not for a while, anyway?'

April grinned. Two months ago, Silvia would have needed wild horses to drag her back through that yellow door in Pond Square. But now? Now she couldn't think of anywhere she would rather be than that poky, creaky room at the top of the house with the view of the spindly tree tops.

'No, I'm not going anywhere, either,' said April. 'But what's all this about?' She held up the parcel.

'You'll see.' She nodded over to Gabriel. 'It's for both of you. Choose a private moment to open it.' She left April standing there as Peter stepped over.

'Two things: one, your father would have been very proud of you. *Is* very proud of you.'

'Stop it,' said April, giving him a hug, 'you'll set me off again.'

'And two, I think Davina would like a word.'

He pointed over to the girl who was standing half hidden on an overgrown side path, beckoning.

'Tell Gabriel I'll catch him up,' said April and followed Davina down the secluded pathway into the trees.

'So where next?' asked April as they walked.

'You'll see,' said Davina.

'No, I mean, what are you going to do next? I'm guessing that Ravenwood is no longer going to be the haven it once was for you.'

Davina sighed. 'I was thinking I'd pop across the pond, see if I can snag myself a silicon valley squillionaire on Rodeo Drive.'

'You're going to *Hollywood*?'

Davina gave a wry smile.

'Going to the one place in the world where having your picture taken is almost mandatory? Not a good move for one of the undead, sweetie. Besides which, I'd miss all this.'

She waved an arm at all the overgrown headstones.

'The graveyard? Really?'

'Not the cemetery per se, no. These paths are not a good environment for a girl who enjoys high heels. But the zillions of vamps in the area, I suppose they are my people in a way – and, well, there's a job to do.'

'Job? What job?'

'Didn't Silvia tell you? I'm going to be sticking around to help her out with her plot to decommission the Suckers.'

April blinked at her, then began to laugh. 'You?'

'Why not me?' said Davina, clearly stung.

'No offence, Davina, but you've spent the last two years working for the vampires in their crazed plan to take over the world. You wouldn't be the first person I'd think of if I wanted to put an end to the blood-sucking.'

'Point taken. Still, they do say "set a thief to catch a thief", don't they? And I think Silvia's going to need someone of my – ah – skill-set if it starts to get hairy.'

April nodded thoughtfully. Perhaps Davina was right; why not her? She was underhand, manipulative and ruthless: not the qualities you'd want in a nursery school teacher perhaps, but ideal for the task facing Silvia. And something else too; when Davina said it might get 'hairy', what she actually meant was 'bloody'. It was unlikely that the vampire community were going to go into retirement quietly. So with Davina in her corner, April felt a little better about leaving her mother to her secret war.

'Can I just ask why? I mean, I'm glad you're watching my mum's back, but why join her?'

Davina looked away, her face sad. 'What else am I going to do? You're right, I can't go back to Ravenwood and our time was running out there anyway. And I figured I might be able to even the scales. If Charles Dickens is right, I'm going to have a hell of a heavy chain to drag through eternity.'

April stopped and looked up. They had walked quite a way into the cemetery now and the atmosphere, so warm and friendly before the funeral, had changed. Was the canopy above them thicker? Had the sun gone in? Then April understood why. They were standing in front of the tomb known as the Sleeping Angel, the one Chessy had told her was dedicated to her memory. April stopped and gave Davina a sideways look.

'Was this where you were taking me?'

Davina nodded.

'So what happened?' asked April. 'To Chessy, I mean.'

'Oh, I didn't have to do anything much – you'd done all the hard work for me.'

April squeezed her eyes shut. 'Don't,' she said. 'I didn't mean to.'

The way you didn't mean to kill Davina's brother, said the voice in her head. *Why don't you tell her about that too?*

She shook her head, trying to clear it. What with the subsequent drama at Ravenwood, April had managed to push the struggle with Chessy to the back of her mind, but every now and then she'd get a flash of that image: the black snakes slithering and hissing down Chessy's neck, the look of horror on her face as she finally realised what was happening.

'Don't feel bad, sweetie,' said Davina. 'She was a bad egg, remember? Made a terrible mess of your grandfather's front step and all.'

April didn't want to think of the body hanging on Gramps' gate – and she didn't want to think about Gramps either. Not today, not now. There was plenty of time for that later.

'But what actually happened to her, to her body anyway?'

'I thought that would be obvious,' said Davina. 'I put her where she was always meant to be.' She raised her eyebrows and nodded towards the sleeping statue.

'You put her *inside*?' gasped April.

Davina flexed a slender arm. 'I'm very strong when roused. Besides, I thought it was rather poetic.'

April frowned.

'Why do you think she tried to kill me? I mean, she kept dropping hints that she knew who the King was. If that was true, why risk killing me?'

'She was insane, darling, couldn't you tell?'

'Yes, but even so. There seemed to be some method in her madness.'

'Oh yes, Chessy was always playing some sort of game, but she was an expert in keeping her hands clean. The vandalism here and at Redfearne's? She will have got some minion to do that for her. And that's why Ling seemed to take over as top dog after I was ousted; you can bet Chessy was pulling her strings, but poor Ling was the figurehead – and a scapegoat if anything went wrong. She would have probably found a way to blame me for sticking Calvin on the gate when she found out your grandfather hated the idea.'

April thought of that night, of the body just hanging there, of the dark pool of blood. She wrapped her arms around herself.

'Can we go?' she said.

They followed the path in a loop around the hill, finally coming out in the courtyard by the chapel. As they passed through the gate, April noticed that Miss Leicester was turned away, apparently staring into a filing cabinet. *Is she making a point, perhaps?* wondered April. She couldn't really blame the woman.

Across the road, April could see the Osbournes' black town car.

'This is it then,' said Davina. 'Wish me luck.'

'Luck? Where are you going?'

'I've got to go and empty the mansion, remove all trace of the Osbourne clan. It's not going to be easy getting Barbara out – might need a crowbar – but we can't stay there, especially after … well, you know: now Nicholas has left the building. I can't imagine Agropharm is going to keep paying the mortgage. I'm thinking of burning it to the ground just to spite them.'

'Where will you go?'

'Pond Square?' Davina laughed at the look of alarm on April's face. 'Relax, I'm joking – it was nice of you to have me to stay, but I think being somewhere so small and creepy would send me mental inside a week.'

That was more like the old Davina: bitchy and insensitive. It was reassuring, somehow.

'No, I'm sure we'll find somewhere more in keeping with the lifestyle I aspire to. Buckingham Palace, maybe.'

April wasn't entirely sure if Davina was joking about that one. They walked down to the car.

'Are you going to stick with Barbara? I mean, she's not actually…' April trailed off, embarrassed.

'Not actually my mother, you mean? No, and she's not

exactly a barrel of laughs, either. Gets through a bottle of gin and a can of hairspray every day. But she's the only family I've got left.'

'I know how that feels,' said April.

They stood there for an awkward moment, joined by their tragedies, but at the same time divided by them. Davina may have finally chosen the right side, but she had still plotted and killed and fed on the blood of innocents. April didn't think they could ever truly be friends, but she'd take an uneasy truce with Davina over all-out war any day.

'Well, I suppose I should say thank you,' said April. 'You know, for Chessy.'

'I suppose you should.' Davina smiled. 'But don't bother; let's call it even. I feel guilty enough about … all the other stuff.'

April laughed.

'*You* feel guilty?'

Davina shrugged and opened the rear door of the car. 'Figure of speech, sweetie. Just a figure of speech.'

Chapter Thirty-Three

If there is a God, thought April, *then He had most definitely created Primrose Hill Bakery.* Her nose practically pressed against the glass counter, she pointed at the swirly red velvet cupcakes, the squidgy chocolate cake and heavenly macaroons, and grinned as Gabriel relayed her orders to the lady in the apron. It was all she could do to stop herself clapping her hands and doing a little dance.

'You've got icing on the end of your nose,' said Gabriel as they walked through the park's iron gates and up towards the hill. April had already eaten the gateau and was busy picking the icing from the cupcake.

'Don't you want any?' she asked, sucking her fingers.

'Vampire, remember? Not big on cakes.'

April's face fell.

'Hey, don't,' he said, bending to kiss the cream away. 'We'll find a way through.'

'Oh, it's not that, more that you reminded me about the last time we were here.'

She thought of Gabriel's face that terrible morning when he had taken the Dragon's Breath and been forced back into his vampire skin. It had been the same expression she had stared into in the hall at Ravenwood. She shook her head to clear the picture away.

'But it worked, didn't it?' said Gabriel, slipping his arm around her waist. 'Most of it, anyway. And we said we'd come back here when it was all over.'

'Is it?' said April as they walked up the steep path. 'I mean, is it really all over? Do you really think my mum will be able to unite the Suckers?'

Gabriel shrugged. 'Who knows? She's certainly got enough power – and enough incentive.'

'Incentive? What do you mean?'

'I mean vampires are vampires, April. They move at night, they love power. And they have little love for Bleeders besides the nutrition.'

'Nice image,' said April, discarding the case of her cake in a litter bin.

'The point is, if Silvia doesn't succeed in pacifying all the vamps, we're in trouble. So she'll move heaven and earth to make sure they toe the line.'

'But what if . . . ?'

He put a finger to her lips. 'No buts, isn't that what you said this morning? "Let's live in the present"? It's good advice.'

She nodded and turned to face the view. It was even more impressive in the summer, the glass towers shining in the sun, the flat bowl of London curving away into the distance. They sat on the same bench they had shared that faraway morning, after the zoo and before the elixir. That bittersweet moment when they had shared their last kiss.

'I'm glad we came back,' said April quietly. 'It's so beautiful up here.'

'You're the most beautiful thing around here,' he said, pulling her hair back and kissing her neck, sending tingles across her skin.

'I suppose we should open this,' said April, pulling the parcel out of her satchel and handing it to Gabriel.

'You do the honours, lady's privilege.'

April had been hoping he'd say that – she loved opening presents. She tore at the paper, grinning with girlish excitement. She had guessed at a photo album or something of her dad's, but then her mum had said it was for both of them. Inside the paper was a plain white polystyrene box. *Curious.* She looked up at Gabriel.

'Open it.'

She slid open the cover and peeped inside – then jumped to her feet, almost dropping it. 'Oh my GOD!' she squealed, her hand flying to her mouth. 'MOTHER!'

'What is it?' said Gabriel, looking in the container. April watched as his expression changed from disbelief, to amazement, then fear. Then he burst out laughing.

'Silvia Dunne!' he laughed. 'You sly fox.'

April sat down and removed the glass vial from its icebox. It was tiny, only about the size of a torch battery, and filled with dark liquid. But not just any liquid. Blood. Thomas Hamilton Vladescu's blood. Silvia must have taken it when April was weeping over Gabriel.

'God, Gabe, what do we do?'

April held the vial up to the light. It didn't look magic or supernatural, it just looked like blood. Could this really bring Gabriel back to her – for ever? Could something so small really do all that?

'What if it doesn't work?' she said. 'Gabriel, what if all those legends are wrong?'

Gabriel smiled and put his hand over hers. 'Then we keep looking for a cure. You were right, baby. Where there's life there's hope – and we'll be together whatever happens.'

Her eyes wide, her fingers shaking, she handed Gabriel the little bottle.

'What if it *does* work?' she said.

Gabriel laughed. 'Then I will kiss you, April Dunne. And we will grow old together.'

April nodded, her eyes still on the vial. 'Good answer,' she said.

Slowly, carefully, Gabriel unscrewed the lid and placed it on the bench. 'Well,' he said. 'Here goes nothing.'

He held out his free hand to April and, nervously, she put hers on top and laced their fingers together, squeezing tight.

'Ready?' asked Gabriel.

'Ready,' said April, looking into his eyes.
'Geronimo,' he said.
And he drank.